LOVE IS BLIND

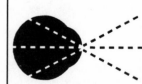

LOVE IS BLIND

LYNSAY SANDS

THORNDIKE PRESS

An imprint of Thomson Gale, a part of The Thomson Corporation

THOMSON

GALE

Detroit • New York • San Francisco • New Haven, Conn. • Waterville, Maine • London

LIBRARY OF CONGRESS CATALOGING-IN-PUBLICATION DATA

Sands, Lynsay.
    Love is blind / by Lynsay Sands.
        p. cm. — ("Thorndike Press large print basic"—T.p. verso.)
    ISBN-13: 978-0-7862-9207-3 (lg. print : alk. paper)
    ISBN-10: 0-7862-9207-5 (lg. print : alk. paper) 1. Large type books. I. Title.
    PR9199.3.S2195L68 2007
    813'.6—dc22   2006032559

Published in 2007 by arrangement with Leisure Books,
a division of Dorchester Publishing Co., Inc.

Printed in the United States of America on permanent paper
10 9 8 7 6 5 4 3 2 1

For Jenny Bent, agent extraordinaire.

CHAPTER ONE

London, England, 1818

" 'Love is a fever . . . in my blood.' "

Clarissa Crambray winced as those words trembled in the air. Truly, this had to be the worst of the poems Lord Prudhomme had recited since arriving at her father's town house an hour ago.

Had it been only an hour? In truth it felt more like several days had passed since the elderly man arrived. He'd entered brandishing a book, announcing with triumph that, rather than go for their usual walk, he thought perhaps today she'd enjoy his reading to her. And Clarissa would have, had he chosen to read something other than this poppycock. She also would have appreciated it more were he not acting as though he were doing her a favor.

For all his words, Clarissa was not fooled. She knew the reason for the sudden change in plans. The man was hoping to avoid

calamity by restricting her to sitting deco-
rously on the settee while he read aloud
from his book of poems. It would appear
that even the aged and sympathetic Prudhomme was growing tired of her continued
accidents.

She couldn't really blame him; he'd been
terribly forbearing up until now. Almost a
saint, to be honest. Certainly he'd shown
more understanding and fortitude than her
other suitors. He'd appeared to accept and
forgive all the times she'd mistaken his fat
little legs for a table and set her tea on them,
had given a pained smile through her tendency to dance on his feet, and had even
put up with her stumbling and tripping as
he led her on walks through the park. Or so
it had seemed. But today he'd found a way
to save himself from all that. Unfortunately,
his choice of reading material left much to
be desired. Clarissa would rather be making
a fool of herself in the park and stumbling
face-first into the cake table than suffering
this drivel.

" 'It gives me wings like those of a dove.' "
Lord Prudhomme's voice quavered with
passion . . . or possibly just old age; Clarissa
wasn't sure which. Truly, the man was old
enough to be her grandfather. Unfortunately, that didn't matter to her stepmother,

Lydia. The woman had promised to John Crambray that she'd see his daughter well married if it killed them both. Lord Prudhomme was the last of the few suitors still bothering with her. At this point, it looked like they were safe from dying. However, Clarissa was in imminent danger of finding herself married to the elderly gentleman kneeling on the floor before her and waving his arms wildly as he professed undying love.

" 'I shall vow my' . . . er . . . 'my' — Lady Clarissa," Lord Prudhomme interrupted himself. "Pray, move the candle closer if you please. I am having trouble deciphering this word."

Clarissa blinked away her ennui and squinted toward her suitor. Prudhomme was a dark blob in her vision with a round, pink blur of a face topped by a silvery cloud of hair.

"The candle, girl," he said impatiently, all signs of the charming suitor momentarily replaced with irritation.

Clarissa squinted at the candle on the table beside her, picked it up, and leaned dutifully forward.

"Much better," Prudhomme said with satisfaction. "Now, where was I? Oh, yes. 'I shall vow my undying . . .' " He paused again and his nose twitched. "Do you smell something burning?"

Clarissa sniffed delicately at the air. She opened her mouth to say yes, actually she did, but before the words left her mouth Prudhomme released a shriek. Pulling back with surprise at the sound, she watched in amazement as the man suddenly leaped to his feet and began to hop madly about, his blurry arms flying and appearing to thrash at his head. Clarissa didn't understand what was happening until the white blur that was his wig was suddenly removed and beat furiously against his leg. She blinked at the pink blob that was his head, then at his actions, and realized she must have held the candle too close — she'd set his wig aflame.

"Oh, dear." Clarissa set the candle down, not releasing it until she knew it was safely on the table surface. Her vision blurred and her sense of distance beggared, she nearly knocked the little man over as she leaped up to help him.

"Get away from me!" Prudhomme yelled, shoving her backward.

Clarissa fell back in her chair and stared at him in blind amazement, then glanced sharply toward the door as a rustling announced the arrival of someone.

Several someones, she amended, squinting at the array of colors and shapes standing just inside the door. It looked as if every servant in the house had heard Prudhomme's shrieks and come running. No doubt her stepmother was there as well, Clarissa thought, and heaved a small sigh at the subsequent shocked silence. She couldn't see well enough to know if those by the door were staring at her with pity or accusation, but she didn't need eyesight to guess at Prudhomme's expression. His rage was a living thing. It reached out to her across the few feet separating them, and then he exploded with verbal vitriol.

He was so angry, most of what Prudhomme said ran together into one mostly incomprehensible rant. Clarissa managed to decipher bits here and there — "clumsy idiot," "bloody disaster," and "danger to society" amongst them — but then, in the midst of his rant, she saw his dark arm rise and descend toward her. Clarissa froze, afraid he might be lashing out, but she wasn't at all sure. It was so hard to tell without her spectacles.

By the time his fist got close enough that Clarissa could see that he was indeed attempting to strike her, it was too late to avoid the blow. Fortunately, the others had apparently suspected he was winding up, and had moved closer while he spoke. Several of them descended on the man midswing, preventing the blow. There was a blurry blending and shifting of color before her as they struggled. Clarissa heard Prudhomme's curses and a grunt from one of the shapes, whom she suspected was Ffoulkes, the butler. Then there was much cursing as the kaleidoscope blur of bodies began to shift toward the door.

"Fie! Shame on you, Lord Prudhomme," Clarissa's stepmother cried, her voice clearly distressed as her lilac blur followed the mass of other colors to the door, then she added anxiously, "I hope once you calm down you shall see your way clear to forgiving Clarissa. I am sure she did not mean to set your wig on fire."

Clarissa sank back in her chair with a sigh of disgust. She couldn't believe that her stepmother would still hope to make a match with the man. She'd set his wig on fire, for heaven's sake! And he'd tried to hit her! Though Clarissa should have known better than to think that would put Lydia off making a match. What did her stepmother care if she ended up married to an abusive mate?

"Clarissa!"

Sitting up abruptly, she turned to peer warily around as the lilac blur that was Lydia reentered the room and slammed the door behind her.

"How could you?"

"I did not do it on purpose, Lydia," Clarissa said at once. "And it would never have happened at all if you would just let me wear my spectacles. Surely being graceful, even with spectacles, will get me more suitors than —"

"Never!" Lydia snapped. "How many times have I to tell you that girls with spectacles simply do not find husbands? I know of what I speak. It is better to be a little clumsy than bespectacled."

"I set his wig on fire!" Clarissa cried with disbelief. "That is more than a little clumsy, and really, this is beyond ridiculous now. 'Tis becoming dangerous. He could have been badly burned."

"Yes. He could have. Thank the good Lord he was not," Lydia said, sounding suddenly calm. Clarissa nearly moaned aloud. She had quickly come to learn that when her stepmother went calm, it did not bode well for her.

CHAPTER TWO

"Mowbray! Been a while since you bothered with the season. What brings you to town?"

Lord Adrian Montfort, Earl of Mowbray, shifted his gaze from the couples whirling past on the dance floor and to the man who approached: the tall, fair, eminently good-looking Reginald Greville. He and Greville, his cousin, had once been the best of friends. However, time and distance had weakened the bond — with a little help from the war with France, Adrian thought bitterly. Ignoring Reginald's question, he offered a somewhat rusty smile in greeting, then turned his gaze back to the men and women swinging elegantly about the dance floor. He replied instead, "Enjoying the season, Greville?"

"Certainly, certainly. Fresh blood. Fresh faces."

"Fresh victims," Mowbray said dryly, and Reginald laughed.

"That too." Reginald was well-known for his success in seducing young innocents. Only his title and money kept him from being forced out of town.

Shaking his head, Adrian gave that rusty smile again. "I wonder you never tire of the chase, Reg. They all look sadly similar to me. I would swear these were the very same young women who were entering their first season the last time I attended . . . and the time before that, and the time before that."

His cousin smiled easily, but shook his head. "It has been ten years since you bothered to come to town, Adrian. Those women are all married and bearing fruit, or well on their way to spinsterhood."

"Different faces, same ladies," Adrian said with a shrug.

"Such cynicism!" Reg chided. "You sound old, old man."

"Older," Adrian corrected. "Older and wiser."

"No. Just old," Reg insisted with a laugh, his own gaze turning to the mass of people moving before them. "Besides, there are a couple of real lovelies this year. That blonde, for instance, or that brunette with Chalmsly."

"Hmmm." Adrian looked the two women over. "Correct me if I'm wrong, but my guess is that the brunette — lovely as she is — doesn't have a thought in her head. Rather like that Lady Penelope you seduced when last I was here."

Reg's eyes widened in surprise at the observation.

"And the blonde . . ." Adrian continued, his gaze raking the woman in question and taking in her calculating look. "Born of parents in trade, lots of money, and looking for a title to go with it. Rather like Lily Ainsley. Another of your conquests."

"Dead-on," Reginald admitted, looking a bit incredulous. His gaze moved between the two women and then he gave a harsh laugh. "Now you have quite ruined it for me. I was considering favoring one or both of them with my attentions. But now you have made them quite boring." He frowned a moment and then perked up. "Ah, I know one woman you cannot size up so easily."

Grabbing Adrian's arm, he tugged him around the room, pausing only once they'd reached the opposite side.

"There!" he said with satisfaction. "The girl in the yellow muslin gown. Lady Clarissa Crambray. I defy you to find someone from the last season you were here to compare *her* to."

Adrian looked over the girl in question.

Tiny — delicate-looking, in fact — and lovely as a newly blooming rose, she had dark chestnut hair, a heart-shaped face, large wide eyes, full lips . . . and appeared about as miserable as he'd ever seen a young woman, a state he suspected had something to do with the older woman at her side. His gaze slid over the matron. Well-rounded with dark hair, she was pretty despite the bloom of youth being gone — or she would be if she weren't wearing a pursed, dissatisfied expression as she surveyed the activity in the ballroom. Adrian glanced back to the girl.

"First season?" he queried, his curiosity piqued.

"Yes." Reg looked amused.

"Why is no one dancing with her?" A beauty such as this should have had a full card.

"No one dares ask her — and you will not either, if you value your feet."

Adrian's eyebrows rose, his gaze turning reluctantly from the young woman to the man at his side.

"She is blind as a bat and dangerous to boot," Reg announced, nodding when Adrian looked disbelieving. "Truly, she cannot dance a step without stomping on your toes and falling about. She cannot even walk

17

without bumping into things." He paused, cocking one eyebrow in response to Adrian's expression. "I know you do not believe it. I did not either . . . much to my own folly."

Reginald turned to glare at the girl and continued: "I was warned, but ignored it and took her in to dinner. . . ." He glanced back at Adrian. "I was wearing dark brown trousers that night, unfortunately. She mistook my lap for a table, and set her tea on me. Or rather, she tried to. It overset and . . ." Reg paused, shifting uncomfortably at the memory. "Damn me if she did not burn my piffle."

Adrian stared at his cousin and then burst into laughter.

Reginald looked startled, then smiled wryly. "Yes, laugh. But if I never sire another child — legitimate or not — I shall blame it solely on Lady Clarissa Crambray."

Shaking his head, Adrian laughed even harder, and it felt so good. It had been many years since he'd found anything the least bit funny. But the image of the delicate little flower along the wall mistaking Reg's lap for a table and oversetting a cup of tea on him was priceless.

"What did you do?" he got out at last.

Reg shook his head and raised his hands

helplessly. "What could I do? I pretended it had not happened, stayed where I was, and tried not to cry with the pain. 'A gentleman never deigns to notice, or draw attention in any way to, a lady's public faux pas,' " he quoted dryly, then glanced back at the girl with a sigh. "Truth to tell, I do not think she even realized what she'd done. Rumor has it she can see fine with spectacles, but she is too vain to wear them."

Still smiling, Adrian followed Reg's gaze to the girl. Carefully taking in her wretched expression, he shook his head.

"No. Not vain," he announced, watching as the older woman beside Lady Clarissa murmured something, stood, and moved away.

"Well," Reg began, but paused when, ignoring him, Adrian moved toward the girl. Shaking his head, he muttered, "I warned you."

"Refrain from squinting, please."

Despite the inclusion of the word *please,* it was not a request but an order, and one Clarissa was heartily sick of hearing. If her stepmother would simply allow her to wear spectacles, she would have no need to squint. She would also not be constantly bumping into things and people. But no, of course she must not wear her spectacles. That would put off suitors.

As if my clumsiness does not, Clarissa thought wearily, and she grimaced inwardly over some of the accidents she'd had since arriving in London. Aside from upending tea trays and missing tables with her plates, she'd taken a terrible tumble down the stairs at a ball. Fortunately, she hadn't hurt herself overmuch, suffering only bruises and stiffness but nothing broken. Then there'd been the little incident of falling out in front of a moving carriage, and of course, recently, setting Lord Prudhomme's wig on fire.

Another sigh slid from her lips as Clarissa recalled Lydia's lecture after the last accident. Her stepmother had decided that — as she was so blind and clumsy without her spectacles — there was only one way for Clarissa to go on. In the future, she was allowed only to sit quietly when in the presence of others. She was not to touch candles, cups, plates, or, well, basically anything. She was no longer to eat in company, but was to claim she was not hungry — whether she was or not. Neither was she to drink. Even walking was out, unless she had her maid to lead her.

Clarissa had cut into this lecture several times with, "But if you would only allow me to wear my spectacles —" But each time, Lydia had responded with a grim, "Never!" And then she had continued on with all the other things Clarissa was to avoid.

By the time Lydia was finished, all Clarissa was supposed to do in the presence of others was sit looking serene . . . which supposedly meant no squinting.

Clarissa turned her gaze away from the shapes swinging past on the dance floor to stare wearily at the pale pink blur of her hands in the yellow haze of her lap. She wished — not for the first time — that her father had accompanied them on this trip. Were Lord Crambray here, she'd have her glasses and be able to properly enjoy the evening. Unfortunately, he'd had estate business to attend. At least that was what he'd claimed, though her father had never much cared for the city, and the claim of estate business might just have been an excuse. Clarissa didn't know. All she knew was that he wasn't here, and it was going to be another boring night.

"May I have this dance?"

Clarissa heard the request, but didn't bother to look up. Why should she? It wasn't as if she could see anything anyway. Instead, she waited unhappily for her stepmother to speak, wondering the whole while who this stranger was that he had not heard of her. Anyone who had heard the tales of her clumsiness surely would not approach.

Realizing that Lydia hadn't yet politely declined the request on her behalf by saying she was too tired, or whatever excuse she would choose, Clarissa glanced to her side with a frown. She found that the pink blur that was Lydia was no longer there. And when a black shape suddenly moved into her stepmother's seat, Clarissa sat back with a start.

A frown forming on her face, she turned, blindly searching the haze of colors around her for her stepmother's bright pink shape.

"I believe the lady who was sitting here a moment ago went off in search of food." The deep voice was so close to her ear that Clarissa felt the man's breath on her delicate lobe. Suppressing a shiver, she turned her attention quickly back to the gentleman at her side. He had lovely, deep, gravelly tones that she found pleasing, and his blurred form appeared quite large. For the millionth time, Clarissa wished she had her spectacles and could see.

"Did she not tell you where she was going?" he asked. "I thought I saw her speak to you before leaving."

Clarissa blushed slightly, and quickly returned her gaze to the smear of movement that was the dance floor, admitting, "She may have. I fear I was distracted by my thoughts and not paying attention."

While she had a vague recollection of Lydia murmuring something to her, Clarissa had been sunk too deep in misery to pay much heed. It was humiliating to sit here catching bits of conversation as people gossiped unkindly about her. Her clumsiness was apparently quite the joke of the season. She'd earned the moniker Clumsy Clarissa, and everyone was wondering what she would do next to entertain them.

"They say you are as blind as a bat, and too vain to wear spectacles," the voice beside her announced.

Clarissa blinked in surprise. But if she was taken aback by his bluntness, she suspected she was no more so than the speaker himself. She heard a small gasp of breath as he finished, as if he'd just realized what he'd said. A quick glance to the side showed that he'd raised his hand as if to cover his mouth.

"I am sorry; I have obviously been too long out of society. I should never have —"

"Oh, bother." Clarissa waved his apology

away and sank back in her seat with a dejected sigh. " 'Tis all right. I *do* know what people are saying. They seem to think that I am deaf as well as clumsy, for they do not worry about saying things in front of me — or at least behind their fans — loudly enough for me to hear." Making a face, she mimicked, " 'Oh look, there she is, poor thing — Clumsy Clarissa.' "

"I *am* sorry," her companion said quietly.

Clarissa waved his words away again, only this time noting the way he dodged as if to avoid a blow to the head. Frowning, she clasped her hands and settled them in her lap, repeating, "There is no need to apologize. At least you said it to my face."

"Yes, well . . ." The man seemed to relax in his seat now that her hands weren't waving wildly. "Actually, it was more a question. I was wondering if you truly are?"

Clarissa smiled wryly. "Ah, well, I am not quite as blind as a bat. I *can* see with spectacles. But my stepmother has taken them away." She threw a dry smile in the general direction of his blurry shape and then shrugged. "Lydia seems to think that I will have more luck setting a fire in some suitable man's heart without them. The only thing as yet that I have set fire to is Lord

Prudhomme's wig."

"Excuse me?" the stranger asked with amazement. "Prudhomme's wig?"

"Hmm." Clarissa leaned back in her chair and actually managed to chuckle at the memory. "Yes. Though if you ask me, 'twas not wholly my fault. The man knew that I could not see without my spectacles. Why the deuce he asked me to move the candle closer is beyond me." Clarissa paused to squint in her companion's general direction. "He is bald as a cue ball without his wig, is he not?"

She thought the man nodded, though it was hard to say. He was emitting small choked sounds it took her a moment to identify. He was fighting desperately not to laugh!

"Go ahead," Clarissa said with a small smile. "Laugh. I did. Though not right away."

The man relaxed somewhat. She could actually feel the muscles in the arm and leg pressed against her own expanding. But he only expelled a small chuckle.

Clarissa squinted again, trying to bring his face into focus. She wanted very much to see his face. She liked the sound of his laugh, and his voice when he spoke was husky yet soft. It was really quite . . . attractive, she decided. And while Clarissa should have moved over rather than allow the intimacy of his hip rubbing against hers with every move, she quite liked that too; so she pretended not to notice.

"How did Lord Prudhomme take this little accident?"

Clarissa gave up trying to see his face and smiled good-naturedly. "Not at all well. He thought it was my fault. He called me quite a few nasty names. I think he would have hit me, too, but the servants wrestled him from the house," she admitted with a small frown. Sighing, she added, "Of course, my stepmother — Lydia — lectured me ad nauseam afterward about everything I must and must not do from now on."

"Such as?"

"Pretty much everything is off-limits," Clarissa said cheerfully. "Let's see, no eating in public, no drinking in public . . . In fact, I am not to touch anything in public: candles, flower vases, anything. I am not even supposed to walk without someone to guide me."

"But did she say no dancing?"

"No. Not as such. But then, she did not have to." Clarissa's smile faded. She hesitated and then tried to explain. "Everything is a blur, you see; so when I whirl about, all

I see are streaks of color and light flashing around. I lose my balance and . . ." She paused and shrugged, but felt a blush creeping over her face as she remembered the last brave soul who had asked her to dance. Clarissa had ended up tripping him, and they had both ended up on the floor. Very embarrassing.

"Just keep your eyes shut."

"What?" Clarissa glanced blankly at the dark blur beside her.

"Keep your eyes closed, and you will not lose your balance," the man suggested, and she saw his hand move closer to her. He was offering it so that she would rise.

Clarissa opened her mouth to refuse, then paused as his hand suddenly enclosed hers, sending a shock of sensation racing up her arm. It was such an odd feeling — excitement, wild excitement — coursing across her flesh.

"I do not. . . ." she began faintly with bewilderment, pausing when his hand lifted her chin and the man bent to stare into her eyes. Close enough to kiss, she thought vaguely. Good God, Clarissa realized, close enough to *see!* For one brief second she stared into the most beautiful set of clear brown eyes she'd ever seen; then he pulled back slightly, out of focus.

"Trust me." It was not so much a request as an order. But Clarissa remembered those eyes, so dark, so kind — and she nodded. Then he was tugging her out of her seat, directing her through the crowd of dancers to the middle of the floor.

"Now . . ." His voice was calm and soothing as he turned her to face him. "Close your eyes," he instructed, lifting her free hand to his shoulder. "Relax."

His voice was almost hypnotic, Clarissa thought vaguely.

"Follow me. I will not allow you to stumble."

Despite having just met him, Clarissa believed him. He would not let her fall as he led her through the dance. And with her eyes closed, she had only her ears and his touch to guide her.

The music was loud and strong, drowning out all conversation. Her companion's touch directed her; a squeeze of the hand, an urgent pressure at her waist. And the only other sensation was the air rushing past as he whirled her around and around, without once tripping or stumbling. For the first time in weeks — since her very arrival in London, in fact — Clarissa didn't feel like a clumsy oaf. It was divine.

When the dance ended, he gave her hand

a squeeze and then drew it through his arm to promenade her through the room.

"You dance divinely, my lady," he said quietly near her ear, gently leading her with his arm and pressure on her hand past the gay colors of the other dancers. Clarissa flushed and smiled a bit proudly, then sighed and shook her head.

"No, my lord," she said demurely. "You give me too much credit. I fear you are the one who dances divinely. I know it is not I, for I have been able to do nothing but stumble and fall when dancing with others."

"Then the fault lies with those others. You are as light and graceful as a feather on the dance floor with me."

Clarissa considered briefly; then, with a sense of justice, nodded her head. "I believe you may be right, my lord. After all, if it were me alone, even your obvious skill could not have made it so easy. Perhaps my previous partners were a bit nervous and awkward."

"How refreshing."

She could hear the smile in his voice, and so Clarissa raised her eyebrows in question. "My lord?"

"Your honesty. I am pleased by your lack of false modesty. It is something that never really bothered me before, yet now seems as fake and unpleasant as the airs everyone puts on when in the city. I find your honesty most refreshing."

Clarissa felt herself blush, and then the first strains of a new song hummed through the air. Her companion paused and turned her into his arms once more.

"Close your eyes," he instructed, and began to move them around the room once more.

Clarissa closed her eyes and relaxed into his arms. She suspected the two of them shouldn't really be dancing this close, but she feared that if she insisted they reduce the closeness, she might return to the clumsy stumbling she'd suffered before. Besides, she quite liked being in this man's embrace. Between that and her closed eyes, she felt coddled and safe.

"Why do you not disobey this stepmother of yours?"

Clarissa blinked her eyes open, tried in vain to see the face dancing before her and then gave up, closing her eyes again. "What do you mean?"

"I mean, why do you not simply wear your spectacles anyway?"

"Oh, I tried that the first day I was in London," Clarissa admitted with irritation.

"I came downstairs dressed for Lord Findlay's ball wearing them. Lydia was livid. She snatched them off my face and broke them right in front of my eyes. Almost close enough that I could see what she was doing!"

"She *broke* them?" He was obviously shocked by the lengths to which her stepmother would go.

Clarissa gave a solemn nod. "Lydia does not care to be disobeyed."

"But if she broke them, how do you see to get around at home?" he asked with dismay.

"I do not." Clarissa grimaced and then admitted with some vexation, "I have to be led around by servants. It is quite tedious."

"I imagine it would be," he murmured.

"Hmm." She briefly reflected upon the humiliation of it all, and then said, "But the worst of it is that I cannot do anything without my spectacles. I cannot embroider, or arrange flowers . . . or anything. And it is impossible to read. Even if I move the book right up to my eyes, I cannot read long before the strain makes my head ache. 'Tis quite boring. I have nothing to do but sit about, twiddling my thumbs."

As he gazed down on her, Adrian murmured sympathetically, a slight smile tugging at his mouth. The pout on this young woman's lips — unconscious though it was — was quite endearing. She was quite lovely, though perhaps not in the traditional way. Her lips were too big for any member of the season to think of her that way, but he himself found them quite seductive. And while her nose was just a bit too pert for today's standards, he thought it cute.

Adrian was so preoccupied with taking in her features, he hardly noticed when the music changed, heeding it only enough to swing her into a waltz as he continued to gaze down at her face. She went on to tell him the trials and tribulations of not having her spectacles. There was quite a long list. Dressing was difficult, and she had to depend entirely on the good humor of her lady's maid. She never knew quite what her hair looked like, and there too had to depend on her maid. As Clarissa explained, she hardly seemed to hear his assurances that her hair was perfection and her gown lovely.

No, the lady obviously wasn't seeking compliments. Blushing furiously, she waved his words away and continued to explain how she had to be led about the house by her maid, for fear of tumbling down stairs, or tripping over something she did not see.

And apparently, mistaking people for one another was a problem, though she assured him she was getting quite good at recognizing voices. There was also the irritating difficulty of obliviously spilling food down her front, albeit only when she was alone, since she was not allowed to take refreshments or food in company. She had taken to wearing a bib to save her wardrobe!

Adrian was biting his lip at the image of her in a bib, and it only got worse as she went on to say she'd nearly set fire to the family town house several times while attempting to light candles. She'd tripped the butler and several of the servants numerous times, and she was positive that they all had begun to hate her. She was sure they cringed whenever she was near, and she'd heard them begin to murmur that she was a walking disaster.

Lady Clarissa was dreadfully cheerful as she admitted all this. Adrian had great difficulty stifling his amusement as she spoke, but managed to withhold his chuckles until she sensed his polite efforts and gave him leave to laugh. The robust humor that escaped him then surprised Adrian. It had been so long since he'd even smiled that laughter was a joy to partake of, and he found his gaze softening on the woman who had brought it about. She was a wonder: adorable, lovely, and so cheerful about the disasters that followed her. Clarissa made his soul feel light and his heart ache with longing.

"You have a nice voice, my lord. A nice laugh too," she pronounced with a smile.

"Thank you, my lady," he replied after clearing his throat of the laughter clogging it. "It is kind of you to say so, but I show my bad manners in laughing at your misfortune. Pray, forgive me."

"Oh, ta ra," Clarissa said lightly. "In retrospect I suppose it is all rather funny — though I doubt that Lydia would agree."

Adrian's humor ended there, and he arched one eyebrow in displeasure, though she could not see it. "Forgive me for saying so, my lady, but your stepmother sounds to be a rather nasty old cow."

"Oh!" Clarissa said, dismayed. "Oh, you must not say that. Ever."

"Why not?" he asked with careless amusement. "I am not afraid of her."

"No, but . . . She would be furious. And she would not like you were she to hear you say such things about her."

"I could not care less if she likes me or not —," Adrian began, but Clarissa cut him off.

"Oh, but you must care. If she does not like you, then she will not allow me to dance with you anymore, and . . . and . . . I do quite like it," she finished with some embarrassment.

The look of scorn on Adrian's face melted away at her confession, and his annoyance softened slightly. "Well, then, I shall have to be sure to treat her with the utmost respect." He watched her pink, embarrassed face for a moment, then added, "Because I quite like dancing with you, too."

Clarissa turned to him and beamed brightly.

Adrian smiled gently down at her, despite the fact that she could not see it, and then some instinct made him peer over her shoulder. He slowed their dancing somewhat as he spotted the woman who had been seated next to Clarissa when Reginald first pointed her out. It seemed her stepmother had returned from stuffing herself, and had found empty the seat where she had left her charge. She was now frowning around the room in search of her errant ward. It did not take her long to spot the chit.

As Adrian expected, the woman looked less than pleased to see Clarissa dancing with him. In fact, she looked horrified.

When she immediately began to make a beeline toward them, he pretended not to see and began to dance Clarissa in the opposite direction, leading her away from her guardian.

He expected the woman to stop and await her charge's safe return when he moved away, but a glance over his shoulder showed her pursuing. He frowned. It appeared the stepmother was the persistent sort. Adrian supposed he should have expected as much; she did rather resemble a bulldog, he thought uncharitably. He then glanced down at the girl in his arms.

"Why is she so determined you should not wear your spectacles?" he asked.

"She wishes me to make a good match. Father will be annoyed should she not manage that, you see."

"Ah. Well . . . actually, no, I do not see," Adrian muttered, changing direction abruptly when he saw that they were in peril of being caught by the stepmother. He was silent for a moment as he maneuvered Clarissa about the floor in avoidance, then glanced down to comment, "Surely you would have a better chance at making a good match were you able to see."

Clarissa gave a deep, heartfelt sigh and nodded. "I must confess, sir, that is my opinion as well . . . However, Lydia does not see it so. She says that I look quite unattractive in my spectacles, and fears that they, on top of my 'unfortunate past,' would quite ruin any chance I have with a respectable man of means."

"Unfortunate past?" Adrian was so startled by the comment, he came to an abrupt halt on the edge of the dance floor.

Clarissa's eyebrows lifted slightly, and she squinted at his face. "You have not heard about the scandal?"

Before Adrian could respond that no, he most certainly had not heard of any scandal, a rather large, dark shadow fell on them both. Glancing to the side, Adrian frowned irritably at Clarissa's tenacious stepmother, who'd come to a breathless pause beside them.

"Clarissa!" the woman snapped, and the young woman in Adrian's arms stiffened as if under the lick of a whip's lash, then jumped back guiltily from the man holding her to whirl to face her stepmother.

"Yes, Lydi—" But her words ended on a gasp of surprise as her arm was seized and she was dragged unceremoniously away.

CHAPTER THREE

"Well, I must say you fared far better than I expected."

Adrian tore his eyes away from the retreating backs of Lady Clarissa and her stepmother to find his cousin at his side once more.

"Did I?" he asked.

Reginald smiled wryly and shrugged. "It seemed to me that you did. After all, she did not stomp on your toes, send you plummeting to the floor, or burn your piffle. I would say that is a good start."

"Hmm." Adrian grimaced. "I was instead chased about the dance floor by a rather large, aging matron who was waving her hands frantically like a mother hen flapping her wings."

Reginald grinned at the description and nodded. "Yes. Poor Lady Clarissa does seem destined to end each day on a rather humiliating note. She has become quite the talk of the *ton*."

"It is not Clarissa who causes herself embarrassment. It is her stepmother."

Reginald looked dubious. "I will grant you that tonight's little performance was all the stepmother's fault. After all, the girl was doing rather well in your arms. However, you can hardly blame the woman for the other fiascoes that have added to her charge's infamy."

"Can I not?" Adrian asked, arching one eyebrow.

"No. Why, Lady Crambray was not even present when Lady Clarissa overset her tea on my legs and burned my —"

"But Clarissa would not have done that if she were in possession of her spectacles — which *is* her stepmother's fault," Adrian interrupted.

"What?"

"Lady Clarissa is without spectacles not because she is too vain to wear them, but because her stepmother took them away and broke them. She refuses to allow the girl to wear the bloody things."

Reginald looked stunned by that revelation — as he should be. "Well, why the devil would the woman do that? The girl is clearly as blind as a bat without them."

"Lady Crambray apparently feels that

spectacles are something of a detriment to marrying a chit off, and that they — on top of an 'unfortunate past' — would make Clarissa unmarriageable," Adrian explained.

"Oh . . . I see." Reginald went silent and thoughtful.

Adrian peered at him. "Do you know about this 'unfortunate past' of hers?" he asked, eyes narrowed.

"What?" Reg glanced back at him, then sharply shifted, looking uncomfortable. "Oh, yes. Well, I have heard about it, of course. Sad, really. Not even the girl's fault. The man went to jail. Still, as I recall, it was quite the scandal at the time. Caused quite a foofaraw, I understand."

"*What* caused quite a foofaraw?"

When Reginald glanced at him blankly, Adrian shifted impatiently. "What was this scandal?"

His cousin's eyes widened. "Surely you recall the tale, Adrian? It was the season after the action near Burgos. . . ." Reginald's voice trailed away as he said that, and his gaze slid to the scar on his cousin's face, then away with discomfort. He murmured, "Oh, yes, you left London and returned to the country early that year."

Adrian grimaced at the polite phrasing. He had not returned to the country "early," he'd done so almost immediately the moment he arrived. The reason, of course, was the scar on his face, the long, jagged scar that zigzagged its way from directly beside his left eye all the way down to his chin beside his mouth. It was his own personal keepsake from the Peninsular War, and from the wound that had brought an end to a promising military career.

His career was not all it had ended, Adrian thought on a sigh. It had also finished the ancient and noble family of Montfort, though he had not realized it at the time. No. He'd returned to England to recover from that injury, which had nearly killed him, grateful to be alive . . . until his first experience at court the following season. He'd been a fool not to realize his disfigurement would cause a stir. Not that he'd believed it would go completely uncommented on. He hadn't been that much of a fool. However, Adrian hadn't expected it to cause weaker women to faint and those with the fortitude to remain standing to cringe in horror.

Yes, Adrian had attended only one ball upon his return. One was more than enough to make him decide to pack his trunks and return to the country estate that was the seat of the earldom of Mowbray. His father had still been alive then, and with uncommon understanding the gruff old man had said nothing about his son's sudden preference to stay on the estate and see to the running of it. He'd merely nodded solemnly and used the opportunity to set out on various and diverse travels with his wife. Travels that had come to an abrupt end when he'd suffered a fatal apoplexy in France. That had been nearly two years ago. It was also the reason Adrian was now — ten years after his last foray into the fray — back at court.

Well, it was the reason behind the reason, he corrected, espying his mother making her way toward him. This was his lady mother's first coming out since her husband's death, and Adrian suspected she would not even be here now were it not for the fact that she was determined to see him do his duty by the family. *That* was why he was here. This last year, as her grief had waned, his mother, Lady Mowbray, had begun to harangue him about his duty to the family name, nagging him about the need to marry and beget an heir. He'd argued with her over it, informing her that no one would have him with his face so hideously marked, but his lady mother had been deaf to his words.

It was well past time he gave up his sulking in the country and learned to deal with his wound was all she'd had to say on the subject. He had a duty to fulfill and had best get around to fulfilling it. And with those uncompromising words, she'd managed — after a year of repetition — to drag him back to court. So here Adrian stood, feeling like a troll among so many fine and glittering people. At least, that was how he'd felt until he'd sat down beside Lady Clarissa.

"There you are, son. Whatever are you doing hiding away here in the corner like a naughty boy?"

Adrian grimaced at his mother's words, feeling just like the naughty boy she suggested. Still, he took her hand in his and kissed it in a courtly manner. "I am hardly in a corner, Mother. I am right out here in plain sight, where everyone may look upon my disfigurement."

Lady Mowbray scowled. "No one is even marking it. You let it bother you far too much. It is much less noticeable now. Time has softened its effect."

"You may be right," Adrian agreed laconically. "At least, no one has fainted at sight of me yet, or run screaming from the room."

Noting her irritation increase, he smiled apologetically and changed the subject. "Reginald was just about to tell me of the scandal attached to Lady Clarissa."

His mother's eyebrows rose. "I did notice you dancing with her, dear. Five dances in a row. I daresay you shall have the gossips' tongues wagging, are you not careful."

"I shall endeavor to be more circumspect," Adrian replied, then turned to arch an eyebrow at his cousin. "Well?"

"Well? Oh, yes!" Clearly nervous in the presence of his aunt, Reginald smiled at her, then explained: "You see, in late summer of 1808 — August, I think it was — Lady Clarissa, a tender twelve, was visiting a friend here in London."

"It was not a friend; it was her aunt, Lady Smithson," Lady Mowbray corrected gently. "And she was fourteen, not twelve."

"Was she?" Reginald frowned slightly. "I see. Well . . . at any rate, shortly after she arrived, a servant followed with a message supposed to be from her mother's maid —"

"Her mother's *doctor*," Lady Mowbray interrupted.

Adrian laughed at his cousin's discomfiture at being corrected once more. Turning a rare smile his mother's way, he suggested, "Since you appear to be more versed on the facts, Mother, perhaps *you* would care to explain this scandal to me?"

She turned away, but not before he glimpsed the tears in her eyes. Adrian guessed they'd been brought on by an excess of emotion, that they were a response to the change in her normally grim son, and he frowned at her reaction; but then she nodded, cleared her throat, and turned back, her face composed.

"Certainly, my dear. My memory was just being refreshed by Lady Witherspoon. She could not hold back the nasty little tale when she saw your interest in the girl," his mother added dryly, seeming recovered. She then shrugged and dove into the explanations.

"It seems that the reason Lady Clarissa was visiting her aunt alone was because her mother was ill at the time. This illness killed her some months later, whereupon Lord Crambray married the present Lady Crambray, a most unpleasant creature by all accounts." She shook her head, then returned to her tale. "At any rate, shortly after Clarissa arrived at her aunt's, a servant arrived with a message addressed to the aunt, supposedly from Lady Crambray's doctor. It claimed Clarissa's mother had taken a turn for the worse and was not expected to last beyond a day or so. The letter instructed the aunt not to alarm the girl by imparting the full severity of the situation, but merely to tell Clarissa her mother needed her — and to send her back at once in the carriage that had transported the servant. Which, foolish as it may seem, the aunt did."

"Why foolish?" Adrian asked.

"The carriage was unmarked," Reginald explained, eager to redeem himself and add something to the tale. "The family crest was missing."

Adrian's eyebrows rose. "Did the aunt not notice?"

"Oh, yes. She even asked about it," Lady Mowbray assured him. "The servant claimed the carriage he had been sent in had suffered a broken wheel on the way to London, and that he had been forced to leave it at a roadside inn to be repaired while he hired another conveyance to finish the journey. He hoped to be able to reclaim the carriage on the return trip if it was repaired."

"A plausible story," Adrian commented.

"Yes, it was rather, was it not?" Lady Mowbray mused consideringly. "Still, the aunt should have at least sent a servant of her own with the girl, or done something else to ensure her well-being." She shrugged. "However, she did not. Lady Smithson merely packed up the girl and her belongings and sent her off in the carriage with this servant."

"Who was not a servant at all," Adrian guessed.

"Oh, he was a servant, all right, simply not in the employ of Clarissa's mother. This servant did not take her home, but stopped at Coventry. There she was led to a private room, where she was met by a Captain Jeremy Fielding and his sister."

"Fielding?" Adrian frowned at the name. It rang a bell.

"Mmm. This Fielding fellow explained that, truly, Clarissa's mother was well on the way to mending, and that Clarissa had really been called away because of her father. He gave some vague claptrap that Crambray's business affairs had taken a sudden turn for the worse, and that while her father had meant to meet her there, he had been forced to leave ere her arrival. I gather they hinted that Lord Crambray was being pursued by the authorities, and that he wished Clarissa to follow. Crambray had supposedly employed this Fielding and his sister to bring her to him safely."

Adrian's mother's expression showed distaste as she went on. "Of course, the girl was just a child, and easily led astray, and I daresay this Captain Fielding cut a dashing and authoritative figure in his uniform. The girl went quietly.

"They traveled for days, supposedly just missing her father here, and there, until they reached Carlisle, where Captain Fielding left his sister and Lady Clarissa alone at an inn and went off to supposedly meet with her father. When he returned, Fielding claimed that her family was on the brink of ruin, and that the only way for them all to avoid the poorhouse was for her to marry, which her father wished her to do at once."

"How would Clarissa's marrying save the family from ruin?" Adrian asked with a frown.

"I am not sure. Lady Witherspoon was not altogether clear on that." Lady Mowbray turned questioningly to Reginald. "Do you know what he claimed?"

"I believe it had something to do with an inheritance she would receive only upon marriage. It was from her grandfather on her mother's side. Once married, she would inherit and the father's bills could be paid, thus saving the family."

"Hmm." There was silence for a moment; then Adrian asked, "I daresay this Fielding offered himself as the martyr willing to aid her in her moment of need?"

Lady Mowbray nodded with a grim little smile. "Kind of him, was it not?"

"Oh, undoubtedly," Adrian agreed.

"So they were off to Gretna Green," Reginald interjected cheerfully. "Married without banns or priest before a prostitute, a thief, and a blacksmith; then they went off on a honeymoon in Calais."

"The witnesses were a landlord of a public house, a tailor, and the blacksmith," Lady Mowbray corrected in arid tones. "And they never made it to Calais; they were stopped at the docks. My," she added a touch archly, "it *is* interesting how rumors get all fouled up with their facts, is it not?"

Adrian was amused at the way his cousin squirmed under his mother's regard, but cut Reg's discomfort short by asking, "Who stopped them?"

"Her father, of course. Well, not her father, really. You see, after the girl left, her aunt regained her senses enough to become nervous about the unmarked carriage. She sent a message to Lord Crambray asking after the mother, alerting them to the fact that something was terribly amiss. Crambray hired several men, who tracked the girl to Gretna Green, then to the boat they had booked passage on to Calais.

"It seems Fielding had told the girl her father was to meet them there once the deed was done, but the runners caught up with them, explained that it was all a bunch of bunk, and brought the girl back in shame. By all accounts she was quite distraught."

"What of Fielding?" Adrian asked, thinking it unfair the girl had suffered anything in this instance. Obviously, none of it was her fault.

"Well, he returned too at first," Lady Mowbray said with a frown. "He was quite sure there was nothing her father could do. They *were* wed, after all. However, Clarissa's father is a clever man. He had Fielding charged with abducting a minor and set about having the wedding annulled. He also promptly removed the girl to the country to get her out of way of the scandal. Not that it helped much," she added under her breath.

"What mean you by that?" Adrian asked curiously.

"Well, her not being here hardly stopped the tongues from wagging," Lady Mowbray pointed out sadly. "This was far too juicy a tale for that. Rumor was rampant. There was rife speculation that perhaps the wedding had been consummated after all. Fielding was quite sure of himself. And then the fact that she'd been removed from public attention led people to wonder if it had not been done to hide the fact that she'd borne fruit from the brief marriage."

"And did she?" Adrian asked.

"No one knows," Reginald put in with a shrug. "This is the first she has returned, and 'tis ten years later."

Adrian raised an eyebrow at his mother, who seemed to be most in tune with the facts of the case up to now. However, much to his dissatisfaction, the older woman merely shrugged as well, and said with obvious reluctance, "It *is* possible. They spent one night at an inn after the wedding, though they were booked into separate rooms. The boat was to leave the day after."

Adrian frowned in displeasure at the uncertainty of this, then asked, "What of Fielding?"

"He fled the country before the trial was scheduled to begin. But Lady Witherspoon said that he returned to England several years back, and was caught. He faced the charges, was found guilty, and sentenced to five years in Newgate. No one has heard anything of him since."

They were all silent again. Adrian was lost

in thought, pondering his own revulsion at the idea that Lady Clarissa's brief marriage had been consummated. With that worry occupying his mind, he peered about the room, unconsciously seeking out the chit and her stepmother.

"They left directly after that ridiculous little scene on the dance floor," Lady Mowbray informed him.

Adrian glanced at his mother with a start, caught the gleam in her eye, and knew she was encouraged by his interest. And he *was* interested.

When he'd first taken a seat beside her, Clarissa had flinched back from him, and Adrian had feared he'd been misled. He'd feared she was able to see his face and was horrified by the scar that marred his former good looks. However, in the next moment, she'd leaned closer and squinted, obviously trying to bring him into focus.

When Clarissa had frowned with frustration and sat back, he'd realized that she really *couldn't* see him, and thus wouldn't be scared off by his looks. Adrian had found himself smiling and relaxing in the company of a woman other than his mother for the first time since arriving back in London. For the first time in years, really.

The time he'd spent with her after that had probably been no more than half an hour, between their sitting and talking and the five dances his mother claimed they'd shared, yet it seemed like mere moments. Adrian had smiled and laughed more in that time than he had in all the years since his injury. For the first time in a long while, he'd felt whole and undamaged.

Any woman who could make him feel like that deserved his interest, and yes, Adrian acknowledged to himself, he was *most definitely* interested. Which would please his mother no end, he thought. However, there was a problem. The very thing that had allowed him to relax in her presence was also the source of the problem. Clarissa could not see him, but she was not permanently blind, merely temporarily so. He worried about what would happen when she could see again, when she saw the horror of the man she had spoken and danced with. How would she react? Would she shrink from him as if he were a monster? Faint in horror at the sight of him? It hurt him to consider either option.

"Shall I find out more about the chit for you?" Lady Mowbray asked, drawing Adrian from his thoughts. He peered at his mother, unable to answer. A large part of him wanted to say yes, but another very large part was afraid, and Adrian hadn't been afraid of anything in a very long time.

Suddenly irritated with the entire matter, Adrian turned away without answering and moved toward the door. He'd had enough of so-called polite society for one night.

"You will not speak to Lord Mowbray again."

Clarissa stared blindly across the coach's dark interior at the blur that was her stepmother. Lydia had not just yanked her away from the man she'd danced with, but had dragged her across the dance floor, out of the ballroom, and straight out of the house entirely. Her stepmother had been so obviously furious that Clarissa had kept her mouth shut as Lydia shouted orders, demanding their carriage be brought around at once. Her silence hadn't seemed to ease the woman's upset, either, and Lydia had dug her fingers painfully into Clarissa's arm as they waited, as if afraid she might flee at any moment and rush back inside to throw herself at the man.

Other than that cruel grip, however, Lydia had ignored Clarissa, giving off a positively frigid air as they waited for the carriage.

Once the coach had stopped before them, she'd practically shoved Clarissa into the vehicle, then taken the opposite seat and glared at her until they were in motion.

"Is that the name of the man I was dancing with?" Clarissa asked, realizing only now that she didn't know the man's name. Had he known hers? she wondered, then glanced warily at her stepmother as the woman's teeth snapped together with a click.

"Yes," Lydia snarled. "Lord Adrian Montfort, the Earl of Mowbray. And you shall stay away from him completely."

Clarissa hesitated, debating whether it was wise to question her stepmother when she was so angry, but she simply couldn't help herself, and blurted, "But why should I stay away from him? He behaved like a perfect gentleman, and if he is an earl —"

"He did not behave like a perfect gentleman," Lydia countered at once. "He danced far too close to you, and he should not even have approached you without a proper introduction."

Clarissa bit her lip. She supposed that hadn't been well done of either of them, but still . . .

"Mowbray was a rakehell when he was younger," Lydia continued. "He ruined many a poor girl. No doubt that is why God saw fit to ruin his looks."

Clarissa bit back the protest she wanted to make at this satisfied claim; it would do no good anyway, she knew.

"You will stay away from him. He can have no good intention toward you. He will merely toy with your affections and further damage your already shredded reputation. Your father is counting on me to see that you marry well. He would never forgive me should I allow you to get tangled up in some scandal with that man."

Clarissa sighed unhappily at this edict, but said little, merely turned to peer at the haze of dark and light speeding past outside the carriage. There was little use in arguing; she'd learned that through the issue of her spectacles. So Clarissa merely swallowed her anger, pretended to be distracted by the passing lights, and replayed her short time with Lord Mowbray in her head.

Adrian Montfort, the Earl of Mowbray. She repeated his name in her head and thought it suited him. He'd seemed terribly nice to her, not at all what she would expect of an earl. The few she'd met before this had always seemed rather arrogant and cold, but Adrian hadn't displayed either tendency. He'd been patient and sweet, so understanding and encouraging. Clarissa could still remember the sound of his smoky voice, the fresh, almost woodsy scent of him, and the feel of his strong arms around her as he'd moved her across the dance floor. She'd felt so safe in his arms, Clarissa found it hard to believe he was a rakehell or debaucher of young women.

A loud sigh from her stepmother interrupted her thoughts, and she squinted warily at the smeared figure on the opposite seat.

"If only you were not so blind," Lydia bemoaned suddenly. "I would not even need worry about you fancying him."

"Why?" Clarissa asked curiously, just barely managing to refrain from pointing out that she wouldn't be blind if she had her spectacles back.

"Because the man is as ugly as his sins," Lydia pronounced. "He used to be considered one of the handsomest of men in the *ton.* However, when the war started, he went off to battle and came back with that huge ugly scar. He is the talk of the *ton* now. No one can believe he would show his face in polite society, ruined as it is."

"Then we are a perfect pair," Clarissa muttered. "Two misfits everyone likes to point at and whisper about."

"What was that?" Lydia asked sharply.

"Nothing." Clarissa turned her gaze back to the passing city streets, blurry as they were, and heaved a sigh. Nothing her stepmother said had lessened Mowbray in her eyes. She simply didn't believe he would ruin her, and she knew he wasn't ugly. Clarissa had seen the scar that marred the side of his face. True, she'd seen it in bits and pieces, glimpses caught only when he'd leaned close to speak, but it hadn't seemed all that awful to her, and the other side of his face was perfect. She had found him terribly handsome.

Clarissa didn't say as much to her stepmother, however. She knew better than that.

CHAPTER FOUR

Clarissa watched the blur of movement in the ballroom and sighed deeply. It had been a week since the De Morriseys' ball, where she'd met the Earl of Mowbray. A mere week, she thought with a sigh. It felt like ten. Life had slid back into its pattern of blind clumsiness on her part, and the tedious — not to mention somewhat dubious — attentions of the elderly Lord Prudhomme. It seemed, despite her little accident in setting him afire, he was willing to continue his courtship. But the man now made sure that any and all incendiary and liquid-bearing items were kept well away from her.

Clarissa was eternally grateful that he was too busy playing host at this, his own ball, to bother her with his attentions, but she was bored. Bored to tears. She was also slightly obsessed with the evening she'd made the acquaintance of Lord Mowbray.

That was the one bright spot in the entire time she'd spent in London to date. And despite her stepmother's orders to avoid him, Clarissa found herself watching every passing blur in the hope that it might be him. She was also listening for the low, smoky tones of his laugh. He had a lovely laugh.

As if her thoughts had produced it, that low, smoky voice was suddenly whispering in her ear, "These *are* rather boring affairs, are they not?"

Turning with a start, Clarissa peered at the dark smudge that had slid into the seat her stepmother had only recently vacated, and blinked rapidly.

"Lord Mowbray!" She beamed at him, then realized how pathetically eager she must seem and said, "I mean, no — no, of course not. Why would you think I was bored?"

Clarissa could hear the amusement in his voice when Adrian said, "I could not help but notice that you were yawning as I joined you just now."

"Yes, well . . . perhaps I was a *little* bored," Clarissa acknowledged, aware she was flushing at being caught yawning, then gave up her pretense and admitted, "Oh, bother! I *am* bored. Terribly bored, in fact. Why, do you know that I have been in London for nigh on five weeks, and the night I met you is the only time anything interesting happened?"

"Setting Lord Prudhomme afire did not raise any interest in you?" Adrian teased.

Clarissa flushed a deeper scarlet, then made a face at him. "That is not what I meant, my lord. I meant that . . . well, I quite enjoyed myself with you. And that was the first — and, so far, only — time I have enjoyed myself in London to date."

"You flatter me," Adrian suggested, his voice gone husky.

"Not at all," Clarissa assured him. " 'Tis true. Why, dancing with you I felt as light as a bird, and I did not trip once, nor even stumble."

"Then let us dance again," he suggested, taking her hand to urge her to rise.

"Oh, nay!" Clarissa cried, tugging her hand free. She then offered an apologetic smile. "I am sorry, my lord, but my stepmother will not be gone long, and if she sees us together she will . . . well, I fear she will be displeased. I hope you are not too offended by my admission of this?"

"Oh, nay," Adrian echoed dryly, and she

bit her lip unhappily. Clarissa had known the news would be insulting, but she had not known how to get around her situation. She certainly hadn't wanted to just send him away thinking that she herself was the one displeased with his company.

Adrian must have spotted her misery, for he suddenly gave her hand a squeeze. "Never fear. I am made of stern stuff. Besides, 'tis not the first time I have heard such a thing said this season, Lady Clarissa."

The words were spoken with a rather distracted air, and Clarissa could tell by the movement of the blur that was his head that he was glancing around. She'd just decided that he was looking for an excuse to leave her when he suddenly turned back and urged her to her feet. "I believe I do not see your aunt, or any of her cronies, nearby just now. If we hurry, I think we might make it out onto the balcony undetected."

"Onto the balcony?" Clarissa echoed with confusion, instinctively following the hand holding hers. He led her through the balcony doors behind them. "Whatever for?"

"To dance."

"Dance?" she repeated with surprise, but then he closed the door behind them, cutting off the music and chatter of the ball-room.

"You would like to dance, would you not?"

Clarissa could hear the frown in his voice and nodded quickly to please him. Then she admitted uncertainly, "But should my stepmother return while I am missing —"

"Oh, yes," Adrian muttered. "I suppose you are right. She might look out here and see us; then we would be in it."

Clarissa was just sighing unhappily, thinking they would return inside now and end this first bit of excitement she'd had since last meeting him, when he suddenly tugged her away from the doors.

"Come along. We shall move farther out into the gardens, where she will not find us. We can dance there."

Adrian was dragging her along and down the stairs to the gardens as he spoke, and Clarissa stumbled to keep up, but she managed to murmur, "No, my lord. I meant that, should she find me missing, I shall surely be in trouble when I do return."

"Ah, well, you can simply tell her you had to attend to personal needs, and had to find a powder room," he suggested.

"My lord!" Clarissa gasped, taken aback that he would mention such things so bluntly. It simply wasn't done. She could hear the grimace in his voice as he made his apologies.

"I am sorry, but I was simply trying to — Damn, someone is coming."

Clarissa forgot his breach of manners, her heart tripping with anxiety as he stilled. "Who is it?"

"I do not know, but I can hear . . . Come." Tugging her to the side, Adrian slid into the bushes, taking her with him. When he paused, she paused as well, some instinct warning her to be quiet as they waited.

It was no more than a moment before two figures came into view, approaching from the direction they'd been headed. Unfortunately, rather than walk by, as Clarissa had hoped, the pair chose that spot to stop and embrace.

"Oh, Henry!" the woman murmured.

"Hazel," came a quavery little voice that made Clarissa frown. She was positive it was the voice of Lord Prudhomme.

"You do not truly mean to marry that wretched girl?" the woman said suddenly. "What of us? What of our grand passion?"

"I love you, Hazel," the quavery voice came again. "And I shall do so until I die, but I must have an heir. Mother is quite insistent on that point."

Clarissa grimaced. It *was* Prudhomme;

she was sure now, as she had met his mother. Lady Prudhomme was a rather horrible old lady. The woman must be at least a hundred years old. Still, she was a frightening harridan for all that, and Clarissa could not blame Prudhomme for his terror of her.

"Yes, but —"

"Shh, my love," Prudhomme hushed. "Just let me hold you and pretend that the dreams I have each night are true. That you are mine and that all this sneaking about is unnecessary."

There was the rustle of silk and a brief moment of silence in which Clarissa imagined the couple to be embracing; then she heard a suspicious sound rather like lip smacking or sucking. Squinting, she tried to peer through the bushes, but all she could see were the smears of what appeared to be a woman in a light-colored dress and the slender dark form of a man. They were very close together. Very close indeed. Their faces looked to be one large blur beneath two seemingly connected fuzzy white wigs.

They were *kissing!* Clarissa realized it with dismay, and she wondered what Lord Achard would think of that. For she had recognized who the woman was the moment

Prudhomme addressed her as Hazel. Lady Hazel Achard was a member of her stepmother's circle — one who was quite often sharp and cold in her attitude to Clarissa. Now Clarissa understood why. The woman was jealous of Prudhomme's courtship of her.

"Oh, Henry, make love to me," Lady Achard gasped suddenly.

"But we just did, my sweet," Prudhomme protested. "I am only a man. I cannot perform again so soon, but must recover from the passion you instill in me."

"Oh." There was a long, drawn-out sigh of disappointment, then: "Were we married —"

"Yes, were we married I could hold you in my arms every night, just as I am now," Prudhomme proclaimed softly. Then he cursed and said, "Damn your husband for his good health!"

"Yes, damn him," Lady Achard agreed. "I wish he would —"

"Shh," Prudhomme interrupted. But Clarissa suspected Lady Achard hoped for the early demise of her poor, unfortunate husband.

"What?" the woman asked, sounding anxious.

"I think I hear someone coming."

The couple broke apart, and none too soon, as another woman came around the path. She stopped in apparent surprise at the sight of them. "Why, Lord Prudhomme. Lady Achard."

Recognizing the voice of Lady Alice Havard, another of her stepmother's friends, Clarissa tried to shrink a little smaller in the bushes.

"Lady Havard," the amorous twosome murmured innocently, as if they had not been in a passionate embrace just moments before.

"Out for a breath of fresh air, Alice?" Lady Achard asked, sounding suspicious.

"Yes. I fear 'tis rather stuffy inside," Lady Havard replied. Then, sounding smug; "In fact, I was just saying so to Lord Achard but a moment ago."

"Arthur is here?" There was no missing the alarm in Hazel Achard's voice. "But he said he was not feeling up to attending tonight."

"Hmmm. He appears to have changed his mind." Lady Havard sounded immensely satisfied. "He asked me if I knew where you were, and I told him I thought you had gone to the table to dine."

"Oh." There was some hesitation, and

then the blur that was Lady Achard turned to Prudhomme. "Thank you so much, my lord. 'Twas most kind of you to take time out to show me your garden. I shall return inside now, I think." She hesitated a moment, then asked a bit archly, "Will you accompany me, Lady Havard?"

"No. I think I should like to see Lord Prudhomme's new fountain. You did mention that your mother had purchased one, Henry?"

"Yes, yes," Prudhomme said at once. "Be glad to show it to you."

"Well . . . I shall be away then," Lady Achard said with obvious reluctance, and her blurred form moved off.

Sure that Prudhomme and Lady Havard would follow, and that she and Adrian could then slip from the trees and go back to the party, Clarissa nearly sighed her relief aloud. However, she was mistaken. The moment Lady Achard was gone, Lady Havard turned on Prudhomme, her voice sharp with jealousy as she asked, "What did she want?"

"Lady Achard claimed she needed a breath of fresh air and asked me to show her the new additions to the gardens, so I did," Prudhomme said innocently. Clarissa rolled her eyes. Goodness, the man was a masterful liar!

"Oh." Lady Havard sounded relieved, but blurted, "When I saw the two of you slip out here, I thought —"

"Hush, my love." The small dark blur that was Prudhomme drew the teal blur of Lady Havard into his arms. "You know there is no other woman for me. I love you, Alice, and I shall do so until I die."

"Yes, Henry." The woman sighed as he kissed a trail down her throat. "It is just that I am so jealous of late."

"There is nothing to be jealous of, my sweet."

Clarissa squinted harder and edged farther forward as Prudhomme leaned back enough to tug some of the teal blur downward. *Good Lord!* She realized with shock that the man had just bared Lady Havard's breasts right there in the garden. At least, that was what Clarissa assumed those blurred blobs were, which Prudhomme proceeded to squeeze and press with loud smacking kisses.

Lady Havard gasped, then grabbed a handful of his wig and tugged his face away from her bosom. "What of that girl?"

"Clarissa Crambray?" Prudhomme's scorn was obvious. "A mere child. What does she know of a passion such as ours?"

"You do still love me then?" she begged.

"Of course," he assured her.

Their blurs blended once more as he offered a moment's reassurance: "I dream of you. I awake with your name on my lips, and imagine that you are mine and that all this sneaking about is unnecessary."

Clarissa rolled her eyes again. Apparently the man did a lot of dreaming — though where he found the time she couldn't say, if he was carrying on with both of these ladies.

"Oh, Henry!" Lady Havard gasped. "Would that I were yours and we could hold each other like this every night."

"Yes," Prudhomme agreed. "Damn your husband for his good health."

Clarissa almost snorted aloud at this familiar refrain, but managed to catch it back.

"Now let me enjoy you for the few moments I do have you," Prudhomme continued, and with that his dark blur suddenly dropped to kneel, then seemed to disappear beneath Lady Havard's skirts.

"Oh, Henry." Lady Havard's shape leaned back against the tree. "Oh, Lord Prudhomme. Oh, oh, oh . . ."

Clarissa stared in amazement, then unthinkingly opened her mouth to ask, "What the deuce is he —"

Mowbray clapped his hand over her

mouth at once, dragging her backward through the bushes.

Grabbing at his arm to keep her balance as they moved, Clarissa glanced at the blur that was Prudhomme and Lady Havard. She really, really wished she had her spectacles. Clarissa had no idea what the man was doing under the woman's skirt, but the moans Lady Havard was emitting seemed to suggest it was pretty amazing. Then Clarissa was dragged out of the bushes on the other side of the path. Adrian allowed her to turn to face forward, then hustled her quickly away.

"What on earth was he doing?" she asked when he drew her to a halt in another small clearing.

Mowbray glanced sharply at her, and she thought he actually blushed, but then she decided she must be mistaken. He finally said, "I shall explain to you someday, my lady. But just now is not the time."

"Why not?" she asked curiously.

"Because you are far too innocent to understand such things. Because you would be embarrassed beyond belief in your innocence. Because . . . because just now I do believe we should return you to the ball," the earl finished, sounding relieved to think of it.

"Oh, but we did not get the chance to dance," Clarissa protested. It did seem that, if she was going to be in trouble anyway, she should at least get to dance first.

"Another time," Adrian promised, offering a gentle smile surely meant to soften the blow.

Clarissa was disappointed, but she allowed him to lead her back toward the noise, music, and lights of the ballroom. "I fear there may not be another time, my lord. Lydia has been doing her best to avoid anyplace you might be. We came here tonight only because she did not think you would bother to attend Prudhomme's ball."

"So that is why I have not been able to find you this week," Adrian muttered, then admitted dryly, "Your stepmother was right. Normally I would not have attended this ball."

"Then why did you come?" Clarissa held her breath, unsure why until she heard his answer.

"Because I knew Prudhomme was considered a suitor, and because I therefore suspected you would come," he admitted.

"Truly?" she asked.

"Yes. Truly."

Clarissa thought Adrian might be smiling too, but she couldn't be sure. Then he smoothed his thumb along her eyes, urging her to stop her squinting as he said, "I, too, quite enjoyed our discourse at the De Morriseys' ball and have looked forward to seeing you again ever since."

"Oh." She tingled with pleasure and sighed. "I wish that . . ."

"What do you wish?" Adrian asked.

Clarissa shrugged unhappily. "I simply wish that Lydia did not feel such antipathy toward you."

He was silent as they walked up the path toward the laughter of the ballroom, then paused to turn her toward him. "Perhaps there is a way to work around that."

"A way?" Clarissa asked with a mixture of curiosity and hope.

"Yes." Adrian peered at her in silence, and then she saw him nod decisively. His fingers tightened on her arm. "Clarissa, should my cousin come to call in the next few days and offer to take you out riding, try to talk your stepmother into allowing it."

"Your cousin?" she asked uncertainly.

"Reginald Greville," Adrian said. "I shall ask him to collect you for me. Your stepmother shall approve. He will bring you out, and I shall meet with the two of you at the park."

Clarissa frowned. She recognized the

name Greville. "I do not think it is very likely he will agree to come collect me, my lord. I fear I have already made his acquaintance."

Adrian chuckled softly. "He told me of your encounter."

"He did?" she asked with dismay. Clarissa hadn't realized it at the time, but Lydia had told her later that she had scalded the man when she'd mistaken his lap for a table and set her tea upon it. She'd rather hoped Adrian hadn't heard about that story. It was humiliating. But then, most of her time in London had been similar.

"Yes, he did. But never fear; I have explained your situation to Reginald. He will be most pleased to help us out."

"Mayhap," Clarissa murmured doubtfully; then she bit her lip and glanced toward the blur that was his face. "He is not a rakehell, is he?" When Adrian went still, Clarissa rushed on. "Because, you see, that is why Lydia is resistant to you. She said that you were a rakehell when you were last at court. Though I am sure she is wrong. But if he is a rakehell as well . . ."

Adrian was silent and stiff for so long, Clarissa began to fear Reginald was a rakehell, but then Adrian relaxed suddenly. "It will be all right."

Clarissa bit her lip, wanting to believe him, but finding it hard to accept that something so wonderful could happen in her life. She had experienced very little joy in the last ten years. First there had been her mother's illness, and then that terrible debacle with Captain Fielding . . . And then Clarissa's mother had died and, while she was still grieving, her father had married the horrid Lydia. Life had been hell in the country, with her stepmother reminding her of her shame every chance she got. The woman was constantly remarking that Clarissa had hurried her mother to her grave with the shameful scandal she'd landed the whole family in.

Clarissa knew Lydia resented and blamed her for the fact that her father avoided London. Unfortunately, Lydia was right. Lord Crambray had avoided the city in the hope that the scandal would eventually be forgotten and that his daughter could yet make a good match. Lydia hated Clarissa for having missed out on several seasons in London, and made little secret of the fact that she couldn't wait to be rid of her.

Yes, Clarissa suspected that resentment and hate were the real reasons behind Lydia's insistence that she not wear her spectacles. She suspected the woman was secretly enjoying every humiliating calamity, especially because her stepmother could then use each accident as an excuse to berate and punish her. And if Lydia had her way, Clarissa would be tied to the hateful Prudhomme for the rest of her life . . . or his. Lydia probably knew exactly how horrid the little man was. Clarissa had noted for quite a while that the two acted friendlier than was warranted given their circumstances, and now she wondered if Prudhomme hadn't proclaimed his undying love to her stepmother a time or two as well and damned Clarissa's father's good health. It wouldn't have surprised her.

"Clarissa? Is that you?"

The sound of Lydia's voice snapping at her through the darkness nearly made her groan. But as she opened her mouth to say good-bye to Mowbray while she had the chance, Adrian shushed her, and his blur seemed to melt into the woods along the path.

"She has not yet seen me. Do not mention me, and simply claim you came out for a breath of fresh air."

"All right," Clarissa whispered, trying not to move her lips as she did.

"And do not forget about my cousin, Reginald Greville. He will come for you tomorrow."

"Clarissa! It *is* you!"

She sighed to herself as her stepmother approached. Whether she claimed she'd come out for air or to escape a raging fire in the house, Clarissa would be in for a lecture, but she would rather it happened away from Adrian.

Whispering good night under her breath to him, she hurried forward to cut Lydia off.

Adrian waited until the two women had disappeared inside the house before slipping out of the underbrush. He didn't bother reentering the house himself, but used the path along the side of the manor to make his way to the front and arrange for his carriage to be brought. Once inside the vehicle, he instructed his driver to take him to one of the more disreputable gaming hells in town, knowing he would find Reginald there. They had both frequented such establishments when younger, but Adrian had lost his taste for such frivolous pastimes after his service in the army. Reginald, who had avoided battle, had not.

As he expected, he found his cousin at the tables, and smiled wryly at the man's shock.

"Devil take it, Adrian!" Reginald gasped,

having turned at the tap on his shoulder. "I thought I should never see you back here. You have shunned such entertainments since returning from the war."

"I have been in the country most of that time," Adrian reminded him. It wasn't worth stating his true feelings on the matter. To start a request for help by insulting a pastime the man enjoyed would be a mistake.

"Well, here, have a seat; join us!" Reginald smiled widely, apparently pleased to have back his old partner in bawdier delights.

Adrian hesitated, then took a seat, unwilling to blurt out what he wanted right there at the table, yet knowing that dragging Reginald from his pleasures was hardly likely to win the man's aid. Resigning himself to several hours in the smoky, desperate environment, he ignored the stares at his scar and mentally prepared all the arguments he would use to convince his cousin once the two got away from the gaming hell. He was going to have to be crafty.

"You must be mad!" Reginald exclaimed two hours later.

Adrian led the way into his town house. He'd convinced his cousin to come back for a drink after leaving the gaming hell, and made his request once the man was trapped in his coach.

Adrian frowned at his cousin's reaction. It was not what he'd hoped for, nor what he'd expected after he'd explained his wish. He had rather been hoping his cousin would be more amenable. "Why mad?"

"Because it is mad to expect me to willingly put myself in such jeopardy," Reginald replied with a laugh. But he followed into the library. "Think of my heirs, or lack thereof, if the chit damages me again."

Adrian rolled his eyes as Reg dropped into one of the leather chairs by the cold fireplace. He himself headed to the rolling table with a decanter of brandy on it, and said, "We are talking about one small woman, not a battalion of Frenchmen."

"Yes, well, Lady Clarissa could do more damage than the entire French army put together," Reginald grumbled.

Adrian frowned, but remained silent, considering his most convincing argument as he poured them each a brandy. He finished pouring, replaced the stopper on the brandy decanter, then picked up the glasses and started back across the room. "I only wish you to pick her up and drop her off. Not spend any real time with her, Reg."

"Yes, but —"

"I would *appreciate* it," Adrian added as he held out one of the glasses to him. They stared at each other silently; then Reginald sighed and reached out to take his drink.

"Oh, all right," he groused, then taunted, "Anything in the name of love and romance. But I hope you remember this when I need a favor."

"I shall," Adrian assured him, and with relief settled into the leather seat opposite.

Reg sighed. "Bravo, old man. So, I will pick up the girl tomorrow for you and bring her to you . . . where?"

Adrian hesitated to answer, knowing this next part was tricky. Finally he said, "We can discuss that in a bit, but first there is one other small detail I have yet to mention."

Alerted by his tone of voice, Reg raised an eyebrow. "And that would be . . . ?"

Adrian avoided his cousin's eyes. "I hesitate to bring this up, but Clarissa's stepmother has a disliking for . . . er . . . rakehells."

Reg raised his other eyebrow. Adrian shifted uncomfortably and added, "Rather like Lady Strummond did."

His cousin's eyebrows now knitted together in suspicion, so Adrian plunged ahead. "I thought mayhap you could use the approach you did to convince Lady Strummond to allow her daughter out of the house."

"Oh, Mowbray, really!"

Adrian winced at his cousin's outrage, but said, "Well, it worked with Lady Strummond."

"Yes, it did, but —"

"It would work again," he insisted. Then he added, "I am sure of it. And only you could pull it off."

"Cousin," Reginald said grimly, "it is one thing to play the fop to get a woman for myself. It's quite another to —"

"Please," Adrian interrupted.

Reginald's eyes widened with incredulity. Adrian Montfort, the Earl of Mowbray, never said *please.* Ever. Suddenly looking uncomfortable himself, he turned his gaze glumly to the cold ashes in the fireplace, then sighed resignedly. "Oh, very well."

CHAPTER FIVE

"A Lord Greville is at the door and wishes to know if the ladies Crambray are in for company."

Clarissa blinked her eyes open and raised her head from the back of her seat to peer toward the doorway and the butler filling it. Her stepmother said, "Who did you say is at the door, Ffoulkes?"

"A Lord Greville," the butler repeated, sounding deadly bored.

Clarissa bit her lip and tried not to look overly excited as her heart began to roar in her ears. Mowbray had said his cousin would come in his stead, and so he had. She crossed her fingers and silently prayed her stepmother wouldn't send him away and ruin everything, then stiffened as she sensed Lydia's gaze turn in her direction.

The woman's voice was full of confusion as she said, "I thought you had already made the acquaintance of Lord Greville?"

Clarissa understood the implication: If he had made her acquaintance, why would he ever return? She managed not to allow the suggestion to upset her, and merely shrugged nervously and offered, "I did. He seemed a very nice man."

"Hmmm." Lydia sounded unconvinced. "I could have sworn I heard that he . . ."

Her voice trailed away, and Lady Havard, who had been taking tea with them and stayed to gossip, said, "I too have heard the whispers that he is a bit of a rogue, Lydia, but I think it is all bunk. Jealousy, most like. He comes from a very good family and is quite friendly with the prince regent."

Clarissa now knew why the woman would encourage Lydia to allow Lord Greville's attentions. No doubt it had to do with her affair with — and jealousy over — Lord Prudhomme; but Clarissa didn't care. She was grateful to Lady Havard, whatever the reason, and held her breath until her stepmother said unhappily, "Oh, very well, Ffoulkes. Show him in."

"Very good, my lady," Ffoulkes murmured, withdrawing from the room.

Clarissa waited impatiently, fingers crossed that the trick would work and she would soon see Lord Mowbray again. The room had gone silent in anticipation, and

Clarissa's ears strained. She clearly heard Ffoulkes open the front door and announce that the ladies Crambray were in.

"Sink me!" a gay voice trilled. "Let me in then. A man could get his wipe prigged out here. I was about to shove me trunk and find some rolling Joe to go in search of a noggin of lightning."

Clarissa was blinking in confusion at these words when Lady Havard announced knowledgeably, "That is cant."

"Cant?" Lydia asked, sounding just as confused as Clarissa felt.

"Slang, dear," Lady Havard explained, the pity in her voice making it plain that they were sadly lacking for not knowing it. " 'Tis all the rage with the young bucks right now."

"Oh." Lydia sounded a tad short. She obviously wasn't pleased to look ignorant. "Well, I rarely follow these new fads. They change so quickly. What did he say?"

There was a brief silence before Lady Havard spoke, and when she did her uncertainty was obvious. "I am not sure. I believe he said something about his hanky being stolen and his gin being hit."

"His gin being hit?" Lydia murmured doubtfully.

"Or perhaps it means hitting the gin," Lady Havard murmured.

"Ah, ladies!" The two words were breathed with delight, and Clarissa blinked and straightened from her listening posture as a blur of color erupted into the room. It was a very active blur of color, one bit waving what appeared to be a hanky about the room as if clearing the way. This most definitely was not Lord Greville — at least, not the Lord Greville she'd met, Clarissa realized with dismay. She glanced anxiously toward her stepmother.

However, rather than appearing taken aback by the obvious impostor, her stepmother was sounding quite charmed. She got to her feet. "Lord Greville, how nice of you to pay us a visit."

"Oh, not at all, not at all. The pleasure is mine." The figure sashayed across the room to Lydia, where he paused and kissed her hand in greeting, then turned toward where Clarissa sat. "Ah, Lady Clarissa, beautiful as ever. Charmed."

Her hand was caught and drawn upward so that a resounding smack of the lips could be placed upon it. The man released her at once, as if her skin were scalding hot, then moved on to Lady Havard. "And Lady Havard — what a delight indeed! I am the most fortunate of men today. Three beautiful women in one room."

85

"You flatter us," Clarissa's stepmother gushed. "Would you care for some tea, my lord?"

"Certainly, certainly. Lovely."

"Do sit down."

"Thank you."

There was a moment of silence as everyone returned to their seats — everyone but Clarissa, who had never left hers — then the others all sighed contentedly.

"Well, this is a surprise, my lord. To what do we owe this visit?" Lady Crambray asked as she poured tea for him.

"Owe?" He sounded surprised. "Why, you owe nothing. I never charge for my company, delightful as it may be."

He gurgled with an almost girlish giggle that made Clarissa's eyes widen in dismay. *Goodness!* She was nearly blind, but not deaf. This definitely was not the Lord Greville she had met. That man had possessed a voice as deep and smoky as his cousin's. His words had been serious and correct. This could not be Lord Reginald Greville, she decided, but the other two women chuckled obligingly at his little joke.

But who was he? Clarissa asked herself. Surely her stepmother and Lady Havard, both of whom had excellent sight, should recognize this man as an impostor if he weren't the real Greville. Yet neither woman seemed alarmed. The only thing Clarissa could think was that it *was* Lord Greville, but that he was putting on some sort of charade. Though she couldn't think why he would behave as he was. He sounded very much like a . . . well, to be frank, he sounded rather feminine.

It was as she had this thought that Clarissa recalled asking Lord Mowbray if his cousin was a rakehell, and warning him that her stepmother would never allow her to ride with one. Obviously the men had decided to put the woman's fears at rest with a performance of masterly proportions.

Clarissa marveled at his acting abilities as Lord Greville confided, "Actually, I was just trying out my new upper ben and calp, and thought to check their effect on the loveliest ladies in London."

Her stepmother and Lady Havard tittered girlishly at the compliment. Clarissa asked what both other women were surely too afraid to show their ignorance by asking, "Er, what exactly is an upper ben and calp, my lord?"

"Why, my greatcoat and hat, girl," Reginald explained in his high, trilling voice. He then jumped to his feet and did a little pirouette before her, presumably showing off his greatcoat and cap as if he didn't know she was blind.

"What think you? Nice fit, is it not?"

Clarissa squinted for all she was worth, but he was still just a whirling streak of chartreuse. It was Lydia who covered for her silence, gushing, "Oh, 'tis lovely. You must give me the name of your tailor so that I may pass it on to my husband."

" 'Tis quite striking," Lady Havard agreed.

Clarissa used a cough to cover her chuckle at the idea of her father even considering wearing such a color. He would have fits. Lord Crambray was very conservative.

Apparently satisfied by their praise, Lord Greville sank back into his seat with a pleased sigh. "I try always to be in fashion. I did wonder if I should not get a matching lally and kickseys as well. What think you?"

"I think that sounds lovely," Lydia murmured with obvious confusion, even as Lady Havard murmured, similarly lost. It seemed the woman's knowledge of cant wasn't as extensive as she would have had them believe.

It was Clarissa who asked, "What exactly would a lally and kickseys be, my lord?"

"Shirt and breeches," Greville explained patiently, and Clarissa's eyebrows flew up at the idea of his wearing a matching chartreuse shirt and breeches beneath the coat. He obviously noted her expression. She could hear the amusement in his voice as he added, "But I thought that might be a bit much, so I dabbled my best white lally and made do. 'Tis for the best, no doubt. I do hate to drop the glanthem."

"I *am* sorry," Clarissa said with confusion. "What did you do to your shirt . . . er . . . lally?"

"I dabbled it . . . *Washed*," he explained at the silence that met his words. "I washed my shirt."

"Oh, yes, of course. Well, that is good," Lydia said, as if she understood.

Ignoring her, Clarissa asked, "And what would glanthem be?"

"Why, money, of course."

"Of course it is!" both older women proclaimed, as if annoyed with Clarissa's obvious ignorance. But she was sure they'd had no idea what glanthem was, either.

"Sink me!" Greville exclaimed with mock horror. "You shall think me cheap. I am not, you know, but Father keeps the purse strings tight. He's old, of course, and does not understand the necessity of fashion. 'Tis absolutely vital one have the proper attire, do you not think?"

When he paused expectantly, Lydia and Lady Havard promptly nodded in agreement. What else could they do should they not wish to appear old?

"Oh, yes, proper attire is vital," they murmured in unison.

Greville heaved a put-upon sigh. "Aye, but everything is so expensive nowadays. Why, I ordered a new pair of hockey-dockeys last week and nearly fainted when I received the bill. And have you seen the price of floggers lately?"

"Floggers?" Lady Havard squeaked. Clarissa could almost hear the woman's eyes blinking in her confusion, but she quickly covered with, "My, yes — very dear."

Clarissa cleared her throat. "I am sorry, but what are floggers and . . . er . . . hockey-dockeys?"

"Floggers are whips, and hockey-dockeys are shoes," Greville explained, then went on to complain, "Only a flat would pay the price they ask for those now." He heaved a distressed sigh and shook his head mournfully. "There is never enough money for a proper outfit. If it would not fret my guts to fiddlestrings, I'd shove my trunk and scamp.

Don't like the idea of having the traps after me and ending up at Tuck 'em fair, though."

"The gallows!" Lady Havard cried with triumph.

When Clarissa and Lydia turned to her in confusion, Lady Havard explained proudly, "Tuck 'em fair. It's the place of execution." She frowned suddenly, trying to piece the rest of his slang together. "Would the traps be the authorities?"

"The magistrate's men," Lord Greville agreed, and Clarissa could hear the grin in his voice.

Lydia, however, wasn't grinning. There was definite horror as she gasped, "Are you saying that the magistrate is after you?"

"Nay! Sink me, I'm the Duke of Moon-struck's son!" Lord Greville sounded shocked that they would for a minute think such a thing, but Clarissa was busy contemplating the Duke of Moonstruck bit. Was that cant too? Or a nickname? For while Lord Greville was a duke, she was quite sure there was no such title as the Duke of Moonstruck.

"Yes, but you just said . . ." Lady Crambray floundered.

"I said *if* I took to scamping they *might* come after me."

"Scamping?" Lydia echoed faintly, obviously feeling rather stupid.

"Took to the highway. Became a highway-man," he explained. "Which, of course, I would not do."

"No, of course not. Well . . . this cant is rather like a puzzle, is it not?" Her step-mother didn't sound altogether happy. Clarissa guessed she didn't like feeling slow, and began to worry that she'd not be allowed to go with Greville despite his efforts if her stepmother got too annoyed. But at that moment, he suddenly flipped out his pocket watch and sat up straight.

"Sink me, my tick says it's time to go," he announced, and Clarissa suspected he'd begun to fear he'd overplayed it himself.

"Go? But you only just arrived." Despite her words, Lydia sounded relieved.

"Aye. Well, I never intended to stay long. I merely meant to stop in and ask if Lady Clarissa might accompany me on a ride through the park. I wanted to show off my upper ben and calp in a more public place, but it would not do to ride the park alone. 'Tis not fashionable, you know."

"Oh, well . . ." There was a hesitation as Lydia glanced toward Lady Havard.

Clarissa could almost hear her step-mother's thoughts. No doubt she was considering the rumors that Lord Greville was a rake and weighing them against the man presently sitting in her salon.

"Oh, let them go," Lady Havard said chidingly. "Lord Greville will take care of her."

It appeared that Reginald's acting had convinced Lydia that there was nothing to fear, for even Lady Havard's chiding encouragement wouldn't have worked otherwise. But Clarissa could see her nodding slowly in permission.

"Very well," she said aloud. "But do not forget your mask, and do be careful and do not . . ."

Excited at the prospect of seeing Lord Mowbray again, Clarissa accepted and donned the mask Lydia shoved at her. Her stepmother's warnings and cautions flew over her head. They were all along the lines of not to touch anything, or to walk without Lord Greville's hand to guide her and so on; and Clarissa had heard these orders often enough that she knew them by heart. She simply nodded dutifully over and over as her stepmother and Lady Havard saw them to the door; then she was hurrying to the open phaeton parked on the street before the house and being lifted onto the bench seat by Greville.

"Well, thank God that is over!"

Clarissa heard the disgusted mutter as

Lord Greville took up the reins of his carriage and set out. The sudden deeper and much more masculine tone of his voice acted as a catalyst, releasing the amusement she'd been holding in. Clarissa burst out laughing, an open, gentle mirth that rolled naturally from her lips and made her cheeks flush with color. When she heard his muttered "damn," however, her laughter faded.

"I am sorry, my lord," Clarissa murmured at once, stifling her laughter. "You must think me terribly ungrateful, and I do not mean to be. 'Tis simply that I can imagine my stepmother's consternation as she tried to follow your conversation and could not. She does hate to appear ignorant."

"That is usually the way of stupid people," Reginald informed her.

Clarissa wasn't sure she'd heard him correctly and frowned in confusion. "My lord?"

Sighing, Greville seemed to relax, though it appeared to take some effort. "I notice you do not mind asking the meaning behind my words."

Clarissa shrugged slightly. "There seems little reason to pretend to any knowledge I lack."

"Aye. Well, my lady, that is a sign of intelligence," he assured her.

Clarissa blinked in surprise. "I do not

understand your meaning."

"Intelligent people have no need to pretend to knowledge they do not have. Only the stupid feel they must feign knowledge about everything and anything. They fear appearing as stupid as they are."

"And intelligent people do not fear appearing stupid?" Clarissa said curiously, wishing to know his feelings on the subject.

"Intelligent people *know* they are intelligent. They also know that one person cannot know all, hence a person is not stupid simply because he is ignorant of one thing or another. They know that, to another intelligent person, they will not appear stupid in asking for an explanation of what they do not know, and so their ignorance on any particular issue does not become an embarrassment."

"Dizzying logic," Clarissa murmured with amusement.

"But you followed it," Greville countered. "Which tells me something."

"And what is that, my lord?"

"That I am an idiot," he answered promptly. "And my cousin is not."

Clarissa blinked. "Excuse me?"

"I said I am an idiot," Greville repeated cheerfully.

"My lord!" Clarissa protested at once, and felt his hand pat hers reassuringly.

"I am. At least when it comes to judging people. I misjudged you terribly."

"You did?" Clarissa marveled.

"Oh, yes. I fear I placed you in the same category as the other silly, vain, and simple-minded girls coming out this season. In fact, I warned my cousin against you."

"Did you?" Clarissa thought he nodded, and she heaved a small sigh. "Well, perhaps you were right to, my lord. After all, I come with a scandal."

She suspected Greville was smiling. He said, "Scandal or no scandal, you are perfect for my cousin. You shall be very happy together."

Clarissa felt herself blushing, and shook her head slightly with amusement at his claim. "You are presuming much, my lord. I have met your cousin only twice. We are but acquaintances."

"Perhaps, but you will not be for long," Greville announced with a certainty that made Clarissa shiver slightly. "My cousin is no fool, and you are perfect for him."

"Now you *do* sound like an idiot," Clarissa murmured, as frightened by his words as she was enchanted by them. "You hardly know me. How can you make such a claim?"

"Because since meeting you he has begun to laugh again," Greville replied seriously. "That is something I have not heard him do for some time. Aye. You are good for him."

Clarissa was wondering over his words when he added, "Treat him gently. He has many scars, and not all of them are readily visible."

Clarissa was about to question those cryptic words when she became aware that the carriage had stopped moving. Glancing around distractedly, she opened her mouth to speak, then paused as a second carriage came to a halt beside them, this one closed. She watched curiously as the door opened and a dark figure leaped out.

"All went well, I see."

Clarissa recognized Lord Mowbray's voice at once, and resigned herself to waiting until later to question Greville further. She smiled at Adrian as he approached, then gasped with surprise as she was suddenly swung from the phaeton to stand on the ground.

"You owe me, cousin," Greville said solemnly.

"That I do," Mowbray agreed, and Clarissa could hear the man's smile. "We shall stay in this area so you can find us easily when it comes time for you to return her."

"As you wish," Greville said; then she heard the snap of the reins and the phaeton moved off.

Once it had disappeared into the green blur of the park, Clarissa smiled in the general direction of Lord Mowbray. She thought he might be smiling back. At least, she believed she heard a smile in his voice as he said, "I thought you might enjoy walking for a bit, rather than getting into my carriage."

When Clarissa's eyes widened in surprise, he added, "I did not think you would be interested in parading about, looking at the other gentry. Besides, even if you did, I fear I got rid of my phaeton some time back and had only this closed carriage to hand."

"Oh." Clarissa hesitated a moment, then said, "You are right in assuming that I am not interested in looking at the other gentry, as seems to be the rage. Not that I could see them anyway," she added with a wry smile. "Still, it does seem less likely that we should be noticed and recognized in the carriage, and should my stepmother hear that —"

"But we wear our masks," Adrian interrupted quickly. "No one shall know who we are."

Clarissa's hand rose self-consciously to

the mask her stepmother had insisted she don ere allowing her to leave with Lord Greville. It was all the rage to ride about in a mask this season, and whatever was the rage, her stepmother insisted she do. "You do not think my clumsiness will give us away?"

Adrian drew her hand over his arm, his voice filled with gentle amusement. "You shall not be clumsy, Lady Clarissa. I shall see to that."

She found herself relaxing at his assurance, and smiled cheerfully as he led her along what she presumed to be a path, but was to her a brown blur. They moved along in companionable silence, but after a time, Clarissa suddenly cocked her ear. "Is that water I hear, my lord?"

Adrian peered around.

"I do not think . . ." he began, then paused briefly before saying, "It has been a long while since I have been here, but I do seem to recall that these gardens have many cascades and fountains. You must be hearing one of those."

Clarissa felt his gaze shift to her, and sensed his smile as he said approvingly, "You have excellent hearing, my lady. I cannot hear it myself, but — as I recall now — there is a fountain near here."

Moments later he spied the fountain and led her to it. They stood at its edge, suddenly oddly uncomfortable.

Clarissa pretended to peer at the green smear of water before her, but her mind was wholly on Adrian. She was agonizingly aware of his presence, and even more aware of the silence that seemed to hang between them like a pall. It was most discomfiting. They had seemed to get along so well at the ball where they met, yet now that they were alone, she could not think of a thing to say. Clarissa was racking her mind when he suddenly gave a small laugh.

"What is it?" she asked, raising her face curiously.

"Nothing," Adrian said, then added, "I was just thinking that I am an idiot. I have been standing here in a panic, searching my mind desperately for some item of conversation to speak on. But it appears that I am a man who has lost all capacity for speech."

Before she could protest, Adrian added, "Around you, Lady Clarissa, I am as nervous as a lad."

"I am nervous also," Clarissa admitted quietly. "And I do not understand how it should be so. We seemed to have no trouble the first two times we met."

"Nay, we did not," Adrian agreed, then

turned her away from the water and said, "Fortunately, I am not a complete idiot, and I did bring something to distract us." He reached into his pocket and withdrew a dark square, then took her hand and filled it.

"A book?" Clarissa asked with surprise.

"Yes."

Aware that he was leading her away from the water, she asked, "Where are we going?"

"There is a small bower just a short distance away that offers some shade. I thought we might partake of it while I read to you."

"You are going to read to me?" Clarissa asked with interest.

"I recalled your saying that — above all things — what you most missed without your spectacles was being able to read. And so I thought to read to you," Adrian explained. "It will not be the same, I know, as being able to read for yourself, but hopefully it will ease your distress somewhat."

"Oh, I am sure it will," Clarissa said quickly, touched that he was so thoughtful, and grateful that he had provided a way for them to avoid conversation until they were both less nervous.

"What book did you bring with you?" she asked curiously as Adrian urged her to settle on a bench in a cool shady spot.

"Ah, well, I brought 'The Rape of the Lock' by —"

"Alexander Pope."

"Aye," he agreed, obviously surprised that she knew the text. "Do you like him?"

Clarissa smiled and nodded, and Adrian audibly sighed. "Well then, I shall begin."

CHAPTER SIX

"Devil take you, cousin! Where have you got to?"

Clarissa blinked in surprise and glanced around at the irritated comment. She recognized Greville's voice even as Adrian's deep, sonorous reading stumbled to a halt; then Reginald's chartreuse figure stumbled into view.

"There you are! Dear Lord, I have been looking for you these past fifteen minutes. I shall be late returning Clarissa. We were to be gone only an hour."

"Has it been an hour already?" Clarissa asked with disappointment. She'd been quietly enjoying listening to Adrian read.

"She was allowed out for only an hour?" Adrian asked with a grimace. He closed the book. "Why such a paltry length of time?"

"How long did you think we'd be expected to be gone?" Reginald asked dryly, as Adrian stood and took Clarissa's hand to help her rise. "We were only going out for a ride."

"Yes, of course," Adrian said with a sigh.

"What's that there?" Reginald asked. "Is that Pope?"

"Aye. Clarissa has missed reading since being deprived of her spectacles, so I thought to read to her," Adrian admitted. He looked embarrassed.

Greville grunted at the thoughtful gesture, but made no comment that might upset either of them. Instead, he turned back the way he'd come. "Let's be off. My carriage awaits, and I can hardly wait to get home and out of this ridiculous coat."

Adrian drew Clarissa's hand through his arm to follow.

"Thank you," she murmured as they followed Greville. "You have a lovely voice, and it was the perfect choice of book. I quite enjoyed your reading."

Adrian shrugged the compliment away. "Aye, well, I had meant to read for only a bit, then to end in conversation. I thought we would have more time."

He fell silent as he herded her around some obstacle — a fallen, ancient tree trunk, Clarissa thought — then he continued, "Which party shall you be attending tonight?"

"The Devereaux."

"I shall be sure to see you there then."

"Oh, yes . . . well . . ." Irritation filled her. "You might as well give up that idea. Lydia has already stated that, should you appear at another party we attend, she shan't leave me alone for a moment. I think she suspects I was with you in the gardens at Prud-homme's. I fear I am a very poor liar. I am sorry."

"Do not be sorry, and do not apologize. I shall arrange something."

Before Clarissa could ask what he meant, he squeezed her hand gently, then lifted her to sit in the phaeton.

"Until tonight," he whispered.

"Lady Crambray. How delighted we are that you could come!"

Clarissa blinked away the boredom that had glazed her eyes and glanced to the pale blue and peach-colored blurs that had appeared beside Lydia. It would be unkind to say she was stunned that someone besides Lady Havard and Lady Achard would claim pleasure in seeing her stepmother, but as those two were usually the only people who spoke to Lydia, Clarissa was rather stunned to hear their hostess and another woman greet her stepmother so.

Lydia seemed rather stunned herself, Clarissa noted, for her stepmother stumbled over her tongue in her effort to reply. "L-Lady D-Devereaux and L-Lady Mowbray. Good evening. How nice to see you. We were most happy to attend, most happy indeed. Were we not, Clarissa?"

Clarissa murmured an agreement, but her attention was on the blue blur that was surely Lady Mowbray. She knew their hostess was wearing pale peach tonight, so that meant the lady in blue was Adrian's mother.

"And this must be the lovely Clarissa." Lady Mowbray moved closer, and Clarissa suspected she was smiling widely. "I've heard a great deal about you, my dear — from both my son and my nephew Reginald."

"Reginald Greville is your nephew?" Lydia asked with interest, nicely sidestepping any comment on Adrian. Her stepmother might not want Clarissa near Mowbray, but she wasn't stupid enough to openly snub him or his family. The Montforts had a great deal of influence in society — at least Isabel Montfort, Lady Mowbray, did. Hence Lydia had been reduced to trying to avoid Adrian rather than flat-out telling him to stay away.

"Yes, he is." Lady Mowbray didn't miss

the lack of comment on her son. At least, Clarissa suspected that was the reason behind the steel in her voice.

"Well, he seems a charming young man," Lydia went on happily, apparently ignorant of her misstep. "He took Clarissa out for a ride in the park the other day."

"So I heard," Lady Mowbray said, and now there was amusement in her voice. Clarissa got the distinct impression that Lady Mowbray knew that Reginald had only taken her to her son. Still, the lady's next words startled her. "In fact, Reginald rhapsodized on so about her, my niece — his sister — was hoping to meet her."

"Oh, well, that would be lovely," Lydia gushed. "Clarissa needs to make friends here in London. It would be good for her."

Clarissa bit her lip, quite sure her stepmother was picturing the boost to their social circle should they be befriended by Reginald's sister. Mary Greville was considered a diamond of the first water. Knowing her could elevate anyone.

"Good, good," Lady Mowbray said. "Then you will not mind if I steal her away for a bit while you help Lady Devereaux."

"Steal her away?" Lydia asked with alarm. Clarissa grimaced, knowing her stepmother was imagining her stumbling, tripping, or bumping into something and blowing this opportunity.

"Yes. Mary turned her ankle today and is forced to rest and keep her foot elevated, so, you see, she cannot come to Clarissa — I shall have to take Clarissa to Mary. It will be fine," Lady Mowbray announced gaily, urging Clarissa to her feet. "The girls will have a lovely time while you are helping Lady Devereaux."

Apparently, Lydia hadn't caught that comment the first time. Now she did, and Clarissa could hear the uncertainty in her voice as she asked, "Help Lady Devereaux?"

"Yes," Lady Devereaux cooed. "I was told you have the most incredible taste in . . ."

Clarissa didn't hear the rest. Lady Mowbray was urging her insistently away from the pair, and hurrying her toward the doors leading into the hall. She went silently, because she didn't have a clue what to say. Clarissa didn't know Lady Mowbray, and wasn't all that certain what was happening. Getting away from Lydia's clutches was a difficult thing at the best of times. At least, it had been since the evening her stepmother had caught her in the gardens after returning from her walk with Adrian. Yet, this had been handled so skillfully . . . It had to have been planned, she thought, and wondered why exactly it had been orchestrated, and where Lady Mowbray was really leading her.

"Here we are," Adrian's mother announced cheerfully, opening a door off the hallway and leading her inside.

Clarissa stepped into the room and paused, her gaze shifting around the blurs that might have comprised a salon. Then her gaze landed on a pale pink confection in a chair by the fire, and she smiled uncertainly.

"This is Mary," Lady Mowbray announced, closing the door. "Mary, this is Lady Clarissa Crambray."

"Hello, Clarissa. It is lovely to meet you."

Clarissa smiled uncertainly, bewildered to find that this had indeed been about introducing her to Reginald's sister. Clearing her throat, she murmured, "I'm sorry to hear about your ankle."

"Oh, my ankle is fine," Mary said cheerfully. "I just have to pretend I twisted it tonight. By morning it will have made a miraculous recovery."

Clarissa stared, wishing she could see the expressions of the two women. She'd never realized how important expression was in communication until she'd lost her spectacles, and her eyesight with them.

Apparently her uncertainty showed, for

Lady Mowbray chuckled softly and moved to her side. "Mary's ailment was invented shortly before we left for the ball, when Adrian asked for my help in getting you away from your stepmother. He seemed to think she would be difficult about his speaking with you."

"And you agreed to help him?" Clarissa asked, uncertain.

"Of course, dear. If Adrian is interested in you, I am more than pleased to help him along."

"But . . ." Clarissa hesitated and then blurted, "My lady, has no one told you about the scandal attached to me?" Silence followed, and she again wished she could see well enough to make out expressions.

Not a moment later, Lady Mowbray clasped Clarissa's hands in her own and said solemnly, "Yes, my dear, I have heard all about the scandal and your brief marriage to Captain Fielding. However, it is my opinion that none of it was your fault. And frankly, I would not care if it were. You are the first woman my Adrian has shown an interest in for ten years. I would not care if you had killed the archbishop of Canterbury; I would still help this along."

Clarissa stood, squinting at the woman in amazement, then was suddenly pulled toward the French doors leading outside.

"Now, come with me, dear," Lady Mow-bray said. "Mary and I are going to sit and visit in here while you speak with Adrian." The woman opened the doors and urged Clarissa through them.

"But what if Lydia —," Clarissa began, only to be interrupted.

"*We* shall deal with your stepmother. Lady Devereaux owed me a favor and will do her utmost to keep your stepmother busy for as long as necessary. And if she fails, I shall handle Lydia myself. Do not worry. Go now. Unless . . . you do not wish to visit with Adrian?"

"Oh, yes," Clarissa said quickly, having heard the concern in the woman's voice. "I do."

"Well, then, off you go." Lady Mowbray's fuzzy image was blocked by the French doors as they closed with a soft click.

Clarissa stared at the blur of curtains and door, then turned slowly and hesitated. She couldn't see very well, but thought there was a path directly ahead. She started to ease uncertainly forward, then paused as a shadow detached itself from the dark haze of trees and moved forward.

"I am glad you wanted to come," Adrian

said, and Clarissa relaxed as she recognized his voice. She should have known he wouldn't expect her to wander through the darkness alone to try to find him.

Clarissa smiled as he took her hand and began to lead her along the path. She said, "Your mother managed to separate me from Lydia."

"So I see." She could hear the smile in his voice.

"I am rather surprised that she did," Clarissa admitted. "But . . . my scandal does not seem to bother her."

"Ah, yes, your scandal," Adrian murmured. "You must tell me about that."

"Have you not yet heard about it?" Clarissa asked with concern. "Your mother said she had, and I hoped it meant you knew about it as well."

"I know what they are saying, but would like to hear the story from you."

"Oh." Clarissa sighed. "Well, there is not really much to tell. I was visiting my aunt, and a servant arrived saying I was needed back home. I rode out of the city with the servant, then we stopped at an inn and Captain Fielding and his sister were there. They said Father was in trouble and had sent them to bring me north, so it was back into the carriage for another long journey.

When next we stopped, Captain Fielding went to meet with Father, or said he was, and returned saying that my father wished me to marry at once, that he needed my inheritance from my mother's father to save the family name." She paused to explain, "I will receive that only when I marry, you see, and Father was supposed to be in debt."

"And Captain Fielding offered himself to help you save the family," Adrian said dryly.

"Yes. I thought it was terribly kind until I found out the truth of it all later." Clarissa made a face. "Anyway, this meant another long ride to Gretna Green to be married, which was followed by yet another long ride. For all the scandal it caused, it was all really rather boring."

"You found getting kidnapped and married boring?" Adrian asked with amusement.

Clarissa shrugged. "Well, it hardly felt like a wedding. We stood in front of a blacksmith with a couple of other people there and said, 'I will,' and bang, it was done."

"And the wedding night?" Adrian asked.

Clarissa frowned. There was a tension in his voice she didn't wholly understand. "There was no wedding night. We could not have annulled the marriage had there been."

"You mean he did not even try to . . . ?"

"He did approach me about it, but we had traveled so much and I was so exhausted . . ." Clarissa shrugged and ducked her head to hide her pink cheeks. She was embarrassed and uncomfortable with this line of questioning. "He did not force me. He left me be and went to sleep in another room."

The tension in his arm, upon which he'd placed her hand, suddenly relaxed, and Clarissa glanced at Adrian curiously, once again wishing she could see his expression.

"I am glad," he said, then added quickly, "Not that I would have blamed you or thought less of you if the marriage had been consummated. I am just glad that it was not."

Clarissa considered his words, then sighed. "The rest of the *ton* thinks the marriage was consummated, do they not?"

"That seems to be the prevailing thought. I am afraid while your father's taking you home to the country to avoid the scandal was understandable, your disappearance allowed a vicious rumor to surface that the marriage had been consummated and produced offspring. Some said you were in the country giving birth to and raising the child from the marriage."

Clarissa's jaw dropped open and she turned to him with horror. "That is what they all think?"

She thought Adrian was frowning, but couldn't be sure until he said grimly, "Perhaps I should not have told you this."

"No, I am glad you did. Better to know what I am dealing with than not." She sighed. "The only problem is, I know of no way to combat such gossip."

"Perhaps there is no way," he said quietly. "Perhaps the only action here is to learn to ignore it and not care what people think."

"Is that possible?" Clarissa asked unhappily.

"I do not know. Does it matter to you what they think? You were so cheerful when recounting your blunders since your spectacles were taken away, I felt sure you did not concern yourself with such things."

"Mostly I do not," she acknowledged. "I know what has and has not happened. I know what kind of person I am. The only time I find it hard is when people whisper behind their fans within my hearing." Clarissa smiled wryly. "I would almost rather they flat-out said these things to me so that I could clear my name."

Adrian reached up to squeeze her hand resting on his arm, then drew her to a halt. "Here we are."

Clarissa turned her gaze forward and

squinted around at the little clearing to which he'd led her. There was something on the ground, a large square with different patches of color. A quilt, she realized, and there appeared to be items on the quilt.

"A picnic?" Clarissa ventured uncertainly. Adrian chuckled and led her forward to sit on one corner of the quilt.

"Yes. I remembered you saying that your stepmother will not let you eat or drink at these functions, and you are left hungry and thirsty. I thought I could remedy that. We have meat, cheese, bread, fruit, and wine."

Clarissa stared at the blur of items around her, tears welling up in her eyes to obstruct her sight further. She'd said she missed reading, so he'd arranged for his cousin to bring her out so that he could read to her. She'd mentioned she could neither eat nor drink and he'd provided her with a picnic.

Incredibly touched by his thoughtfulness and consideration, Clarissa decided Adrian must be the sweetest of men.

"And . . ." He produced something light-colored with a flourish, and Clarissa blinked in confusion until he said, "Your bib, my lady. To prevent any little accidents from giving us away. You may feel free to pretend I am one of your servants and wear it with me. Shall I help you don it?"

Clarissa gaped, then burst out laughing, her tears drying before any had left her eyes. Adrian was definitely the most wonderful of men. He made her laugh and was considerate as well, and she sat still for him to put the bib on her.

" 'Tis not really a bib," he announced as he settled it around her neck. " 'Tis just one of Cook's towels, but it was the best I could do at short notice."

"Thank you," Clarissa murmured. Adrian finished and settled back on his corner of the blanket. "This is all lovely. And I am starved."

"Then we shall eat," he said cheerfully, and began to offer her food. There was cold roast chicken, cheese, a scrumptious sourdough bread, and strawberries, grapes, and apples to choose from. They ate and chatted and laughed an awful lot, and Clarissa thought she must be happier than she'd ever been in her life.

The food was long gone, and Clarissa was laughing at a tale Adrian had just told about troubles with his cantankerous old butler, when she sensed him stiffen and saw his head shift so that he was looking somewhere over her shoulder. Her laughter dying, Clarissa turned to see that a woman in pale pink stood just inside the clearing. Mary, she realized a moment before the girl spoke.

"Aunt sent me to tell you Clarissa has to return now," Reg's sister said apologetically.

Adrian and Clarissa were both silent for a moment; then Adrian said, "I shall bring her back directly. Tell her thank you, and thank you, too, Mary, for your help this night."

"I am glad you enjoyed it. You get little enough pleasure, cousin," the girl said softly, then turned and disappeared back into the night.

Clarissa glanced at Adrian, sorry that it was time for their picnic to end. Neither spoke as he helped her to her feet and removed her bib; then he took her hand to lead her back along the path. When they reached the door where he'd collected her, Clarissa turned her face up to his.

"Thank you, my lord," she said solemnly. "I had a lovely time. I have not enjoyed myself so much since . . . well, since the last time we met," Clarissa admitted with a smile. "I am the most fortunate of women to have a friend such as you."

She sensed the way Adrian stiffened at her words, but didn't understand until he said huskily, sounding disappointed, "A *friend,* Clarissa? Is that how you see me?"

She could feel herself flush, and lowered

her head to hide her face as she admitted, "I did not wish to presume on your —"

Adrian cut off her words by catching her under the chin with one finger, lifting her face, and covering her mouth with his own.

Clarissa went still as their mouths touched, his sliding over hers, soft but firm, brushing in a gentle, insistent caress. Her lips parted slightly as a little sigh escaped; then she felt something press forward into her mouth. Clarissa was so startled that she froze for a moment at the intrusion. When she realized that it was Adrian's tongue, she stiffened even further, shock claiming her. Then his tongue swept through her mouth and she tasted the sweetness of wine mixed with his very own taste, and she sighed again, her body relaxing and her mouth opening further as he tilted her head to the side.

Clarissa had been married but never kissed. She supposed that was odd, but it was how things were. She'd never experienced the excitement and pleasure that were suddenly rushing through her, and found it all a bit overwhelming. Clutching at Adrian's arms to help keep her balance, she really didn't kiss him back at all at first, but stayed still beneath his ministrations until his tongue lashed hers, goading her on.

Uncertain at first, Clarissa moved her own tongue forward and reciprocated, gasping in surprise at the sparks that seemed suddenly to erupt between them.

A groan sliding from his throat, Adrian slid his arms around her, pressing her close to his body as his mouth crushed hers again and again. Clarissa slid her own arms around his neck, nearly strangling him as she tried to get closer still. She felt one of his hands drift down to her bottom and press her forward until she rubbed against a hardness that her mind was too slow to understand just then; then he suddenly released her and stepped away.

Clarissa stared blindly, aware that she was panting. It took her another moment to recognize that Adrian's breathing was ragged as well. His voice when he spoke was a growl, and he said, "You had best go in now."

He opened the door and turned her with a gentle hand, careful to keep a distance between them as he propelled her inside, promising, "I shall see you soon."

Clarissa heard the door close behind her and released a little sigh. Her mouth curved into a soft smile. *I shall see you soon.* Those were the loveliest five words she'd ever heard, she thought, her arms rising to wrap around herself.

"Did you have a good time then?" a voice asked.

"Of course she did. Look at that smile."

Clarissa gave a start, flushing as she recognized Lady Mowbray asking the question and Mary answering. She found the two women approaching from the fireside, and was suddenly worried that they had witnessed the kiss Adrian had given her, but neither woman said anything the least bit embarrassing, or reprimanded her for her poor behavior in allowing such intimacy. There were smiles in their voices as they fussed over her, straightening her hair and brushing wrinkles out of her dress. Lady Mowbray then led her from the room and back to the ball.

They had just reached the door to the ballroom when Adrian's mother paused and turned to face her.

"Clarissa, my dear. I truly . . ." She hesitated, took a breath, and touched Clarissa's hand. "I have never seen my son so happy as he has been in the short time since he met you. I want to thank you for that. Whatever happens, thank you for that."

"He is a very special man," Clarissa murmured, blushing.

"Yes. But not everyone sees that," Lady

Mowbray said sadly. "Some cannot see past the scar on his face."

"Like my stepmother," Clarissa suggested quietly.

"She is only one of many," Lady Mowbray assured her, then heaved a little sigh and added, "We had best go in now. Your stepmother will be frantic by this time." And taking her arm, Lady Mowbray led her into the ballroom and across the floor to her stepmother.

"There you are!" Lydia was on her feet by the time they reached her, and Clarissa could hear the anger underlying her words. "You have been gone for two hours."

"That is my fault," Lady Mowbray said with a smile. "I am afraid the girls were getting along so well, I did not have the heart to bring an end to it."

"Well, I am glad," Lydia murmured, but Clarissa frowned, recognizing that her stepmother wasn't appeased. Something was wrong.

"Well, the two of you must come to tea soon," Lady Mowbray went on cheerfully, not knowing Lydia well enough to recognize anything amiss. "I shall invite you and Mary, too, so that the girls can have another visit."

"That would be delightful," Lydia replied.

Lady Mowbray hesitated and then nodded. "Till we meet again then."

Adrian's mother gave Clarissa's hand a little squeeze, then turned and left them alone. The moment she was out of hearing, Lydia took Clarissa's arm and urged her to move.

"Where are we going?" Clarissa asked warily. Her stepmother led her across the ballroom.

"Home," the woman snapped.

Clarissa bit her lip, but she remained silent as they left the Devereaux home and waited for their carriage. Lydia didn't go on the attack until they were safely seated inside with the door closed.

"You were awfully flushed when you returned from your 'visit with Mary.' " Lydia's voice was cold and emotionless.

Clarissa went still, feeling extremely wary. "We were seated by the fire. It was a bit warm."

"And your lips were still a touch swollen from kissing Lord Mowbray outside the salon doors."

Clarissa felt herself freeze inside. "You saw?"

"I saw," Lydia agreed in a voice full of rage. "Lord Prudhomme wished to speak to me, and we went for a short walk in the

123

gardens. We saw you on our way back, and watched from the trees as you let Mowbray paw you like an animal and —"

Lydia paused abruptly, as if too sickened to continue. But Clarissa hardly noticed; she had stiffened at the mention of Prudhomme and a walk in the garden, distinctly recalling what she'd witnessed of the man's walks in the garden with other women.

"How you can let that man touch you?" Lydia snarled. "Here you have a good man like Lord Prudhomme willing to overlook your scandalous past, and you choose to — once again — throw yourself toward ruin. This time with Mowbray."

"Prudhomme? A good man?" Clarissa asked with amazement. Then she realized she'd never told her stepmother what she'd seen in the gardens.

"Yes. A good man," Lydia snapped. "He is willing to overlook the scandal, your clumsiness, and even the kiss he witnessed."

"Is that not kind of him," Clarissa said dryly. "I suppose in return I am to overlook his affairs?"

"What? Whatever are you talking about?" Lydia asked, but there was far more than curiosity in her voice. Clarissa was sure she heard panic there, and wished like crazy that she could see well enough to make out the woman's expression.

"I mean Lady Havard and Lady Achard," she explained slowly. "The night you found me in the garden, I witnessed him toying with both women."

"What?" Lydia said. "What are you rambling about?"

"I am saying that I nearly ran into him and Lady Achard in the gardens, but ducked into the bushes." There was no need to mention Adrian at this point. "I overheard them talking. It seems they had just made love. He proclaimed his undying devotion, cursed Lord Achard's good health, as he was keeping them from proclaiming their love to all; then Lady Havard interrupted to announce that Lord Achard was at the ball. Lady Achard hurried back to the ballroom, and Prudhomme proceeded to proclaim his undying passion and love for Lady Havard, cursing Lord Havard's good health in exactly the same words he used with Lord Achard. Then he proceeded to disappear under Lady Havard's skirt."

Silence met her announcement. While Clarissa couldn't make out Lydia's expression, she could tell that her stepmother had gone pale.

"You are lying," the woman said shakily.

"No. I am not," Clarissa replied. She

added, "I was not alone. I was not the only one to witness this."

"Who else?"

Clarissa hesitated. She was already in trouble over Mowbray, and hesitated to bring him up. On the other hand, perhaps Lydia would stop pushing Prudhomme at her if she could be convinced of the truth.

"Mowbray," she said at last. "You may ask him if you do not believe me."

Clarissa never saw the slap coming, but she certainly felt it. The pain was sharp and sudden and her head jerked to the side from the impact. Reaching up, she clasped her cheek and slowly turned to squint at her stepmother.

"We will not speak of this any more," Lydia said. "But you will not be seeing Mowbray again . . . ever."

Clarissa sat stiff and still, inwardly seething. In all the years Lydia had been her stepmother, Clarissa had never once been hit.

The carriage door opened. They'd arrived at home without her even noticing. Clarissa nearly tripped over her skirt in her haste to disembark the carriage. The footman caught her arm to steady her. She murmured thank you as she pulled away and hurried up the path to the front door.

Ffoulkes, or someone Clarissa presumed was Ffoulkes, opened the door as she approached. She sailed in and hurried straight upstairs, and had just reached the privacy and safety of her room when Lydia caught up to her.

"Clarissa," her stepmother hissed, catching her arm in a painful grip and opening the door. Releasing a slow breath, Clarissa turned to face her stepmother, then simply waited, unwilling to speak and draw more anger down upon herself.

"I never want to speak of this night again," Lydia repeated firmly. "But I just want to be clear that you will not see Lord Mowbray. How you could let him touch you . . ." The woman was clearly still furious, her breathing heavy as she paused and — no doubt — glared at Clarissa. "Your father would never forgive me if I let that man ruin you. And Prudhomme will not be welcome in our home anymore either. Courting you while . . ." Her voice cracked, and Clarissa was even more convinced that Lydia had somehow been involved with the man. If he hadn't already been having an affair with her, he'd certainly worked hard at obtaining one. The woman was struggling under strong upset.

After a moment, Lydia gave up the

struggle and turned away to hurry off to her own room. When that door slammed shut, Clarissa allowed the tension to drain from her body with a sigh. She then stepped into her bedroom, and started as a figure appeared from behind the door.

"I am sorry, my lady," her maid, Joan, said. "I did not mean to startle you. I was waiting for you to return so I could help you undress."

"Of course you were," Clarissa said quietly, and let the door close behind her. She was still getting used to the girl's silent ways. Her old maid had been slightly more outspoken, likely due to her age.

Joan set to work, but there was a tension about the girl while helping her undress that Clarissa wasn't used to. After several minutes, she finally said, "What is it, Joan? I can tell you want to say something, but —"

"I am sorry, my lady," the maid murmured, then blurted, "Your gown is wrinkled, you have a mark on your face where it appears you have been slapped, your lips are slightly swollen as if you have been kissed, and I overheard what Lady Crambray said about Lord Mowbray. It seems obvious that something has gone on between the two of you. My lady, he . . . they say his heart is as deformed as his face, and that he . . ." Her voice trailed off as Clarissa turned a hard look her way. "I am just worried about you, my lady. You are sweet and kind and good, and — I think — a little naive. I would not wish to see him take advantage of you."

Clarissa turned away, anger burning inside her. Adrian had shown her nothing but kindness and consideration. He listened to what she said, to the things she missed or wished for, and he set out to give them to her. And he hadn't once tried to take advantage of her. For a moment, Clarissa considered telling Joan to mind her own business, but then she decided Adrian deserved better; he deserved for her to defend him. Besides, she wanted at least one person on her side, even if it was only her maid.

Settling onto the dressing table chair for Joan to let her hair down, Clarissa cleared her throat and recounted the night she'd first met Adrian, then the second time, and so on, not leaving out a single detail. Once she finished recounting everything, right up to the conversation Joan had overheard between Clarissa and her stepmother, Clarissa fell silent and waited.

"He sounds wonderful," Joan said in a quiet voice. "Nothing like those tales people whisper behind his back."

"He *is* wonderful," Clarissa said, and blinked away the tears that had gathered in her eyes. It was ridiculous, but she was extremely grateful that the maid thought well of Adrian. His own family did, of course; but they would. It was nice to have some objective validation of her own feelings for the man.

"Well," Joan said, finishing brushing out Clarissa's hair. "I think you should continue to see him. If he arranges another picnic, enjoy it."

"Really?" Clarissa asked.

"Certainly," the maid said firmly, then added, "My lady, I have not seen you this happy in all the time I have worked here. Your eyes light up when you talk about him, and a soft smile claims your lips. 'Tis obvious that if you are not in love with him already, you soon will be."

Clarissa blinked in surprise at the girl's suggestion, and remained silent as she finished preparing for sleep. Joan then turned down the covers, watched her slip into bed, wished her good night, and left the room. The maid's words were still playing through Clarissa's head as Joan pulled the door closed.

My lady, I have not seen you this happy in all the time I have worked here. Your eyes light up when you talk about him, and a soft smile claims your lips. 'Tis obvious that if you are not in love with him already, you soon will be.

Was it true? she wondered. Was she falling in love with him? Or, was she even *already* in love with him?

Clarissa didn't know. All she knew was that she liked Adrian, that she was bored and weary when he wasn't around, and that she seemed to come alive only when he appeared. She laughed with him, and enjoyed talking to him and now that he'd kissed her . . . it seemed to be all she could think about — that, and the next opportunity she might have to experience those kisses again. All of that seemed to suggest that she was falling in love with the man. And if she was . . . it was the most wonderful feeling in the world. Clarissa couldn't wait to see him again.

She just didn't know how it would happen.

CHAPTER SEVEN

"Your shawl, my lady."

Clarissa blinked in confusion as Joan suddenly appeared at her side with the garment in hand. "My shawl?"

"Yes. You said you were chilly and asked me to bring you your shawl," Joan repeated firmly, then bent and *tsk*ed over a spot on Clarissa's skirt. "I fear we did not get all the punch out of your dress from the night you spilled it at the Brudmans' ball. Perhaps you should accompany me upstairs to change."

"What?" Clarissa squinted down at her skirt. Not that she would have been able to make out anything anyway, but she was sure this wasn't the gown she'd been wearing when she'd spilled the punch. That had been her forest green dress.

"Yes, yes, take her upstairs to change, Joan," Lydia said with obvious irritation. "The girl cannot be in a stained gown at my first ball. I do hope no one has noticed."

"I am sure they did not, my lady," Joan said soothingly, her hand firm as she pulled Clarissa to her feet.

"But . . ." Clarissa began only to be shushed by Joan, who rushed her through the ballroom and out of it. The maid didn't let her speak until they were in the hall, when Clarissa was allowed to whisper, "But this was not the gown I was wearing when I spilled punch at the Brudmans' ball."

"I know, my lady," her maid admitted, "but Lady Crambray has a bad memory, and I needed to get you out of there."

"Why?" Clarissa asked with surprise.

"Because there is a boy at the door with a message for you, and he will not give it to anyone but you."

"Oh," Clarissa said. "I wonder what it is?"

"I do not know, my lady. But it was just fortunate I happened to be passing the door on the way upstairs, else Ffoulkes might have answered, and then your stepmother would know."

Clarissa grimaced. Ffoulkes was very proper and upright, and would certainly have informed Lydia. With Clarissa's luck, it would be a message from Adrian and she would never have known what it was, because Lydia would have snatched the letter and burned it right in front of her.

"Do you think it is from Adrian?" she asked Joan hopefully. She hadn't seen him since the night of the Devereauxs' ball, a week ago, and all she'd been able to think of was how he'd treated her to a picnic and then kissed her. She'd been missing him terribly.

"I do not know, my lady, but if it is, you must tell him not to send messages like that. Tell him to send the boy to me in future. It will not raise eyebrows if a poor boy brings *me* a message. I can claim he is my little brother."

"Do you have a little brother?" Clarissa asked curiously as they approached the front door.

"No," Joan admitted. "I have no family at all anymore."

"I am sorry," Clarissa murmured, but they reached the door, and Joan merely shrugged and opened it to reveal a small boy of perhaps six on the front stoop.

"Here she is," Joan said, gesturing to Clarissa. "Now, give us the message."

The boy peered up at Clarissa, his eyes huge in a dirty face. He pulled something from inside his shirt and held it out. "I was told I'd get a coin for me trouble."

"Oh." Clarissa stared, nonplussed, and then turned to Joan. "My coin purse is up in my room."

"Here." Joan dug a small bag out of the folds of her skirt and handed over the money. "Off with you now."

"Thank you, Joan," Clarissa said as the maid closed the door. "Take a coin from my change purse to replace it."

"I would not presume to go into your purse, my lady," Joan murmured, then glanced up the hall as Ffoulkes appeared and started to walk toward them.

Taking the note from Clarissa, the maid tucked it between them as she took her lady's arm to lead her to the stairs, saying loudly, "Come, we had best take care of getting you changed, my lady."

Clarissa waited until they got to her room to open the message and try to read it. Of course, she couldn't read a darned thing without her spectacles, so Joan took it from her to read.

"It says, 'Meet me at the fountain.' 'Tis signed, 'A.M.' "

"A.M.? It *is* Adrian," Clarissa said happily.

"You must tell him to send the messages to me from now on," Joan reminded her with worry. "If Ffoulkes had got this and given it to your stepmother . . ."

"Yes," Clarissa agreed, then glanced

around with surprise as the maid herded her to the door. "Should I not change first?"

"After," Joan said firmly. "If I change you now and he wrinkles your gown as he did last time, I shall just have to change you again."

"Oh, yes, of course," Clarissa said, but she was blushing at how her gown had gotten wrinkled the last time. He might kiss her again, she realized, and she felt her toes curl up in her shoes at the very idea.

Joan walked her down to the main floor using the servants' stairwell, checked to be sure the hallway was empty, then hustled her out the French doors in the dining room to avoid guests or staff. Stopping at the door, the maid turned to her. "Can you make it from here?"

"Yes." Clarissa nodded. One of the advantages of the town house was that she knew her way around it and its grounds pretty well. She was certain she could make her way to the fountain without assistance.

"Good, then I shall wait here to sneak you back upstairs. It will give the two of you some privacy," Joan said. At the last moment she added, "Be careful."

"I will," Clarissa assured her, but could hear the frown in Joan's voice as the servant replied.

"Maybe I should come with you. You could —"

"No, no," Clarissa said quickly. "I shall be fine. And I will try to hurry."

"No, take your time. I do not want you rushing and hurting yourself," Joan insisted, then opened the door and urged her out.

Clarissa slid through the door and made her way quickly but carefully toward where she knew the path would be that led down to the clearing with the fountain. She found the path easily enough and hurried along, excited at the prospect of seeing Adrian. It seemed so long. Lydia had canceled all their outings this past week and had refused any and all visitors. No matter who approached, Ffoulkes had answered the door with the announcement that the ladies Crambray were not in to visitors. Clarissa wasn't sure if it was meant as a punishment, or intentionally to keep her from Adrian, but in the end the result was the same: she hadn't seen him in a week.

Clarissa had been surprised to find that Lydia refused even to see Lady Havard and Lady Achard. The three women had been inseparable before this. It was more suggestion that Lydia had been having an affair with Prudhomme as she'd suspected, and that she was now refusing to see any of them out of humiliation.

Clarissa saw the blurry shape of the fountain ahead, and picked up speed in her eagerness to reach it and see Adrian. And then . . . *crash.* She didn't see the branch she ran into. Light exploded inside her head, along with pain, and Clarissa stumbled forward several feet and felt herself falling.

When next she opened her eyes, it was to an anxious voice calling her name over and over. It took a moment for her to realize it was Adrian. Blinking, Clarissa winced as pain made an appearance. It was no little headache type of pain either, but a serious hammering along the front of her forehead. Clarissa quickly closed her eyes again.

"Oh, thank God," Adrian murmured by her ear, and she thought she felt him press a kiss to her brow.

"Adrian?" She forced her eyes open again. His face was dark above her, but almost in focus for a change.

"Are you all right?" he asked. "When I found you in the fountain, I thought you were dead."

"In the fountain?" Clarissa asked with confusion, and frowned as she raised a hand to touch his face. Water dripped down her arm. "Why am I wet?"

"You were in the fountain," Adrian repeated — slowly, as if the reduced speed might make it easier for her to comprehend. He eased her to an almost upright position in his arms. "How are you? Are you seeing double or anything?"

"I do not think so." She forced herself to sit up fully and take her own weight, then peered around the darkness surrounding them. She could see enough to know they were right beside the fountain. Adrian was wet, too, and she supposed it had happened when he'd pulled her out.

She turned to peer at the fountain, knowing exactly how it looked despite her blindness. The edifice had stood as long as she could recall, it being her favorite spot as a child. It was huge around the base, but really quite shallow, with perhaps a foot and a half to two feet of water. Enough to drown in, she supposed. "I was *in* the fountain?" she echoed.

"Yes."

"What was I doing there?" she asked with confusion.

"Floating," Adrian said. "I thought you'd fallen in and drowned."

"Fallen in." She recalled hurrying out to meet him, running into the branch and then crashing forward . . . She must have stumbled into the fountain, Clarissa realized with a frown. Then she decided it was good she hadn't changed into a clean dress after all.

"I got the shock of my life when I saw you lying there," Adrian continued grimly. "What were you doing? How did you end up in there?"

"I was coming to meet you, as you asked, but hit my head on a branch. I remember falling forward before I blacked out, but . . ." Clarissa frowned, then shook her head. "I must have stumbled."

"Meet me?" Adrian asked.

She frowned at the surprise in his voice. "Yes, I got your letter. I —"

"My lady?"

They both turned to peer at the dark shape that hurried down the path toward them. "I am sorry to intrude, but your mother is asking after you. We must go, my lady. I have to get you changed and . . ." There was a pause; then Joan asked with alarm, "What have you done to your dress?"

" 'Tis all right, Joan. I fear I had a little spill," Clarissa said. Adrian helped her to her feet.

"Oh! I knew I should have accompanied you." The maid shook her head, sounding exasperated as she added, "I shall insist next time. Now, come, we have to go."

"I have to go," Clarissa echoed apologetically as Joan began to tug her away. "I am sorry we did not get the chance to talk, my lord. I came as quickly as I could in response to your note. Perhaps we will meet again soon."

"Note?" Adrian frowned as the pair disappeared down the dark trail and back through the woods to the house. He hadn't sent any note. But it was possible Reginald had found it impossible to talk to Clarissa alone, and slipped her one. Adrian had asked his cousin to approach her as soon as he arrived, and to ask her to meet him here by the fountain. This was the only place Adrian had known to suggest for a meeting to take place. He'd never seen the Crambray home, inside or out, but Clarissa had mentioned the fountain during their picnic at the Devereauxs' ball. She'd thought that the Devereauxs could do with a fountain just like it.

Sighing, Adrian turned to peer at the structure. He could understand why Clarissa liked it; most peaceful it was to stand and listen to the soothing sound of water. Mind, it hadn't been nearly so peaceful when Clarissa's body had been floating within.

Adrian shuddered and ran his hands over his face to wipe away the memory. It was the very last thing he'd expected to find after climbing over the back gate and into the yard. His whole plan had been born of desperation. It had been a week since he'd seen Clarissa and shared a first kiss. He had gone home that night feeling on top of the world. His plan had worked beautifully. The picnic had been a great success. She had been pleased. The kiss had been a wonderful bonus. Adrian hadn't intended to take such liberties, but she'd stood there, her eyes glowing with happiness in the moonlight, her lips a soft curve as beautiful and velvety-looking as the petals of a rose, and he hadn't been able to help himself. He'd wanted to sip of that glowing happiness curving her lips.

Once he'd kissed her, however, Adrian had realized the mistake he'd made. She was soft and warm and melted into him like butter dissolving into toast, and he'd wanted to do much more than kiss her. That was why he'd made himself end the kiss so soon. He'd left the Devereauxs' feeling both excited and eager to see her again.

Adrian had made many plans since on

how best to separate her from her step-mother at future balls, to get her alone to read to her or maybe dance in the gardens, or picnic again, or perhaps even kiss. He'd enlisted his mother's aid, both of his cousins, and even some of their friends to prepare for the opportunity. But it was all to no avail. Clarissa and her stepmother hadn't attended a single ball since.

Adrian had even finally hired a man to find out what they were doing that might keep them away from balls, to find any information that he might exploit to see her. However, it appeared they'd been doing nothing. Neither woman had left the house this whole last week. It would have concerned Adrian greatly, except his man had learned by bribing a staff member or two that neither lady was ill; Lady Crambray had simply canceled attendance of all balls and refused all visitors. Even Reginald had been turned away when Adrian had talked him into trying to collect Clarissa for another ride through the park.

Adrian had feared that Lady Crambray somehow found out about their little picnic, and he had become sure of it when Prud-homme made a sarcastic comment to him at one of the balls he'd attended. And so, the moment Adrian heard about the ball her stepmother planned, he'd come up with a scheme to get to speak to Clarissa.

While he hadn't been invited to the ball, and neither had Adrian's mother or his cousin Mary, nor even Reginald, one of Reginald's friends had, and Reginald had accompanied that friend tonight. His sole purpose in coming had been to send Clarissa out here to meet with Adrian, who would climb the back gate, find the fountain, and wait for her there. Adrian had left home early, intending to be waiting long before Reginald arrived to send Clarissa out, and so he had been shocked to arrive at the fountain to find her floating in it. He'd thought his heart would stop at the sight of her slight body floating in the shallow water, her gown and hair billowing about her in the moonlight.

"Adrian?"

He stilled at that whisper, and glanced toward the path where Reginald appeared and hurried toward him.

"There you are." His cousin paused at his side, glancing around at the spot chosen for the rendezvous and nodding in approval. "This should do nicely."

"For what?" Adrian asked with confusion.

"For your meeting with Clarissa," Reginald explained. Then he added, "Speaking of which, I have yet to see her and tell her to come out here. Her maid apparently took her away to change her gown or something, and has not yet returned. I only came out to let you know that so you would not worry. I am sure she shall return to the party soon, and I shall ask to be shown the gardens and bring her to you.

"But never fear; I will not stay with you," he added reassuringly. "I shall leave as soon as I have brought her, and will wait by the house to escort her back in when the two of you are finished."

Adrian stared at Reginald, confusion suffusing him. "You mean, you have not yet given her the message?"

"No. As I say, she is up in her room at the moment, and has been since I arrived."

"But she said she got my note." Adrian frowned. "I thought you had perhaps had trouble talking to her alone, and had given her a note instead."

"No." Reginald frowned. "You mean she was here? You have already seen her?"

"Yes," Adrian murmured thoughtfully. "She was here when I arrived, floating unconscious in the fountain. She ran into a branch and knocked herself out, apparently. Landed in the water."

Adrian suddenly turned to survey the

fountain, then the path. Reginald made a sound of disgust and said, "Lady Crambray is an idiot. That girl is going to end up dead in one of these accidents, and all because of her ridiculous refusal to allow spectacles."

"I begin to wonder if these are accidents," Adrian said.

Reginald blinked. "Oh?"

"Well, I did not send her a note. And if you did not give her a message, Reginald, who did?"

His cousin frowned. "You did not send her a note?" he repeated.

"No. Why would I? You were to give her the message for me. Besides, I know she cannot see without her spectacles. She could not read a note. I would never send her a written message."

"Her maid could read it to her," Reginald pointed out.

"Yes, but that is not the point. The point is, I did not send it."

"Right. Oh . . . I say!" Realization struck. "If you did not, who did?"

"I do not know." Adrian frowned and moved to the path to peer up at the branches overhead. None of them was low enough for Clarissa to hit her head on them. Not if she'd been on the path. He supposed she could have been off the path a bit, but that would have been noticeable. In fact, it would have been a struggle for her to get through the foliage that lined the path in her long skirt.

Adrian turned and peered back at the fountain again, recalling the wound on her forehead. How could she have stumbled from the edge of the path to the fountain to fall in? Even if she'd been dazed and still on her feet . . .

"What are you doing?" Reginald asked, moving to his side.

"Clarissa said she hit her head on a branch and fell into the fountain."

Reginald glanced around, then shook his head, echoing Adrian's own thoughts. "That is not possible. There are no branches for her to have hit her head on."

"I know," Adrian said with a frown. "But someone gave her a message to come out here; then she somehow ended up with a head wound and floating in that fountain. If I had not come along, Clarissa would have died. In fact, I feared for her life when I first saw her."

Reginald was silent, his eyes moving over the fountain and then shifting to examine the trees. They returned to the fountain. "You think someone lured her out here . . . to do her harm?"

Adrian remained silent. When spoken out loud it sounded ridiculous, but . . .

"Why?" Reginald asked, apparently taking his silence as an affirmative. "Why would anyone harm her?"

"I do not know," he admitted.

His cousin frowned and then said, "And who else knows about the two of you? Am I not the only one?"

"I am not sure. Mother and Mary know, of course, but they would not be behind this." Adrian frowned. "But Prudhomme may know as well."

"Prudhomme?" Reginald said with surprise.

Adrian nodded. "I think he might have spotted us in the garden that night Mother arranged it for our picnic. I did not see him, and I could be wrong, but he made a snide comment to me the other night about 'kissing Clarissa in the moonlight.' "

"Hmm." Reginald frowned, then asked, "What about her maid?"

"Whose maid? Clarissa's?" Adrian frowned and then nodded. "I suppose Joan must know. She is the one who fetched Clarissa back to the house, because her mother was looking for her. She was not surprised to see me here." Adrian shook his head and added, "But she knows Clarissa cannot read without her spectacles."

"Hmmph." Reginald frowned suddenly and asked, "How *did* Clarissa read it, then?"

"I do not know," Adrian admitted.

They were both silent for a moment; then Reginald said, "What makes you so sure this was not just an accident — like all her other accidents?"

"Because I did not send her a message except through you," Adrian reminded him.

"Yes, but . . ." His cousin frowned and then suggested, "The letter could have been a prank, and the rest just an accident."

"There is no branch for her to have run into," Adrian pointed out. Then he added, "And now I am starting to wonder about these other accidents as well. She's had an awful lot of them — falling down stairs, stepping out in front of a horse and buggy . . ."

"Oh, now, Adrian! I fear you are losing my support here. Clarissa is as blind as a bat without her spectacles. She set her teacup in my lap thinking it was a table," Reg pointed out. "She set Prudhomme's wig on fire. A fall down the stairs, and her having stepped in front of that carriage — that is hardly surprising."

"I suppose so," Adrian acquiesced, but then he added, "I need to talk to her."

"There is probably no way to get her out here now. 'Tis growing late. Besides, her stepmother was heading off to look for Clarissa when I stopped to talk to her and asked where the girl was. She was changing. It does not sound to me like she was likely to let Clarissa out of her sight for long. Perhaps we should give it up for tonight and think of a better plan for tomorrow."

Adrian gave a grunt that might have been agreement, but his gaze was on a window on the second floor of the house. Candlelight had filled the room several moments before, and he could now see the silhouettes of two women. When the taller began to undress the smaller, he realized it must be Clarissa and her maid. He watched as her clothes were stripped away, article by article.

"Did you hear me, Adrian?"

He glanced reluctantly to the side to see Reginald frowning. "What?"

"I said, I am going to return to the party, make my excuses and go home."

"Very well," Adrian murmured, his gaze flashing back to the window. He was vaguely aware of his cousin saying something and moving off, but the bulk of his mind was focused on the scene taking place in the bedroom.

He continued to watch right up until the

women disappeared, taking the candlelight with them; then Adrian knew what he had to do. He had to climb up to her room and wait for Clarissa to return. Then he would ask her about tonight and the other accidents she'd encountered. He was sure from this he would learn whether there was something for him to worry about or not.

Satisfied with his plan, Adrian made his way closer to the house to survey the tree outside her window. It looked like it would be an easy climb.

"The party ended earlier than expected."

Clarissa smiled faintly at Joan's observation and gave a weary shrug.

"Yes. Lydia will not be pleased. I escaped just as the last guests were leaving, to avoid her wrath."

A successful party was one that lasted until nearly dawn. By that accounting, Lydia's party *wasn't* a success. Her stepmother would be livid. The woman was short-tempered at the best of times; she'd be impossible to live with tomorrow. Clarissa muttered to herself as Joan undid her gown.

"How is your head?" the maid asked as she began to remove the dress.

Clarissa grimaced at the reminder she

didn't need about her head wound. Fortunately, the branch had hit her high and mostly on the side, leaving any mark hidden in her hair, but she didn't have to see it to know it was there. Her head had been aching most of the evening. However, all she said was, "It will be fine by morning, I am sure."

"Is it aching?" Joan asked with concern. "Would you like a draft?"

"No, no. Thank you, Joan, but I shall be fine."

The maid hesitated, then nodded and carried her gown over to lay it upon the chair by the wardrobe, to be cleaned on the morrow. "That reminds me, did you tell Lord Mowbray to send future messages to me?"

"No. We did not really get the chance to talk. I did not even get the opportunity to ask him why he wished to see me," Clarissa admitted, and heard Joan tut-tut as if she had wasted an opportunity. But there had been no opportunity to waste! The maid had rushed her back to the house to change into a fresh, dry dress before she could really talk. If she and Adrian had shared even a minute to speak, Clarissa would have asked him why he'd wished her to meet him. Still, since Lydia had been heading upstairs to find out what was taking them so long when they'd started down, Clarissa supposed her maid's decision had been a good one.

"There," the woman said, dropping a nightgown over Clarissa's head. "I brought you warm cocoa to help you sleep."

"Thank you, Joan. Truly, for everything," she added solemnly.

"You are welcome, my lady," the maid said quietly as she moved to the door. "Sleep well."

Clarissa heard the door click shut as she turned to make her way to the bed. Joan had set the candle on the bedside table for her so that all she had to do was blow it out. She did so, careful not to get too close to the flame, and then lay down. Her head ached and she was exhausted — far too tired even to bother with the cocoa, lovely as it smelled.

Clarissa then lay there, wondering why Adrian had wanted to see her and wishing they'd had a better chance to interact. Life was always more exciting when he was around. She smiled as she drifted off to sleep.

CHAPTER EIGHT

Clarissa was dreaming about Adrian. He'd taken her out on a lake in a small boat, and was reciting poetry to her as he rowed across the placid water. Unlike the poetry Prudhomme had read, this was beautiful, heart-wrenching prose about unending passions and undying love. But he paused suddenly, tilted his head, and said, "Clarissa? Where the hell are you? Ouch! Dammit. Clarissa?"

Frowning, she blinked her eyes open and was suddenly awake. But the dream didn't end: Adrian's voice followed her.

"Clarissa? Say something. I cannot see a damned thing."

"Adrian?" she murmured sleepily.

"Clarissa?" His voice was a whisper in the darkness, coming from somewhere beyond the foot of her bed.

Awake now but still confused, Clarissa gave her head a shake. She must still be dreaming, she thought. It was the middle of the night. He couldn't really be in her bed chamber. Could he?

"Ouch."

What on earth . . . ? Sitting up in bed, Clarissa stared into the dark with incredulity. "Adrian?"

"Yes. Where are you? I cannot see a damned thing. Keep talking. I shall follow your voi— Ouch! Dammit. Why is there furniture in the middle of the floor?"

The bed shook as he bumped into it, and Clarissa squinted into the darkness and asked in an amazed whisper, "What are you doing here?"

"I need to talk to you, and since we cannot seem to meet in the normal way, I — What is that?" he paused to ask with surprise.

"My foot under the blankets," she answered dryly, giving her toes a wiggle; then she reached out toward him. Clarissa was used to being blind, but usually she could at least see colorful blurs. This was much worse. She touched what she thought must be his chest. At least, she hoped it was his chest. His hand covered hers, and Adrian allowed her to pull him forward, leading him around toward the head of the bed.

"Do you have a candle? 'Tis dark as night in here."

Clarissa couldn't hold back her laugh, but covered her mouth to muffle it, and pointed out, "It *is* night in here."

"Well, yes, but . . ."

"If I light a candle, it might be seen and attract attention. Just sit and tell me what was so important you had to climb through my window," she said. She added, "I presume that is how you got in here?"

"Yes," Adrian breathed, and the bed sank under his weight. Clarissa immediately shifted to make more room, and he followed, clearing his throat before saying, "Sorry. I do not think I am properly awake yet."

"Awake?" Clarissa asked with surprise. He had to be awake. How could he have climbed into her room otherwise?

"I fell asleep in the tree outside your window while waiting for the party to end and for you to retire," he admitted.

Clarissa frowned with concern. "You could have fallen and hurt yourself!"

"Yes, well . . . I did not intend to sleep when I climbed the tree," Adrian pointed out.

"No, of course not," she realized.

He cleared his throat again, clearly overcome with self-consciousness, and said, "This is most improper."

Clarissa pointed out with amusement, "Most of what we do appears to be."

"Yes, I suppose." She could hear the smile in Adrian's voice. But when he next spoke, his words were more solemn. "I wanted to ask you about the message you said you got from me."

"Yes, of course. I am sorry we did not get the chance to talk. What was so important?"

"I did not send that message."

"You did not?" Clarissa asked blankly.

"No."

"But it was signed 'A.M.' "

"But I did not send it," he said firmly. "And for future reference, I never sign anything 'A.M.' "

Clarissa considered briefly. She wanted to ask if he was sure, but she supposed that was a stupid question. He'd certainly know if he'd sent a letter or not. Finally, she asked, "Who did? And why?"

"That is the question that concerns me, Clarissa." She could hear the frown in his voice, and he admitted, "It makes me wonder whether your accident was an accident. It also makes me wonder about these other accidents you have been having. Tell me about your fall down the stairs."

Clarissa felt her eyebrows rise. "It was nothing odd. I was supposed to always have a servant walk with me, but I was too impatient that morning," she said, admitting unhappily, "I also felt foolish that I needed an escort, so I went down on my own. I was fine until I got to the staircase, but then I tripped over something at the top and tumbled down."

"What was it you tripped over?"

Clarissa blinked in surprise. "I do not know. I twisted my ankle and was a bit banged up. Joan and Ffoulkes made a fuss over me. I did not think to have them look to see what I tripped over."

"Hmm. And no one mentioned there being something on the stairs?"

Clarissa shook her head, then realized he couldn't see and said, "No."

Adrian pondered, then asked, "What about the time you were almost run down by a carriage?"

"Oh." Clarissa sighed at the memory and then quickly explained. "I was bored to tears and heard Cook mention she was going to market. I wanted to pick out some fruit, so I went with her. She took my arm to walk me there. We stopped at a vegetable stall at the edge, and she let go of me to look at the vegetables. She let go of me for only a moment, but that was all it took. A heartbeat later someone bumped into me. I was not expecting it, and was startled off balance. My foot twisted on the cobblestones and I fell forward onto my knees; then I heard a great commotion and glanced up to see a huge blur kicking out above me. A carriage had been coming. But the driver managed to stop just short of me, and the horses were apparently rearing." Her expression solemn, Clarissa added, "I was really very lucky. I have always been very lucky, I guess."

"Who was it that bumped into you?" Adrian asked.

She shook her head. "I do not know. Cook came rushing over and asked if I was all right, then started yelling at the driver because he was yelling at me, and then she hustled me home for Joan to change me and clean up my scrapes and went back to the market alone." She scowled. "I never did get my fruit."

"Hmm." He was silent for a moment. "Clarissa, earlier tonight, did you actually *see* this letter I supposedly sent you?"

She was sure he'd leaned closer on the bed. Clarissa could feel his breath on her ear, and it made her shiver. Clearing her throat, she answered, "Of course I saw it.

The boy insisted he was to give it only to me. Joan had to fetch me from the ball to accept it."

"Did you read it?" he asked.

"No," Clarissa admitted, beginning to frown. "I could not read it properly. Joan had to read it for me."

Adrian considered that, then asked, "Do you still have the letter this boy supposedly brought?"

"Supposedly?" Clarissa asked. "You keep saying that, but I *saw* the letter, Adrian. There *is* one."

"Yes, but you could not read it."

"Joan did." When he remained silent, Clarissa frowned. "What on earth are you thinking?"

"I do not know," Adrian admitted on a sigh. "Ffoulkes and Joan were nearby and the first to reach you when you fell, and Cook was with you at the market. Yet no one seems to have bothered to find out what you tripped over, or who pushed you into the street."

"Bumped me. I was not pushed," Clarissa corrected. "And both times everyone was too busy ensuring I was all right to look into these things. I did not think of it either. And goodness, I am sure the staff hates me for all the accidents I have caused and all the times I unintentionally stepped on their toes or hit them with something without meaning to, but surely you are not suggesting my father's entire household wants me dead?"

"No. No, of course not," Adrian said quickly, then sighed. "Can you please just light a candle and find the letter?"

Clarissa hesitated, a little snort of laughter slipping out. "As if light would help me."

Shaking her head, she slid out of bed and began to make her way to her dressing table. Clarissa kept her hands out before her as she moved carefully forward, but still she found the table by stubbing her toe on one leg of it. Wincing, she bit back a curse not dissimilar to those Adrian had supplied earlier, and lowered her hands to find the tabletop. She had a vague recollection of Joan setting the letter on her dressing table once they'd reached the room. It must be here some — *Ah,* Clarissa thought as her hand brushed against paper. Picking it up, she turned to head back to the bed.

Light suddenly erupted in the room. Clarissa froze halfway to the bed and blinked in it. Apparently Adrian had found the candle at her bedside. While she stood blinking, he turned from the table and moved to her. Clarissa held out the letter and waited as he read it.

"Well?" she asked finally, when enough time had passed for him to have read it.

"It says what you said it did, but 'tis not my handwriting," he explained. Then he muttered, "Of course it isn't; I knew I had not sent it."

"But then who did?" she asked. "The only people who know about us are your cousin and my maid . . . and Prudhomme."

"Prudhomme *does* know? You are sure of this?" Adrian asked sharply.

"Aye. He was walking in the gardens with Lydia the night you presented me with that picnic. They saw us kissing at the salon doors," Clarissa admitted. "So Lydia knows as well."

"I suspected Prudhomme knew," Adrian murmured, lifting his head. Clarissa knew he was looking at her. She was suddenly terribly aware that she stood in nothing but her nightgown. Clarissa could almost feel his gaze moving over her, and a little shiver trailed through her in reaction. She had the sudden urge to cross her arms over her chest, but resisted.

The silence drew out a long time; then Adrian spoke, his voice husky as he announced, "Clarissa, I am going to kiss you."

She breathed in, excitement rushing through her at the announcement, only to have it drain away when he recanted. "No. I am not."

"You are not?" Clarissa asked. Disappointment took the place of the anticipation coursing through her.

"This is all terribly improper." Adrian sounded distressed.

"But I should like you to kiss me," Clarissa admitted with a frown.

"Oh, please do not say that." Adrian almost groaned. "I am trying to be a gentleman."

"Do gentlemen not kiss ladies?" she asked with a small smile, then reminded him, "You kissed me at Prudhomme's ball."

"Yes, but that was different," he assured her.

"Why?"

"You were not half-dressed and in your bedchamber."

"I could dress."

A soft laugh slipped from his lips, and Adrian suddenly leaned forward. Clarissa went still, her heart briefly stopping; then she melted into him as his lips moved across hers.

It seemed the heat and excitement of her response had not been because of the small bit of wine she'd had the night of Prudhomme's ball. She felt that same wild excitement now, and hadn't had a drop to drink.

Clarissa's body seemed to know just what to do, and molded itself to Adrian. Her hands crept around his neck to hold him close, and then his tongue intruded as it had before. This time she wasn't surprised by its sudden appearance. Instead of stiffening, she went weak in the knees, and would have slid to the ground if not for his arms tight around her.

Clarissa sighed into his mouth, moaning with pleasure. And in the next moment she gave a startled gasp as Adrian scooped her up and moved to sit on the end of the bed.

"I should not be doing this," he murmured against her cheek as he broke the kiss and let his lips travel to her neck and ear.

"No, we should not," Clarissa agreed, her hands sliding over his shoulders and upper chest as she tilted her head to give him better access.

"I am not showing you the proper respect." His words were breathed with regret, and Clarissa shuddered as tingles ran through her body, rushing all the way down to her toes. At that moment, respect seemed highly overrated. Certainly if this was disrespect, she seemed to like it. Perhaps she wasn't a proper lady after all.

"Tell me to stop," Adrian murmured, kissing the length of her throat.

Clarissa opened her mouth, then gasped as one of his hands closed over her breast.

"Oh," she breathed, arching into his touch. "Maybe . . . maybe in a . . . Ohh." She sighed as he kneaded the soft flesh through her gown, and her body was assaulted by waves of alien sensation. Her muscles were all flexing and curling with excitement, and heat was pooling in her lower body. This was amazing.

"Maybe what?" Adrian asked, sounding a little out of breath.

"Maybe you should kiss me again," Clarissa gasped — though she was sure that hadn't been what she'd intended to say at all.

A growl slid from Adrian's lips, then they covered hers, and Clarissa slid her hands into his hair, unable to keep from knotting them there as she opened her lips to receive him. Her body had suddenly come alive in a way that she'd never experienced. Whole parts of it, which she'd hardly been aware of, or had neglected as unseemly to notice, were making their presence known as she kissed him back.

Inexperienced as she was, there was the fear at the back of Clarissa's mind that she didn't really have a clue what she was doing and might be doing it poorly or wrong; but that was eased when Adrian groaned at the back of his throat and his kiss became even more heated, more demanding. She must be doing something right — or at least passably — to elicit such a reaction, she decided vaguely, then felt the mattress against her back and realized he'd laid her down.

"Just a little," Adrian panted as he broke away again.

"Yes," Clarissa gasped, though she hadn't a clue what she was agreeing to. She didn't really care, so long as these feelings didn't stop.

"Just a little kissing and touching, and then I shall stop — I promise," Adrian said, and Clarissa understood what he meant and thought it a fine idea. Except for the stopping part. Clarissa didn't want this to ever end. She'd never felt so wonderful, so alive.

It wasn't until his mouth replaced his hand that Clarissa realized that he'd somehow gotten several buttons of her nightgown undone, and had tugged it off one shoulder to bare her breast. His warm lips closed around her nipple, and Clarissa nearly flew off the bed with surprise at the shocking charge sent through her body.

"Oh," she breathed, her legs shifting restlessly and her hands moving over his head, then shoulders. Then she caught her hands in his waistcoat and tugged. It took a moment for her pleasure-drugged mind to realize that wouldn't work, and she began to push to remove it instead, shoving the garment off his shoulders and down his arms as far as she could. Fortunately, her actions hampered his movements enough that he took over the task and removed the jacket for her.

Clarissa let her hands drift over the soft cloth of his shirt, clenching it in her fingers and dragging upward, eager to touch his naked flesh.

Adrian broke away and said, "No," but the word wasn't very firm-sounding. It was more of a plea. And when he shifted up to kiss her, Clarissa ignored his no and tugged his shirt the rest of the way out of his pants, sliding her hands underneath to move them curiously over the skin of his back.

Adrian groaned into her mouth, tangling his hand in her hair, his kiss becoming more forceful, his tongue thrusting with demand as his body ground against hers, pressing a hardness against the aching need between her legs. Clarissa shuddered in his arms, her nails digging slightly into his flesh as she pushed back, her legs parting of their own volition.

"Oh, God, Clarissa," Adrian breathed, pausing to press little kisses on her eyes, nose, cheek — basically anywhere he could find. "We have to stop."

"Oh, Adrian," Clarissa said, then stiffened and cried out as his hand slid between her legs and pressed her gown against the spot that was now aching so. Her attention was split between the pressure he was applying between her legs, and the kisses he was trailing down her throat and across her collarbone. She was tugging hard on his shirt, twisting it around his upper chest, and knew she was hampering him, but she wanted it off. She wanted to feel him.

"Tell me to stop," Adrian begged, pausing to rip his shirt up over his head before bending to again lick and nip and suckle at her breast.

"Oh," Clarissa gasped, her nails digging into his flesh. Her hips arched and her legs fell apart as he began to rub. "Oh, yes — please do not stop."

Adrian released a chuckle against her breast, and her body pulsed to the vibration. Then he left off and kissed her lips.

His hand slid from between her legs, and Clarissa moaned into his mouth in protest, but she stilled as he caught at her nightgown and began to draw it up until his hand could slip under the hem. Her legs quivered in anticipation as his touch glided up her thigh. They then locked instinctively around him as he reached her center once more, this time with no cloth to impede him.

Clarissa gasped again into his mouth, her body bucking then quaking with building tension and need. His fingers drifted over her damp, tender flesh.

"Just this. I will not make love to you, I promise," Adrian murmured, kissing the corner of her mouth. "But I have to touch you and taste you."

"Yes, just touching," Clarissa agreed, ready to allow anything if he just did not stop. Her hands were drifting over his skin, her head twisting on the bed as his mouth trailed down again to find her breast. It stayed there only a moment, however, before he shifted and moved lower.

Clarissa's bliss was startled out of her, and she stiffened up like a board when he suddenly shifted to kneel between her legs, his mouth replacing his hand. Shock and horror were her first reactions, and she grabbed for his head, trying to pull him away.

"I do not . . . You should not . . . What — Adrian!" she said uncertainly, some of her protest dying away as his tongue, teeth, and mouth moved over her. Her body began to respond, despite her mind's reticence.

Letting go of his head, Clarissa grabbed for the bed, clutching at the sheets in desperation. Her world had begun to rock. She was vaguely aware that her hips had taken on a mind of their own and were thrusting themselves upward, eagerly meeting his kisses and caresses; then Adrian shifted, forcing her legs still so they couldn't interfere with his actions.

"Oh!" Clarissa stared blindly up at the shadows the candlelight cast overhead, her entire focus on the feelings within her.

"Oh!" She now knew why there were so many babies in the world.

"Oh!" She thought Adrian was the cleverest man in England, perhaps the world.

"Oh!" She suddenly understood the design of the universe.

"Oh!" There definitely was a God.

"Oh!" Was that smoke she smelled?

Frowning, Clarissa blinked her eyes several times, trying to clear away some of the passion clinging stickily to her thoughts and slowing her brain. She inhaled again, deeply, and definitely smelled smoke. Her gaze shot to the candle Adrian had lit, but it seemed fine, one little circle of light in her hazy vision.

It must be my imagination, Clarissa thought vaguely, but she was having trouble thinking at all with Adrian doing what he was doing. Her legs were now trying to wrap themselves around his head, wholly uncaring of what she thought she smelled or where it might be coming from. Clarissa even realized that one of her hands had released the bedsheet and was tangled violently in his hair, urging him on as her body rode his caress.

Afraid she might be hurting him, Clarissa forced herself to release his hair and grabbed at the bed again, but her hips still kept trying to thrust and twist, though they were helpless to do so against his hold. The tension in her was building to an unbearable level, and Clarissa's body was straining in response, her hands ripping at the sheets, her toes curled under, her head thrashing on the bed, her teeth clenched, wishing for something to bite — then she gasped in another breath and there was no mistaking the scent of smoke.

Clarissa stiffened, her head whipping around, trying to find the source. But before she could she was distracted again, a groan ripping from her throat as Adrian's teeth grazed the nub that appeared to be the center of her excitement. Her body vibrated, the tension pulling tighter, and Clarissa sucked in a breath on a gasp. She gave a choked cough as more smoke tickled her throat.

Trying desperately to think past the excitement and passion assaulting her, Clarissa pushed herself up to peer around the room. Her eyes found the blurred square of the door to her room and stilled. There appeared to be light on the other side, light seeping under the crack at the bottom of the door, and from that light she could see thick black smoke.

Clarissa instinctively reached for Adrian's head to get his attention, but he caught both her hands in his free one, using his weight to hold her legs in place as he continued his assault.

"Adri— Oh!" Clarissa gasped as he suddenly pushed one finger into her. Her body bucked and clamored for more, begging her to shut up.

"Adrian," she gasped with determination. "Fire. Burning."

"I burn for you too," he raised his head long enough to say, then bent once more to the task of driving her crazy.

"No. Oh . . . no." Clarissa tried again and was struggling to free her hands, but he had a firm grip, and her own thrashing just changed the sensations enough that her excitement was peaking again.

Her eyes locked on the light under the door, and on the smoke now billowing in, and she wondered that he couldn't smell it. But then, he was rather busy down where he was. Renewing her efforts, Clarissa managed to drag one hand free of his and immediately caught at his hair, tugging — and not kindly — as she tried to get his attention. Unfortunately, her body really couldn't care less what else was happening; even as she struggled to get him to raise his head, her hips were still thrusting themselves eagerly upward, and she had no doubt he thought her hair-pulling was just excitement.

Groaning deep in her throat, Clarissa fell back on the bed, her head twisting, and she screamed, "Fire!" as the tension finally broke and her body bucked with release. It seemed to go on forever, wave after wave of pleasure riding her, until she was left a quivering, limp mass.

Adrian raised his head, and through the blissful fog that had descended over her mind, Clarissa was aware of his shifting up the bed to lie beside her. He took her boneless body in his arms and held her, pressed a kiss to her forehead, then frowned, sniffed, raised his head, sniffed again and said, "Is that smoke?"

"Yes." Clarissa sighed, a smile feeling permanently affixed to her face. "The house is on fire."

"What?" She found herself suddenly dumped back onto the bed as Adrian launched himself up and hurried to the door. He tried to open it, frowned, then tried again, using both hands this time, as if that would make a difference. When the door still didn't open, he felt its surface, cursed, and hurried back to the bed. "Why didn't you tell me?"

"I did try," Clarissa said. "I said, 'Fire,' and, 'Burning,' and tried to pull your head away."

"Oh, yes," he said. "I thought you were . . . Never mind."

He glanced toward the window, then caught her hand and pulled her off the bed. "Come on; we have to get out of here."

Clarissa stood and nearly crumpled to the floor, but Adrian caught her and frowned. "What's the matter?" he asked.

"My legs are a little shaky," she admitted with embarrassment. "Just give me a moment."

"Oh." He hesitated, then scooped her up in his arms and carried her to the window.

"What are we doing?" Clarissa asked.

"The door is hot. The fire's right outside. We shall have to go out the window."

"Oh, dear," Clarissa breathed as he set her on her feet by the window and leaned to peer out. She wasn't the most coordinated person at the best of times. Even with her spectacles, she had proven slightly clumsy. The idea of trying to climb out of a window half-blind was not an attractive one.

"You will be fine. I shall help you," Adrian said reassuringly, then swung one leg out the window and straddled the ledge. She saw him reach out; then his lower body suddenly slid off the ledge and out of sight. Clarissa stepped up to the window and peered out. The good news was that she couldn't see how high up she was. Clarissa hated heights. The bad news was, she couldn't see anything. Then she felt Adrian touch her.

"Take my hand. I shall help you."

"Okay." Clarissa took a deep breath. Grasping his hand, she held on tightly and settled sideways on the ledge, trying to straddle it as he had but finding her nightgown hampered the exercise.

After an embarrassed hesitation, Clarissa reminded herself that he'd already seen what was under the thing, and yanked it up to her thighs to manage the maneuver. She then turned to try to see Adrian, and was actually able to make out his frame. It helped that his shirt was snow white, whereas the sky and surrounding trees were dark.

"Just swing out to me and I shall pull you onto the branch." Adrian's voice was calm and reassuring, and Clarissa forced herself to concentrate on that and ignore her fears.

She swung her other leg over the ledge, then took a breath, tightened her hold on his hand and pushed herself forward. For one heart-stopping moment she swung in midair; then Adrian yanked on her, pulling her to him, and she grunted as she slammed into the branch he sat on. Clarissa started to slide downward, and for a second she thought she'd fall anyway, but then his grip tightened and Adrian pulled her against his side. She hung there next to him, her body crushed between the tree branch and his side, and nothing under her feet but air.

Adrian hesitated, then said, "I am going to lower you to the ground."

"I would rather you not," Clarissa murmured, clutching at his arm. "Can you not just raise me up?"

"Yes, but the ground is easier, Clarissa. We are not that high. Besides, if I did pull you up, we would just have to climb down. This way I can lower you to the ground and then drop down beside you."

Clarissa bit her lip and twisted her head to peer down at the yawning black blur below. "You are sure it is not far?"

"I swear it is not. Your bedchamber is only on the second floor, Clarissa. This branch is just a bit lower than that, and once I stretch you down, your feet should almost be touching the ground."

"Oh." She sighed. "All right then, but please do not drop me."

Rather than lower her, Adrian suddenly lifted her a bit more, just enough that he could press a kiss to her cheek. "I will not drop you; you are far too precious to me."

Before she could react to his words, he shifted one hand to clasp hers, then leaned to the side and began to lower her. Clarissa clung to his hand and closed her eyes, sure she was too heavy and that he would drop her.

"You are just above the ground now, love. Let go and drop."

"Do I have to?" she asked unhappily, and heard his strained laugh.

"I am afraid so." That strain in his voice finally made up her mind. Taking her courage in hand, Clarissa released her hold.

Adrian released her as well, and she started to fall, but a start was all she got before she landed with a jolt. She couldn't have fallen more than a couple of feet, if that.

"Oh," Clarissa breathed with relief.

"She's here!"

Relief fled as quickly as it had descended at that faint call. Clarissa whirled toward the sound of the voice, and thought she saw the figure of one of the footmen at the corner of the house. Biting her lip, she glanced up to see Adrian dangling overhead.

"Umm, Adrian," she said, trying not to speak too loudly but wanting to be heard over the snapping and crackling of branches overhead and the soft curses he was uttering as he tried to untangle his shirt from where it was caught.

"Just a minute, love. I shall be right with you." He grunted.

Clarissa glanced back toward the footman to see that he was hurrying toward her . . . and around the corner behind him came the whole household. And behind them came half the residents of the other town houses on the block. All of them were rushing forward en masse to see if she was all right.

Clarissa stared at the blurred faces as they approached, hardly aware of the murmurs of relief they were uttering. Then Adrian dropped to his feet before her, blocking them from view.

"There, you see? That was not so bad, was it?" he asked, slipping his arms around her and bending to press a kiss to her lips.

"Lord Mowbray!"

Adrian stiffened, straightened slowly, then turned to face the mob. Clarissa saw him look her way, and was suddenly aware of a chill. Glancing down, she saw that the top of her gown was still undone and now gaping open, baring a good deal of her flesh to the crowd. Biting her lip, she pulled it closed. Adrian looked down and recalled his own half-dressed state.

Clarissa had just realized how compromising a situation they were in when Adrian straightened his shoulders and said, "Lady Crambray, may I ask for your stepdaughter's hand in marriage?"

CHAPTER NINE

Clarissa chewed her toast and avoided looking at Lydia. She could not see the woman's expression anyway, not without some spectacles, but she could actually feel the woman's glare every time her head turned.

Her stepmother was furious, and had been ever since the night of the fire. She hadn't said anything, not even after the flames had been put out and they'd been allowed to return to their beds. Fortunately, the fire had started in the hall near Clarissa's room, and while it had blocked anyone from getting to her from inside the house to warn her, it had destroyed only that end of the hall and her own room, and the rest of the house was fine except for two of the servants' rooms and the salon under her, which had sustained some water damage. Yes, the rest of the house was perfectly fine except for a bit of smoke damage.

Clarissa was now residing in a guest room.

She was also terribly short of gowns until hers could be replaced, though two or three had been scrounged up for her to wear in the meantime.

Directly after proposing that night, Adrian had suggested Clarissa and her stepmother stay at his mother's home while the town house was repaired, but Lydia had refused with an icy disdain that made it clear she would not be moved on the matter. She had been treating Adrian coldly ever since. He bore it, and both he and Clarissa did their best to ignore her silence and glares when he came to visit. There was little else to be done.

The worst part of it all was that Lydia had not left them alone since that night. Clarissa had no idea why. The banns had been read, the wedding was set for two weeks to the day after the fire, and all was in order. The woman should be happy. After all, she'd landed her stepdaughter an earl. But it was obvious that she wasn't happy.

Clarissa sighed and took another bite of toast, her thoughts running over the same worries and fears that had filled her mind since the night of the fire. Part of her was happy at the prospect of marrying Adrian. Certainly he was preferable to Prudhomme, and she liked him. Then there was the fact that the marriage bed would be far from a trial, if the things Adrian had done to her in her bedroom were any indication.

In fact, Clarissa thought she could be very happy married to Adrian . . . if their relationship had run a normal course and he'd proposed of his own accord rather than circumstances forcing him to do so in order to save her honor. She feared it was something he might come to resent later. Clarissa didn't want her own happiness at his expense. She'd rather suffer through scandal alone than do that. She'd survived it before, and could again. In fact, that was what Clarissa had expected when she saw all those people coming upon them and realized they'd been caught. Adrian's asking for her hand had stunned her as much as it seemed to infuriate Lydia.

The door to the dining room opened, and Clarissa glanced around, then paused, squinting to try to see better. She saw a tall shape with silver hair that wasn't a wig.

"Father?" she asked uncertainly.

"Hello, Clary," John Crambray called. She was immediately enveloped in the scent of saddle oil and the smoke from his pipe tobacco as he hugged her close.

"What are you doing here?" Clarissa asked with amazement.

He straightened. "Did you think I would not come see my little girl married?" he chided. "As soon as I received Lydia's message, I headed for London."

Clarissa's gaze shot in Lydia's direction. Her stepmother hadn't mentioned writing.

"I brought some of your clothes from home," John Crambray added. "Your stepmother's note said yours were ruined before they could put the fire out."

Clarissa nodded. "Yes, Daddy. Thank you."

"We shall have to get some new ones made for balls and such; most of what you left behind weren't fancy." He paused, eyes narrowing. "Where are your spectacles, Clary?"

"Clarissa broke them," Lydia lied smoothly. "I sent a message home to have her spare set sent to town so that she could see whom she is marrying, but I sent it after the first message I sent, so it may not have arrived until after you left."

Clarissa gave a start at this news. Her stepmother hadn't mentioned this, either; but judging from her tone of voice, Lydia considered it a spiteful act and not a kindness to arrange for her to regain her spectacles. Clarissa couldn't for the life of her understand why.

"Well, accidents do happen," her father said, drawing Clarissa's attention back his way. Then he announced, "I am very happy for you, daughter. I have always liked Mowbray. He's a good man."

Clarissa noted the way that Lydia stiffened, but she was more concerned with her own surprise. "You know Adrian?"

"Yes, of course I do. His father and I were good friends, mostly through correspondence since your mother died. Adrian's father was an excellent businessman. He could wring profits out of any rocky outcropping. We were always writing back and forth about our properties. When he retired and Adrian took over, I began to correspond with the son instead."

"I did not know that," Clarissa murmured.

"There is no reason you should. I did not bring up our correspondence with you. I doubt it came up in conversation with him either," John Crambray remarked easily.

"Oh." Clarissa stole a glance at Lydia as her father took a seat at the table. Her stepmother's expression was grim, and as a servant rushed forward with a cup of tea for her father, he nodded a thank-you.

It was then that Clarissa realized her father never showed affection to her stepmother, and while he had greeted his daughter with a hug, he hadn't greeted Lydia at all. It occurred to her then that her father never did, and she wondered about the two of them and what sort of relationship they had. Perhaps there was a reason for the lady's bitterness and even her anger, and perhaps it really wasn't anything to do with Clarissa at all.

"Why do you not show her the gallery?"

Adrian blinked at the suggestion from John Crambray, then smiled wryly at getting caught staring at Clarissa while speaking to her father.

"Go on," the man suggested. "The two of you remind me of her mother and myself when we were your age. Each of you is constantly following the other with your eyes, always aware of where the other is." He smiled reminiscently, then sighed. "I miss her still."

Adrian raised an eyebrow. "What about . . . ?"

"Lydia?" Lord Crambray sighed wearily. "She was a mistake. I thought Clarissa needed a mother to help her into womanhood, especially after the scandal. I also did not want the burden of the household falling on her shoulders when she was so young. I wanted a marriage of convenience.

I knew I would never love another woman like I did my Margaret." He shook his head. "I thought Lydia understood that. She *said* she understood. But in the end, she did not understand at all. Lydia thought that I was still just grieving, that I would eventually get over it and come to love her as she felt I should. When she realized that wouldn't happen . . ." He shrugged, his gaze finding his daughter.

"Clarissa is her mother's child. She looks like her and is the living embodiment of Maggie . . . who — in Lydia's mind — is her rival for my affections."

"I see," Adrian said quietly. It explained a lot of Lydia's behavior.

"I am glad to see you and Clarissa found each other. I think you shall be as happy together as her mother and I were. Now, go show her the gallery," Lord Crambray repeated. He added, "I would suggest a walk in the garden, where you would have more privacy, but 'tis raining, so the gallery is the best I can offer."

"Thank you." Adrian nodded and crossed the room to collect his soon-to-be bride. She was sitting with his mother, his cousin Mary, and Lydia, and for the first time since Adrian had met her, Clarissa looked as if she was enjoying herself at a ball. In fact, she looked happy. She was chatting away with his mother and Mary. This time it was Lydia who looked unhappy. Her demeanor was sullen and miserable. If it weren't for how unhappy she constantly worked to make Clarissa, Adrian would have felt sorry for her.

It was the first ball either of them had attended since the fire. Lydia had refused to allow Clarissa to attend any without her, and had refused to attend herself, claiming she couldn't bear the scandal. Now, with John's arrival, everything had changed. He'd insisted they come out tonight, and had insisted Adrian accompany them, having him ride over in their carriage. Lord Crambray was making a point of including him in their family.

"Adrian?"

He smiled at the certainty in Clarissa's voice as she looked up at him. Despite her inability to see, Clarissa always seemed to recognize him.

"Yes," he said, then added, "Your father suggested I show you the gallery."

Lydia appeared as if she were about to protest, but closed her mouth with a sigh. She could hardly override her husband, though she looked like she wanted to.

Beaming widely, Clarissa took the hand he offered and got to her feet, then walked with him out of the ballroom. "I did not realize you and Father were good friends," she murmured as they started up the hall toward the gallery.

"Well, we are not the best of friends or anything, but we do correspond several times a year. He's a nice man."

"I like him," Clarissa agreed lightly — then gave a grin that showed that her feelings for her father went far beyond liking.

Adrian smiled and admitted, "Actually, I did not realize he was your father. I mean, I did not connect you to the John Crambray I correspond with." He gave a laugh. "He has invited me to your home several times over the last couple of years. If I had realized he had you for a daughter, I would have accepted."

Clarissa was smiling at this comment as they entered the gallery and Adrian was so enchanted watching her that he didn't see the woman in his path until he crashed into her.

"Lord Mowbray."

Adrian glanced down sharply, his mouth tightening as he saw whom he'd run into: Lady Blanche Johnson.

His gaze slid warily over her ice-blond hair

and lush body. Adrian hadn't seen her for ten years, and would have been happy to go another fifty without the privilege. This woman had hurt him more than all of the cringing and fainting and overheard insults he'd suffered during his last visit to court ten years ago put together. She was a viper. Only, this woman had not turned from his scarred face. She alone had smiled and cooed and flirted and welcomed his touch . . . It wasn't until she'd lured him back to her home and seduced him that he'd learned why. As they lay, still sweaty and panting, the lady had laughed with exhilaration and announced that she'd always found freaks exciting, and that she had the best sex with them.

Adrian had lain frozen on the floor of her boudoir, where their passions had overtaken them, his stomach churning as she'd told him of some of her other lovers. It seemed a dwarf and a hunchback had been tied as favorite until him, but he had given her the best ride. "Freaks are always so eager to please, you understand," she'd told him.

Adrian left London two hours later. There had seemed little reason to stay. Most of the *ton* found him hideous to look on, and he was not interested in being a freakish toy for anyone.

"My, my, you look as yummy as ever," Blanche announced, running a familiar hand up his chest.

Adrian caught the hand in a hard grip that should have been painful, but all that flashed in Blanche's eyes was excitement. He should have realized she would like pain. He grimly tossed her hand away.

"Lady Johnson, may I introduce my fiancée, Lady Clarissa Crambray," he said coldly, a warning in his eyes.

"Hello." Blanche did not even bother to glance Clarissa's way; her cold, flat gray eyes were too busy eating him alive. "What a lucky girl you are, to have landed yourself such a stallion."

Adrian saw Clarissa's eyebrows rise and a small frown pull at her lips, and felt anger roar through him. Lady Johnson was playing dangerous games.

"After you take your little friend home, you should drop around to my place for a . . . friendly drink, my lord. I would be most happy to receive you," Blanche murmured. Her hand returned to his chest, then dipped dangerously low to brush toward his groin.

Adrian knocked the hand away, this time with barely controlled violence. Her behavior was an insult to Clarissa, and he would not allow it.

"One 'friendly drink' with you was more than enough, Blanche," he said dryly, deliberately neglecting her title. And, turning his back in another deliberate insult, he caught Clarissa by the arm and moved them past the blonde, leaving her standing in the doorway.

"She seemed . . . interesting," Clarissa said faintly as he led her down the gallery of paintings.

"Actually, she is not very interesting at all," he assured her.

"Oh."

She was silent so long that Adrian glanced over to see her biting her lip. He suspected she wanted to say something, but she held her tongue as they passed another couple. Once they were alone again, she finally said, "Adrian, I do not want . . . I mean, if you do not really wish to marry me, you need not."

Adrian stopped walking, his head whipping around, and anxiety claimed him. "What?" he asked, then said quickly, "Clarissa, Blanche means nothing to me. I have not seen her in ten years!"

"Oh, that is all right, my lord. I am not saying this because of her. It is just . . . I know you proposed only because of our being caught that night. I do not want you to marry me only to prevent a scandal."

"Do you not want to marry me?" Adrian asked, his voice harsher than he intended.

"Oh, yes," Clarissa said, too quickly for it to be a prevarication, and he felt himself relax until she added, "But I would not choose my happiness over yours. I would rather suffer the scandal than —"

Her words ended on a gasp of surprise as Adrian caught her arm and hustled her out of the busy gallery. He led her to the next door in the hallway, opened it, saw that there were people inside, and closed it abruptly to glance around. It seemed to him that he had to prove to her both that Blanche meant nothing and that he did indeed want to marry her, and not only to prevent a scandal. Certainly the events of that night had rushed things along faster than he'd expected, but Adrian was sure he would have asked for her hand eventually. He needed her to understand that, and knew of only one way to assure it. However, he needed privacy to do it as well.

Adrian glanced up and down the hall, then pulled her to the next door, opened it, saw that room, too, was occupied, and moved to the next. When that room also turned out to be occupied, he glanced around with frustration and spotted the wardrobe. The hall was empty but wouldn't be for long, so he rushed her toward the wardrobe.

"What are we doing?" Clarissa asked in confusion as he opened both doors and pushed the clothes inside out of the way to make a small space. Rather than answer, Adrian checked outside once more to be sure the hallway was empty, then stepped into the wardrobe, tugged her up with him, then pulled the doors closed.

"Adrian?" Clarissa said uncertainly, but that was all she got out before his mouth covered hers. He kissed her with all the passion she stirred in him, all the passion stored up from days of watching her laugh, talk, walk, and smile.

Obviously confused and startled, at first Clarissa was stiff in his arms, but then she released a little sigh and melted against him, her arms creeping around his neck.

Adrian groaned as she began to make little mewling sounds of pleasure and stretched against him like a cat. Those sounds and movements had driven him wild each of the two previous times they'd kissed. The first time he'd been terribly aware of his mother just on the other side of the French doors, and that had given him the strength to end their kiss and send her in to return to the party.

The second time had been in her room, and there had been no one on the other side of the door, nothing to force him to remain in control. Despite his protests at the time, Adrian had gladly gone wild and begun to do all the things he wanted to do to her . . . and he would have done them if the fire hadn't interrupted. Now the two of them were in a wardrobe, and he was forced to maintain some control or risk making love to her up against the inner wall. Which was certainly not the best option for deflowering a virgin.

Sadly, his body didn't seem to care. As Clarissa continued to sigh and mewl and stretch and rub against him like a cat, his body responded, growing hard and erect, and he found himself rubbing back. Adrian told himself that was all they could do, kiss and rub, but his hands didn't listen, and one moved down to catch her by the bottom, pressing her lower body closer against his, while his other hand found one breast and squeezed.

"Oh, Adrian." Clarissa gasped, and Adrian was moved to break their kiss to let his lips travel to her throat as he slid one leg between hers in the narrow confines, settling her there so that she rode his thigh. It elicited another moan that made his erection surge in his breeches.

Adrian suddenly wished to God they were already married. If they were, he'd take her home right now and . . . His mind suddenly went blank, his body stiffening as Clarissa's hand found his erection and investigated.

"What is it you have in your breeches, my lord? It keeps poking me," she murmured breathlessly.

All Adrian could get out was a small whimper. He wanted to beg her to touch him harder, to reach into his pants and take him in hand without cloth to hinder her. Another part, however, was aware that they were in a damned cupboard, and he wanted to plead with her to leave off touching him before he lost control.

"How long until the wedding?" he asked.

Clarissa paused, breathing heavily, and tried to work it out. A moment later she said, "A week, my lord."

"Oh, God. So long," Adrian muttered.

"Not so long; it just feels that way."

Adrian stiffened. The comment had come from a third voice. For a brief moment, he thought someone was in the wardrobe with them, but then he realized that it had come from outside. It was dark in the cupboard and he couldn't see Clarissa, but Adrian had no doubt a look of abject horror had claimed her face. She had gone stiff against him.

Adrian hesitated, then whispered, "That wasn't your father's voice, was it?"

But before she could answer, the person on the other side of the cupboard chuckled. "Yes."

Cursing, Adrian disengaged himself from Clarissa as much as he could, straightened his shoulders, and opened the cupboard door. Stepping out, he half expected to find a glove slapping his face and to be offered swords or pistols at dawn; however, what he found was John Crambray leaning against the wall opposite, looking vastly amused.

Adrian managed a chagrined smile. "Sorry," he muttered. "Clarissa thought I was marrying her only to save her from scandal, and I was trying to prove to her that I want her for herself, scandal be hanged."

"Is that what you were doing?" Clarissa asked with surprise. She had followed him out of the wardrobe.

Adrian opened his mouth to answer, then got a look at the state of her and quickly set to work trying to straighten her clothes before anyone saw. John Crambray immediately began to help, tending to the bits of hair Adrian had unintentionally pulled from the coiffure on top of her head.

"Yes, that is what I was doing," he said as they worked. "Why else would you think I pulled you into the cupboard?"

"To kiss me," Clarissa said simply, and Adrian blinked, glanced at John Crambray's amused face, then sighed.

"Yes, Clarissa," he said. "But I kissed you to prove that I want you. To reassure you that this is not just some act of chivalry on my part."

"Oh." She looked bemused and then asked, "Well, why did you not just say so, my lord?"

"From the mouths of babes," John Crambray said with amusement. Then he explained, "Because men do not think like women, Clary. Women talk, but men *do*. It is why they use the term '*man* of action.' "

"Oh, I see," Clarissa said. But it didn't really sound like she did.

Adrian sighed to himself and stepped back to peer at her. Her gown was straight, but her father appeared to be having some difficulty with her hair. It looked nothing at all like it had before the wardrobe.

Lord Crambray peered at Clarissa's hair, frowned, then glanced at Adrian. "Do you know how to fix this?" he asked.

"No." Adrian grimaced. Brightening, he realized, "But my mother may. Wait here and I shall go and bring her back."

John nodded, then turned to speak to Clarissa as Adrian hurried away. Adrian found his mother still seated with Lady Lydia and Mary, and he explained the problem to her in a whisper. She stood at once and headed out of the ballroom, but when Adrian turned to follow, Lydia murmured, "She shall have her spectacles again soon."

Adrian froze and turned back. "Excuse me?"

"I sent a message to Crambray to have her spare spectacles sent to us here in London. They should be here soon." She smiled. "Then she will be able to see properly and know just what she is marrying. Clarissa seems happy now. I wonder how happy she shall be when she can see properly."

"She shall still be happy," Mary said firmly. Getting to her feet, she took Adrian's arm. "Come, let us join Clarissa and your mother."

Adrian allowed his cousin to lead him out of the ballroom, his mind awhirl. Clarissa would have her spectacles soon and would be able to see him? He blanched with horror. She would *see* him.

"Are you all right?" Mary asked as soon as they were out in the hall. "You turned white when Lydia said Clarissa would have her spectacles back."

Adrian didn't respond. He didn't know what to say. No, he wasn't feeling all right. He felt sick, actually. But he couldn't tell Mary that.

It seemed he didn't have to. His cousin squeezed his arm and said quietly, "Clarissa will love you just as you are, Adrian."

He wanted to believe her — he really did — but pain and fear were clawing at his chest, and he asked, "Where's Reginald?"

"I believe he went in to play cards with some of the men," Mary said. Curiously, she asked, "Why?"

"I must speak with him," Adrian answered, and patted her hand. "Thank you, Mary. Now, there are Mother and Clarissa ahead. I shall find you again once I have spoken to Reg."

Mary nodded absently. "But what happened to Clarissa's hair?"

"It got a little messed up, and Mother is helping to fix it," Adrian explained. He frowned as he saw that Clarissa's hair actually looked worse now than it had before.

"You thought your *mother* could help?"

Mary asked with horror. She came to a grinding halt.

Adrian frowned. "Yes. She's a woman; she knows more about this than . . . Why are you shaking your head?"

"You must never let your mother near Clarissa's hair. She is hopeless with such things." Mary turned back toward the ballroom with a sigh. "I shall ask Lady Guernsey if her maid would be willing to help."

Adrian watched her walk off, then glanced back at Clarissa and the others, frowning at the way his fiancée's hair was now piled high atop her head and leaning like the Tower of Pisa. There had been only a couple of wisps loose and in need of fixing when this had started. John had somehow managed to make it look a little worse, and now his mother had definitely made it even worse. He would take Mary's advice to heart and be sure not to enlist his mother's aid for such things in the future.

Shaking his head, Adrian turned to make his way to the room where he knew the men and a few women were playing cards. He spotted Reginald at once. His cousin crowed as he approached, obviously having just won a round.

"Reginald, I need to talk to you," Adrian

said, moving behind his chair.

"Go ahead," Reginald said, as he continued to rake in his winnings.

"In private," Adrian murmured apologetically.

"Can it not wait until I have finished this game?" Reg asked.

Adrian hesitated and debated the matter. "No," he said finally.

Reginald heaved a sigh and got to his feet. "Deal me out of this hand. I shall be back directly."

"Thank you," Adrian said as they moved across the room to talk.

"Any time, cousin. Now, what is so important?"

"Lydia sent for Clarissa's spare spectacles from home," Adrian said grimly.

Reginald stared. "And . . . ?"

Adrian frowned as he pointed out, "She will be able to see me."

Reginald raised his eyebrows and repeated, "And . . . ?"

"Well, I cannot let that happen," he pointed out. "If she sees me, she —"

"Adrian, think," Reginald interrupted. "She is going to see you eventually. You did not plan to carry on where Lydia left off and keep her blind indefinitely, did you?"

"No, of course not, but —"

"But what?" Reginald asked.

"I need more time."

"For what?"

Adrian hesitated, then said, "Mayhap if she comes to love me before she sees me . . ."

Seeing the pity in his cousin's eyes, Adrian turned away. He swallowed hard, trying to remove the lump that had suddenly lodged itself in his throat. He was a grown man, but felt like a six-year-old threatened with losing his best friend.

"Adrian." Reginald placed one hand on his shoulder and eyed him solemnly as he turned. "First, your face is not as bad as you think. Second, I do not think Clarissa would care even if it were. And third, if she does, and if it affects her feelings for you, then 'tis best to know now, is it not?"

Adrian's shoulders slumped with defeat. "Mayhap."

"All will be well." Reginald patted his shoulder, and turned away. "Go enjoy her company. You are finally able to see her without elaborate plans and sneaking about, and now you're worrying about other things. Go kiss her senseless!"

Adrian watched Reginald return to his game, then gave a sigh and walked out into the hall. His eyebrows rose as he saw that

Clarissa, her father, and his mother were all missing. At first he assumed that meant that they had fixed her hair and returned to the party. Adrian decided to find her, but then he heard his mother's voice, followed by Clarissa's. Pausing, he peered up the hall. The door to the room right next to the wardrobe was open, and it hadn't been before. Moving up the hall, he peered inside. His eyes widened incredulously.

"What on earth have you done to her?" he gasped, hurrying into the room. Catching Clarissa by the hand, he pulled her out of the clutches of the two people who were in the process of utterly destroying her coiffure.

"Is it as bad as it feels?" Clarissa asked unhappily, one hand moving over her hair.

"No, of course it is not," Lady Mowbray said quickly; but she was biting her lip and couldn't seem to look at Clarissa without wincing. Adrian wasn't at all surprised. Her lovely hair had become a tangled mess, tucked and stacked and wrapped here there and everywhere else. It bore absolutely no resemblance to a hairstyle at all, but looked more like someone had dropped a bird's nest upside down on her head.

He shook his head. "Mother —"

"Do not 'Mother' me, Adrian. I am not

the one who messed it up in the first place. Dragging the poor girl into the wardrobe — a *wardrobe,* for heaven's sake — and messing it up?"

Adrian ground his teeth together, but merely said, "Where is Mary? She was going to ask Lady Guernsey if her maid would help with this."

"Was she? Well, isn't she clever?" Lady Mowbray sounded impressed, but frowned. "But she has not come with a maid. Besides," she said with a defeated sigh, "I doubt even a lady's maid could do much to repair this mess we've made. I fear Clarissa's hair needs a proper brushing out and redoing."

"Hmm." John Crambray pursed his lips and said, "Well, 'tis growing late anyway. Perhaps you had best take Clarissa home in the carriage, son. Have my driver take you home afterward; then send him back for myself and Lydia."

"Yes, of course." Adrian glanced at Clarissa, relieved when she didn't appear to be terribly upset at the turn of events.

Adrian's mother and Clarissa's father saw them out. Lord Crambray then had a word with the driver before turning to lead Lady Mowbray back into the house.

Chapter Ten

"I am sorry," Clarissa murmured as the carriage began to move.

Adrian glanced at her with surprise. "For what?"

"That your evening had to end because of my hair."

A small laugh burst from his lips. "That is nothing for you to apologize for. I messed it up in the first place."

Clarissa nodded, apparently accepting that it was his fault. She didn't look upset, he noted, and she cleared her throat and asked, "Did you mean what you said?"

"When?"

"That you are not marrying me to avoid scandal, but actually *wish* to wed me."

Adrian smiled faintly. Clarissa's face was all screwed up as she squinted and tried to see him. It was obvious his answer was important to her. "Yes, I meant it."

Clarissa bestowed a smile on him that was

like sunshine after a hard rain. Adrian had to swallow or choke on the sudden lump in his throat.

"I am glad, my lord. I wish to marry you too. It is not just the scandal for me either," she assured him solemnly.

Adrian let slip a little sigh. She looked so beautiful and sweet and —

"Are you going to kiss me again?"

Adrian's thoughts scattered like leaves in a breeze. "What?"

"I like it when you kiss me," Clarissa explained. "And I would not mind at all if you wished to kiss me again. So . . . will you?"

"No," he said abruptly.

She looked hurt. "Why? Do you not want to — ?"

"Of course I want to," Adrian said dryly, and her hurt look disappeared.

"Then why will you not kiss me?"

Adrian frowned. "Most ladies would not ask such things."

"I am not most ladies," Clarissa replied. "Besides, Father always said, 'Do you not ask, you will not know.' And I want to know. Why will you not kiss me if we both want you to?"

Adrian scowled, but of course she couldn't see his scowl, so it didn't cow her in the least. Letting out an exasperated breath, he decided to tell her the truth. She'd asked for it, after all. Besides, it might encourage her to be more circumspect. "Because if I kiss you, I will want to touch you."

"I *like* it when you touch me," Clarissa answered promptly.

"But if I touch you," Adrian went on, "then I will want to make love to you."

"I think I might like that, too."

Adrian raised an eyebrow. "You *think?*"

"Well . . ." Clarissa hesitated and then asked, "Was what you did to me in my room the night of the fire lovemaking?"

"No," Adrian answered, his voice harsh as he recalled the event. It seemed so long ago, and yet like only a moment. He could remember the taste of her, the way she'd moved beneath his seeking hands and mouth. God, he had an erection again just at the thought! He realized with disgust that he had no control around her at all.

"It was not?" Clarissa said with a frown. "Then what was that?"

"I . . . It . . ." Adrian scowled, at a loss for how to explain. "Yes, it was, sort of. But it was not . . ." He paused and glared at her. "Has no one explained these things to you?"

"No." Clarissa tilted her head and then shrugged. "Never mind, my lord. You need not speak of it if it makes you uncomfortable. I am sure Lydia will explain things to me the day of the wedding."

Adrian blanched in horror. The woman would terrorize Clarissa with tales that would leave her a quivering mass of fear and anxiety; he was sure of it. He would have the devil of a time soothing and comforting her, and the whole night would be one long, awkward, fear-ridden trial. He could not let Lydia explain things to her. Someone else would have to do it.

"I shall have my mother explain things to you," he decided. "If Lydia tries, just tell her to stop, and do not listen to anything she says."

"Oh, no," Clarissa said with a firm shake of her head. "I would be too embarrassed to have your mother talk to me about such things. Besides, it would be a deliberate insult to Lydia, and I begin to think that there is more to pity about Lydia than to dislike her for."

"I will not have Lydia scaring you with tales of blood and pain and —"

"There will be blood and pain?" Clarissa asked with horror.

"No," Adrian replied, silently cursing his big mouth.

"Well, then, why would you say that?

There *is* blood and pain! You just don't want me to know."

"Dammit," Adrian muttered. Now he'd mucked everything up.

"How much blood and how much pain, my lord?" Clarissa looked terribly anxious now. He cursed himself again.

"Clarissa —" Adrian began, but she interrupted.

"Nay, my lord. You cannot fob me off. I will know," she insisted, then just as quickly said, "Never mind, I do not wish to discomfort you. I shall ask Lydia the moment she and Father return tonight. Mayhap this will bring us closer together, and she and I can become friends."

Dear Lord! Adrian sat up and said firmly, "I refuse to allow you to ask Lydia."

"We are not yet married, my lord. You cannot refuse to allow me anything."

Adrian's eyes widened at the unconcern she showed at ignoring him. "Do you intend to disobey me so nonchalantly once we are married?"

"I fear I probably shall," Clarissa admitted, her tone apologetic. She then quickly added, "Though never nonchalantly — and only when I do not agree with whatever it is I am disobeying."

A burst of laughter slipped from Adrian's lips, and she tilted her head curiously.

"You do not seem angry, my lord."

"Nay," he said. "In truth, I suspect very few women enter marriage intending to obey. I find it refreshing that you admit to it."

"Oh." Clarissa shrugged. "Well, I do try to be honest, my lord."

"Right." Adrian sighed, straightened his shoulders, and said, "If I tell you about it myself, will you leave off letting Lydia terrify you?"

"Aye."

"Well, then, I shall do my best to educate you," he muttered. Sitting back, he considered where to start.

After several minutes of his thinking, Clarissa asked, "My lord? Are you not going to tell me?"

"I'm thinking," he growled.

And he was. He was racking his brain, trying to sort out how to explain things. This was not something he should *have* to explain. He was a man, dammit! Men did not explain sex to virgins. Or at least, they should not have to. But it looked like he was going to have to. It was that, or he could let Lydia make a nightmare of their wedding night.

"Perhaps I can help, my lord."

Adrian blinked at the suggestion, and turned to stare at her with bewilderment. "Help?"

"Aye," Clarissa said, then added, "Well, I am not completely ignorant. I did grow up in the country and have seen stallions cover mares."

" 'Tis not the same thing between a man and woman," Adrian said at once — but the comment had brought to his mind an image of doing just that — mounting her like a stallion. He could imagine the soft lines of her back, the curves of her buttocks, the —

"Are you sure?" Clarissa interrupted his musings. "I once surprised the stablemaster when he had one of the milkmaids bent over a bale of hay in the barn, and —"

"Oh, God, please stop." Adrian gasped as his mind made a leap, projecting an image of Clarissa in a milkmaid's dress, bent over a bale of hay, her skirt up around her hips and him pounding into her from behind.

Banishing the image from his mind, he took several deep breaths, then corrected himself by explaining desperately, "It *can* be approached in such a manner, but not the first time. The first time 'tis better to approach it face-to-face."

"Oh, I see," Clarissa murmured, and he

was just breathing a sigh of relief to have the task over with when she asked, "Why?"

Adrian cleared his throat. "Because the first time can be rather uncomfortable for you."

"Was it uncomfortable your first time?" Clarissa asked.

"No."

"Then why must it be uncomfortable my first time?"

It was a perfectly reasonable question, but Adrian had no intention of explaining. He couldn't. He didn't have a clue how to go about it, and didn't intend to try. Not until she said, " 'Tis all right, my lord. I shall ask Lydia," and reminded him of all his previous fears.

Cursing, he sat up straight and said, "You have a . . . There is this . . . Ask her," he finally ended lamely, and felt an immediate ass for doing so. It would have been easier to show her — easier than explaining, certainly. And another part of his brain, the part that had all the improper but fun ideas, pointed out that were he to show her here, tonight, he needn't fear her refusing to marry him next week; Clarissa would no longer have a choice, whether she was disgusted by his scar or not.

"Like this?"

"Hmm?" Drawn from his thoughts, Adrian glanced to the side to see that Clarissa had turned to face him on the bench seat.

"Would we be facing each other like this?" she asked.

"No, you'd be on your back, and I'd be over you," Adrian answered absently — but then he frowned as that picture filled his mind. It was an image of Clarissa lying on her back, face wreathed with excitement, her head twisting as it had the other night.

"Why must I be on my back?"

Adrian blinked the image away and glanced at her, trying to concentrate on her question. "Well, you do not *have* to be. It can be done with me on my back and you on top instead." But that image immediately rose in his mind: him lying back on a bed, his hands covering and caressing her breasts as she rode him.

"Are there many ways to do it, my lord?"

"Yes." Adrian couldn't help but notice that his voice was growing deeper and huskier. All this talk was rather affecting.

"What are some of these ways?" Clarissa asked.

Adrian's mind was immediately swamped. He tried to banish images of all the ways he could make love to her, then cleared his throat and said, "Well, there are the ones I just mentioned; then there is one where I would be sitting up with you on my lap, or —"

"Really?" Clarissa interrupted. "How would that be done?"

Adrian stared at her. His thoughts were a muddle, part of him wanting to just get the deed done here and now and ensure she would have to marry him, and the other part arguing that that was no way to get a wife, and that she deserved better than the discomfort of the carriage for her first time. Not to mention, there was the respect issue. It showed little respect to take a woman in a moving carriage.

But really, his body didn't care about respect, or consideration. It didn't even care about trapping her into marriage. His body was just excited by all this talk, and it was urging him on.

Without realizing what he intended, Adrian suddenly reached out, caught Clarissa about the waist, and lifted her onto his lap so that her knees rested on either side of his thighs.

She gasped in surprise, her hands clutching at his shoulders for balance as she settled astride him. Her eyes went wide.

"Like this?" she asked, sounding dubious.

Adrian urged her closer until they were nearly chest-to-chest. His voice was husky, almost impossible to hear. "Yes. And . . . you would move up and down."

"Up and down?" Clarissa asked uncertainly. She hesitated, then raised herself up, lowered herself, then rose back up again. "Like this?"

"Yes." Adrian watched her breasts rise and fall before his eyes — lowering to about mouth level, rising to eye level, then lowering again. Up and down, up and down. He licked his lips, watching the flesh of her breasts jiggle as she moved. If he leaned his head forward just the littlest bit, he might actually lick the tender flesh in motion before him.

"This is hard," Clarissa commented.

"Yes. I am," Adrian agreed, thinking she referred to his erection. Then he realized she was referring to the constant up-and-down motion, that it was a strain on muscles unused to the exercise, and said quickly, "I mean, yes, it is."

"But we could not kiss like this, could we? With me moving up and down?" She sounded concerned about the fact. But then, Clarissa had already told him she liked his kisses.

Catching her by the back of the head, Adrian drew her down to him. He covered her mouth with his, and thrust his tongue out to urge her lips apart before she could open them herself.

Clarissa stopped moving and settled against his chest with a little sigh. Her lower body came to rest, warm and heavy, where his erection pressed firmly against his breeches. Adrian groaned, his body shifting beneath her, instinctively pressing upward against her. If he just slipped his hand down and rearranged their clothes, he could make her his now, Adrian thought. And the moment the thought was born, his hands reached down to find the hem of her skirt — only to discover that she was kneeling on it.

"What other ways are there, my lord?" she asked as he broke the kiss. He was glancing down, trying to see if he couldn't somehow get her skirt out of the way.

Adrian hesitated, wondering at an answer, then suddenly surged forward. Clarissa gasped and held on for dear life. He set her on the bench seat opposite, landing on his knees between her legs on the floor of the carriage.

"Oh. This is nice. We could easily kiss this way," Clarissa murmured, smiling widely.

"Yes," Adrian agreed, reaching for the hem of her skirt. But that was when the carriage came to an abrupt halt. He was so startled, the small jerk sent him crashing to the carriage floor, pulling Clarissa down on top of him.

Adrian groaned as pain radiated through him — her pelvis had impacted with his groin. Then he glanced to the door in alarm as it suddenly opened. Both he and Clarissa stared out at the footman, who gaped back with an expression that was at first startled, but quickly became amused.

"Oh." Clarissa brushed her hair out of her face and smiled with embarrassment. "We fell off the seat."

"Yes, my lady," the man said.

Adrian caught Clarissa around the waist and quickly set her back on the bench seat, then scrambled upright and out of the carriage, trying for dignity and failing miserably. Once on his feet outside the carriage, he glared at the smirking footman, then turned back to offer Clarissa his hand to help her out.

Despite not being able to see, Clarissa must have sensed that the footman was laughing, for she felt moved to say, "We were not doing anything, James. Lord Mowbray was just showing me some . . ." She paused, a frown creeping over her face. She'd realized she couldn't really explain that either.

"He was showing you some . . . ?" James prompted with an amusement that ensured this tale would be told in the servants' quarters this night.

"Some . . . thing," Clarissa ended lamely.

"Ah. He was showing you some . . . thing." James was nearly killing himself trying not to laugh. He nodded. "Yes, my lady. I am sure he was."

Adrian scowled. His servants wouldn't have dared shown him such an attitude, he thought; then he sighed. Who was he kidding? They would have done as much and more. Good servants were so hard to find nowadays.

"I believe we are to take you back now," the footman commented to Adrian as he began to walk Clarissa up the path.

"Yes," he replied stiffly. "I shall just see her to the door."

"Very good, my lord."

"Very good, my lord," Adrian grumbled under his breath, wondering why the man even bothered pretending respect.

"Thank you, my lord, for your instruction," Clarissa murmured as they paused by her front door.

"Oh, I . . ." Adrian blinked as he noticed the state of Clarissa's hair. Half of it had fallen out of its bun, and now ran in a river of tangles down one side of her head. The other half leaned precariously in the other direction.

Adrian sighed and reached up to release it all. Her silken locks fell around her face in waves, and looked quite lovely despite the tangles, he noted. They would look glorious spread out on his pillows.

Adrian leaned down to kiss her, pausing only a hairbreadth away as the door suddenly opened beside them.

Sighing, he stepped back and murmured, "Good night."

"Good night, my lord," Clarissa answered, and she turned to enter the house.

After Adrian watched the door close, he turned to make his way back to the carriage.

"My lady!"

The door to her room burst open, and Clarissa blinked as she sat up in bed.

"What is it?" she asked with alarm as Joan rushed into the chamber.

"Your spectacles have arrived!" The maid sounded as excited as if they were her own.

"Oh!" Clarissa whipped off her blankets with excitement. Joan, who had been rushing up to the bed, gasped. Clarissa heard a clack against the wall to her right, followed by a tinkling that made her freeze.

"What happened?" she asked with dread. A small moan sounded from her maid.

Joan hesitated, and when she spoke, her voice was choked. "Oh, my lady. You caught my hand with the edge of your blankets when you threw them aside, and you knocked the spectacles clean out of my hand."

Clarissa's shoulders slumped. "They hit the wall, did they not?"

"I fear so." Joan moved around the bed.

Clarissa watched reluctantly as the maid moved to the wall and stooped to pick up her spectacles. When she picked up several somethings, and they clicked and chinked in her hand as she worked, Clarissa lowered her head to her hands with dismay. Her spectacles were in pieces. And it was all her own fault.

"I am sorry, my lady," Joan murmured, and Clarissa glanced up to see the girl standing at the side of the bed, hands cupped before her, no doubt holding the shattered remains.

"It was not your fault, Joan."

"If I had been holding them tighter, or —"

Clarissa waved the words away and shook her head as she stood. "It was not your fault. Now, help me dress please. Lady Mowbray is taking me to the modiste today for the final fitting of my wedding dress."

"Yes, my lady." Joan set the remains of the spectacles on the bedside table, and started to help her get ready to meet the day.

Clarissa was quiet as they worked, her mind on the spectacles she'd just destroyed, and her clumsiness that had caused it. The situation was enough to depress her. She tried not to let it. Spectacles were replaceable. She could get new ones made, perhaps quickly even — but wished she had them now. At least, part of her did. The other part wasn't so eager. It might be silly, but Clarissa was worried about how Adrian would react once he saw her in them. Lydia had made such a big deal of her wearing the things, she found herself somewhat nervous at his reaction. Would he take one look at her in spectacles and head for the hills?

Clarissa didn't really think he would, but really, there was nothing attractive about spectacles to her mind, and she wished she didn't have to wear them.

"There you are, my lady," Joan murmured.

The maid had been subdued throughout her ablutions and dressing, and Clarissa knew she was blaming herself for the accident. Which was just silly. It hadn't been anyone's fault, really. It had been an accident, like the many other accidents that had plagued her since Lydia had taken her first pair of spectacles away.

"Shall I walk you down now, my lady?"

"Yes, please, Joan," Clarissa murmured, and stood to take the arm her maid held out.

The upper hall was empty. They didn't run into anyone on the way down, no one until they reached the main floor. And it was just her luck that Lydia happened to be walking up the hall as they arrived in the foyer.

"There you are," her stepmother said, moving toward them. "Ffoulkes said your spectacles had arrived. Why are you not wearing them?"

Clarissa felt Joan's arm tense, and she patted it reassuringly even as she said, "I fear there was an accident and I broke them."

"What?" Lydia growled, and immediately turned on Joan. "How could you let this happen?"

"It is not Joan's fault," Clarissa said firmly. "I knocked them out of her hands in my excitement at their arrival."

"I should have been holding them more

tightly," Joan said with distress, and Clarissa could have smacked her for speaking up. She was sure Lydia would have left her alone otherwise, but the maid's words brought Lydia's wrath down on her.

"You stupid, stupid girl!" she snarled. "Pack your bags. I want you out of here at once."

"Yes, my lady." Joan started to pull her arm from Clarissa's grasp, but Clarissa held her in place.

"Joan is *my* maid, Lydia. I was going to seek permission to bring her with me when I marry, but as you are firing her, I guess I need not ask." She turned to Joan and said gently, "You really should pack, Joan. If you wish to come with me, you will need to."

"She is not staying under this roof. She —"

"Lydia!" John Crambray appeared in the door of the breakfast room, his expression grim. Obviously he'd heard everything and wasn't pleased.

Lydia turned slowly, reluctantly, toward him. Her voice was sullen as she asked, "Yes?"

"Enough," Clarissa's father said firmly. "If Clary wishes to take Joan with her as lady's maid, then she is welcome to do so. Joan will stay here until Clarissa leaves, then accompany my daughter to her new home at Mowbray. It will ensure that Clary does not feel alone there."

He turned his attention to the maid. "Do you wish to go with her?"

"Aye, my lord, I would be honored," Joan said quickly.

John Crambray nodded. "Then you would be best to start packing. The wedding is in only two days."

"Thank you, my lord." Joan hesitated, and turned to Clarissa. "Do you need me any more, my lady?"

"No. I shall be fine. I will just have some tea and toast while I wait for Lady Mowbray," Clarissa replied, patting her arm. "You go start seeing to whatever you need to do ere we leave."

"Yes, my lady. Thank you, my lady."

Clarissa watched the girl's blurred figure hurry away; then she turned back to her father and Lydia. She hesitated uncertainly. Her stepmother stood still and silent, but Clarissa could feel the waves of anger rolling off her.

"Come, Clary," her father said quietly. "You shall need more than toast and tea if you have a day of fittings ahead."

Nodding, Clarissa moved to join him in

the doorway, thinking the whole time about Lydia. She suspected the woman had tried to fire Joan only out of spite. She wished she knew how to repair the rift between them. Lydia had appeared to resent her from the beginning, and that resentment seemed only to have grown over the years. Clarissa had no idea what had caused the resentment, so had no idea how to make amends.

She consumed three sausages, two eggs, black pudding, toast, and three teas before Lady Mowbray arrived. Her father sat with her throughout the meal, chatting about the news, the weather, the coming wedding, and various and sundry other things to keep her company. When Lady Mowbray was announced, Clarissa stood and kissed her father good-bye, then hurried out to join Adrian's mother in the foyer.

Presumably having been up in her room, Lydia was descending the stairs as Clarissa did so. Suspecting that her mood would not have improved any, Clarissa didn't pause to wish her a good day, but rushed her soon-to-be mother-in-law out of the house.

"My," Lady Mowbray murmured as they settled in her carriage. "Lady Crambray had a face like thunder. Is she not a morning person?"

Clarissa sighed and briefly considered saying no, she wasn't; then she decided the truth would serve better, and she regaled Lady Mowbray with the story of her own clumsiness in breaking her spectacles, and of Lydia's blaming Joan.

Lady Mowbray made murmurs of consolation, but agreed it was no one's fault. Accidents happened, after all. Then she said the oddest thing: "Adrian will be relieved."

Clarissa blinked at the strange comment, turning quickly to peer out the window to hide her concern. Did he dislike spectacles so much then? Was he abhorring her decision to wear them? She had hoped to ask Lady Mowbray if they might not stop to see if she could find a new pair in town, but now hesitated to suggest it. Frowning, she pondered the matter as they rode through the city streets.

She continued to consider as she stood patiently for the dressmaker to fuss, pluck, and tuck in the creation everyone had assured her was lovely. And once finished, and the dressmaker had helped her undress then turned her attention to Lady Mowbray's gown for the wedding, Clarissa wandered to the front of the shop, her thoughts still distracted.

"Is there something I might get for you,

my lady? A tea, perhaps, while you wait?"

Clarissa recognized the voice of the dressmaker's assistant, and so she paused to ask, "Is there a shop near here where they make spectacles?"

"Oh, yes. Just two stores up from here," the girl said, happy to be of help.

"Thank you," Clarissa replied. Her gaze slid to the back room of the shop. The dressmaker would be dressing Lady Mowbray in there, fussing and plucking at her gown. So, when the assistant moved off, Clarissa hesitated only a moment, then slid out the door. There, she paused. The girl had said two shops up, but hadn't said which way. Clarissa hesitated, then went left. She would try one way first, then the other if she did not succeed.

As it happened, Clarissa chose the right direction. She found out by stopping at each store and pressing her face to the glass to see what was displayed within. Two shops up, she found what she was looking for. Just entering the shop made her feel good. She was that much closer to being able to see again.

"Can I help you, my lady?"

Clarissa turned with a start and squinted at the man who moved so silently that she had neither heard nor seen him approach.

Forcing herself to relax, she said, "I need spectacles."

"Well, then, you have come to the right place, my lady. I have a wide selection."

And it was as simple as that. Clarissa left the shop several moments later with a new pair of spectacles perched on her nose and a wide smile on her face. It was wonderful. It was bliss. She could see again!

Clarissa peered up and down the street, looking at passing people, taking in the fine details of their clothes and the small lines on their faces, then turned her attention to the horses and carriages. Wonderful! A pleased little sigh slid from her. After a moment, she headed back toward the dressmaker's shop at a quick clip, wanting to get back before Lady Mowbray noticed her missing. In fact, she didn't think she would inform the lady of her little trip just yet. Not about her new spectacles. Clarissa wished to feel Adrian out on the issue first. If he truly had some disgust for spectacles, she would wait a bit before wearing them in front of him . . . just long enough for him to start to love her. Once he loved her, surely he would not mind so much that she needed them.

At least, that was what she hoped. Clarissa had no desire to go through life blind.

Pausing outside the dressmaker's shop, Clarissa took one last clear look at the world around her, then removed the spectacles with a little sigh and slipped them into the small bag inside her skirts. They would be her little secret for now. She would enjoy them when she was alone, and keep them tucked away otherwise until she knew where Adrian stood on the issue.

Half-blind once again, Clarissa stepped into the dressmaker's shop and had just moved toward a bit of cloth on a side table when Lady Mowbray came breezing out of the back.

"Are you ready to go, dear?" the woman asked. "I thought we might have tea at Adrian's today. That way you can get to meet your staff."

Clarissa's eyebrows rose. "Adrian has his own home in town?"

"Oh, aye. He bought it when he was young and wild and wanted a place of his own to misbehave." Lady Mowbray gave an amused shake of her head. "Now he keeps it just to annoy me, I think. And to avoid my nagging him to attend this party or that play."

Clarissa smiled faintly. "Tea with Adrian sounds lovely, my lady."

"Come along, then." Adrian's mother took

Clarissa's hand to lead her from the shop, adding, "Clarissa, dear . . . I know you do not get along well with Lydia, and I want you to know that if ever there is something you need, anything at all, or if you simply need someone to talk to, I would like you to feel free to talk to me. I am very pleased to count you as my daughter, and would like to treat you as one."

Clarissa swallowed the sudden lump in her throat and nodded. "Thank you, my lady," was all she could say.

CHAPTER ELEVEN

"There you are." Adrian set the bag of coins on his desktop and settled back in his chair with a sigh. Martin Hadley scooped it up.

Adrian had used Hadley for the first time several years ago, when things had begun to go missing from his family estate. The man had been recommended to him by a neighbor, who had used Hadley on several occasions and found him quite competent at handling such matters. Hadley had taken a job at the Mowbray country estate as a footman — or at least had appeared to. In truth, his sole occupation had been finding out where the Mowbray silver and heirlooms were going. He had caught the maid responsible within a week of his arriving on the scene.

Adrian had been properly impressed. He'd used Hadley again on other occasions, and had had enough faith in him that he hadn't hesitated to call when he'd found himself frustrated in his efforts to meet up with Clarissa. He'd hired Hadley to find out what functions she and her stepmother were attending in the hopes of finding a way to steal Clarissa away. Now, of course, that was no longer necessary, because of their engagement, and so Adrian had decided to settle his account, which was what he was doing today. But that wasn't the only reason he'd wanted to see Hadley.

"Thank you, my lord. I appreciate your settling your debts quickly. Few enough do, and have to be chased down for payment." The bag of coins safely stored in his pocket, Hadley relaxed in his seat and raised an eyebrow. "You mentioned in your note that you might have another matter for me to consider?"

"Yes. It, too, is in regards to Clarissa." Adrian frowned, his gaze sliding to the window overlooking the gardens behind the house. "There is a possibility someone is out to harm her."

Hadley's eyebrows rose. "My lord?"

Adrian glanced back. "I presume during your previous investigation you became aware of the exceptional number of accidents she has been suffering."

Hadley nodded slowly. "It would appear the lady normally wears spectacles, but her stepmother took them away. The girl is uncommonly accident-prone without them, and miserable on top of it."

Adrian felt himself relax a little, encouraged that the man had sorted out that bit. No one else but himself seemed to have. Hadley was a good man. He would figure out this new situation.

"Yes, most of those accidents were probably caused by her missing glasses, but there are one or two I wonder about."

Hadley pursed his lips, then said, "My guess would be that her fall into the street, where she was nearly hit by a carriage, is one of them."

Adrian nodded, unsurprised that the man had heard the tale. Hadley was known for his thoroughness.

"And the other?" the man asked.

"The night of our engagement, Lady Crambray held a ball. I made plans with my cousin Reginald Greville on how I might see Clarissa. He was to accompany a friend to the ball, find Clarissa, ask her to dance or otherwise take her aside, and tell her to meet me out by the fountain.

"With this plan in motion, I went to the ball a little earlier than he, in order to make my way to the fountain and be waiting there when she arrived. That being the case, imagine my surprise when I got to the fountain and found Clarissa floating in it."

Hadley's eyebrows rose and he sat up straight. "What happened?"

"She said she got a message from me, rushed out to the fountain to see me, and — in her haste — ran into a branch."

Hadley frowned. "How did she end up in the fountain?"

"Clarissa says she recalls stumbling forward, and must have tumbled into it as she blacked out."

Hadley blew a silent whistle between his teeth and sat back, then shook his head. "Well, it is plausible enough, my lord. Why do you think it might not have been an accident?"

"Because I did not send her a message."

"Your cousin —"

"Was to speak to her personally, which he never managed to do, because she was already floating in the fountain when he arrived," Adrian said. "Clarissa received a *written missive* telling her to meet someone there. It was signed 'A.M.,' but I did not send it!"

Hadley sat up again, a frown pulling at his face. "That is troublesome. But she recalls running into a branch?"

"She is blind without her spectacles. Clarissa would not know what she ran into," Adrian pointed out. He added, "If she ran into anything at all. As far as I could tell, there were no branches low enough to strike her. Even if one had, it is difficult to believe she could have stumbled so far."

"I should like to see this fountain and the area around it, I think," Hadley pronounced, and Adrian nodded.

"I will arrange it," he said; then he glanced at his pocket watch and murmured, "Actually, my mother was taking Clarissa out for a fitting this morning, and mentioned something about having tea with her afterward. We could join them, and I could ask to see the fountain by daylight. You could accompany me."

"How would you explain my presence?" Hadley asked curiously.

Adrian shrugged. "As a friend, or my assistant."

"Your assistant is the better option," Hadley decided. "You can claim you want me to see the fountain because you are considering having one put in at your country estate and you want me to see what you're looking for."

"That would work." Adrian nodded slowly and got to his feet. "Come; we can head over there now."

He led the way out of his study, but had barely stepped into the hall when Jessop appeared, moving toward him at an unhurried pace.

"Are you going out, my lord?" the man asked with an air of deference that was normally absent. Adrian knew it was present now only because Hadley was.

"Yes. My mother mentioned having tea with Clarissa after their fitting, so we are going over there. They should be done with that by now, should they not?"

"I would not know, my lord," Jessop said in a tone so dry it almost crinkled.

"Hmm." Adrian scowled faintly, then said, "Have the carriage brought around front, please."

"Very good, my lord." Turning on his heel, Jessop headed back up the hall. Adrian moved to collect his own coat and hat and Hadley's, then led the way outside.

"Are you starting to question the carriage accident because of this debacle by the fountain?" Hadley asked as they donned their coats and waited for the carriage.

"The fact that she was lured to the fountain by a letter I did not send made me wonder," Adrian said. "That, and the fact that she was bumped into the street. And then there is the fact that she has no idea who bumped her. And there is her fall down the stairs."

"I had not heard about that one," Hadley said. "What happened?"

"Clarissa normally has someone to escort her, usually her maid. This time, she said she grew impatient with being escorted and so decided to make her own way below. She tripped over something at the head of the stairs. No one appears to know what she fell over, however." Adrian frowned. "It may sound silly, but I would have thought that, when they found out she'd tripped, they would have looked at the top of the stairs to see what it was she stumbled over. No one appears to have done that."

Hadley remained silent, considering, and Adrian shifted impatiently. "I know there is no evidence to support that both accidents were anything but accidents, but it troubles me now. Yes, after the fountain incident."

"Her apparent clumsiness is certainly convenient if someone is causing these accidents," Hadley murmured thoughtfully.

"That did occur to me, too," Adrian agreed.

"The stepmother took the spectacles away. Are you thinking she is behind these mishaps?" Hadley chewed on his lip. "She certainly seems to hold some strange dislike for the girl. At least, that's the way it appears to me. Mind you, I was not looking into that aspect of things, so I could be wrong there."

"You are not wrong," Adrian assured him. "I believe Lydia identifies Clarissa with the girl's dead mother, whom she somehow sees as a rival for her husband's affections."

"I see," Hadley said, then fell silent as the carriage arrived. Adrian told the driver where he wished to go, then got into the conveyance, and they rode in silence to the Crambray house.

"Lady Clarissa is not at home," Ffoulkes announced the moment he opened the door and spotted Adrian waiting in front of the house with Hadley.

Adrian replied, "I was to meet Lady Clarissa and my mother back here for tea after their dress fittings."

"They have not yet returned," came the butler's response.

Adrian was just beginning to think they would be reduced to waiting in the carriage, when John Crambray appeared in the hall behind the sour-faced old butler and said, "Adrian, hello. Come in! Clarissa and your mother should be back soon, unless they stopped somewhere else. Let the men in,

Ffoulkes, and show them to the salon to wait."

"Very good, my lord." Ffoulkes opened the door and stepped to the side to allow the guests entry.

"Unfortunately, I was just on the way out," Lord Crambray said apologetically. "I am meeting an old friend at the club; otherwise I would keep you company."

"That is all right, my lord. Perhaps I shall just show Hadley here the fountain while we await the women's return. I am considering putting one in at my country estate, and I'd like his opinion on it."

"Oh, by all means. Clarissa quite enjoys that fountain. She often sits and reads by it. Or, she used to," he corrected with a grimace. "When she still had her spectacles. Speaking of which, her spare pair arrived this morning."

Adrian stiffened at this announcement, only to relax as Lord Crambray added, "Unfortunately, there was a little accident and they were broken."

The relief that claimed Adrian was almost palpable. He felt his entire body relax . . . until Clarissa's father continued: "I shall have to take her to a shop here in town and purchase a new pair before the wedding."

"There is no need for that, my lord,"

Adrian said quickly. "I shall take care of it."

Lord Crambray hesitated before nodding. "As you wish," he said. Then much to Adrian's relief, he turned to head out the door. "Enjoy the fountain. I am sure Clarissa and Lady Mowbray shall return shortly."

"This way, gentlemen," Ffoulkes announced, and turned to lead the way up the hall after closing the front door behind his master.

Adrian spoke up once the butler had led them to the French doors in the salon. "We can find it from here," he said.

"As you wish." Ffoulkes gave a nod and turned away. "I shall see to it that Cook is preparing the tea for when the ladies return."

Adrian opened the French doors and led the way out. He'd never approached the fountain from this direction — the night of the ball he'd come in over the back gate — but he had no problem finding where he needed to go. He knew the fountain was in the back right corner of the property, so he simply kept taking paths that led in that direction.

"Here we are," he said as they emerged in the clearing.

Hadley paused, glancing at the fountain, then turned and peered toward the path from which they had just stepped. "Did she come this way?"

"That is the path she and Joan took back, so I am assuming it is the path she took here," Adrian said. He followed Hadley to peer at the trees at the end of the path. None was low enough to have caused her a problem. Neither he nor Hadley had to duck his head even to walk underneath, and Clarissa came up only to Adrian's chin.

Hadley turned back to survey the fountain.

"Clarissa thought she hit her head on a branch coming off this path," Adrian said. "And then she recalls stumbling a step or two forward before she fell and blacked out."

Hadley surveyed the fountain a good ten or more feet away and shook his head. "That is not how she ended up in the fountain," he said.

"I did not think so either," Adrian admitted unhappily.

"And she certainly did not hit her head on a branch coming off the path. Even if she had stumbled off the path, the branches are pruned high enough that she wouldn't have hit anything."

"Yes," Adrian agreed.

"I am afraid you are right, my lord," Hadley said, moving toward the bushes on the left of the path and using his foot to move the undergrowth aside. He peered at the ground. "It does not appear possible that this could be an accident."

"No." Adrian frowned and turned to survey the fountain, recalling the manner in which his heart leaped in his chest as he'd spotted her floating in the water. He'd thought he'd lost her then, and it hadn't been a happy thought. Adrian had known he was interested in her and enjoyed her before that, but it was then that he realized his feelings ran far deeper. Yes, he very much feared he was well on the way to loving this woman.

"Oh-ho! What have we here?"

Adrian glanced back toward Hadley at the grim comment, and saw him bending to pick something up. The man straightened a moment later with a long, wide branch in hand. Frowning, Adrian moved to his side.

"Do you think that was the branch? Do you think Clarissa broke it off when she hit it?"

"Not unless she sawed at it first," Hadley said dryly, pointing.

Adrian noted the marks halfway through the branch on the heavy end, then looked at the strand of long brown hair caught in the bark. Hadley removed the hair and raised an eyebrow. "Clarissa's, by my guess. It looks the right color."

Adrian nodded.

"So, someone cut this down ahead of time, lured her out to the fountain, and knocked her out with it. They then dumped her in the fountain, no doubt expecting her to drown. Your plans to meet up with her here are the only thing that saved Clarissa that night."

Adrian felt a cold kernel of fear begin to grow in his chest. Only his hopes of seeing her that night had saved her. And if he'd chosen a different spot to meet her, or a different night, Clarissa would now be dead. The very idea froze his heart in his chest. The depth of his upset was a bit startling. Adrian hadn't known her long, and yet her happiness and safety were already terribly important to his welfare.

Hadley tossed the branch down and brushed off his hands. "What of the fire?"

Adrian blinked. "The fire?"

"That same night. I understand there was a fire here. You and Clarissa were found together in a somewhat compromising situation, and you announced your intention to marry her."

"Ah, yes. I had forgotten about that."

Adrian's mouth tightened. "The fire occurred directly outside the door to her room. A candle was supposedly left burning on a hall table there and somehow tipped over and started a fire — or at least, that is what they say happened."

"You do not believe it? Is it because of this — ?"

"Clarissa's door was locked, or possibly jammed shut from the outside. Not that it mattered; the door was too hot by the time I noticed the fire and went over. The fire was roaring on the other side. We had to go out the window. However, had she been alone and asleep . . ."

Hadley nodded grimly. "I shall begin to look into the incident at the market when she was nearly trampled. It is possible it was just that — an accident. Still, I shall ask around and see if anyone remembers that day and saw anyone nearby who might have pushed her. I could talk to the staff here about the day she fell down the stairs, as well, but —"

"Nay." Adrian shook his head. "I would rather not alert anyone to the fact that we suspect someone is trying to hurt her."

Hadley nodded. "Now, what about Clarissa? If someone is trying to kill her as we suspect, they may redouble their efforts before she marries you."

"I took care of that. I am paying three of the Crambray footmen to keep an eye on her. I arranged it the night of the fire," Adrian said grimly.

"And what about the maid?" Hadley asked.

Adrian shrugged. "She is already supposed to keep an eye on her; she walks her around. Besides, I feared she might tell Clarissa, whom I don't wish anxious or afraid. She is already under a lot of stress with the preparations for the wedding."

Hadley nodded. "Three should be sufficient. There is —"

"Adrian Maximillian Montfort!"

Stiffening, Adrian turned to the path as his mother came into sight leading Clarissa. He was obviously in trouble; his mother only ever used his full name when she felt he had done something wrong. But he couldn't seem to find the wherewithal to care. His brain slipped a gear at the sight of Clarissa.

She was wearing a lovely cream-colored dress, and her hair — while pulled back at the sides — was mostly down as it had been that night in her room. He liked it better this way than all tucked up in one of those convoluted 'dos women all wore to balls.

She looked lovely.

"Oh, do stop gawking at Clarissa," his mother said impatiently, apparently put out. "She will be your wife soon enough, and you may gawk to your heart's content. At the moment, *I* would like your attention."

Adrian blinked and turned reluctantly, asking with resignation, "What have I done wrong?"

"Do you not recall my mentioning having tea with Clarissa today?" his mother asked grimly.

Adrian's eyebrows rose. "Yes. In fact, Hadley and I decided to join you. It is why we are here."

"Well, that is lovely," Lady Mowbray said with a smile. It hardened as she added, "Except, we were to have it at *your* house."

Adrian blinked. "My house?"

Lady Mowbray heaved an exasperated sigh. "Yes, Adrian, your house. You were to arrange it with your staff so that they could make the house spic-and-span and present themselves in their Sunday finest so that Clarissa could meet them all and get acquainted — both with her new home and its staff — before the wedding."

"Oh." Adrian stared at her, nonplussed. Come to think of it, he did have a vague recollection of a comment about tea with

Clarissa, followed by one about Clarissa meeting the staff, which he hadn't understood at the time but which made perfect sense now. They weren't yet her staff, but they soon would be, and by having tea in his home she would have been able to become acquainted with them.

It was a very good idea. Crucial, even. Clarissa's life and home would change with their wedding. She would have a new residence and new staff, and meeting them ahead of time was really important. It was a shame he hadn't paid more attention to his mother.

Lady Mowbray heaved another put-upon sigh, then glanced at Hadley. "Mr. Hadley. My son has mentioned you to me."

Adrian stiffened, afraid she would give away what the man did for him, but she was clever enough not to, and simply said, "Clarissa, this is Mr. Hadley. He assists Adrian with projects from time to time. Mr. Hadley, this is my soon-to-be daughter-in-law, Lady Clarissa Crambray."

"Lady Crambray."

Hadley moved forward to take her hand, offering a smile as his eyes moved over her head. Adrian knew he was searching for the wound from the night of the fire. However, there was nothing left to see. It had been a week and a half since the accident, and while there had been a bump and bruise at the time, there was no longer. Had Adrian been able to get hold of the man sooner, there might have been something to notice, but Hadley had been off in the north of England to handle another matter for another lord. He'd returned only the night before, and had come to see Adrian first thing this morning.

"Good day, Mr. Hadley," Clarissa murmured. "What do you assist Adrian with?"

Adrian stiffened at the question, but needn't have bothered. Hadley was quick on his feet and lied without hesitation. "Oh, this and that. A bit of everything, really."

"Oh," Clarissa said, but still looked curious.

Hadley continued, "In fact, his lordship was just telling me this morning that, for his next project, he wishes to create a fountain out at Mowbray in the fashion of the one at your father's home here in town, which is why he invited me to tea with you two ladies today. He thought this way we could get acquainted, and I could take a look at it, so I know what I am talking about when I approach workers about making one," he explained. Adrian marveled at the man's skill.

"Oh, of course." Clarissa smiled widely. "That would be lovely. Now, Mr. Hadley shall be returning to your house for tea with us then, shall he?"

"Er . . ." Adrian frowned. "I believe Ffoulkes was seeing that Cook would make tea here."

"We explained the mix-up to Ffoulkes when we arrived," Clarissa said. "He said not to worry, that he would tell Cook not to bother. He did not think she could have gotten much farther than putting water on to boil."

"We also explained the mix-up to Jessop," his mother announced. "And he was going to see to it that your cook got started on tea at once, so it would be ready when we returned."

"You were at the house?" Adrian asked.

His mother nodded. "How do you think we learned you were here? Jessop told us. We explained to him that you were confused, and that we were to have tea in your home, and then we followed you here to bring you back."

"Oh, well, then . . . I guess we could head home," Adrian murmured, wondering how upset his staff was with him at the moment. He'd learned long ago that angering one's help could mean a good deal of discomfort.

They walked back along the path to the house, and were actually preparing to get into the carriage when Hadley said, "Actually, my lord, perhaps it would do me better to get to work on this latest project rather than join you for tea, lovely as that would be."

"Oh, yes. Yes, of course." Adrian turned to offer his hand. "Thank you, Hadley. I shall look forward to hearing from you."

The man shook his hand with a nod, then turned and made his way off up the street.

"Is Mr. Hadley not joining us after all?" Clarissa asked as Adrian got into the carriage. He took the empty bench seat across from the ladies.

"No. He has business to take care of," he said vaguely, settling on his seat, his eyes sliding over her. She was like a ray of sunshine in that light-colored dress, and Adrian marveled that she grew more beautiful to him every time he saw her.

His mother began to chatter about their fittings that morning, and Adrian listened with half an ear as they made the short journey to his home. His mind was conjuring thoughts of his last ride in a carriage with Clarissa, and he decided it was probably a good thing that he didn't live far from his mother's house. Despite Lady Crambray's presence, he felt himself stir in his breeches.

At his home, Jessop had the front door open before Adrian and his companions had quite reached it. "Welcome home, my lord."

One look at the man's face, and Adrian knew he was in the doghouse with his butler and probably the rest of the staff. He didn't need the sneer that greeted him to know that. He supposed the servants had been rushing about like crazy, cleaning and dusting. Not that his home or servants were not always neat and clean, but they would have put a little special shine into things, or at least tried to in the short time since they'd learned their new lady was coming.

Yes, if they'd had more warning about Clarissa's visit, they would have done all in their power to make a good first impression. However, they hadn't, because he hadn't paid attention to his mother, so he hadn't informed them about the planned tea today, which was why Jessop was presently glaring at him as if he were some form of pond scum the man had just noticed on the rug.

"Never fear, Jessop," Lady Mowbray said as she led the way inside. "I have already lectured him on not listening to me and not warning you."

"Very good, my lady," the butler said. But his glare did not ease.

Adrian grimaced, then turned to Clarissa, who was squinting around at his entry. It was a dark blue-and-slate color scheme, which suited her perfectly, making her stand out in her cream-colored dress. She looked as if she belonged in his home.

"Do not even bother to glare, Jessop. He is obviously too taken with his fiancée to pay any notice. I fear my son is quite useless, and will continue to be for quite some time — at least until after he has married our lovely Clarissa. Do you not think she is lovely, Jessop?"

"Quite lovely, my lady," Jessop agreed.

"They will give me beautiful grandbabies, do you not think?"

"Most assuredly, my lady."

Spotting the blush that rose on Clarissa's face, Adrian turned a glare on the speakers and said, "We are present and listening, you know."

"So, you *do* hear me on occasion," Lady Mowbray commented dryly, then slid her hand through Jessop's arm. She led him up the hall, saying, "Come along, my good man. We shall go see what Cook has managed to whip up to save the day. Adrian is really quite fortunate to have staff as clever and quick as all of you. No matter what crises arise, you all handle them with the greatest aplomb — and I must say it always impresses me."

Adrian rolled his eyes as he listened to his mother butter up the butler. Still, within moments the whole household would be killing themselves to please her, and not one person would be upset at the chaos into which they'd been thrown by unexpected guests.

"I am sorry if we are causing a fuss," Clarissa said quietly. "We need not stay for tea if —"

"Nonsense," Adrian interrupted. He stepped forward to draw Clarissa into his arms, only to pause as his mother called over her shoulder, "Show her around your home, Adrian. It will be hers soon, and she should at least know something about it before she comes here to live."

Letting his arms drop to his sides, Adrian sighed and took Clarissa's arm to lead her to the staircase. "I will show you upstairs first."

"If you are not down in a quarter hour, I will come looking for you," his mother's voice floated back as she disappeared into the kitchens with Jessop.

Adrian grimaced as he led Clarissa upstairs. The wedding was only a day away; surely there was no longer a need to observe the proprieties?

CHAPTER TWELVE

Clarissa woke up early, realized it was her wedding day, and simply couldn't get back to sleep. She lay in bed for a few minutes thinking excitedly about the day ahead — and the night — then recalled her new spectacles. Sitting up abruptly, she retrieved them from the small detachable pocket she usually wore under her skirt and popped them onto her face.

A little sigh slid from her lips as the world came into focus. Most of the time everything around Clarissa was a blur, and her head was slightly achy from squinting. Her spectacles might not look good on her, but when she was wearing them the world around her certainly looked better.

It had been difficult not to wear them, not to scream with joy to everyone that she could finally see. However, she still felt it was better to keep them a secret until Adrian formed a tendre for her.

If he formed a tendre for her, she thought. Clarissa was almost afraid to hope that he might. She knew he found her attractive and seemed to like her, but that didn't ensure a lifelong abiding love would follow.

Finally able to see, Clarissa contemplated slipping down to the library to fetch a book, but feared she did not really have time. And before she could decide on anything else, the click of her doorknob turning sounded loudly in the silent room. Clarissa snatched her spectacles off and grabbed for her pocket. She had just managed to slide them out of sight when Lydia entered.

Her stepmother was carrying something, but Clarissa couldn't make out what it was. She watched the woman place the object on the dressing table by the door, then walk over to the bed. Suddenly wary, Clarissa watched narrow-eyed as Lydia approached. She wished she could pop her spectacles on again and see the woman's expression; she had no idea why Lydia was here on the morning of her wedding, but suspected it wasn't for a good purpose.

"Your father thought I should explain the facts of the marriage bed to you," Lydia announced without preamble, and Clarissa almost sighed. This would *not* be pleasant, she was sure. Adrian had seemed to fear that the woman would attempt to make her miserable and afraid, and Clarissa suspected he was right. She tried to tell herself that she wouldn't allow Lydia to do so, but really, one had to wonder: if there was nothing to fear in the night ahead, then why had Adrian been anxious that her stepmother could make it seem so? And what was that comment about pain and blood? What had he been so reluctant to explain?

"I shall tell you exactly what my mother told me," Lydia announced. "Come."

Clarissa hesitated, then pushed her linens and blankets aside and followed her stepmother to the dressing table where she'd set the items she'd carried in. By leaning close and squinting, Clarissa could see that there was a small silver truncheon and a pie of some sort. Lydia picked up the truncheon.

"This is the approximate size of the man's apparatus, and quite similar in size," she announced. "Imagine it is a key to your lock."

Clarissa pursed her lips at this announcement and wondered if the hardness she'd felt nudging her from between Adrian's legs was the key in question. She had a vague idea of where her lock was, though she'd never explored the area. Adrian had, however, and quite thoroughly to her mind.

"This pie is your lock," Lydia announced. "Your lock is not open and perfectly suited in size to the man's truncheon or key. It is small and narrow, and has a thin layer of skin called the . . . well, most often it is called the maiden's veil."

Clarissa glanced sharply at Lydia's face, noting the woman's sudden evident discomfort. Apparently, getting this technical bothered her. But Lydia struggled on.

"The man has to break through that veil the first time. Like so."

Clarissa gave a start as her stepmother slammed the truncheon down, stabbing it through the top of the pie with a violent thud. Clarissa stared at the broken crust and then reached up to wipe away the juice that had squirted out and splashed her face. The pie was some sort of berry or cherry and — blind though she was — Clarissa could see that the juice seeping out around the half-buried truncheon was a deep red.

"To quote my mother," Lydia said grimly, "you will bleed. And it will hurt as you would expect. But if you are very lucky, he will finish quickly and leave you alone to sleep and weep in privacy. I somehow doubt Lord Mowbray will be so considerate."

Leaving behind the mess she'd made, Lydia turned to the door and opened it. As she walked out, she said dryly, "Enjoy your wedding night."

Clarissa watched the door close, then moved weakly to sit on the dressing table chair. She didn't seem able to tear her gaze away from the pie. The barely golden, almost white crust was stained with — and soaking up — the red juices of the smashed fruit. The truncheon still stood up out of it, proud and hard.

"Damn," she breathed. Clarissa had sworn to herself that she would not allow Lydia to upset her, but this was . . . well, it was upsetting.

"My lady?"

Clarissa turned at Joan's voice, and stared at her maid's blurred image that slipped into the room. "I saw your stepmother leaving as I approached. Is everything all right?"

"I . . ." Clarissa paused and cleared her throat, then promptly forgot what she'd intended to say. She asked instead, "Do we really have a maiden's veil, and does the man really have to break through it?"

"Well . . ." Clarissa could hear the reluctance in her voice.

She bit her lip. "It *is* true, is it not?"

"Well, yes. But —"

"And will there be blood and pain?"

Joan sighed. "My lady, you should not have let Lady Crambray upset you. The first time is painful for most women, but —"

"Most?" Clarissa interrupted hopefully. "Then 'tis not always so?"

"I have heard that some women suffer little in the way of pain," Joan assured her.

"Heard," Clarissa echoed. "Heard? But do you *know* anyone who did not suffer pain and bleed?"

"Well . . ." Joan hesitated, then closed the bedchamber door and approached with an air of determination. "Never you mind. Come. I am sure Lord Mowbray will make it as easy on you as he can. We should get you ready now."

"But —"

"My lady," Joan interrupted. "Do you wish to marry him or not? Would you really prefer to marry Lord Prudhomme or someone of his ilk? Because I assure you that I do not think Lord Prudhomme would at all concern himself with your comfort or well-being."

"Nay," Clarissa agreed, then stood with a sigh. "Let us get me ready then. I am to marry today."

She felt a distinct lack of enthusiasm, and she knew it was reflected in her voice. She had been looking forward to the night ahead until Lydia's little talk; she'd thought it would be like the night in her room, when Adrian made her toes curl and her heart beat rapidly and excitement had coursed through her like water in a river after a hard rain. Now she knew it would involve pain and blood, and she was suddenly very sorry she'd been born a woman. After all, surely it was better to be the truncheon than the pie.

The priest was old and stiff, and looked no more pleased to be there than Clarissa felt at the moment. It had turned out to be a cold, rainy day, unusual for the middle of summer. Clarissa couldn't help but think it wasn't a good portent of what was to come.

"Clarissa?"

She glanced around, startled by Adrian's murmur, and frowned. Everyone seemed to be looking at her. At least, it appeared that way from what she could see.

"Do you . . ." the priest began in weary tones that suggested he'd done this once or twice already.

"I do," Clarissa interrupted quickly, embarrassed to have been caught daydreaming at such an important time. Then she realized what she'd said, and sighed to herself. In truth, she was no longer sure she wanted to "do" anything. Not if it meant Adrian was going to truncheon her pie.

Too late to worry about that, though, Clarissa supposed. She'd accepted her fate and now Adrian was doing the same; and it was as good as done. She was Lady Clarissa Montfort, wife to the Earl of Mowbray. And she didn't need to ask if he wished to truncheon her. It seemed rather obvious he would.

"I now pronounce you man and wife. You may kiss the bride."

The words had barely registered before Adrian turned her into his arms and kissed her. Clarissa remained stiff under his embrace, her mind a mass of confusion. As little as eight hours ago she'd been excited and happy at the thought of marrying him. Now all she could think of and see when she closed her eyes was that club smashing that pastry.

Adrian must have noticed her reticence, for he pulled back from the kiss and peered at her with a frown of concern. Clarissa forced a smile in an effort to try to reassure him; then everyone seemed to move at once. There were scrolls to sign and congratulations given, and then she found herself bundled into a carriage and heading to her home. Her *father's* home, she corrected herself. It was no longer her home. From now on, her home was with Adrian.

"Shall we go?"

Clarissa glanced up sharply from the drink she'd been clenching. She knew her eyes were wide with alarm. This was the moment she'd been dreading since arriving at her father's for the wedding celebration.

Biting her lip, Clarissa turned to glance around the crowded room. Surprisingly enough, while she'd been shunned by nearly everyone since her arrival in London, the wedding party had turned out to be a large one. There were, of course, Lady Mowbray and Adrian's cousins, Mary and Reginald, as well as her own father and stepmother, but then there were also Lord and Lady Havard, Lord and Lady Achard, Lord Prudhomme and his mother, and several people whose voices she recognized but whom she wouldn't know on the street if she could see them, because she'd never glimpsed them close enough to make them out.

Aware that she had yet to answer Adrian's question, Clarissa swallowed, tried for a cheerful smile . . . and failed miserably. Her voice was a mere squeak when she asked,

"So soon?"

She thought she saw Adrian's eyebrows rise, but his voice was quiet as he said, " 'Tis quite late, Clarissa. Nearing midnight."

She knew that wasn't late for a ball, but this wasn't a simple ball. It was their wedding party. Still, she tried desperately: "Yes, but everyone is still here. Should we not stay until the last guest leaves? After all, the party is for us."

"Clarissa," Adrian said patiently. "It is tradition that the bride and groom leave first. Everyone is waiting for us to go."

"Oh, I see." Unable to think of any way to further delay the departure, Clarissa reluctantly put her drink down. "I should collect my things."

"The servants took them during the ceremony," he said gently.

"Oh . . . Well, Joan —"

"Joan is there too," Adrian said. "Come, we should say good-bye."

"Oh." Sighing, Clarissa allowed him to lead her first to her father and Lydia, then to Lady Mowbray. It all seemed to be moving terribly fast. The next thing Clarissa knew, she was bundled into the carriage. She sat tense and anxious in the corner, her mind consumed with what was to come.

Adrian was just as quiet in the opposite

corner, but she could feel his eyes on her. Clarissa knew her behavior was disturbing him, and she racked her mind for something to say to ease the tension. Anything. But her mind was filled with the image of the truncheon smashing into the pie, and the red juice spilling out.

Adrian's servants — hers now too, she realized in some deep part of her mind — were all lined up at the door when they arrived home. Everyone was smiling and nodding in greeting, and Adrian officially introduced her to each member of the staff. Clarissa listened to all the names, but forgot every one the minute he steered her to the stairs.

As he started walking her up, she felt as if she were being led to the gallows. Every nerve in her body was screaming with fear and tension, and she tried to sort out what would happen. She almost moaned when Adrian opened a door revealing a bedchamber.

When she hesitated in the doorway, he pushed her gently inside. The door closed softly behind her, and Clarissa turned to stare at it wide-eyed. Her husband hadn't entered with her. She felt her shoulders sag with relief. There was to be a brief reprieve.

"*There* you are!"

Clarissa stiffened at the sound of Joan's cheerful greeting, and she whirled to see the blurred image of her maid bustling forward, all cheer and energy. Clarissa wanted to ask what she was smiling about, but restrained herself.

"Was the wedding lovely? How was the party that followed? Did you dance? Was the food delicious? Cook and the staff worked ever so hard to make everything just right." Joan rattled on as she began to tug at Clarissa's clothing.

Clarissa must have answered, but she couldn't have said later what those answers were. Her head was awhirl as the maid worked, and her panic deepened as each item of clothing was stripped away to leave her more and more vulnerable.

Too soon, she was stripped and bathed, and she found herself in a lacy nightgown and tucked into bed.

"There we are. You look lovely," Joan assured her, as if she thought Clarissa would care. The maid then wished her good night and left the room.

Clarissa remained frozen where she'd been placed, in the center of the bed, her gaze moving dully around the dark shadows all around. She could not see much beyond the candle on the bedside. After some hesitation, she reached for the small bag she'd removed as Joan had undressed her. The maid had set it on the bedside table, and, reaching inside, Clarissa found her spectacles and perched them on her nose. She peered around at what was now her bedroom.

She had seen it the day before, when Adrian had given her the tour of the house, but then it had been daytime. It had seemed very pretty at the time, what with its red-and-gold color scheme. It looked much different in the glow of candlelight. Dark and gloomy, was her opinion — the red that had seemed so gay in daylight now appeared to her the color of thick blood.

Sighing, she let her gaze return to the bed in which she sat. It was huge, much bigger than her bed at home. At her *father's* home, she corrected herself again. She was a married woman now, with her own home and staff and husband. The last thought made her grimace, and Clarissa removed her spectacles and tucked them back in her bag to keep them hidden. She then lay back on the bed, contemplating the possibility that if she pretended to be asleep, Adrian might leave off the consummation until tomorrow.

But that seemed the coward's way out,

and Clarissa feared that if she did that, it would just leave her to worry and be anxious over it all day tomorrow until the task was finally done. If there was one thing she had learned in her short life, it was that it was always best to get unpleasant tasks over with quickly and get them out of the way. Besides, it would be good to know what she would have to face each night of her life from now on — *if* she would have to face it each night. How often did husbands wish to consummate? If there was no pain for them and they enjoyed only the pleasure of what she'd experienced the other night, Clarissa feared Adrian might wish to consummate often.

She frowned at the idea: his truncheon in her pie every night for the rest of her life . . . ?

It couldn't be like that, Clarissa decided suddenly. Lady Havard and Lady Achard wouldn't have been so eager to have affairs with Lord Prudhomme if it were like that every time. Perhaps it was only the truncheon part that hurt. She already knew that there were things a man and a woman did together that could be quite pleasurable. So it seemed reasonable that only the end part, the actual key-in-the-lock part, hurt.

Clarissa made a face. It seemed a shame to end such pleasure with such unpleasantness, and she found it hard to believe the pleasure made the pain all worthwhile. Still, Lady Havard and Lady Achard had seemed eager to indulge. Come to think of it, she realized, there had been no sign of anxiety about the pain to come in Lady Havard's moans and sighs that night. Of course, Clarissa now understood what Prudhomme had been doing under the lady's skirts and why she'd been sighing and moaning . . .

Clarissa blinked as it occurred to her to wonder if she herself had made the same sounds when Adrian was doing those things to her. She didn't recall making noise, but then, between the fire and the sensations Adrian had been causing in her, she'd been a little distracted. She would have to pay more attention the next time, Clarissa decided — then grimaced at the idea of a next time. It would not end nearly so pleasantly.

Just thinking of all this made Clarissa glance impatiently toward the dark section of wall where she recalled seeing the door that led to Adrian's adjoining room. It was late and had been a long, stressful, and tiring day. Clarissa wanted to sleep. Where was her husband? Could he not show a little consideration and get the deed done quickly so that she could rest?

Really, it did now seem to her a good idea to get it over with as swiftly as possible. She shifted impatiently in bed, then pushed her linens and blankets aside and got to her feet.

Picking up the bedside candle, Clarissa moved carefully toward the wall where she thought the door was, wishing she could put on her spectacles to find it. Life would be so much easier if she did not have to wait on wearing the things. She certainly hoped her husband came to have a tendre for her quickly, so that she might wear them again. Really, if he realized how much she was willing to suffer for him even in going through with the truncheon-and-pie-ordeal, he should half love her already. Clarissa had no idea how other women put up with it, but she already knew it would not be the joyful part of her marriage.

Blowing a wisp of long hair out of her face, she stretched out a hand to prevent herself from walking into the wall, relieved when she felt a solid surface beneath her fingers. She then moved sideways along the wall until she came to the door. Clarissa paused, allowing herself to take a deep breath and build some courage. This was for the best, to get the nasty deed done, she assured herself. Surely it couldn't take too long? A quick unpleasantness and then she could relax and sleep. Forcing a bright smile onto her face, she found the door handle and turned it.

Adrian rolled onto his side in bed and released a pitiful sigh. Once his manservant, Keighley, had helped him undress and bathe, he'd sent the man away and sat, trying to decide what to do. His instinct had been to go directly to Clarissa and consummate the marriage . . . and what a pleasant thought that was.

Unfortunately, there appeared to be something wrong with Clarissa. She had seemed perfectly fine and happy about the wedding yesterday, but today, from the moment she had entered the church he'd been aware that something was wrong. She'd been distracted and anxious throughout the ceremony, then quiet and tense through the celebrations, always shifting a half step away when he moved to her side. It was as if she could not bear to be near him. And then, she hadn't been eager to leave and come to her new home.

Adrian wasn't sure what the problem was, and was afraid to ask. He worried that she had somehow seen his face and now loathed being near him. It seemed just like something Lydia would do, borrowing someone's spectacles for Clarissa to wear so she could peer out the window to see exactly whom she was marrying. If that was the case, the happiness he'd been experiencing, that he had envisioned continuing on in the future, would be lost forever.

Over the last few weeks, Adrian's mind had been constantly weaving dreams and fantasies of a happy home life. A home full of love and laughter, with the cries and giggles of children, Clarissa loving him, her smile greeting him in the morning, her presence to share the long days and nights . . .

But now it seemed like all that was slipping away, and the very idea made his heart hurt. Worse, Adrian was afraid to ask her what was wrong. He was also afraid to approach her about the bedding and have her turn from him in revulsion. So, in his cowardice, he'd decided to let her alone tonight. It had been a long day, Adrian had told himself; he would be considerate and let her sleep, then see how she was on the morrow. If it had been just the stress of the wedding and moving to a new home, Clarissa should be more cheerful tomorrow, and perhaps he could approach her then. But if not . . .

Adrian silently cursed the injury that had stolen his looks and left him an ugly beast. He wished he were handsome for her, wished that when she got spectacles, she would still look on him with love and adoration and attraction. He had always felt ten feet tall around her. Until today.

The sound of the door opening interrupted his bitter reflections, and Adrian glanced over his shoulder with confusion. His eyes widened as he saw the connecting door between his own room and Clarissa's open. Candlelight spilled in.

"Adrian?" Clarissa appeared in the opening, squinting. "Why is it so dark? Are you here, husband?"

Adrian had opened his mouth to say yes, but paused at the word *husband. Husband.* It was the first time she'd addressed him as such, and his heart squeezed in his chest at the title. *Husband.* He was her husband.

And she was his wife, Adrian realized, gaping at the thin, lacy gown she wore. It was sheer and sexy as hell, revealing more of her body than it concealed, and more than just his heart was reacting. Her hair had been let down and brushed until it shone. It lay in glossy waves around her lovely face.

"Adrian?"

Clearing his throat, he sat up in bed. "I am here. What are you still doing up? I thought you would be asleep by now."

Much to his amazement, Clarissa looked annoyed.

"It is our wedding night, my lord," she said — as if that explained everything.

Adrian wasn't too sure what it explained, though. It seemed as if she had come in search of him, which he found hard to believe after the way she'd been acting all day.

"I thought you were tired and would wish to sleep uninterrupted tonight," he said uncertainly.

"What?" Clarissa squawked, and there was no mistaking her ire at this news. "You'd make me wait another whole day and evening before we consummate our marriage?"

Adrian blinked. She sounded truly upset. "Well, you were so tense and anxious all day, I thought to show some consideration and —"

"I do not wish consideration, my lord. I wish to get it over with," she announced grimly.

It was nice to know she was so eager, Adrian thought, then frowned as Clarissa started forward, bumping the small table beside the door and sending an unlit candle tumbling to the floor. Muttering under her breath, Clarissa knelt, holding her lit candle out as she felt around in search of the other that she'd knocked off the tabletop.

Adrian hesitated, then shifted the linens and blankets on his bed aside and got to his feet. He was completely and utterly nude, but she was practically blind without her spectacles. Not that it would have bothered him to walk around nude in front of her. While his face was scarred, his body was unmarred and in perfect condition. Still, Adrian would have shown her innocence some respect and not revealed himself so soon if he'd thought she could see properly.

"Here, I shall get it," he said as he crossed the room to join her.

Adrian had held his hand out, intending to help her to her feet, but Clarissa only raised her head to glance at him. At least, he thought that was what she'd intended to do, but her eyes never made it to his face. They reached his groin and froze there, and she suddenly went white.

"Dear God," she breathed. "Your truncheon is huge."

At least, Adrian thought that was what she said, though he barely heard the murmur and could be mistaken. Certainly if that was what she'd said, it made absolutely no sense.

Any concern or curiosity over her words died an abrupt death when she moved the candle closer as if to get a better look. It was obvious her depth perception was off. Adrian almost got his own piffle burned — and not just with some hot water, as Reginald had — and without the barrier of cloth to protect his body! Catching the candleholder, he took it from her with one hand and urged her to her feet with the other.

"Come, then. If you wish to tend to this tonight, I would be more than happy to accommodate you," Adrian assured her. He walked her to the bed. Had she been able to see, his desire would have been in no doubt. His piffle had become as stiff as a pole at the prospect.

He set the candle on the bedside table as Clarissa climbed into bed, then turned back to find her climbing out the other side. As he stared at her blankly, she stood on the opposite side of the bed, wringing her hands as if they were damp towels she was washing.

"You have to get into the bed if you wish . . . Well, I do not suppose it has to be in the bed," Adrian allowed uncertainly. But truly, despite her claim that she wished to get to it, she did not look eager to do so. Tilting his head, he eyed her uncertainly. He finally said, "Clarissa, is there something wrong?"

His wife shook her head mutely and continued to wring her hands, her eyes wide and — in his opinion — alarmed.

Deciding she must be a bit nervous about the bedding, and that he should approach the task carefully and gently, Adrian did not order her back into the bed, but walked slowly around to join her on the opposite side, thinking to kiss away some of her anxiety. But the moment he rounded the bottom corner, she turned and scrambled into the bed again.

Adrian smiled faintly, thinking she was as changeable as the wind. He started to climb onto the bed, only to pause when she continued across and scrambled off the other side.

Straightening slowly, Adrian stared as she turned to face him across the expanse, once more anxiously wringing her hands.

"Clarissa," he said slowly. But that was as far as he got before she blurted, "I do not think I wish you smashing my pie with your truncheon."

Adrian stilled and blinked. There was that *truncheon* word again and he had no idea what she was talking about. Smashing her pie with his truncheon? That did not even make sense. "I fear I have no idea what you are talking about, wife."

Clarissa gave a little jerk at the last word, then said, "I mean, I do not want you breaking my veil with your key."

Rather than helping him understand, her words simply confused him further. "What?"

"My lock is too small for your truncheon."

"Are you speaking in tongues?" Adrian asked. "Clarissa, I have no idea what —"

"Lydia explained everything."

And Adrian went still, the light suddenly going on in his head. He should have realized earlier. "Lydia," he repeated.

Clarissa nodded fervently. "You said to ask her about why this would be uncomfortable. I did not ask, but she explained anyway."

"I see." He sighed. Her odd behavior today suddenly made sense: Lydia had scared the hell out of her, and she'd spent the past ten hours dreading the night ahead. And it was all his own fault, he acknowledged. He *had* told her to ask Lydia rather than explaining about her maiden's veil himself.

Running one hand wearily through his hair, Adrian said, "And Lydia said that I would smash your pie with my truncheon?"

Clarissa nodded. "She said her mother told her it was like a man was the key and the woman was the lock, and that he would put his key in her lock, but that that was all lies. It is much more messy than that, and painful too, and then she took a little silver truncheon and smashed it into a cherry pie and said the top crust of the pie was the veil that the man had to break through with his truncheon. And I am not altogether certain, as I do not have my spectacles, but from what I can tell, you appear to have a very big truncheon, my lord."

The last was said in a most woeful tone, as if it were a bad thing indeed, and Adrian had to bite back a smile. In truth, there was nothing amusing about any of this; Lydia had managed to make his wedding night much more difficult than it had to be. But still, he was relieved to know it had nothing to do with her having somehow seen and been repulsed by his face.

"Clarissa?"

"Yes?" She looked as wary as a doe, eyes wide and alarmed, chest rising and lowering swiftly as her breaths became shallow and swift.

"Do you like my kisses?" he asked patiently.

Her expression became even more wary, as if she sensed a trap in the question somewhere. However, after some hesitation, Clarissa nodded and said, "Yes, my lord. I very much like your kisses."

"And do you like when I touch and caress you?"

Clarissa shifted on her feet as if preparing to fly, but nodded.

"And did you like what I did to you in your room?"

Clarissa bit her lip, but nodded again.

"Then what if we just did that again?"

"Just kissing and touching and . . ." Even in the firelight he could see her face flush pink. "The other?"

"Yes," Adrian lied. He had every intention of taking it farther than that, but first he had to get her relaxed and prepared. Telling her ahead of time that this was what he intended would not aid his efforts.

Clarissa relaxed a little. "You do not mind if we do not . . ."

" 'Smash your pie'?" Adrian supplied dryly when she hesitated. "No, I do not mind."

Clarissa let out a little sigh and smiled, one of those wide, beaming smiles that made him feel like the most attractive man in the world. She didn't even bother to answer his question verbally, but instead crawled into the bed and settled under the covers, then turned to smile at him expectantly.

Adrian heaved a little sigh of his own, sure they were past the worst of it, then pulled back the blankets and linens and eased carefully in beside her.

CHAPTER THIRTEEN

Clarissa felt the bed depress beside her as Adrian slid under the linens, and that was as long as she lasted before throwing herself at him. Her husband gave a muffled grunt of surprise as she plastered herself to his chest and kissed him wildly across the face, cheeks, nose, and forehead.

"Thank you, thank you, thank you, thank you," Clarissa murmured between each kiss. She peppered everything she could reach. "Thank you for being so patient and understanding. You are the best husband in the world. Truly, my lord, I am the luckiest of women."

His breath brushed her ear as a soft chuckle escaped his lips. "I am happy you are pleased."

"Mmm." Clarissa smiled, slipping her arms around his neck as he slid one hand to her back and the other into her hair. "Please kiss me, my lord husband."

"As you wish, my lovely lady." His mouth closed over hers, and Clarissa immediately opened to him, a little murmur of pleasure sounding in her throat as he tipped her back on the bed and rolled atop her. This was what she liked. This, she enjoyed. His lips on hers and his body pressed close sent little shivers tingling through her body and made her toes curl. Clarissa thought they should always just do these things. She saw absolutely no reason for pie smashing at all, really. Unless they needed to do that to have children, she realized. She supposed they would eventually have to get to the pie smashing if that were the case.

Adrian's hand found her breast through the thin cloth of her gown, and Clarissa's ability to think died a quick death. Gasping into his mouth, she arched into his touch, her hands digging into the flesh of his shoulders as he caught her nipple between thumb and finger. He rolled and tweaked gently, sending little shocks of excitement through her.

Clarissa was shifting her legs restlessly, and as if in answer to her unconscious demand, Adrian shifted to his side and caught her hip in his hand. Drawing her onto her side with him, he then slid one of his legs between hers. His bare skin against hers was the most erotic thing Clarissa had ever felt. It was also the way she knew her gown had ridden up; but she didn't care. It felt so good, she found herself shifting her legs to make things easier. She then closed them when his thigh reached the seat of her pleasure and began to apply a gentle, insistent pressure. It felt so good, she found herself pressing down onto it.

Clarissa was aware of the way her body was contorting in an effort to get the most out of Adrian's caresses, but only in a subconscious, vaguely uninterested way. Most of her attention was on the excitement and pleasure he was creating and building in her.

Adrian broke their kiss, and she threw her head back with a gasp and pressed herself more firmly into his embrace, wanting more but not sure of what. Her new husband seemed to know, however. His mouth burned a trail across her cheek to her ear, then down to the base of her throat, where he nibbled briefly as his hands set to work on her gown.

Clarissa heard the sound of ripping cloth, but in the next moment her husband's calloused hand had closed over her breast again, and she cried out. This was so much better! His rough skin on her sensitive flesh made her buck in his arms with shock and excitement.

Then his lips left her neck, and they moved over her collar and down until they found their way to her breast. Clarissa moaned as his mouth closed hot and wet over her flesh; then she gasped and jerked as he gently bit at the nipple. She felt her knee hit something hard between his legs, and heard his groan as he went completely still.

"I am sorry, my lord," Clarissa gasped. "Did I hurt you?"

Adrian was silent for a moment. He had let her nipple slip from his mouth and squeezed his eyes closed, an expression of pain on his face. Clarissa bit her lip, afraid she had hurt him so much that he wouldn't wish to continue.

"Shall I kiss it better?" she asked. The words slipped out without a thought. It was an offer her real mother had often made when she was a child and skinned a knee or banged an arm. But the question seemed to cause Adrian more pain, for his body went even stiffer against her, and his eyes opened. He was close enough that she caught a glimpse of fire in them; then he shifted and his mouth covered hers, ravishing.

This was no gentle kiss, no careful exploration; it was a devouring, a demanding, a wanting that raised an immediate response of hunger in Clarissa so strong that she kissed him back with just as much passion and need. The kiss became almost a battle, and when he finally broke it and Clarissa resurfaced, she found that she was again on her back and he had shifted to settle between her legs, removing the threat of her unintentionally kneeing him again.

She was panting, but blinked and stilled, holding her breath as Adrian pressed a gentle kiss to first one eye and then the other. Clarissa blinked open her eyes slowly, and peered up at him, and found he was close enough that she could see his beautiful face. Even the scar on his cheek did nothing to mar the perfection of him. Clarissa smiled softly, feeling her heart tighten in her chest at just the sight of this dear man. He had found her miserable and alone, and set out to try to make her happy with picnics and prose.

"I . . ." Clarissa began, and then caught herself as she realized that she'd been about to say, *I love you.*

She blinked at him with confusion, and her mind tried to wrap itself around the thought as well as the feeling behind it. Surely she couldn't love him. Not yet. It was all far too soon, far too much, far too easy. Was love this easy?

Her thoughts were distracted when his hands began to wander again, and she focused her gaze on him as he shifted to kneel between her legs, moving out of focus so that he became a blur. Still kneeling there, he ran his hands over her stomach and then up to cup both breasts. Clarissa glanced down at herself to see that her nightgown had become a belt about her waist, leaving her exposed from the hips down and the waist up. Adrian was taking advantage of the exposure. She could feel his eyes eating her up as his hands glided over her tender white skin. He fondled her, and she felt him watching her face as he did.

Self-conscious under his gaze, Clarissa struggled not to arch into his touch, and bit her lip to keep from making a sound; but when he concentrated on her nipples again, a low moan ripped from her throat. She felt bereft as his hands left her breasts, and couldn't keep back another moan, but then his hands coasted down her stomach to catch her at the hips. Clarissa twisted restlessly on the bed, wishing he would kiss her again, or . . . well, do something.

She'd barely had the thought when Adrian

let one hand dip between her legs and drift over the damp flesh there. Clarissa squeezed her eyes closed and jerked under the touch, her own hands knotting in the linens. She could feel her teeth grinding together as her excitement jumped to an almost unbearable level. Then her eyes shot open as Adrian bent to press his face to her belly, brushing it first one way, then the other, as if wiping his face on her flesh. Finally he shifted lower, his mouth tickling as it trailed over the flesh of her hip.

Clarissa knew his intentions, and still she jerked wildly and went stiff as a board, her knees bending and heels digging into the bed as his head dipped between her legs. It was too much. Too much. She couldn't bear it, Clarissa thought, and then she became aware of the small mewls and moans that were struggling out of her throat and mouth. Embarrassed, she tried to stop them, tried to regain enough control to end the sounds. As if aware of her struggles and determined to ensure they failed, Adrian slid one hand back up her body to knead and squeeze one breast, and Clarissa gave up the battle, allowing the small sounds freedom to become louder.

She began to thrash under his ministrations, her head twisting wildly on the bed, her hands tearing at the linens, her heels alternating between digging into the mattress and then pressing into his sides. And just when Clarissa thought she couldn't bear it another moment, Adrian slid a finger into her and upped the pressure, so that she gave up her hold on the linens and grabbed for the headboard above her. Clarissa pulled at it so that she was almost dragging herself up away from him, even as her hips pushed up off the bed into his caresses.

Eyes squeezed closed, body in an agony of excitement, Clarissa didn't even notice when Adrian shifted his position and rose up over her. When his mouth covered hers in a kiss, she automatically kissed back, sucking at his tongue for all she was worth. And in the next moment Clarissa was crying out in shock as something large and hard pressed into her.

Both of them froze and remained completely still. Then Adrian slowly lifted his mouth from hers and she could see him clearly as he peered down at her with worry.

"Are you all right?" His voice was harsh with strain.

Clarissa swallowed, then shifted her lower body tentatively, only to realize that they were fully joined. He had put the key in the lock. "Y-you smashed my pie?"

It was a question. She thought that might be what had happened, but had felt hardly a pinch of pain, and wasn't at all sure. And while her excitement had died an abrupt death from surprise at the intrusion, it certainly hadn't been anything like Lydia described.

Adrian rolled his eyes, but his voice was solemn. "Yes. I smashed your pie." He closed his eyes and took a deep breath, then said, "I am sorry; I thought it best to get it out of the way. Are you okay?"

Clarissa nodded slowly, taking in his tense expression. Of the two of them, he seemed to be in more pain. At least, that was how it looked. It certainly wasn't pleasure on his face at the moment and she asked, "Are *you* all right?"

"Yes." The word wasn't very convincing, coming through his gritted teeth as it was. "Does it still hurt?"

Clarissa shook her head and admitted, "In truth, my lord, it did not hurt much at all to begin with."

"But you cried out."

"It startled me," she admitted.

Adrian hesitated, then asked, "How does it feel?"

"Odd," Clarissa said honestly. She offered a wry smile. "And a bit disappointing."

Adrian's eyebrows rose. "Disappointing?"

"Well, I was . . ." Blushing, Clarissa lowered her eyes to his chest and admitted, "I was enjoying what you were doing, my lord. And would have liked to have experienced the . . . er . . . completion of it, as I did that time during the fire. But now I just feel — What are you — Oh!" Clarissa gasped with surprise as he shifted his weight to one arm and slid his hand between them to touch her.

"You . . . Oh, that is . . . Oh, husband," Clarissa breathed. Her hips began to move of their own volition as he caressed her, and her previous excitement leaped back to life.

"That is . . . that is . . . that is . . . Ohhhhh." She moaned, her hands catching at his upper arms and clenching tightly.

Adrian chuckled, and when he bent his head to kiss her, Clarissa murmured her pleasure into his mouth. She gasped as he removed his hand and withdrew slightly from her body. But before she could complain, he slid back into her at an angle, allowing his body to rub against the spot he'd previously caressed.

Clarissa groaned deep in her throat, her hips and legs shifting instinctively to increase the caress of his body. Her nails dug into his back to urge him on, and he withdrew once more, to plunge forward.

This, then, she thought with wonder, was the truncheon and the pie, the lock and the key, the man and the woman. His body was filling and pleasuring hers even as it pleasured itself — or at least, she hoped he was experiencing pleasure. It was hard to tell; Adrian was not expressing himself as she was; he wasn't making the soft sounds in his throat that Clarissa couldn't seem to hold back.

She suddenly realized that, while he'd caressed and kissed and touched her, she had yet to do more than clutch at him as if he were a life raft in rough waters. She spent a moment trying to think of a way to make things more enjoyable for him, wondering if she should kiss and caress Adrian's nipples as he had hers, but then the excitement was back at fever pitch and it was difficult for her to think coherently. In the end, Clarissa put the thoughts away for later consideration and simply held on to Adrian as the anchor he was, the only thing keeping her body and soul together as he drove them both to the edge of the world and pushed them off.

"Here you are!"

Clarissa snatched the spectacles off her nose and stuck them into the pocket inside her skirts, then turned quickly toward her husband's voice as he crossed the library to her side.

"I woke up and you had gone," he growled just before claiming her mouth in a swift kiss.

Clarissa sighed with pleasure into his mouth, and snuggled against him as her arms slipped up around his neck. She'd woken at dawn and slid from his bed to return to her own room to dress. Joan had not been there yet, and she had been too impatient to wait, so she had dressed herself. Clarissa had a project she wished to attend to before the whole household was up and about.

She had wanted to search the library and see if there was not some book of instruction on how a wife could please a husband. Donning her clothes, she had grabbed her spectacles, slipped from the room, and made her way below to the library undiscovered. She'd spent the last hour on the hunt.

Unfortunately, Clarissa had not come up with a single volume on the subject. Most books seemed more inclined to suggest that she could please her husband best by running a smooth household and budgeting well. Such advice wasn't at all what Clarissa had in mind.

Her thoughts scattered as Adrian suddenly scooped her into his arms and turned toward the door. Clarissa gasped into his mouth.

"Husband, you are not dressed," she broke their kiss to say, surprised to feel nothing beneath the soft silk cloth of his robe.

"And neither should you be at the moment," he announced. Carrying her back across the room to the door, he added, "We have just got married. We are not expected to leave the bedchamber for at least a week."

"We are not?" she replied.

"Nay. It is a law — or should be," Adrian added with a grin. He started up the hall toward the stairs.

"Nonsense! How could we visit the happy couple if they decided to stay in bed?" a new voice said.

Adrian stopped abruptly, and both he and Clarissa glanced toward the speaker. Reginald Greville stood in the main entry with Adrian's butler, Jessop. Both men appeared to be smiling, and Clarissa was suddenly quite glad that she, at least, was dressed.

When she kicked her feet, Adrian frowned, but he understood the silent message and set her down. Clarissa kissed him on the cheek to soften her defection, then turned to smile at her husband's cousin.

"You are the first guest in my new home," she announced with a smile, moving up the hall to greet him.

"The first of many, I am sure," Reginald said lightly. "In fact, I know. Aunt Isabel and Mary intend to drop around later today. And no doubt your father shall come around to see how you are faring. In fact, I am sure half of the *ton* will drop by, determined to look you over after your first night as a wife."

Clarissa glanced over her shoulder toward Adrian, who gave a growl. She fully understood his reaction. She too would be happy to avoid such a throng of visitors so soon after their wedding, for it suddenly occurred to her that the people would know exactly what she and Adrian had been doing until the wee hours of the morning. Perhaps not all the hows and whys, but certainly they would know the wedding had been consummated. The idea of so many people knowing something so personal was daunting.

"Jessop," Adrian snapped.

"Yes, my lord?" The butler seemed to stand a little straighter under the verbal lash.

"Arrange for both carriages to be prepared and brought around. Then send Joan and my manservant to us. We leave for Mowbray within the hour."

Clarissa's eyes widened as her husband moved purposely forward and caught her hand to tug her toward the stairway.

"But what about Lord Greville?" she asked as he pulled her up the steps. "He has come to visit. We cannot just leave him here and —"

"He did not come to visit," Adrian assured her calmly.

"Did he not?" she asked. Uncertainly she glanced back to the door and at the blurred figure standing there.

"Nay. My cousin is never up this early. He is on his way home to bed, and was good enough to stop in along the way to warn us that if we stayed here, we would be bombarded with guests."

"He was?" Clarissa said with amazement.

"Yes. He was," Adrian assured her, and then called over his shoulder, "Thank you, Reg. Good-bye."

"Yes, thank you, Lord Greville," Clarissa called.

"You are most welcome, cousins!" Reginald Greville laughed, then turned to let himself out of the house. Adrian and Clarissa reached the landing and headed down the hall toward their rooms.

Now that he knew that guests intended to

descend on them, Adrian was galvanized into action. He led Clarissa to her room, and he pushed her gently inside with the order to write a letter to her father explaining that they had decided to travel to Mowbray to relax after the wedding. Adrian liked her father, and he had no wish to make the man worry at the unexpected departure.

That being the case, he also suggested Clarissa invite Lord Crambray to visit on his trip home from London, which he knew was supposed to take place in a week or so. Adrian was hoping that he would have had enough of his little wife by then, and that he wouldn't mind the intrusion on their time together. He also hoped — quite fervently — that the man would be returning home alone, without Clarissa's stepmother. The woman was a menace, and one whose neck Adrian wouldn't mind wringing. He wanted to avoid her at all costs.

"Yes, husband," Clarissa murmured. Then she asked, "What should I have Joan pack?"

"Everything," Adrian replied quickly.

Her eyes widened with surprise. "Everything?" she asked with amazement.

He frowned. Adrian himself hated London, and hoped not to return for a good long while. However, he had a wife now, and he had to take her wants into consideration.

"Did you wish to stay in London for the season?" he asked uncertainly.

"Oh, no," she said so quickly that Adrian knew she wasn't just saying it to please him. He felt himself relax. She added, "I fear I am like my mother, and do not have much taste for polite society."

"Very good." Adrian smiled and then kissed her for being so perfect, before straightening and reiterating, "Have her pack everything, then."

Nodding, Clarissa turned into her room, nearly tripping over the leg of a chair beside the door. Adrian frowned, catching her and drawing her away from it. It occurred to him that they hadn't made arrangements to get her new spectacles, and he briefly considered delaying their departure to do so . . . but then he let the thought drift away. They could arrange for spectacles in the village at Mowbray, maybe. He was still reluctant for her to be able to see him so soon. Last night had been a good start to the marriage, but Adrian would like just a couple more weeks to solidify their relationship before she saw his scar.

Troubled by his own selfishness, Adrian frowned and pulled her door closed, then moved on to his own room. Really, he acknowledged to himself, Clarissa's life would be made much easier by having spectacles. Not to mention safer. As it was, she was in constant danger of tumbling down stairs or setting herself afire. But he was so afraid of her reacting badly to his scar . . .

Adrian's hand ran absently over the mark in question as he entered his bedchamber. Just a couple more weeks, he promised himself. Then he'd be sure to get Clarissa her spectacles so that she could read and move about safely. In the meantime, he would read to her so that she wouldn't miss it. Adrian didn't care if she spilled food on her clothes, so that wouldn't be a problem; and he would ensure that every member of the staff at Mowbray was apprised of the matter and kept an eye out to maintaining their mistress's safety. He would even make it the main priority.

Satisfied with his decision, Adrian tossed his robe on the bed and moved to the wardrobe to begin pulling out clothes. He was half-dressed when his manservant, Keighley, entered the room. The man immediately moved to help him finish dressing, but Adrian waved him away and directed him to start packing and enlist all the aid he needed to manage the endeavor as quickly as possible.

Once dressed, Adrian made his way to Clarissa's room and found her just finishing her letter. Joan was there, hard at work packing all the clothes she'd just unpacked the day before. Telling the maid he would send someone up to help her, Adrian led Clarissa downstairs and handed her letter over to Jessop, who would give it to one of the lads to run over to Lord Crambray. Then he escorted her into the dining room. As expected, Cook had already prepared a meal to break their fast, and they both ate heartily after their strenuous activity from the night before.

The servants were still packing when they finished eating, but Adrian had expected as much, and he told Jessop to have the trunks loaded and strapped to a second carriage when they were packed. Joan and Keighley would follow with the belongings while he and Clarissa took the first carriage. He then rushed her out and saw her inside the carriage before having a word with the driver.

"My," Clarissa breathed as he joined her a moment later. "When you set your mind to something, it certainly happens quickly."

Adrian smiled at her dazed expression, then leaned down and kissed the tip of her nose. He felt a momentary pang. "You do not mind leaving the city so soon? I know you were enjoying your father's company."

"And I shall do so again when he stops at Mowbray," Clarissa said quietly. Then she assured him, "Nay, my lord. I truly do not mind. I fear I would have found any company today overwhelming."

Her blush suggested the reason for her discomfort had something to do with what they'd been doing last night, and Adrian smiled again, then scooped her onto his lap. Clarissa gave a small squeal of surprise, grabbing at his shoulder as he settled her against him.

"Are you sore today?" Adrian asked huskily, bestowing a light kiss to her brow, then each eye.

"No," Clarissa whispered. "Should I be?"

"I do not know," Adrian admitted. He kissed her softly on the lips, smiling as she melted against him. Then he whispered, "Clarissa?"

"Hmmm?" she murmured, tilting her head as he nipped briefly at her ear.

"Do you recall the trip in the carriage where you asked me about the different positions a man and woman might use when —"

"Yes," Clarissa interrupted, blushing prettily.

"Well . . ." Adrian paused to nibble at her neck, enjoying the little shivers that went through her. *He* caused those shivers of pleasure and excitement, and could cause much more. Last night Clarissa had screamed with her release the second time he'd made love to her. He was graced with a most responsive and sensuous wife, and knew how fortunate he was in that. Clarissa was still shy and innocent, but once he excited her, she shed most of her inhibitions and lost herself to the experience.

"Well?" she echoed, urging him to complete the thought.

Smiling, Adrian slid a hand up her leg under her skirt, then bent his head to press a kiss to the swell of one breast above the neckline of her gown. His other hand caught the neckline and tugged it downward until the breast popped free. He smiled when he saw that the nipple was already erect — just as he was. They were like fire and tinder, burning each other up.

"Well," Adrian murmured against the exposed flesh. He paused to give it a little lick before continuing. "I was recalling your saying that carriage journeys were long and boring."

"Very little is boring with you around, my lord," Clarissa said with a little laugh, then groaned as he caught her nipple in his mouth and grazed it with his teeth.

"Mmm," Adrian breathed around her excited flesh, smiling when she shuddered and arched her back. Then he added, "I was wondering if you would like to pass the time here in the carriage by trying the position I showed you?"

Clarissa's breathing had grown labored, and she shifted on his lap, spreading her legs more as his hand crept up her thigh.

"Which one, my lord?" she asked breathlessly, reminding him that he had indeed shown her two positions before the carriage stopped and dumped them on the floor.

Adrian didn't answer. He closed his lips around her nipple, drawing on it slowly while his fingers finally reached the center of her.

"Oh, husband." Clarissa moaned, clutching at his head, and Adrian groaned as she shifted her hips in response and her bottom pressed against his erection.

"Which one?" she repeated more urgently, her hands tangling in his hair.

Adrian released her breast and withdrew

his hand from between her legs. He then worked at the décolletage of her gown until he had her two breasts exposed.

"Both," he breathed, covering them with his hands. "Both positions and perhaps others. It is a long journey."

"Oh," Clarissa groaned. "My lord, I do believe I shall enjoy this journey far more than I did the trip to London with Lydia."

"I certainly hope so, wife." Adrian chuckled. "After all, I do have an advantage over your stepmother."

"You have many advantages over her," Clarissa assured him, her voice husky. She kissed him softly on the lips, and then asked, "But of which do you speak?"

"Mmmm." Adrian took a moment to kiss her, then reached out to pull the curtain closed on first one side of the carriage, and then the other. "I have the key to your lock."

Clarissa blinked, then chuckled softly, but her laughter died as he bent to claim her lips again.

CHAPTER FOURTEEN

Adrian peered down at the slight woman in his arms, a smile playing about his lips. Clarissa was settled straddling his lap, her bare breasts and face plastered against his equally bare chest. She was sleeping the sleep of the exhausted, and it was all Adrian's fault. He'd clearly worn her out with his lovemaking.

He peered at her silky, flawless skin, her tipped-up nose, and her slightly parted lips, and felt his heart turn over in his chest. Just looking at Clarissa made Adrian want to hold her, and just holding her made him want more. Unfortunately, it wouldn't be long before they arrived at Mowbray, and there really was no time to wake her for another experiment in the best position to travel by carriage on a long journey.

Clarissa made a little snuffling sound in her sleep, and Adrian's heart took another turn. She was so adorable, he thought, raising a hand to brush a finger lightly down her cheek. His lady wife immediately frowned, and muttered irritably in her sleep as she slapped the hand away. Adrian's chest rumbled with laughter, and that seemed to displease her as well, for she swatted at his chest as if to make it stay still.

Shaking his head, he hugged her to his breast and briefly closed his eyes, hardly able to believe his luck. It was Adrian's considered opinion that he had the most incredible wife in the world.

At the moment the top of her gown was a wrinkled mass around her waist. Her skirt was also gathered up, and her body was almost glued to his by drying sweat. Yet, did this worry her? Was she fretting over the state of her gown, which he'd managed to rip in his eagerness? No. Clarissa was unconcerned to the point that she'd fallen asleep.

Of course, Adrian realized, he was in no better shape. His breeches were tangled around his ankles, and his shirt was torn open with half the buttons missing. And he didn't much care himself. At least, he didn't until the driver gave a sudden shout. When Adrian lifted the curtain he'd drawn closed, he saw with horror that they were rolling up to Mowbray.

Adrian was so shocked to realize they'd arrived — and when they were so unprepared to meet anyone — that he jerked slightly forward, sending his wife to the floor in a flurry of skirts.

"Oh, Clarissa! I am sorry," he murmured, letting the curtain drop back into place as he leaned forward to help her. His sweet wife was squawking sleepily and trying to dig her way out of the ocean of fabric entwining her.

Adrian managed to lift her up off the floor, but her dress promptly slid off to pool on the bottom of the carriage. Frowning, he settled her on the bench beside him, then bent to snatch the dress up. He handed it to her, saying urgently, "We have arrived. We have to dress. Quickly."

"What?" she asked with bewilderment. "What do you mean, we have arrived?"

"I mean we are here, at Mowbray." Adrian jerked the curtain aside to show her, then realized she could not make out much without her spectacles, so he explained: "We are already halfway up the drive. We must dress quickly."

Clarissa didn't waste time asking questions. She immediately began struggling with her gown, trying to sort out the material.

Relieved that she grasped the urgency of the situation, Adrian turned his attention to his own clothing. He quickly drew his breeches up his legs, then lifted his butt off the seat to tug them up to his waist, only to collapse back down as the carriage jerked to a halt. Reaching out, he managed to keep Clarissa from crashing to the floor. They slid forward and then slammed back against the padded bench seat.

Struggling under the waves of her gown, Clarissa muttered what sounded very much like, "Damn, damn, double damn," and continued her battle. Adrian gave up on his breeches to try to help her, shifting yards of material as he searched for her head. It looked to him as if she'd tried to pull the gown on, but was having trouble finding her way out through the neck. He'd just found the top of her head amid all that material when the carriage door started to open. Adrian promptly gave up on Clarissa and turned to stop it.

He glanced back, and her head was popping up out of the dress. Clarissa's arms, though, were still trapped inside the gown, apparently unable to find appropriate exits.

Leaving her to sort it out, Adrian quickly finished doing up his breeches, then tugged his shirt closed over his chest, fastening what buttons were left. Once finished, he glanced at Clarissa. With some surprise, he saw that she had the dress on properly and done up, and was making a vain effort to brush the wrinkles out of her skirt. She felt her hair and asked, "Do I look all right? They will not be able to tell, will they?"

Adrian bit his tongue, unwilling to admit that her hair was sticking up every which way, and that it — along with her ripped and wrinkled dress — was definitely going to spill the proverbial beans.

Clearing his throat, he decided to take the chivalrous route: He lied. "They will never guess a thing."

"Oh, good."

Clarissa sighed and, before he could say another word, reached for the door and threw it open, nearly braining his butler, who had apparently approached the carriage to see what was amiss.

Fortunately, for all his age Kibble was quick on his feet, and he managed to dance back out of the way before he got clobbered. He just as quickly danced forward again to catch his new mistress as Clarissa tripped over the hem of her gown and tumbled forward.

She landed with a squawk against the man's thin chest, then managed to get her feet back under her and squinted up at the butler's bulldog face, trying to make out his features. For his part, the butler gaped back. His eyes moved over her well-kissed lips, mussed hair, and rumpled clothing with a sort of horrified wonder.

Cursing himself for not being quick enough to get out first and aid her from the carriage as he should have, Adrian quickly followed her disembarkation. He then took her by the upper arms and pulled her away from his butler. Drawing her back against his chest, Adrian rested his hands on her shoulders and proudly faced his estate employees.

"Clarissa, this is my staff. The gentleman who saved you from falling is my butler, Kibble. He used to be my tutor when I was a boy, but he took the role of butler when my parents' butler, Fitzwilliam, died."

"Hello, Kibble. Thank you for keeping me from falling on my face," Clarissa said with embarrassment, offering a smile to the grizzled old man.

"It was my pleasure, my lady," Kibble assured her, in a rare show of charm and dignity.

"And this is my — *our* — housekeeper, Mrs. Longbottom," Adrian continued, turning her slightly so that Clarissa faced the woman he'd secretly called Longface as a boy. Truly, the name was more suitable. The woman was short and round, with nothing long except her face.

"Mrs. Longbottom." Clarissa smiled and nodded at the woman before Adrian turned her again, this time to face a passel of servants that he listed quickly.

"This is Marie, Bessie, Antoinette, Lucy, Jean, Jamie, Frederick, Jack, and Robert," he announced.

"Hello," Clarissa said weakly, and Adrian squeezed her shoulders in encouragement. He paused to inhale the scent of her as it wafted to his nose. Damn, she always smelled so good.

Blinking that distraction away, Adrian continued. "Do not worry; I know there are a lot of names, but you will get to know them all in time."

"I am sure I will." Clarissa determinedly straightened her shoulders.

Adrian squeezed her again, then added, "There are several servants not present at the moment, but you will get to know them too. In the meantime . . ." His gaze swept the small crowd. "Staff, this is my wife, Lady Clarissa Montfort, the new Countess of Mowbray."

"Countess?" Clarissa glanced sharply over her shoulder in his direction.

"The wife of an earl is a countess," Adrian pointed out gently, and smiled with amusement at her startlement. Apparently, his wife hadn't considered the social gain of marrying him.

"Yes, but . . . Oh," Clarissa said with realization, and his smile widened.

No, she really hadn't considered his title before marrying him, Adrian realized. What bliss! What wonder! His wife had married him for himself. If there had been questions before, there were none now. He was truly the luckiest of men.

Unfortunately, his reaction set off his servants.

"Is that a smile?" Kibble asked, his bulldog face showing astonishment. He turned to the housekeeper. "Surely that is not a smile on our lord's face?"

"I do believe it is," Mrs. Longbottom replied with a grin.

"What could have caused it, do you think?" Kibble asked.

"Why, I do believe 'tis the little bundle in his arms. That is who has made our lord smile so, Kibble."

"Nay. A little slip of a thing like her? Taming the beast?" the butler continued. "Could it be?"

"I'd be smiling if she were *my* lady," Frederick announced loudly. He received a swat to the head from Lucy for his trouble.

"I do believe you are right, Mrs. Longbottom," Kibble decided, and quite suddenly he dropped to one knee before Clarissa, took one of her hands in both of his, and lifted it gently to his lips. He pressed a reverent kiss to her fingers. "You must be an angel, for only an angel could turn our lord from the grim and gloomy Gus he was, to this laughing example. From this moment forward, my lady angel, you have my undying devotion. My life is yours."

Adrian groaned and rolled his eyes. Kibble had been his tutor as a lad, and was as much a parent in his way as Adrian's own mother and father had been. Unfortunately, it left him in a somewhat elevated position; part family, part staff, wholly annoying and above his station. He was also something of a ham, which just made everything worse.

"All right, Kibble," Adrian said dryly. "Enough. You shall scare Clarissa."

Kibble merely arched an eyebrow. His gaze was kindly as it drifted over Clarissa's grinning face. "You must mean I am scaring you, my lord, for the lady is nowhere near looking frightened."

Adrian smiled and bent to press a kiss to his wife's forehead, then turned her toward the door. "It has been a long journey. I am sure Clarissa would like a bath and then a short rest before dinner. Lucy, would you see her to her room?"

"Of course, my lord." The little blonde smiled widely and turned toward the stairs.

"Take her arm, please, Lucy," Adrian instructed. "I fear Clarissa's spectacles have been broken, and I would not have her stumble and fall before we can replace them."

"Of course, my lord." The girl moved back to quickly draw her new lady's arm through her own, then led her more slowly to the stairs and up them.

Adrian watched until the two women reached the landing and disappeared up the hall, then turned to find that his staff had crowded around at his back to also watch them leave. He scowled, but they weren't paying any attention, so he cleared his throat irritably.

Kibble glanced at him sideways. "Are you coming down with a cold, my lord?"

Adrian sighed. This was the problem with staff who had been around when you were born, who had seen you running about the yard with your nappies drooping around your knees: No respect. Ignoring the distinct lack of proper deference, Adrian walked toward the salon door. "I would see everyone in here, please."

"Does that include your wife and Lucy? Shall I go fetch them back?" Frederick asked hopefully.

"Just get in here," Adrian snapped, pausing at the door to the salon and scowling until the group trooped past into the room. He then followed the last one in and pushed the door closed.

"One of you will have to pass this information on to Lucy once she returns, but I will not have you mentioning this conversation to Clarissa. In fact, I will fire the first person who speaks of it to anyone after this talk, including one another. I will not have her overhear one of you and worry. Is that understood?"

"Excepting, of course, when one of us tells Lucy," Kibble pointed out.

"Yes, yes, except then," Adrian muttered with a sigh. Kibble had always made a point of correcting him. It was the man's opinion that communication was most important, and the most important part was getting it right.

"Very well, my lord," the man said, and

he took up a relaxed yet attentive pose. "Please proceed."

Adrian's mouth thinned. The phrase *please proceed* was the same one Kibble had used when he wanted him to recite or explain something he'd taught Adrian. It always made him feel about ten years old, facing his tutor — which, of course, he was. At least, Kibble had once been his tutor.

Sighing, he let the matter go and said, "First off — as you heard me tell Lucy — Clarissa's spectacles have been broken and she cannot see well without them. It makes her a tad accident-prone, and she has suffered several calamities in town because of it."

"What kind of calamities?" Frederick asked.

Adrian hesitated, then decided it was better to tell them so that they were aware of what they were up against. "She has set teacups in laps she mistook for tables, tumbled down stairs, set wigs alight with candles, and things of that sort."

"Dear heavens!" Mrs. Longbottom murmured, concern creasing her brow. "We shall have to keep an eye on the girl until her new spectacles arrive."

"Yes, exactly," Adrian said. "Her maid is

supposed to watch her, but the girl is not always around. Clarissa herself will not always allow it, and grows impatient with having to be nannied. So, I want you all to keep an eye on her. That chore takes precedence over everything else until she has her spectacles. I will not see her hurt."

"It shall be done," Kibble said firmly. "How long will it be before new spectacles arrive?"

Adrian shifted uncomfortably, unable to meet the man's gaze. He muttered, "I am working on that."

Kibble's eyes narrowed, and Adrian suspected the butler sensed his prevarication; the man had always been able to see through his lies. Before Kibble could question further, Adrian spoke again.

"This is not the only problem," he said quickly, regaining some of his earlier confidence. "There may be someone trying to harm Clarissa."

This brought expressions of surprise to the faces around him, and he continued, "Some of the accidents she has had may not have been accidents at all."

"How do you mean, my lord?" Mrs. Longbottom asked.

Adrian deliberated, but again decided it was better that they knew what they were dealing with. He did not truly believe that Clarissa would be under threat here. He was sure whoever had been attempting to harm her would not try again now that she was married to him and safely ensconced in his country estate. However, since Adrian had no idea why anyone would wish to harm her in the first place, he couldn't be completely sure, so he quickly explained about her fall down the stairs. He then told of her being pushed in front of the moving carriage, as well as the fall into the fountain, and the fire when her bedchamber door had been locked.

There was complete silence as everyone contemplated his information; then Kibble asked, "Just how long has she been without spectacles?"

"A while," Adrian answered evasively, then cleared his throat and said, "So, as you can see, I have some concern for her well-being, and would appreciate all of you keeping watch for strangers on the property, or anything that might do her harm."

"I will watch her night and day, my lord," Frederick vowed, apparently moved to chivalry by the tale of Clarissa's woe.

"I am sure that will not be necessary, Frederick," Adrian said dryly. "But I would appreciate you all being alert when you can."

"Very well, my lord, we shall watch her most carefully," Kibble agreed. "If that is all, perhaps everyone could get back to work?"

"Yes, that is all," Adrian said. As he moved to settle himself in a seat by the fire, he heard the rustle of clothing and the shuffling of feet as the salon emptied out, then glanced around with a start at the clink of a glass from the wheeled table that held the brandy. Everyone had left but Kibble, who was now pouring brandy into two snifters. Setting the glass cork back in the decanter, the butler carried the snifters over and handed one to Adrian before settling into the plush cushioned seat beside him.

Adrian wasn't at all surprised. This was a common ritual when Kibble wished to speak to him. His only concern was what the man might want to discuss.

"She has not seen your face," the man said. It was not a question.

Adrian's mouth hardened, and he glared into the cold hearth, refusing to respond.

"You said that her spectacles were broken. Why did you not get her a new pair ere bringing her here to Mowbray?"

Adrian shrugged resentfully, and raised his glass to swallow a good portion of brandy.

"You are afraid she will be repulsed by your face." Again, the butler's words weren't a question.

"I plan to get her new spectacles in a week or so," Adrian snarled, guilt making him angry.

Kibble was silent for a moment, his gaze thoughtful. He too peered into the empty hearth; then he asked, "Has she no money of her own?"

"What? Yes, of course." Adrian frowned. He knew Clarissa had money; his mother had mentioned to him that on the way back from one of their fittings she'd purchased a small bottle of perfume. He'd since learned that she'd received a small allowance from her inheritance ever since she'd turned twenty. Of course, all of it had been settled upon her on their wedding day, and some of the papers they'd had to sign that day had been to arrange money in an account she had access to. The rest was to be invested. "Why would you ask that?"

Kibble shrugged. "I just wondered, my lord."

Standing, the butler downed the last of his brandy, then carried the dirty glass with him to place it on the brandy table before leaving the room. "You cannot keep her blind forever," were his last words as the door closed behind him. It was a comment Adrian was growing heartily sick of.

He glowered at the empty hearth and drank the rest of his brandy, then stood and moved to the table to pour himself another. He didn't need his butler poking at his conscience; it was already making enough noise on its own. It was screaming at him that surely Clarissa would be safer if she could see properly and recognize any approaching danger. It was also claiming that just knowing someone might be out to harm her would put her on alert, perhaps help to keep her safe. But he had arguments for each point. Surely, several eyes were better than just her own. And he had put his entire staff on orders to watch out for her, which should keep her safe enough.

As for her being more alert were she to know about the dangers possibly stalking her, this was true, but it would also make her anxious, and Adrian really didn't want her anxious or afraid. Clarissa was blossoming now that she was out from under her stepmother's thumb. He didn't want anything to change that and make her grow timid and afraid.

Both were perfectly valid arguments, Adrian told himself as he carried more brandy back to his chair. It was just too bad he knew the real reason he didn't want her to have spectacles.

Sighing, he flopped into his chair once more and stared into the depths of his drink, mulling over the unfairness of life. He had found the perfect woman, someone he liked, desired, and enjoyed spending time with. Someone who made him laugh and — in his opinion — made him a nicer, softer person. Clarissa was also not repulsed by the very sight of him. But, he feared, that was only because she could not see him. While her presence made him more patient and kinder to others, it also made him cruel to her, the one person he loved. For surely it was cruel to leave her without sight when she could have it, to rob her of her ability to read and really experience and enjoy life, all for his own selfish reasons.

Sighing, Adrian set his full brandy glass on the table and stood with resignation. He would have to arrange for Clarissa to have spectacles. He would have to give up his own chance of happiness to ensure hers.

Shaking his head, Adrian left the salon and started upstairs. He would go tell her now that he would take her to the village tomorrow to see if they could arrange spectacles for her. That way he could not play the coward and change his mind again.

He had reached only the third step when he heard the muffled sounds of a commotion in front of the house. Pausing, he turned back and walked down to the door to pull it open, eyebrows rising at the sight of the second coach from the city pulling to a stop in the drive. As he watched, the door opened and a weary Keighley stepped down, turning to offer a hand to Clarissa's maid. Joan looked just as exhausted from the journey as Adrian felt.

"That would be Lady Clarissa's maid?" Kibble inquired, reaching his side and peering out at the pair now moving toward the door.

Adrian nodded. "They will be tired after their journey, Kibble. Show Joan to her room and let her eat and relax. Tomorrow is soon enough for her to start back to work. The same for Keighley."

"Very good," Kibble murmured, then said, "Lucy saw Lady Clarissa undressed and into the bath, but is below now. Shall I send her back up to help Lady Clarissa out of the bath and to dress for dinner?"

"No. I shall help her," Adrian said, and he turned to head to the stairs. "But have our meal sent up to my wife's room on trays. We will dine there and have an early night."

Eyes wide behind her spectacles, Clarissa turned the page of the book she was reading and continued to devour the tale of an unfaithful wife and the punishment her husband was exacting. It had looked to be the sort of book that could be helpful, but when she'd sneaked down to raid the Mowbray library, she hadn't had much time to look.

Yes, Clarissa had asked Lucy if Mowbray had a library, and where it was situated, while they were walking to her new room. And when Lucy had finished showing her around her chambers and then slipped below to order a bath, Clarissa had popped her spectacles on and followed. This was the first likely prospect she'd come across in the few moments she'd allowed herself, and, afraid of getting caught, she'd hurried back upstairs. She had managed to regain the room and hide the book under her pillow just before Lucy reentered.

The woman helped her undress and took down her hair while the bathwater was carried in. Clarissa had then dismissed her, assuring the girl she would prefer to bathe unattended. Once the maid was gone, Clarissa had retrieved her spectacles and book and sunk into the tub to read.

Clarissa turned another page and continued on with the story, marveling that it had been written by someone named Maria de Zayas. A woman! That was still a rarity in society, and this book had been written a good many years ago. As it turned out, it really wasn't very helpful in giving her ideas on ways to please her husband as yet, but it was interesting for all that, and Clarissa read it with pleasure. She had been parched for a glimpse of the written word these last weeks, and she was now soaking it up like a flower did rain after a long drought.

Clarissa was in the process of turning the page when she heard the telltale sound of the doorknob turning. Alarm racing through her, she snatched the spectacles off her face and pressed the book and spectacles flat against her chest as she glanced over her shoulder toward the door. Her mouth fell open to tell Lucy that she really didn't wish to be disturbed when she recognized the dark hair and much larger shape of her husband.

Panic a living thing in her chest, Clarissa didn't even think, but she dropped her hand with the book and spectacles down into the water. She hid the condemning items under one leg, then racked her brain for what to do next.

"How is your bath?" Adrian asked, and she could hear the smile in his voice as he approached.

Clarissa's mouth opened and closed, any answer evading her as she sought some way to keep him from coming all the way to the tub. If he came that far, he would no doubt feel a need to help her bathe; then that help would turn to hindrance as he kissed and caressed her, and then he would either be in the tub with her, or scooping her out of it. Either way the book would be revealed.

The only answer seemed to be to keep him from approaching the tub. To manage that feat, Clarissa did the first thing she could think of. Adrian was halfway across the room when she suddenly stood up out of the water.

As she'd hoped, his footsteps stopped, and he appeared simply to be gaping at her openmouthed. Water ran down off her body to splash back into the tub. Clarissa could feel his hot gaze moving over her naked flesh, and knew she was blushing, but desperate times called for desperate measures.

Before her husband could regain his wits, she stepped out of the tub and crossed the small amount of space between them. Clarissa didn't say a word; she didn't even do anything but walk to him. The moment she was within range, Adrian reached for her and drew her into his arms. His mouth covered hers and his hands roved over her, and then he turned while still kissing her and maneuvered her to the bed.

As her legs backed against the mattress, Adrian broke their kiss and murmured, "I thought you might be too tired after the journey."

Smiling, Clarissa pressed a soft kiss to the corner of his mouth, then dropped to sit on the side of the bed and reached for the fastening of his breeches.

"I suspect I will never be too tired for you, my husband," Clarissa assured him. As she helped him shed his clothes, she told herself not to forget to retrieve the book and her spectacles from the tub at the first opportunity . . . which had best be before anyone went near it.

CHAPTER FIFTEEN

"Are you sure you would not rather —"

"Nay," Clarissa interrupted Kibble quickly, then forced herself to regain patience and managed a smile. "I would really rather just lie down for a little while. A short nap is what I desire."

"You are not sickening, are you, my lady?" the butler asked with concern.

Clarissa managed not to scowl. Honestly, the Mowbray staff worried like a bunch of old ladies — even the young male members of the staff. One or the other, and sometimes several at once, had been trailing her at all times during the last four days. And, did she try to slip away to her room for a moment's privacy, they became quite distressed.

"I am fine," she insisted firmly. "It is just that I have been getting little sleep of late and wish for a nap."

"I see." Kibble frowned. "Well, if you are

not ailing . . ."

"I am not ailing. Please be sure no one disturbs me. Tell Joan I will not need her." She had reached her door, the butler following her the whole way and one of the footmen close behind him. Clarissa forced a smile for their benefit, then escaped into her room and firmly closed them out. She then leaned against the door with a sigh.

Good lord, Clarissa thought with exasperation; then she removed the library book from the folds of her skirts where she'd been hiding it, and tossed it on the bed. Giving her head a shake, she slid her hand through the small slit in the side of her skirt to find the pocket that hung from her waist. Clarissa retrieved the bag, took her spectacles out, and popped them onto her nose to survey the chamber. There was one chair. It stood before her dressing table. Determination coursing through her, she moved to drag it over to the door to prop it under the doorknob.

Satisfied that no one would be able to slip in and surprise her from that direction, Clarissa turned to contemplate the door that led into Adrian's room. There was no chair for that door, and for a moment she considered just leaving it as it was, but the fear of

Adrian coming in and catching her in her ugly spectacles made her sigh.

Without a chair to prop against this second door, she was forced to resort to a larger and bulkier piece of furniture. The dresser was the closest item. Moving to its side, Clarissa bent to the task of pushing the heavy wooden item in front of the door, wincing at the squeal of wood on wood as she forced it across the hardwood floor. Muttering under her breath, Clarissa redoubled her efforts, hoping that speed would make up for the loud sound.

"My lady?" Kibble's voice came muffled through her bedroom door, sounding anxious. "Is all well?"

Pausing with the dresser half in place, Clarissa rolled her eyes. "Yes, Kibble, I am fine."

"I thought I heard an odd sound, like something heavy being moved," the man said. She could hear the disapproval in his voice.

Clarissa blew a stray strand of hair out of her face and said, "Yes, I was just moving something. Making the room my own."

There was a long silence, and Clarissa was beginning to hope he'd accepted that answer and gone away when he said, "Do you think you might open the door for a moment? Just so that I can be assured that you are all right?"

Clarissa groaned under her breath, then moved to the door to the hall. She removed the chair from in front of it, took off her spectacles and hid them in the folds of her skirt, then opened the door. "See? I am fine."

Kibble slowly looked her over, his eyes narrowed in suspicion as if he feared she might not be telling the truth; then his gaze slid past her to survey the room.

Clarissa bit her lip, hoping against hope that he wouldn't notice the dresser . . . but of course he did.

"You have blocked off the entrance to his lordship's room!" The butler sounded as startled as he should be by such an occurrence.

"Yes, I did," Clarissa said quietly. "It is only a temporary arrangement, Kibble. I wish for a few moments of rest, just a little privacy, and thought to ensure that no one troubles me."

Kibble considered her silently, then glanced around the room again. She was close enough to see his mind working behind those fiercely intelligent eyes, and found herself growing nervous. When his gaze suddenly paused and narrowed on something in the room, Clarissa couldn't resist turning to see what he'd found. Of course, she couldn't see a thing without her spectacles, just blurry shapes.

"There is a book on your bed," Kibble announced, and Clarissa felt her heart sink. She'd forgotten all about the book she'd tossed on the bed moments earlier. Trying to keep her expression bland, she turned back to the man.

"Is there? Perhaps Joan left it here."

"No doubt," he said agreeably, then added, "Shall I take it back to the library so that it is not in your way?"

"No, 'tis fine," Clarissa said quickly, then added, " 'Tis just a book. I shall put it on the bedside table and she can collect it later."

"She may wish to read it while you are resting," he pointed out. "After all, you said she was to take the afternoon off."

Clarissa ground her teeth as she saw her opportunity to spend a few quiet moments reading slipping away. Feverishly trying to come up with a way to keep the book, she tilted her head and listened when someone called out from the main floor.

Kibble turned to glance up the hall, then excused himself and moved to the head of the stairs. Peering down at the entry below, he asked, "What is it?"

Clarissa had found that her hearing had improved since her spectacles were taken away. It was as if her body were trying to make up for the loss of one sense by increasing others. She heard well enough that she caught Frederick's answer that a carriage was approaching up the drive.

Kibble unintentionally verified what she'd heard, glancing back her way and saying, "Excuse me, my lady. It would appear we have company." Clarissa then watched his blurry image disappear down the stairs.

Closing the door behind him, she glanced at her curtained windows. Unexpected guests? Who could it be? she wondered. Popping her spectacles on, she moved to the window to peer curiously down at the front of the house.

There was indeed a carriage making its way up the drive, but it wasn't until it had almost reached the front of the house that she recognized the crest on the side. Drawing a sharp breath, Clarissa turned and hurried to the door. She was opening it before she recalled her spectacles. Snatching them off her face, she tucked them back into her pocket and made her way quickly to the stairs. Those she made her way down very carefully, one hand tight on the banister as she went. She'd learned her lesson the hard way, what with her tumble down the stairs in London, and had no desire to repeat the action.

Kibble stood in the open front door, surveying the carriage as the first passenger disembarked. As she reached his side, Clarissa could see the suspicious scowl on his face. She realized he hadn't a clue who it was. To clear up the problem, she launched herself past the butler saying, "Daddy! We were not expecting you so soon." Her father turned and caught her up in a bear hug, and Clarissa heard Kibble begin to shout orders to prepare rooms and warn Cook there would be guests for dinner.

"How is my girl?" Lord Crambray asked, letting her go and giving her the once-over. "You look healthy and happy."

"I am." Clarissa smiled at him widely, then said, "But we did not expect you until the end of the week. Is anything wrong?"

"No, no," he assured her. "I just finished my business sooner than expected and thought I would spend the extra time visiting you and your new husband. Where is he, by the way?" Her father glanced around inquisitively.

"Adrian rode out to check on a paddock that needs repair," Clarissa explained, linking their arms. "He should be back soon."

Clarissa caught movement out of the corner of her eye, and she turned to see the blurry shape of a woman in a gown in the doorway of the carriage. Lydia had come as well, she realized, and she retrieved her arm at once. "I am sorry. Here I am talking away and Lydia is still waiting to disembark."

"Oh." John Crambray turned back to the carriage, murmuring an apology as he took his wife's hand to help her out.

Clarissa hesitated as the woman reached the ground and began to brush down her traveling dress. A part of her felt that she should kiss and hug the woman in greeting as she had her father, but Lydia never welcomed such displays, and so Clarissa found herself hesitating. Finally she decided that — whether Lydia liked it or not — she was a part of this family and would be treated as such. Straightening her shoulders, Clarissa stepped up to the woman, kissed her cheek, and hugged her.

Lydia stiffened in her embrace, and Clarissa could feel her surprise. She let her go, then took her father's arm and her stepmother's, and ushered them to the front door.

"Come, you should meet Kibble and everyone else. How long can you stay?"

"I think we can manage almost a week before we have to continue home. If your husband does not mind," Lord Crambray added quickly.

"Her husband does not at all."

Clarissa paused and glanced to the side as Adrian approached from the direction of the stables. She smiled softly as he greeted her father and stepmother and welcomed them to Mowbray; then they all went in.

"I hope you do not mind our being here?"

Adrian glanced at the man riding beside him: Lord John Crambray. It was the morning after the arrival of the Crambrays, and Clarissa's father had ridden out with him to inspect the property. Adrian had thought everything was going well between them before this, but . . . "No, of course not, my lord. Why would you think otherwise?"

John Crambray shrugged, but the smile on his face was wry. After a moment had passed, he admitted, "Well, I do understand that the two of you are newly married and probably wish to spend as much time getting to know each other as possible."

Adrian smiled faintly. While he had originally hoped that Clarissa's father would delay a visit until he'd had his fill of his new wife — or at least until they could be in the same room without his wishing to rip her clothes off — Adrian was beginning to realize that might not be for a very long time. He could hardly hope to keep her to himself for the next two or three decades.

"We have a lifetime ahead of us. I can hardly begrudge you a few days' visit."

John Crambray smiled and said, "You love my daughter."

Adrian stiffened in his saddle. He was still coming to grips with what he felt for Clarissa. Every day with her was an adventure. This morning he had awoken to find his sweet young wife kissing and caressing his erect member. She had taken to surprising him with such aggressive actions over the last few days. She seemed as eager to please him as he was to please her, and it warmed his heart every time she showed this tendency. It made him hope that she might be coming to care for him as he wanted.

"I can tell you love her," Lord Crambray announced, then added, "which is why I do not understand why she has still not got spectacles."

Adrian stiffened further, then forced himself to relax. He said, "They are on their way. I had to send to London for them. But they are a surprise, so I would appreciate your not telling Clarissa."

Lord Crambray looked relieved, and nodded. "As you like."

Adrian grimaced. If it were truly to be as he liked, Clarissa would never have spectacles. However, with his conscience to trouble him, he had finally set out to get her a pair. In the end, Adrian had not told Clarissa of his plan and taken her to the village as he'd originally intended — Clarissa had managed to distract him from that when he'd arrived in her room and she'd stood up naked in her bath. By the time he'd thought of the subject again, he had decided to order them himself. While he hadn't explained why he wished to know, he'd asked Clarissa where she'd gotten her last pair of spectacles, and had sent a messenger with money to the city to get another pair. All without her knowing.

Adrian told himself it was because he wanted to surprise her. However, he suspected the truth was that, so long as she didn't know they were on the way, he could delay giving them to her for another day or so even after the spectacles arrived.

Sighing, Adrian set his heels to his horse and urged it to a trot as the house came into view ahead. He had no desire to talk anymore.

The house was quiet when Adrian and his

father-in-law entered. They found Lydia reading in the salon, but the servants were making themselves scarce. Adrian had no doubt it was in an effort to avoid Lydia. She could be demanding and unpleasant to deal with. Apparently Clarissa was not the only one she liked to make miserable; she seemed to pick on anyone weaker than herself, anyone she saw as being lower. His servants seemed included in that category.

Leaving Lord and Lady Crambray, Adrian headed above stairs to change out of his mud-spattered clothes. He stripped and dressed by his wardrobe, his gaze moving repeatedly to the connecting door leading to Clarissa's room, and he wondered where she was and what she was doing. He often found himself wondering that when they were apart.

I can tell you love her, John Crambray had said, and Adrian was starting to fear it was true. He'd come to care for his wife's pleasure more than his own; hence the reason he'd ordered the spectacles. He suspected that to be a sure sign that he did indeed love her, and Adrian found himself marveling over that.

Clarissa was easy to love, that was certain, but more than that astounded him. Adrian had expected that finding a wife would be a struggle — a struggle even without the added task of actually caring about and loving her. And yet, everything had been relatively easy with Clarissa right from the start.

In fact, the only real trouble he'd encountered had been Lydia, and she appeared to trouble most people. Clarissa herself had been open to Adrian right from the beginning.

"There you are, my lord," Keighley said as they finished getting Adrian into new clothes. "Will there be anything else?"

"No, thank you, Keighley," Adrian replied, but as the man moved to leave the room, he asked, "Do you know where my wife is?"

"I believe she is in her room at the moment, my lord. One of the footmen is in the hall watching her door and that is usually a clear indication that she is on the other side."

"Thank you." Adrian moved to the connecting door as the man left the room. He was eager, as always, to see her, and didn't bother knocking. But when he tried to open the door, he found it blocked.

The door opened a slight bit, then hit something. Frowning, he pulled the door closed and tried again. When the same thing happened, he stared at the door and called, "Clarissa?"

Silence answered him.

"Clarissa?" he called again, this time accompanying it with a knock. "Clarissa? Are you in there? There is something blocking the door."

When he got no answer, Adrian turned and hurried out into the hall. He spotted Frederick lurking there. "Is Lady Mowbray in her room?" he asked.

"Aye, my lord." Frederick straightened his shoulders, taking up a military pose.

"Is she alone?" Adrian asked. He moved to her door and turned the knob. The knob turned, but after the door moved inward a bare half inch, it stopped.

"Aye, my lord. I have been watching this door since she entered, and no one has gone in or come out." Frederick frowned and moved closer as he saw that Adrian was struggling. "What is wrong?"

"The door is jammed with something," Adrian muttered, then pounded on the wood. "Clarissa? If you can hear me, call out!"

Both men remained silent as they waited; then Adrian turned impatiently away and hurried back through his bedroom. He was sure that the adjoining door had shown some give — certainly more than the hall door. Trying it again, he found it still blocked, but this time he put his weight behind the effort and grunted. The door opened a bit more.

"No one went in, my lord," Frederick assured him, sounding worried. "I did not take my eyes off the door for a moment."

Adrian didn't comment. All of his concentration was on the door he was slowly but surely forcing open. The screech of wood on wood told him that some heavy piece of furniture had been shoved in its path. Unfortunately, while the perimeter of the room was bare hardwood, a rug covered most of the floor and was making the barricade difficult to push forward. If Adrian could just have slid the item sideways, he would have had no problem. However, that wasn't possible.

"Can I help, my lord?" Frederick asked anxiously. "Perhaps if we both put our weight into it . . ."

Adrian glanced toward the man — a boy, really, no more than sixteen, and skinny as a rail — but he was anxious, and any help was welcome, so he nodded grimly. "Put your shoulder to the door and push when I say."

Frederick moved up beside him, bracing

his shoulder against the wooden surface, and when Adrian said "Push," they both put their weight behind the effort. This time the door gave several more inches and Adrian was able to see into the room. Clarissa was lying on the bed and looked asleep, but her face appeared extremely pale.

"Again," Adrian ground out, and they pushed for all they were worth, this time managing to shove the door — and what he could now see was a dresser — far enough inward that he thought he could slip through the opening.

Frederick watched anxiously as Adrian forced himself through. They both released a sigh of relief when he finally made it.

"Is she all right?" Frederick asked, starting through the opening now himself as Adrian rushed to the bed.

"Clarissa?" Adrian caught his wife's face in his hand and turned it toward him, his heart stopping in his chest. It hadn't merely been panic making him think she was pale. Clarissa was as white as a sheet, and completely unresponsive.

"Is she all right?" Frederick repeated as he reached the bed.

"Get help," Adrian barked, brushing one shaky hand over Clarissa's face.

"Yes, my lord." Frederick headed for the

connecting door again, but Adrian called him back.

"Move the chair from the hall door and go that way," he ordered, seeing what had blocked that entrance. His gaze slid around the rest of the room, but everything else seemed to be in order. And there was no one else present.

Frederick left the door open as he hurried from the room, and Adrian could hear him shouting for help as he raced down the hall. With the hope that assistance would soon arrive, Adrian turned back to Clarissa.

She looked so small and fragile lying there. He lifted her off the bed, pressing her to his chest, unable to peer at her lifeless face anymore. She hardly seemed to be breathing, and he was terrified that she would die on him. Adrian wouldn't have that; *couldn't* have it. Clarissa was his, and he wouldn't lose her. She was too important. She was everything.

Dear God, he did indeed love her — so much so that he would rather die himself than live out his life with nothing but her memory.

"Stay with me, Clarissa," he murmured, rubbing her back helplessly. "Do not leave me. I need you."

"My lord?"

Adrian glanced to the door as Kibble rushed in. The butler was followed closely by Clarissa's father and several servants.

"Frederick said that her ladyship was ill. What has happened?" Kibble asked, rounding the bed to where his master sat on its edge.

"I do not know. She is pale and will not wake up," Adrian explained, his voice cracking.

"Let me see," Kibble said. And as John Crambray started to crawl across the bed on the other side, Adrian lay Clarissa gently back, and the three men bent over her pale form.

"Dear God, she is as pale as death," Lord Crambray said.

"Almost gray," Mrs. Longbottom agreed, appearing and crowding up next to the bed with the others as Kibble lifted Clarissa's eyelids and peered at her eyes, then bent to sniff her mouth.

Adrian watched his butler's actions with bewilderment until the man suddenly straightened. The alarm on Kibble's face was the most terrifying thing Adrian had ever seen.

"We need to make her purge. She has been poisoned."

"What?" Lord Crambray and Adrian

cried, but Kibble wasn't listening; he'd turned his attention to the bedside table and a half-eaten bit of pie. As they watched, he bent to sniff. His mouth tightened. "It was in the pie."

"But we all had some of that last night," Adrian protested.

"Not this piece," Kibble muttered. He glanced around. "I need something to stick down her throat."

"What?" Adrian asked in alarm.

The butler turned a grim look his way. "Mayhap you and Lord Crambray should leave."

"No. I am staying," Adrian said with determination.

"Then you save her — if you can," Kibble announced, and turned to head for the door.

"No! Kibble, get back here! We need you," Adrian said sharply.

"Then you have to leave," the butler demanded, turning back. "I cannot work on her with you interrupting and questioning my every comment and order. You are slowing me down and will simply get in the way."

When Adrian hesitated, desperate for Kibble to help yet reluctant to leave his wife's side, John Crambray touched his arm. "Come, he is right. This is no place for us.

Let us get out of his way and go below stairs."

"But what if she —" Adrian cut off the thought. He'd been about to say, *what if she dies?* He didn't want Clarissa to be alone if that happened. But then, he didn't want it to happen at all.

"Either you leave or I leave, my lord," Kibble said heartlessly.

Adrian felt his shoulders sag in defeat. Kibble was the smartest man he knew. The butler had not just been a teacher before taking the role as butler here at Mowbray. In fact, when Adrian had come of age and not needed his tutelage anymore, the man had gone off to join the army. He'd been in battles in countries Adrian could not even pronounce, and most of that time had been spent bandaging, tending, and saving the injured.

In Adrian's opinion, Kibble had probably forgotten more about caring for the injured and ill than most doctors knew. That was how they'd met again: Kibble had saved his life after the battle that had stolen his looks. He'd then agreed to accompany Adrian home to look after him as he mended and had simply stayed, taking on the mantle of butler when Fitzwilliam died. If Adrian were to trust Clarissa to anyone, it would be to this man.

"I will call you as soon as there is any change," Kibble said, softening as he saw the concession in Adrian's stance. "Any change either way, and I shall call you back at once."

Adrian gave one brief nod, then allowed Lord Crambray to lead him from the room. The two men were silent as they walked up the hall to the stairs, their ears straining to hear the orders Kibble was barking like a sergeant.

"She will be fine," Lord Crambray said quietly, but Adrian could hear the fear in his voice and realized that Clarissa was the man's only daughter, the child of his love match with his wife Margaret. He had to be at least as upset as Adrian.

Forcing himself to buck up, Adrian managed to murmur something of an agreement and led Clarissa's father down to the salon, thinking a jolt of brandy would do them both some good. But as he pulled the door open and stepped into the room, he paused to see Lady Crambray seated calmly on the settee, her face expressionless.

"So, what is it now? Has she set this house afire too? Or perhaps she has stumbled and stubbed her toe?" the woman asked.

Adrian felt the blood boil through his body, but it was John Crambray who answered. Stepping up to Adrian's side, he glared at his wife with a show of true dislike. "She has been poisoned. And since you are the only person I know who hates her enough to do such a thing, I would not look so smug. It will be you who hangs if she dies."

CHAPTER SIXTEEN

Clarissa opened her eyes slowly and peered at the empty bed beside her. Apparently, Adrian had already awoken and left. This was unusual. Generally, if he woke up first, he would stir her awake with kisses and caresses. It was a lovely way to start each day.

Though, Clarissa supposed, today she would not have enjoyed it as much as usual; she was feeling a bit weary, and for some reason her throat and tummy were sore. Hoping she wasn't coming down with something, Clarissa released a little sigh and rolled onto her back, then nearly screamed at the sight of the wrinkled old face leaning over her.

"Kibble." She gasped, clutching the linens and blankets to her chest and staring at him, wide-eyed. "What —"

"How are you feeling?" the butler interrupted calmly.

"I . . ." Clarissa blinked, her mind now fully awake and beginning to function. The last thing she recalled was lying down to rest in the late afternoon, but the light in the room suggested it was early to midafternoon now. Frowning, she explored her mind, poking at half memories and disjointed recollections of Mrs. Longbottom and Kibble holding her up and murmuring soothingly as she was sick.

"I was ill," she said slowly.

"Yes," Kibble acknowledged.

"You and Mrs. Longbottom looked after me."

"Along with the rest of the staff," Kibble said quietly. "We were all quite concerned, my lady."

"Oh." Clarissa frowned. "What happened? Was it a flu?"

"What do you recall?" the butler asked.

Clarissa bit her lip and thought back. "I came to my room to escape Lydi— I mean, for a little privacy," she interrupted herself quickly. While her stepmother was a trial, Clarissa would not speak of that to servants. She had been glad that her father and husband got along well, and had been happy when they'd ridden out together; unfortunately, it had left Lydia behind to torment her with sly comments about what a trial her marriage bed must be, and how horrified Clarissa would be when she finally saw her husband's ugly face — if he ever allowed her to have spectacles again. He might just keep her blind, her stepmother suggested.

Holding her temper and keeping her secret that she already owned spectacles, Clarissa had escaped to her room to read. She'd blocked both doors as usual, and settled down with a book. Clarissa didn't tell Kibble this part, however. She was still reluctant to reveal her glasses.

"I came to my room to rest for a bit," Clarissa said. "There was a slice of pie on my bedside table."

"You did not bring it up yourself?" Kibble asked.

"No. I thought perhaps Frederick had left it for me. He seems always to be trailing me around and bringing me small gifts." She shrugged. "I was not hungry, but was loath to hurt his feelings by ignoring it, so I took a couple of bites."

"Thank God you were not hungry," Kibble murmured with a sigh, and Clarissa glanced at him in surprise.

"Why?"

Kibble hesitated and then said, "Never mind. Please finish telling me what happened."

Clarissa considered insisting he explain, but then decided she would find out in a moment and shrugged. "That is it. I had a couple of bites and then relaxed on the bed. I recall that my stomach started to hurt, so I decided to sleep. I thought a little nap might set it to rights."

Kibble was silent for a moment and then suddenly held something up. Clarissa couldn't at first tell what it was. When he perched them on her nose, she realized it was her spectacles.

"They were caught in the blankets when I moved you," he announced. "As was a book from the library."

Clarissa bit her lip, warily eyeing him, but the butler's face was expressionless, neither accusatory nor angry. "This is why you were blocking the door," he said. "Lord Mowbray does not know you have these."

It wasn't really a question, but Clarissa responded as if it were. "No. He does not know." She hung her head.

Kibble nodded. "How long have you had them?"

"Since the day before the wedding," she admitted in a small voice.

"I suspected this when you kept slipping away to your room," Kibble told her. "It made no sense to me that you had money of your own and had not used some to replace your spectacles."

"I could not at first! Not at home. Lydia was constantly with me. But I slipped out to get them the day before the wedding while at the dressmaker's with Lady Mowbray," Clarissa admitted.

Kibble nodded. "Why have you not told Adrian?"

Clarissa noted the lack of proper title in the servant's reference to her husband, but knew the two men had a special relationship, almost that of a father and son, so she was not too surprised. She was not eager to answer his question.

When she remained silent, Kibble asked, "Is it because you have seen your husband clearly with them and find him repulsive? Did you wish not to have to look on your husband?"

Again, there was no judgment or condemnation in his tone, but Clarissa was horrified.

"No! Of course not," she cried. "Adrian is beautiful. His scar hardly affects his looks at all. He has the deepest, most beautiful brown eyes, and the sweetest lips, and . . ."

Realizing what she was saying, Clarissa paused and felt a blush course up over her skin.

"You love him," Kibble said with satisfaction.

"Yes. I believe I do," she admitted shyly.

With her spectacles on, Clarissa had no difficulty seeing the smile that now transformed the butler's face. Kibble obviously loved Adrian as well, and was pleased to know his wife cared for him.

They smiled at each other for a moment; then Kibble frowned and asked, "But why are you hiding your spectacles from him?" When Clarissa bit her lip and avoided his gaze, he said, "Is it for his sake?"

"Yes," she answered unhappily — though it was really for both their sakes. Clarissa did not wish for him to have to look on her in ugly spectacles, but also, should he find her ugly, she did not wish to lose what little bit of his affection she had gained.

Kibble frowned. "But do you not understand it would touch him more to know that you can actually see him and still love him than to let him think you do not know what he looks like?"

Confused, Clarissa lifted her gaze to his face. "What?"

Kibble frowned, then asked, "Are you not hiding your spectacles so that he is not uncomfortable under your gaze?"

"*Him* uncomfortable under *my* gaze?" she

asked with bewilderment. "No. Why would he be uncomfortable under my gaze? I love him just as he is. I think he is handsome and smart and sweet and —"

"Then why do you not wear them and tell him so?" Kibble interrupted.

Clarissa blinked, thinking the butler must be slow. Taking pity on him, she explained, "Because the spectacles make me *ugly.*"

Kibble blinked in surprise, and it was his turn to ask, "What?"

Clarissa sighed. "Lydia says that they make me ugly. And when Lady Mowbray heard that my spare pair of spectacles had been broken, she said that Adrian would be relieved. I fear he would not find me attractive in them."

Kibble jerked back as if she'd hit him. He stared at her with a stunned expression, then said, "You refuse to wear the spectacles because you fear Adrian will not find you attractive."

"Yes," Clarissa acknowledged miserably. She stiffened when the butler suddenly burst out laughing. Scowling, she snapped, "What is so funny?"

"Oh, my lady, if you only knew," he got out between gasps of breath and howling mirth. "Oh, the two of you are so precious.

Each so in love, and afraid of rejection from the other."

Clarissa glowered, not at all happy with the man's amusement.

"Oh, dear."

Clarissa turned to find Lady Mowbray filling the doorway, an exasperated expression on her face. Shaking her head, she moved into the room to join them. "I apologize, but I was eavesdropping in the hall. Clarissa, I fear you misunderstood me."

"Lady Mowbray," Clarissa said with surprise. "When did you get here?"

"About an hour ago," Adrian's mother admitted. "I decided to visit and see how you and my son were getting along. I would have been here last night, but one of the carriage wheels broke. We had to stay at an inn overnight while it was repaired."

She draped herself over the empty side of the bed and patted Clarissa's hand. "Had I known you were ailing, I would have found a hack and carried on."

"There was no need. I am fine," Clarissa murmured, but she was touched by the assurance.

"No, my dear. It is quite obvious you are not fine," Lady Mowbray countered. "You have been working under a misunderstanding."

Clarissa's eyebrows rose. "A misunderstanding, my lady?"

Adrian's mother opened her mouth, then paused. When she did speak, Clarissa was sure the words were not what she'd originally intended to say.

"I would be very pleased if you would call me Mother, Clarissa. I have always wanted a daughter, but could not have any more children after Adrian. I would be happy to fill the hole left behind by your mother's death, if I might. I gather Lydia is not . . . well, she has never had children of her own, so perhaps is not the best for the job," she said charitably.

Smiling, Clarissa squeezed the woman's hand holding hers and whispered, "Thank you . . . Mother."

Lady Mowbray beamed, her eyes overbright with what Clarissa suspected to be a light glazing of tears. But before they could say anything else, Kibble cleared his throat.

Once he had their attention, he suggested, "Perhaps you could explain this misunderstanding, Lady Mowbray, so that Lady Clarissa *does* understand and can work toward fixing things?"

"Yes, of course." The woman sighed, then squeezed Clarissa's hand again. "My dear girl, when I said that Adrian would be relieved to hear that your spectacles were broken, it was not because he does not like them or would find you less attractive in them. It was because he fears that once you have spectacles, you will not be attracted to him any longer."

"What? Why would he think a thing like that?" Clarissa asked with surprise.

"His scar, dear," Lady Mowbray answered.

"Oh, pish-posh," Clarissa muttered with a wave that illustrated the level of importance her husband's scar held for her. "He is lovely even with it. Why, goodness — without it, it must have been almost painful to look on him!"

Lady Mowbray nodded and admitted, "He was as beautiful as any Greek god. As beautiful as an angel. And he still is, in my opinion. But . . ." She sighed. "The ladies of the *ton* demand perfection in all things, and look on him as a fallen angel."

Clarissa found her eyes narrowing with anger.

"Of course, at first the wound was much worse. He attended court directly afterward, while he was still swollen and scabbed. That *did* distort his face a good deal at the time, and the ladies of the *ton* — ever determined to prove their 'delicacy' — fainted at the sight of him." She made a disgusted face. "It started with young Louise Frampton. She had carried a tendre for Adrian for years, and was truly distressed and *did* faint when she saw what the battle did to him. But no one had warned her ahead of time, and she was also laced too tightly." Lady Mowbray added dryly, "Our Louise was a bit on the largish side, and when she heard that Adrian had returned, she had her maid stitch her up tight. The poor girl felt an idiot afterward for fainting, then felt even worse when she heard that other girls had taken to doing it to prove they were as delicate as she."

"Oh, dear," Clarissa murmured.

Lady Mowbray nodded sadly. She added, "I know something happened with Lady Johnson as well, though I am not sure what, but it all worked to send him home. Adrian packed up and returned to Mowbray at once. And he stayed here." She peered sadly into the past. "No matter how often I or Mary visited and told him his scar was much improved and he should return to society, Adrian would not listen. Finally I realized that I would have to get tougher with him, else he would stay out here and never leave. I began to nag."

Clarissa bit her lip to keep back the amused smile that wanted to claim her lips. Lady Mowbray had made the announcement with a shudder of horror that bespoke how she felt about having to nag.

"And I was unrelenting until he finally gave in and attended court this year."

"I am most grateful you did," Clarissa said firmly, squeezing the woman's hand. "Else I never should have met him."

Lady Mowbray smiled. "This is true. Had I not nagged him into going to London this year, the two of you might never have met."

"Yes." Clarissa frowned as she considered the possibility: never meeting him, never dancing with him, never kissing him, never . . . Why, she might be married to Prudhomme this very minute, she realized, and probably ready to throw herself off a cliff! She shuddered at the very idea of the wrinkly old man touching her in the ways Adrian did. *Dear God!*

"Well," Lady Mowbray murmured. "Let me do one more thing and instruct you now to let him see that you have spectacles. He needs to know that you can see him and still love him. And you need to see that he will love you with or without spectacles." Adrian's mother patted her hand, then got gracefully back to her feet. "Now, I should go along to my room. And we shall keep this little visit between ourselves. Somehow I do not think my son would be pleased to learn that I saw and spoke to you before he did. He has apparently been up pacing the salon all night, waiting and worrying."

Clarissa's eyebrows flew up at this news and she glanced at Kibble in question.

The butler's bulldog features shifted into a grimace, and he nodded. "I forced his lordship to leave while we tended to you, Lady Clarissa. He — of course — did not wish to go, but he was questioning my every order and just generally getting in the way. I had to be firm."

Clarissa's eyes widened. She was surprised to know anyone could make Adrian do something he did not wish to do.

"However," Kibble continued, "I also promised to fetch him if there was a change. I shall get him now, but first would like to say that Lady Mowbray is right. You should really tell him that you know what he looks like, and that you love him the way he is. The man is as self-conscious of his looks as are you with your spectacles."

Kibble escorted Lady Mowbray from the room, leaving Clarissa in a quandary. Was it true? Had she been going without her sight for nothing?

Clarissa frowned over the matter. The very fact that Adrian had not mentioned her getting new spectacles had convinced her she had read the situation correctly, and that he did not think they would look good on her. However, his mother and Kibble had cast a new light on the matter. If what they said was true, her husband was self-conscious of his own looks.

She shook her head. Scar or no scar, Adrian was the handsomest man of the *ton.* Clarissa found it hard to believe he did not realize how attractive he was. He seemed so confident and commanding all the time . . .

Clarissa's thoughts scattered when the door to her room started to open. Out of habit she snatched off her spectacles and slid them under her pillow. She was so used to hiding them, she did not even think twice about it.

"Clarissa."

She recognized her husband as he entered and strode across the room. It seemed to her that his entire being screamed of worry.

A second man entered behind him, then another, and while Clarissa thought the second man was her father, she had no idea about the third. Adrian dropped against the side of her bed and scooped her against his chest.

"Thank God you are all right," he said, hugging her tightly and stroking her hair. "We have been worried sick."

"Yes, we have," her father said, and she felt his hand rub her back. "We were up all night waiting for you to wake up."

"I am sorry to have worried you so," Clarissa murmured, hugging Adrian back and reaching for her father's hand.

"Nay. 'Tis not your fault." Both men spoke at once, and all three of them smiled; then Adrian released Clarissa and sat back to peer into her face. He was close enough that she could see the lines of worry around his eyes.

"We knew by about midnight you would survive, but Kibble could not tell us if you would wake up with all your faculties still in place, or if your mind would be damaged somehow."

"Oh." Clarissa managed a smile. "I think my faculties are fine."

Adrian smiled and kissed her gently on the nose.

"We are glad you are well," the third man said.

Clarissa frowned, thinking she recognized the voice, but unable at first to place it.

"Do you think you could tell us what happened?" he added.

Her eyes widened. "Mr. Hadley," Clarissa said with surprise as his name suddenly clicked into place. "Whatever are you doing here?"

"I sent for him," Adrian said. "He arrived an hour ago."

"Oh."

"Do you feel up to answering the question?" her husband asked with concern.

"Yes, of course. I am fine, really," she assured him, giving his arm a squeeze.

"Then can you tell us exactly what happened?" Hadley repeated.

Clarissa wondered why he was asking the question. Why he was even there, really. But with all three men waiting in what felt like an impatient manner, she decided to answer first and then ask her own questions.

Clarissa quickly repeated what she'd told Kibble, about coming to the room for a bit of privacy and then eating some of the pie, her stomach bothering her, and then sleeping. The room was silent for a moment as she finished; then Adrian murmured, "Kibble said that your not eating much of the pie may have saved you from being more ill."

"Then 'tis good I was not hungry," she said wryly.

"Indeed," Hadley agreed.

"You could have been killed," her father said harshly, apparently upset that Clarissa seemed to be taking things so lightly.

"That was undoubtedly the plan," Hadley murmured.

"Kibble does not think there was truly enough poison in the pie to kill her," Adrian said soothingly. "Even if Clarissa had eaten the whole piece, he does not think she would have died. He suspects she just would have been sicker."

"Poison?" Clarissa said with alarm. "In the pie?"

She saw their heads turn as the three men glanced at one another, but no one seemed eager to respond. "You are suggesting that I was poisoned?"

When they were all silent again, she asked, "What is happening? Why would someone wish to poison me?"

Adrian blew a little sigh out between his lips, then said, "Clarissa, I have asked you this before, but are you *sure* there is no one who would wish you harm?"

Clarissa stared at him. She did recall his asking if she had any enemies, anyone who would wish to do her harm. It had come up so naturally in that conversation after making love that she hadn't thought anything of it. He'd told her a tale about a friend who had found out someone was trying to kill him, and then he'd murmured that he didn't think he had any enemies who would wish him dead, and did she? Clarissa had thought they were just talking. Now she realized he'd been worrying that someone was out to harm her. But why?

"No, of course not," she decided. "Why would anyone wish me harm? I have never hurt anyone in my life. Perhaps they were trying to poison you and I ate it by mistake."

"Me?" Adrian said with surprise. "Why would you think someone was trying to kill me?"

"Well, my lord, why would you think they are trying to kill me?" Clarissa replied, growing a bit testy. "After all, you are the one who does not listen to your mother when she tells you things. Perhaps there are others you do not listen to and who are trying to get your attention."

Adrian's mouth twitched with amusement; then he said solemnly, "No one is trying to kill me, Clarissa. The pie was meant for you."

"How do you know?" she asked.

"Well, for one thing, I was not even in the house. And I am not the one who rests in the afternoons; you are. Besides," Adrian pointed out, "it was in *your* room."

Clarissa grimaced unhappily at that logic; then her eyes narrowed. "But you asked me about someone trying to harm me days ago. Did you think then that someone was trying to hurt me? And if so, why?"

Adrian hesitated and sighed. "Clarissa, you have suffered innumerable accidents since your arrival in London for the season."

"Because I have not had my glasses," she pointed out.

Clarissa didn't think he agreed that this was the reason behind her accidents, but he didn't argue. In fact, he didn't say anything. His head was turned, and he seemed to be looking at Hadley.

Before Clarissa could say anything else, Adrian kissed her forehead and stood. "I need to have a word with my man. I will return shortly."

The two men left the room, and her father took Adrian's place on the side of the bed, but his attention was on the door through which the men had just left. Both Clarissa and Lord Crambray could hear the murmur of voices as the men conversed.

Knowing her father wished to join in whatever conversation was taking place but was reluctant to abandon her, Clarissa sighed and waved him off. "Go on. Join them. I wish to get up anyway. Perhaps you could send my maid to me and order a bath sent up?"

"Yes, yes." Lord Crambray patted her hand with relief and escaped. Clarissa heard the murmur of voices pause as he joined the other two; then it began again and moved off up the hall.

Shaking her head, Clarissa sat up and slid her feet off the bed. She had stripped off her soiled gown and drawn on a robe before it occurred to her that she didn't have anything to read in the bath. She was in the mood for a good long soak after the trials of what had happened and all she'd learned, and she liked to read in the tub.

After a hesitation, Clarissa headed for the door. She would just slip down to the library and find something to read. She'd be quick about it and — if she was very lucky — would not run into anyone. Clarissa had a lot to think about, but was not in the mood for thinking just now. After she'd relaxed a bit in the tub with a book, she would consider what her husband feared was going on, as well as what she'd learned from Lady Mowbray and Kibble.

CHAPTER SEVENTEEN

"I do not understand," Lord Crambray said, following Adrian into his office. "Are you telling me that you have known for some time that someone was trying to kill Clarissa and you did not say a word to me? Or to her?"

Adrian frowned as he walked around his desk and dropped into his chair. Put into those words, it did not sound very good.

"His lordship did not wish to worry or upset your daughter, Lord Crambray," Hadley said when Adrian remained silent. "He felt she was under enough stress with the wedding preparations and such. He *did* see to it that she was well looked after."

"Not well enough, obviously," Lord Crambray said grimly. He turned back to Adrian to say, "And while I understand your wishing to protect Clarissa, there is no excuse for not telling me. I should have been told."

"Yes, you should have," Adrian admitted

with a sigh, and ran one hand through his hair. He had managed to mess everything up. Again. "I apologize. I ever seem to be doing things wrong where your daughter is concerned. I fear my faculties are not all there whenever she is involved."

At this admission, Lord Crambray's anger seemed to run out of him like water out of an upturned pail. Sighing, the older man ran his hands through his own hair, then fell into one of the two seats in front of Adrian's desk.

"You mentioned fires, and being pushed in front of carriages, and falls down the stairs." Clarissa's father frowned. "Lydia mentioned none of this in her letters to me. Please tell me . . . what the hell has been going on?"

Nodding, Adrian sat up and leaned his arms on his desktop, carefully explaining everything that had happened since he'd met Clarissa, including things he'd heard had happened before they met. As he spoke, Hadley moved to the table along the wall and poured three snifters of brandy. He handed one to each lord, taking the third for himself as he settled in his own chair. He remained silent as Adrian finished speaking.

"Dear God," Lord Crambray murmured

once Adrian was quiet. "Who could be behind all of this?"

"I do not know," Adrian said grimly. "Clarissa seems to think they are all just accidents, but —"

"No." John Crambray shook his head firmly. "If it were not for the incident at the fountain, I might believe that, but no. The note that was not from you and her ending up unconscious in the fountain — it's all just too much to be a prank or an unhappy accident."

Adrian nodded in silent agreement.

"What are we going to do about this, son?" Lord Crambray asked.

Adrian sighed and then glanced to Hadley, who had arrived at the house just as Kibble came below with the news that Clarissa was awake. Adrian had given the man a brief explanation of what had happened as they'd rushed upstairs, but he had yet to hear why he was here.

"I hired Hadley," he said. "Mr. Hadley has handled several situations for me in the past, and I hoped he might be helpful this time." Adrian raised an eyebrow at the man. "I gather you are here because you have news?"

"Aye, I have news," the man admitted, his expression grim. "However, I fear you will not like it."

Adrian frowned. Sinking back in his seat, he gestured for Hadley to continue.

"I looked into each incident, and then I looked everywhere I could think to look, my lord. Most people have skeletons in their closets, and I thought this was where we would find the snake causing all these accidents."

"And?" Adrian prompted.

"And every lead turned into a dead end," Hadley said with a frown. "There is nothing in your wife's past that would leave someone with ill will toward her."

"What of Lydia?" Adrian asked, casting a quick apologetic glance at his father-in-law.

"Aye, well . . ." Hadley glanced uncomfortably toward Lord Crambray, then said, "The stepmother does appear to have it in for Lady Clarissa, but I do not think she would take it so far as attempted murder. I could keep an eye on her if you like, but . . ." He shrugged.

"I have already told my wife," Lord Crambray said grimly, "that if she *is* behind this I will wring her neck myself. I shall keep an eye on her."

Adrian grimaced sympathetically at him, then asked Hadley, "What of the business with the captain?"

"Captain Fielding, aye." Hadley sat up a bit. "Well, I did look into that too. After all, it is about the only thing in Lady Clarissa's life that might have caused anger toward her. Howbeit, the man died during his term in prison, so your culprit cannot be him. And from my investigations in that area, I've learned that he had no family but for a mother and sister. The mother died of a heart attack when he was first imprisoned, and the sister not long afterward in a fire in the row where she rented a room."

"I see," Adrian murmured. "As you say, this is hardly good news. Someone is trying to kill my wife, yet there is apparently no one who has motive."

"Well, now. I didn't say I haven't found a likely culprit, merely that you wouldn't like what I learned."

Adrian's eyebrows beetled, a frown tugging at his mouth. "Explain."

"Well, as I said, I looked into those areas you suggested. I also looked into a couple others. In my experience, my lord, murder is most often based on greed. So I was positive that it would be the case here . . . and I was right."

Adrian's eyes narrowed. "Why would anyone kill Clarissa for greed? The only one who would benefit at this point is myself. I am her only heir, as far as I know." He blinked. "I hope you are not suggesting —"

"No, no, of course not," Hadley said quickly. "You would hardly hire me to look into the matter if you were trying to kill her. Good lord, everyone else has accepted everything as mere accidents. You're the only one looking for a person out to harm her."

"Well, then, who, man?" Lord Crambray said impatiently. "Whom have you set your sights on?"

"Lord Greville."

Adrian blinked, sure he'd misheard or misunderstood. "What?"

"Lord Greville, your cousin," Hadley repeated firmly.

"Reginald?" Adrian said with disbelief. "What on earth would make you think that he would harm Clarissa?"

"He is presently your heir," Hadley pointed out.

"No, he is not. Clarissa is," Adrian corrected. "She has been from the day we married."

"If she is alive," Hadley agreed. When Adrian began to shake his head, Hadley added, "He seems to me to be the one with the most likely motive."

"Motive be hanged; it cannot be him. First

of all, the accidents were taking place long before I even met Clarissa — the carriage incident and the fall down the stairs, for instance. And his inheritance would hardly have been a motive for him to hurt her before she and I met. Second, Reginald is my friend as well as my cousin. He helped me in wooing Clarissa. And money would not be a motive for him; he is at least as well-off as myself."

Lord Crambray nodded solemnly after each of Adrian's points, agreeing with every one. Hadley just shook his head. "What if those first accidents were just that: accidents? The carriage incident and the fall down the stairs might have been. We really have nothing that proves otherwise. If that is the case, he might have simply taken advantage of that history of accidents."

Adrian frowned at the possibility, then said, "Why has he not attacked me?"

"If he kills you first, Clarissa inherits. If he kills her first, then kills you, he inherits," Hadley pointed out.

Adrian shook his head and repeated, "He is wealthy and hardly in need of my funds."

"Ah, well, you see, that is the news I learned. It seems Lord Greville is not as well-off as he likes to appear. In fact, he is nearly bankrupt. The creditors will be dragging him off to debtors' prison any day now if he does not do something about it. However, were you and your wife to die unexpectedly, all his financial problems would be solved."

Adrian frowned at this news, taken aback, but still opened his mouth to protest. He was forestalled by Hadley raising one hand.

"He also had opportunity. When the fire and the fountain incidents occurred, he was right there, not only in London, but at the Crambray house."

Adrian relaxed. "But he is not *here,* so could not have poisoned Clarissa." He shook his head firmly. "It cannot be Greville."

"I am afraid he *is* here," Hadley countered apologetically.

Adrian stiffened. "What do you mean?"

"When you returned to the country, Greville did as well. He has been staying at the neighboring Wyndham estate since the day after you arrived here. 'Tis only a half hour's ride away, and I have learned through inquiry that he is off 'hunting' most of the days and sometimes at night," Hadley informed him.

Adrian dropped back into his seat with something resembling a moan, his face pale as he considered the damning news. Hadley nodded sympathetically.

"I fear he is your culprit, my lord. I would stake my life on it."

"You are staking Clarissa's life on it," Lord Crambray said grimly.

Adrian shook his head as he tried to absorb the possibility. He and Reginald used to be as close as brothers, and while it was true that they had grown apart over the last ten years, they had seemed to pick up their friendship right where they had left off. Adrian had counted on him for help in wooing Clarissa; he'd listened to the man's advice and accepted his comfort. It couldn't be him.

"I know it is hard to believe, my lord," Hadley said sympathetically. "I know the two of you were close. But that was over ten years ago. Closer to twelve. You went off to war at twenty and returned two years later, wounded. I gather you did make one foray into London after that, but have spent most of your time here, taking care of the estates. Twelve years is a long time. People change. Affections change. Circumstances change. Priorities change." He paused and let Adrian consider that, then added, "I think your cousin changed."

Adrian frowned. He just could not believe

it, and said so. "Nay, I know Reginald. He is not behind this. He would never hurt either Clarissa or myself this way. We may have grown apart, but our friendship returned once I came back to London. And he simply would not do it."

Hadley looked doubtful. "Your cousin is a rapscallion, my lord. He has ruined more than a few virtuous girls. His feelings have never proven very deep, from what I can see."

Adrian waved that away. "That is all rumor and gossip. Reginald never ruined anyone. The only women he bedded were experienced ones. The few so-called 'good girls' who were ruined were liars trying to trap him into marriage by getting caught alone in a room with him. They thought the threat of scandal would move him to marry. Unfortunately for them, Reginald saw no reason to ruin his life for any scheming little fortune hunter."

"I am afraid I have to agree with Adrian," John Crambray said suddenly. "Murdering Clarissa seems a bit extreme. Why would he not have at least tried to break them up first? Turn Adrian against Clarissa, or her against him? It does seem . . ." His words trailed off as he saw Adrian's expression change; then he asked sharply, "*Did* he try to turn you against each other?"

"Yes. No. I do not know." Adrian frowned. "Reginald *did* try to warn me off her that first night at the ball. He told me she was clumsy and had burned his piffle, and that I could be taking my life in my hands by going anywhere near her. But after that he helped me see her. He dressed as a fop to convince Lady Crambray to let her go out for a ride in the park with him, just so I could see her and read to her for a bit. And he tried to see her to get her to meet me at the fountain. . . ."

They were all silent for a moment, and then Hadley got to his feet. "Well, I shall continue to look into the matter, my lord. But from here now, I think, since a poisoning occurred here. There is no more I can learn in the city. However," he added quietly, "I do think it is Greville. He was there. He is here. And he knew about the two of you, so he could have written that note and signed your initials to it and would — quite rightly — expect Lady Clarissa to rush out to meet you."

"What about Prudhomme?" Adrian asked abruptly. "He knew about Clarissa and me."

Hadley shook his head. "Prudhomme is happily pursuing his affairs with married women in London. He could not have poisoned that pie. I will have to focus now on people who were both in London and are now here. That is, if you wish me to continue my investigations," he added.

"Yes, of course," Adrian said quietly. "I asked Kibble to arrange for a room for you when he came to tell me Clarissa was awake. He should be able to tell you which one is yours."

Nodding, Hadley turned and left, and Adrian sat back in his seat, a frown pulling at his face.

Lord Crambray and he both sat silently for several moments, each lost in his own thoughts; then Clarissa's father said, "He is right about one thing."

Relieved to have his contemplation interrupted, Adrian glanced at John Crambray. "What is that?"

"The killer has to be someone who was both in London and is now here."

Adrian nodded.

"Shall we make a list?" Clarissa's father asked.

Adrian sighed. "Reginald would be on it, of course."

"And Lydia," John Crambray suggested. "She was both there and here, and — in fact — was the one who took away Clarissa's spectacles, making her accident-prone."

"You know about that?" Adrian asked with surprise.

Clarissa's father nodded. "Lydia claimed Clarissa broke her spectacles, and my daughter let her get away with it, but I have known for a long time that Lydia dislikes my daughter. She wouldn't dare treat her with anything but respect in my presence, but of course, here in London . . ." He shrugged. "I feared without my presence she would treat her less kindly. I decided I'd best come to the city after all, and was arranging my affairs so that I could come when I got word of your marriage. 'Tis why I was able to leave so quickly."

"Ah," Adrian said. He shouldn't be surprised at this news, and part of him wasn't. He had already come to the conclusion that Clarissa's father was an intelligent man.

Sighing, Adrian continued with their list. "I suppose we should add the servants. Both Joan and Keighley were in London and here."

"Keighley is your manservant, is he not?" Crambray asked.

Adrian nodded. "He was not in her life before I was, but if the first accidents were just accidents . . ." He shrugged.

"Unfortunately, neither servant has a motive," Crambray said wearily. "Lydia does. She hates Clarissa."

"And there's Reginald, who needs money if Hadley is right," Adrian suggested.

"Do you doubt him?" Crambray asked.

Adrian shook his head. "No. He is a very thorough man."

Crambray nodded, then got to his feet. "I think I should go have a chat with my wife."

Adrian watched the door close behind Clarissa's father, then turned to peer out the window of his office at the rolling hills and green fields of his estate. His thoughts were awhirl. He found it hard to believe that Reginald would harm anyone, but . . .

His thoughts died as a movement out of the corner of his eye made his head whip around toward the door. Outside his study in the library, Clarissa was standing in the now open door. He took one look at her face and knew she had been listening.

"How much did you hear?" he asked quietly, standing to move around the desk.

"Most of it, I think," she admitted. "I came down to the library for a book right after my father followed you out of the room. I did not intend to eavesdrop, but your office door was cracked open. I heard everything.

"I do not think Reginald would harm me,"

she went on as Adrian paused before her, resting his hands on her waist.

He sighed and pulled her forward against him, then placed his cheek against the top of her head. "Neither do I. But someone is."

"But why?" she asked plaintively.

Adrian squeezed her a little tighter, wishing he could have kept her from this knowledge. She sounded so bewildered and hurt. "I do not know, Clarissa. But I will find out," he vowed. He pushed her back to look down into her face and said, "In the meantime, you should not be out of bed."

She shrugged. "I am not tired, and I feel fine."

"Clarissa, I nearly lost you last night. I would have you stay in bed at least a day to recover," Adrian said firmly. When she opened her mouth to protest, he added in a pleading voice, "If not for your sake, then for mine. I swear I nearly had an apoplexy when I found you so pale and unmoving. I do not want to lose you."

Adrian was close enough that Clarissa could see the lines of strain around his eyes. He really had been worried, she realized, and she felt her heart tighten. Maybe he truly had come to care for her. Perhaps he would not mind so much that she wore spectacles. Mayhap he would still want her anyway. But she supposed that was a matter to test another time.

Clarissa closed her mouth on the protest she'd been about to give and hugged him tightly, blinking rapidly to dispel the tears that glazed her eyes.

"Mmm," Adrian murmured. "It is good to hold you. I feared for a while I would never get the chance to do so again."

Clarissa sighed against his chest, enjoying the gentle play of his hands over her back through the silk of her robe. The caress was almost absentminded, and she suspected he wasn't even aware of what he was doing. But as his hands brushed the sides of her breasts in passing, she was aware, and — as always — her body responded.

Smiling softly, she leaned back and said, "I shall make a deal with you, husband. I shall go back to bed . . . if you join me."

She saw him smile at the offer. Adrian's eyes drifted down over her. He said huskily, "While I am tempted, wife, you are not well enough for such things yet."

Clarissa raised her eyebrows. He was more than tempted. She could feel his erection pressing against her, and she knew he was just trying to be considerate. As usual. But she didn't desire consideration right now.

"Not well enough?" Clarissa asked softly. Smiling wickedly, she took a step back from him into the library and undid the sash of her robe. While he watched, she drew the flaps open to reveal nipples already hard with desire. She allowed him to look his fill, then released the sides of her robe and took his hands to place them over her breasts so that he could feel how hard the tips were. "My body does not agree with you, husband. It seems to think I am well enough."

"Clarissa," Adrian growled in warning. "No."

"Your mouth says no, but your body says yes," she murmured, slipping a hand down to run one finger along the length of the hardness in his breeches.

A fire lit in Adrian's eyes as she caressed him through the material. His voice was husky as he said, "You have grown bold since our wedding night, wife."

Clarissa bit her lip, then cupped him with her whole hand. Tilting her head, she asked, "Do you mind?"

"No," he growled, moving forward.

Clarissa backed slowly away, smiling, leading him toward the couch in the library. "Good. Because I want to make you as happy as you make me."

"And how do you plan to do that?" Adrian asked. Clearly amused, he allowed her to lead him across the room.

"I have been reading books, my lord, in search of ways for a woman to pleasure a man."

"Without spectacles?" Adrian asked, then warned, "You shall strain your eyes more."

"You are worth it, my lord," Clarissa murmured, not mentioning her spectacles. She no more wanted to discuss them just now than he seemed to want to discuss Reginald or the matter of who was trying to harm her.

"And what have you learned from your books?" he asked, slipping his hands inside her robe to hold her at the waist. She bumped up against the sofa and came to a halt, then sighed at the feel of his rough hands on her soft skin.

"I learned that I can please you exactly as you please me."

"Oh?" he asked.

"Yes." She smiled and ran her hands up his chest as Adrian's own hands slipped around behind her. Clarissa murmured with pleasure as they dropped to her behind. He urged her closer, lifting her against him so that they were groin-to-groin.

"I love your strength," she whispered, rubbing her mouth along his chin. "I love your body; I love your mind; I love the pleasure you give me. Let me pleasure you."

Adrian growled deep in his throat and covered her mouth with his. His kiss was hot and thrilling and she caught her arms around his neck and moaned into his mouth, tilting her head for the best effect. His hands were hard on her behind, his erection hard on her front. His lips and tongue were hard as they explored her. It would be easy to believe he was hard through and through, but Clarissa knew that hardness simply guarded the softness inside.

"We have to go upstairs," Adrian muttered, breaking their kiss.

"Still trying to send me to bed?" she taunted as he set her on her feet. The moment his hands released her, she dropped to her knees before him and reached for his breeches.

"Clarissa," he growled, trying to catch her hands, but she was quick and had already tugged his breeches down, her hands out of reach.

"Yes, my lord?" she asked innocently, as his erection popped out and bobbed briefly before she caught it in one firm hand. Adrian sucked in a hard breath, his body jerking into her touch.

"Oh, God, you shall be the death of me," he groaned.

"I sincerely hope not, my lord husband," Clarissa murmured, contemplating his staff and wondering exactly how to pleasure him. One of the books had mentioned something about this, but it had all been terribly metaphorical and not really instructive, except to assure her that as he had used his mouth to pleasure her, she could do the same to him.

Shrugging inwardly, she leaned forward and simply popped him into her mouth. That seemed the best way to go about it. He was long and hard and yet soft at the same time, like velvet over steel. Clarissa held him there, then moved her mouth forward . . . and decided she was doing things right when she heard him suck air in through his teeth.

"Dear God." He gasped, catching one hand in her hair.

Clarissa took that to mean she was doing it right, and ran her mouth down his length again. It seemed the natural thing to do. It was the same action he'd used when making love to her, and it did seem her mouth was just replacing her body.

"Clarissa, you have to stop," Adrian said

harshly; then he added, "Please."

When she ignored him, he ground out, "We have four guests and almost two dozen servants running around. Someone could come in."

Noting that the muscles of his thighs were quivering, Clarissa ran a hand along one with fascination as she drew her mouth along his length again.

Adrian gave up talking and was reduced to breathless pants, and it seemed to her that he had grown harder under her ministrations. The hand she was using for balance brushed his feet, and she slanted her eyes downward with surprise to see that his toes were curled. It seemed she could do that for him just as he did for her.

This was all new to Clarissa, and fascinating because of it, but she thought she preferred it when he made love to her. His body enveloped her then, his arms around her, his erection filling her, his mouth kissing her. She really liked that the best — but she also liked the idea of pleasing him, so she was terribly disappointed when he suddenly bent and caught her by the shoulders to force her away.

"Husband," she protested as he quickly jerked his breeches back up. It was all the complaint she managed to get out before he finished with his pants and caught her up in his arms.

"Upstairs," he panted, apparently still breathless. "You may do whatever you like to me, but upstairs, where we need not fear being interrupted."

Appeased by that promise, Clarissa relaxed in his arms and let him carry her from the library.

CHAPTER EIGHTEEN

Clarissa watched silently as the servants filled a bath for her. Adrian had promised to have one sent up when he'd gone below, and had kept his promise. She felt bad about the time of day, knowing that early morning was the staff's busiest time, but she'd never had her bath the day before and really felt she needed one after the strenuous activities of the day and night — strenuous activities that had resulted in a long sleep, followed by more strenuous activity and more sleep.

Adrian had had a sleepless night to make up for, and Clarissa, it seemed, hadn't been as recovered as she'd thought. They'd spent more time sleeping than making love, though both had been wonderful.

Clarissa's attention returned to the bath as the last of the water was poured in; then she watched as the room emptied out until only she and Joan remained. The moment the door closed behind the last person, Clarissa moved to the bedside table to retrieve her spectacles from the small bag resting there. She'd decided at one point during the night, while laying, staring at Adrian's sleeping face, that she'd heed Lady Mowbray's and Kibble's advice and start wearing her spectacles. However, Clarissa had been made so self-conscious about them for so long, she wanted to start out slowly. She'd wear them in front of Joan first and see how the maid reacted. Then perhaps she'd move on to other servants, and then finally her family and husband.

Straightening with the spectacles in hand, Clarissa hesitated, then perched them on her nose, calmly retrieved her book from the drawer of the bedside table, and turned to walk to the tub.

"Shall I —" Joan's words ended abruptly and were followed by a thud as she dropped the bar of soap she'd been carrying.

Clarissa glanced at the maid sharply, trying to decipher her expression. She didn't like to admit it, but it looked to her as if Joan's face held horror. Just as she came to that conclusion, the maid forced the look away and managed a pitiful smile. "I . . . you . . ."

Clarissa waved her to silence. She had no

desire to discuss her spectacles. She was suddenly too depressed to be bothered with explanations, and certainly didn't wish to hear any lame claims that they looked "nice" after the maid's initial response.

Joan hesitated, then remained silent on the subject as she took Clarissa's hand to steady her as she got into the bath. However, she caught the maid repeatedly peeking at the spectacles as she did.

With the truth of her spectacles no longer a secret, at least with Joan, Clarissa didn't insist on being left alone to bathe, but allowed the maid to help her wash her hair. Once finished, Joan moved off to deal with what clothes she'd wear while Clarissa tried to relax in the water and read for a bit. It was difficult to relax, however. She was terribly aware the entire time that Joan continued to cast surreptitious glances her bespectacled way.

"Are they so ugly?" Clarissa asked finally, and Joan stiffened guiltily.

"What, my lady?" the maid asked.

"Am I so ugly in the spectacles?" Clarissa clarified. "You looked horrified at first, and now keep staring at them."

"Oh, no, my lady," Joan assured her quickly. "I was not horrified. They look fine. I was just surprised. I did not realize that

Lord Adrian had sent for a new pair. What you saw was surprise, not horror."

"Hmmm." Clarissa murmured doubtfully, then peered close at the maid. She'd seen the blond woman every day for the last few months, and her face was familiar, but still Clarissa was seeing new aspects now with the spectacles on. Joan was quite lovely — surprisingly so for a maid. But then, Clarissa supposed there was no reason a maid could not be beautiful. It just seemed to her that the prettier women tended to get better jobs, such as shop assistants. Shrugging, Clarissa set the matter aside and returned to her book, but found herself now too restless to enjoy it. She was made more self-conscious by her spectacles than she'd ever been about her nudity in front of the maid.

Setting her book aside with a sigh, Clarissa turned her attention to bathing, her mind worrying over what to do. The plan had been to wear the spectacles in front of Joan, and if that went well, wear them in front of others. Unfortunately, it didn't seem to her that this had gone at all well.

Still, she would have to wear them in front of Adrian at some point, or spend the rest of her life mostly blind, with stolen moments here and there where she sneaked off to her room to wear them.

Clarissa grimaced at the idea. It sounded almost like being unfaithful. Besides, if her mother-in-law and Kibble were to be believed, Adrian was afraid she would find him unattractive if she saw him properly, and it seemed unkind to leave him with that opinion. She was going to have to wear them in front of him eventually. She'd always known that, of course, but would really rather delay a little bit longer.

Not much longer, Clarissa assured herself. It seemed to her that Adrian was actually growing attached to her. He'd certainly seemed worried about her, and relieved that she was recovering yesterday. But still . . .

"Coward," she muttered under her breath, and stood in the tub. Leaning forward to reach for the linen Joan had laid nearby, she paused when the maid rushed over to hand it to her. "Thank you," she said. Using the soft linen to quickly dry her upper body, Clarissa stepped out of the tub to dry her legs and feet before following Joan to the clothes the maid had set out for her.

Half an hour later, Clarissa was dressed and headed below; her hair still a tad damp and her spectacles still perched on her nose. She was trying to be brave about it, but wasn't at all sure she wouldn't snatch them off and hide them should she run into her husband.

One step at a time, she told herself. Everything would be fine.

Lydia was alone in the breakfast room when she entered, but there were empty plates suggesting that her father and Adrian and possibly even Lady Mowbray had been in and gone. One look at her stepmother's face was enough to tell her why. Lydia had a face like thunder this morning. Clarissa sighed to herself, knowing it meant her stepmother was going to be difficult. She almost turned and slipped back out of the room, but Lydia had seen her, and escaping now would have been rude.

"I see you have spectacles." Lydia smiled unkindly as Clarissa walked to the sideboard to fill a plate with food from the offerings there. "They must have arrived this morning. Have you seen your husband with them yet? Do you now realize what you have cursed yourself to with your outlandish behavior? Are you miserable now?"

Clarissa allowed the questions to wash over her as she filled her plate. It wasn't until after she'd made her way to the table, sat down, opened and spread a napkin on her lap, and picked up her fork that she finally said, "I have had the spectacles since the day before my wedding, Lydia."

Silence filled the room at her announcement, and Clarissa took the opportunity to get a bite or two of food into her mouth. She was lifting a third forkful to her lips when Lydia finally snapped out of her surprise.

"You married him knowing how horrid he looks?" Lady Crambray asked. "My God! Are you mad? How can you stand for him to touch you?"

Sighing, Clarissa lowered her fork. "Actually, Lydia, I not only married Adrian knowing how he looked; I knew how he looked before he ever kissed me or made love to me. I saw him the first night at the ball when he danced with me. Every time he bent close to hear what I said, I caught a glimpse of his face." Clarissa met her stepmother's gaze head-on. "I found him attractive then, and find him attractive still. I am sorry you do not. But then, you are not the one who married him."

She began to eat, aware that Lydia was staring at her once more. Her stepmother was eyeing her as if she were a puzzle she was unable to make out.

"You are actually happy with him," Lydia finally said, wonderingly. And then, sounding bewildered, she asked, "How can you be happy with him?"

Clarissa lifted her head, sadly eyeing the woman across the table from her. Lydia truly did not seem to understand.

"Because he is good and kind," she explained softly, then went on. "Because he treats me like a princess. Because he makes me laugh. Because he makes me happy. Because he took the trouble to read to me when I could not read to myself. Because he fed me and gave me wine when I could not eat or drink at balls. Because when he kisses me my toes curl, and when he makes love to me I cannot contain my passion."

Oddly enough, Lydia's reaction to these words was to pale and blanch as if Clarissa had struck her. Then several other emotions crossed her face: anger, resentment, envy, confusion. Finally, she simply looked lost and dejected.

Clarissa pondered the woman's reaction, as she took up her fork and returned her attention to her food. Several moments passed before Lydia recovered sufficiently to go on the attack again; then she asked, "Has he seen you with your spectacles on? I bet he has not. I have not noticed you wearing them before this. Does he dislike them then?"

Swallowing the food in her mouth, Clarissa set her fork and knife down on either side of her plate. She then dabbed at her mouth with her napkin, set it back in her lap, folded her hands neatly together, raised her eyes back to Lydia, and did what she should have done several years ago. She asked, "Why do you want so much for me to be miserable? Why do you hate me so?"

Jerking in her seat as if slapped, Lydia said, "Do not be ridiculous. You are my stepdaughter. I do not hate you."

"But you do wish me to be miserable."

"Life is miserable, Clarissa," the woman said harshly. "All those dreams you have of children and happiness? A loving husband and home? Forget them. Fate is a fickle bitch, and even when she gives you what you think you want, you soon learn you have nothing at all. It is better to learn while young how hard life can be than to grow up soft and coddled and have it taught to you in heartbreak."

Clarissa stared at her stepmother silently, feeling as if she were very close to understanding. After a moment she asked, "Were you soft and coddled, Lydia?"

"Oh, yes." She gave a brittle laugh. "I was spoiled beyond imagining. Anything I wanted I could have. Anything I needed was there."

"Until you married my father," Clarissa guessed.

Lydia stared down at her plate. After a pause, she said quietly, "I wanted him from the moment I saw him. I saw how he was with your mother and —"

"You knew him while my mother was alive?" Clarissa asked with surprise.

Lydia nodded, her downward gaze almost ashamed. "They loved each other so. I envied your mother. When she died, I thought, 'Brilliant! Now it is my turn.' And I went after him."

Her hand moved to her teacup, and she gave a short laugh. "Oh, not outright, of course. I was there to comfort and soothe him, to murmur sympathetically about how hard it must be for you without a mother. How hard for him, too. You needed someone to guide you into womanhood, especially after the scandal. And raising a child alone and running a household must be a terrible burden alone."

"And he married you," Clarissa said quietly. She recalled that Lydia had been kind to her upon first arriving at Crambray. They had laughed a time or two. And then, slowly, she had withdrawn and grown cool, then cold, then downright unpleasant. Not just with Clarissa, but with everyone.

"Yes. He married me," Lydia said miserably. "As I say, I always got what I wanted."

"But you didn't, did you?" Clarissa said with realization. "Because you did not really want my father; you wanted the sort of relationship he and my mother had."

"Yes," Lydia said wearily, then gave a wry smile. "You always were a clever girl. Had I been half so clever, I would not have ruined my own life." Sighing, she ran a hand over her hair, then shook her head. "Oh, he is good and kind in his distant way, but I felt nothing when he kissed me. This toe curling and uncontainable passion you speak of is alien to me. I blamed him for it. He married me to mother you and run his home, and that was all he really cared about. You were the daughter of his precious Margaret, and he showed you more affection, attention, and consideration than he ever showed me, his wife.

"But I could have lived with that," she went on quietly. "Most marriages are simply business arrangements. I could have been content with his mild affection and lack of interest if only I had borne children of my own. But that never happened." Her hand tightened around the teacup handle until her knuckles were white, and Clarissa feared she might snap it with her anger. "I have been with your father for many years with no sign of a child."

Clarissa's eyes went blurry even with her spectacles on, and she realized they were filled with tears of empathy. Blinking the tears away, she cleared her throat and said, "You had me. I would have been your daughter."

"I did not want you," Lydia said harshly, and her eyes were hard; then she looked away with shame. "I am sorry, Clarissa, but you were full grown when I came to Crambray. A woman already, formed in personality and attitudes . . . and an exact replica of your mother, who'd had the marriage I wanted but could not seem to have." She grimaced and shook her had. "I wanted what your mother, Margaret, had: a husband to love and cherish me, and a baby of my own. My own daughter to look like me and to spoil and coddle."

Clarissa nodded slowly. "And I am sure my mother would have liked what you had."

Lydia blinked in confusion. "What is it I have that she did not?"

"Her health," Clarissa said. "Mother was always frail and ill. She did not have the strength to do much. A slight chill could make her ill for days. And all our love could not keep her healthy and alive."

A flash of shame sparked in Lydia's eyes, and she looked away, her mouth going tight.

"I am not telling you this to humiliate you," Clarissa said quickly. "I am telling you that, with all she had that you want, she did not have it all. Perhaps no one does."

Lydia turned slowly back, curiosity replacing her shame. "Was she happy?"

Clarissa sighed and glanced into the past, recalling her mother's laughter and smiles despite how ill she often got. Margaret Crambray had never shown how wearying it must have been for her, or how frustrating. She had been unendingly cheerful and smiling through all her ailments. It was why they had loved her so.

"I think a part of her must have been terribly unhappy," Clarissa said finally. "I know I should have found it frustrating myself. However, she never showed it. Mother once told me that happiness is a choice. If you choose to mope and be glum, you shall be; but if you wish to be happy and determine to enjoy what life has to offer, then you can have that as well.

"She said that nothing is all good or all bad, that life offers everyone a mix of both — though sometimes it does not seem so, and bad is all we can see in our lives, while in the lives of others we see only good and feel envy. She said we must enjoy the good despite the bad, else life can beat us down and leave us hopeless, and that is no way to live."

"Your mother sounds very wise," Lydia said quietly. There were tears in her eyes. "I wish I had got to know her while she lived. Mayhap with a few words of wisdom from her I might not have made such an irreparable muddle of my life."

"Is it irreparable?" Clarissa asked. Lydia gave a harsh bark of laughter.

"Oh, I do not know," she said dryly. "You tell me. I am growing old and fat — a matron, in fact — and am married to a man who hates me, with a stepdaughter who hates me."

"I do not hate you," Clarissa said quietly.

"Your father does."

"He —"

"Please." Lydia held up a hand. "Do not try to tell me he does not. At first I think he was just indifferent. He loved your mother, and she died while still young. She will always be young and beautiful in his eyes. I could never compete with her, either then or now. But with the passing of time came contempt. I suppose I deserve it. I have been miserable in my disappointment and have made you all miserable too. Now your father does not even like me anymore." She lifted stark eyes to Clarissa and said, "He loathes me so much he even believes that I am trying to kill you." Lydia shook her head, a wounded look in her eyes. "How could he think that? I understand that he does not like me, but does he not know me at all after all these years?"

"I am sure he does not really believe it," Clarissa said, her heart going out to her stepmother. She had never seen Lydia so vulnerable. She'd never realized how unhappy the woman was. Or, to be more exact, she'd known Lydia must be unhappy to cause so much misery for everyone else, but had not understood — or troubled herself to find out — why. It had never occurred to Clarissa to wonder why she hadn't any half-brothers or -sisters. Or to wonder what dreams Lydia had and if they'd come to fruition. It seemed Lydia had lived a charmed life as a child, and had not been as lucky in adulthood.

"He accused me of it flat-out, and warned me that if anything happened to you he would see me hang. I do believe he does indeed think I am behind these accidents," Lydia said. She sighed. "And that, too, is my own fault, since I insisted on taking your spectacles away."

"I am sure he does not *really* believe it," Clarissa repeated. "It is just that the men have decided it must be someone who is here now and was also in the city, and that is a very short list."

"And I am on it," Lydia muttered, sitting back with a sigh. "I suppose I shall never earn anything but loathing from your father now."

Clarissa was silent for a moment, then said tentatively, "Lydia, if my mother was right and we can choose to be happy . . . I mean, perhaps if you were not always moping about and making everyone else unhappy, maybe Father would find his way to caring for you."

Lydia stared at her blankly for a moment; then her eyes sharpened. "Speaking of making everyone else unhappy . . . why are you being so nice to me, when I have been so horrid to you?"

Clarissa frowned. "I realize now that I was a selfish child when it came to you. I fear I took you for granted. It never occurred to me that you might want children of your own or that my father was not perfect. I knew you were unhappy, but just thought it was your choice. I did not trouble myself to care." She frowned and then said sincerely,

"I am sorry, Lydia. I am sorry for your disappointment, and I am sorry that I was not more aware."

"You were a child," Lydia said. "I was not. I should have handled the disappointments better. If I could not have children of my own, I should have been grateful to have been given the chance to be a mother to you. I overheard Lady Mowbray talking to you the morning you woke after the poisoning. I was on the way down to the salon from my own room, and passed yours along the way. I heard her say that she had always wanted a daughter, but had not been able to have any more children after Adrian, but that she would like to be a mother to you." She frowned. "I should have taken that opportunity myself."

Her gaze was full of regret as she continued. "I am sorry, Clarissa. I wish . . . I wish I could do it all over again. If I could, I would do it differently. I would be your friend and a mother."

"It is not too late. We can start fresh now and be friends," Clarissa offered. "I am willing."

Lydia smiled uncertainly. "Really? After all the horrible things I have done? Could you really forgive me and start anew?"

Clarissa waved her hand dismissively.

"You were not so horrible, Lydia. Mostly you just were cranky a lot of the times, and I avoided you then. It was only in London that you truly started to be bothersome. However," she added quickly, as a shamed look covered her stepmother's face, "all of that led to my meeting and marrying my husband, so I can hardly complain, can I? He makes me very happy."

A small, relieved smile curved Lydia's lips. "I am glad you are happy, Clarissa. I can see that you are. I can also see that he is attentive and kind and caring with you. I suppose that goes a long way toward making up for that hideous scar."

Clarissa blinked in surprise. She truly did not understand everyone's fixation on his scar. It was just a part of him, like an ear or a finger, and she thought it added character to his handsome face. Yet Lydia obviously found it ugly and distressing.

Shaking her head, Clarissa said, "I was thinking about going down to look around the village today. Would you care to go with me?"

Lydia stilled, her eyes going wide, like those of a child being offered an unexpected treat. "Truly?"

"Aye." Clarissa laughed. "Well, if we are to become friends we must do things together, must we not?"

"Aye, I suppose we must," the woman said slowly, then beamed. "When shall we go?"

"Right now, if you like," Clarissa offered. "I am finished eating."

"Oh!" Lydia leaped to her feet, excitement on her face. "I need to fetch some coins from my room in case we find something to buy." She started for the door, then turned back to ask, "Are we taking the carriage or walking?"

"I thought we might walk," Clarissa said, rising to join her by the door. "It is not supposed to be far. However, if you would prefer to take the carriage —"

"Nay, nay. A walk would be nice." She turned and bustled into the hall, chattering excitedly. Clarissa smiled. Lydia's new attitude made her feel bad that she'd not confronted the woman on matters and had this talk a long time ago. They might have been the best of friends had she done so.

"Clarissa."

Jerking to a halt at her husband's voice behind her, Clarissa snatched the spectacles off her face and slid them through the slit in her skirts. She was aware of the startled glance Lydia cast her way, but ignored it as she turned to face Adrian. "Aye, husband?"

"Where are you off to?" he asked, his narrowed eyes sliding from her to her step-mother.

"I shall just run up and fetch some coins," Lydia murmured, moving away. "I will not be a moment."

Clarissa watched the woman's blur disappear upstairs, then turned back to Adrian. "I was just going to walk down to the village and have a look around."

"Not with Lydia?" he asked sharply.

Clarissa sighed, knowing he would give her trouble about this. "I know you think she was the one behind the poisoned pie, my lord, but she and I have had a nice long talk this morning, and I truly do not think it was her. Lydia is unhappy and prone to make others unhappy because of it, but she is not trying to kill me."

"Clarissa —" Adrian began grimly.

She interrupted. "You must trust me on this. Lydia is not the culprit. I would stake my life on it."

"You *are* staking your life on it," Adrian snapped. "And I will not have it. I refuse to allow you to go to the village alone with her."

Clarissa squinted, trying to bring his panicked expression into better focus, and smiled. Leaning up, she kissed him softly on the lips. "You are so cute when you get all demanding and bossy, my lord. Truly, it makes me just want to take you upstairs and throw you on the bed."

Adrian's tension eased somewhat, and a small smile pulled at his lips. "Throw me on the bed, huh?" He slipped his arms around her waist. "I may be willing to sacrifice some time to the endeavor, if you are very persuasive."

"How persuasive?" Clarissa asked, running her tongue sensuously along his lower lip.

Adrian growled. Catching her by the back of her head, he denied her retreat and claimed her mouth. His tongue swept between her lips, and she moaned and arched against him, always easily excited by the man.

Clarissa's arms crept about Adrian's neck, and she gasped as his hands clamped firmly onto her bottom and lifted her against him so that their bodies rubbed together. But at the sound of footsteps quickly pounding down the stairwell beside them, they both stiffened. Adrian reluctantly set her back on the floor, and she broke their kiss. They both turned as Lydia reappeared.

"I am ready," the woman said cheerfully, then paused, her eyes widening as she seemed to realize what she'd interrupted. "Oh," she said uncertainly. "Shall I —"

"I am ready too," Clarissa interrupted firmly, slipping from her husband's slack hold and moving to join Lydia by the door. "Come along. Lucy says there is a lovely little tea shop in the village that serves the finest tea cakes around."

"Clarissa," Adrian growled, but Clarissa simply pulled the door open and urged Lydia out.

"We shall be back soon," she cried cheerfully, following her stepmother out the door and pulling it closed behind them. She then hurried Lydia up the drive, unsure that Adrian wouldn't come chasing after them. Really, he was so difficult where her well-being was concerned! Slipping her spectacles out of the small bag under her skirt, she popped them onto her nose.

"I could not help but notice that you removed your spectacles when your husband appeared," Lydia murmured suddenly as they reached the end of the drive. They slowed to a walk on the way up the lane. "He does not know you have them, does he?"

"Nay," Clarissa admitted on a sigh.

"Why?"

Clarissa shrugged. "As you said, I look

ugly in spectacles. I do not wish him to see me in them."

"Oh, Clarissa," Lydia said sadly. "You do not look ugly in spectacles. I am so sorry I said that. I was just being . . ."

"Difficult?" Clarissa suggested lightly.

"A bitch," Lydia countered. Sighing, she shook her head. "I do not even know what I was thinking when we were in London. We got there, and you are so beautiful and young, and have your whole life before you . . . while I am growing old and fat and am beyond hope."

"Oh, Lydia." Clarissa took her arm and hugged it to her. "You are hardly old and fat."

"None of it matters," Lydia said, pulling her arm away and then slipping it tentatively about Clarissa's waist. When Clarissa did not withdraw, she relaxed a little, the half embrace becoming more natural. "The point is, you do not look ugly with spectacles, and I apologize for ever saying you did."

"Apology accepted," Clarissa said. "Now, enough of this old business; we have shops to visit. I wonder if they have a baker who makes those little cream-stuffed buns."

Lydia's eyes widened with delight. "Or

those shortcakes with chocolate and cara-mel!"

Smiling, Clarissa slid her arm around Lydia. "We always did have similar taste in food."

"In *sweets,* you mean." Lydia laughed.

"And books," Clarissa added. "You were forever reading the books I wanted to read before I could get my hands on them. And clothes," she added. "I have always liked your fashion sense."

"Really?" Lydia asked. She seemed sur-prised.

Clarissa nodded solemnly. "You have a good eye for color, and seem to have a natural instinct for what will look good on you."

"Thank you, dear." Lydia glowed with pleasure, and the two women began to nat-ter about fashion as they walked.

CHAPTER NINETEEN

Adrian watched the door close behind his wife, his eyes wide with horror and disbelief. Despite their conversation before the wedding on the subject of her obeying him, she'd just flouted his authority with such unconcern . . . and in a matter of such import. He could not believe it. Cursing under his breath, he whirled and started up the hall, yelling, "Frederick!"

"Yes, my lord?" The boy had not been far away from his mistress, and now appeared from a door in the hall.

"Take three of the other male servants and follow your mistress and her stepmother. Stay close," he ordered. "Do not let them out of your sight for a moment. And if that woman tries anything the least bit threatening, you have my permission to stop her however you deem necessary."

His Adam's apple bobbing as he swallowed, Frederick nodded. "Yes, my lord."

Adrian watched the lad hurry away to do his bidding, then stood there in the hall, clenching and unclenching his fists. He wanted to go after the women himself, but he and Lord Crambray were supposed to be meeting with Hadley to map out a plan of action. Maybe he should just follow anyway; a plan of action would do little good if Lydia had already killed Clarissa.

Whirling back toward the door, he hurried forward, only to come to a halt when Kibble stepped out of the salon.

"It is not Lady Crambray," he announced calmly.

Adrian stilled, his head cocking to one side. "You sound very certain of that."

"I am," Kibble said. "From what you told me and from what I saw when Lord and Lady Crambray arrived and Clarissa greeted them, I deduced that the stepmother was the most likely suspect. And so I set two of the footmen to watch her. They have been following her since her arrival, and she did not place the poisoned pie in Lady Clarissa's room."

In his relief, Adrian reached for the wall as all the strength seemed to trickle out of him. He did not doubt for a moment that what Kibble said was true. Nor was he surprised that the man had taken matters into his own hands. He was a take-charge kind of butler, a leave-over from his time in the royal army.

"I am glad she is not," Kibble went on. "Lady Clarissa and her stepmother had a fine talk this morning. I do believe the two of them may become closer. It may help make Lady Crambray a little less miserable. She is very unhappy."

"You were eavesdropping," Adrian accused.

Kibble shrugged. "You told us to watch Lady Clarissa. I was just following instructions."

Adrian smiled faintly. Kibble had missed his calling. He would have been a fine spy for His Majesty's army. The man knew absolutely everything that went on in this house — or almost everything, he thought grimly. It would be handy if the man knew who actually had put the poisoned pie in Clarissa's room.

Nodding, Adrian turned and walked back up the hall to his office, knowing that Kibble would follow.

"I understand that Mr. Hadley, Lord Crambray, and yourself are going to meet for a strategy session. I should like to be present — if you do not mind," Kibble said as Adrian took a seat behind his desk.

"That would be fine," Adrian replied, turning to peer out the window. "We will be having it as soon as Mr. Hadley gets back from the village."

"The village?" Kibble raised an eyebrow.

"He received a message this morning and said he had to go to the village for something," Adrian explained with a shrug. "I imagine he should return soon."

"Very good." Kibble turned and headed for the door, then paused and glanced back to reiterate, "I know you have a great deal of antipathy for Lydia because of her treatment of Clarissa, but I think these two will be much closer now, and I also think it would behoove you to give the woman another chance."

"I shall take your advice into consideration, Kibble," Adrian murmured. He wasn't promising anything. He would wait on that matter, to see how the woman behaved toward Clarissa, and then make his decision.

"Very good, my lord." Kibble nodded.

As the butler left the room, Adrian turned his chair to face the window. While he was glad that Clarissa and Lydia might find their way to a new relationship, and was happy for his wife's sake that her stepmother wasn't the one trying to kill her, it did leave him with something of a conundrum. While it had removed one suspect from the list, it had removed the suspect he most liked: Lydia was the suspect he would have *preferred* to be the culprit. With her off the list, the alternatives were greatly reduced. In fact, Reginald had become the prime suspect.

Frowning unhappily, Adrian stared outside, but he wasn't seeing the rolling lawns or surrounding trees. He was seeing Reginald when they were younger, the two of them running across the grounds, laughing and joking as they got into mischief. He was seeing Reg as a young man, eyes shining as he thought up some new adventure they could try. Adrian was seeing him as a man, and possibly the murderer trying to take his wife's life.

"Son! What are you doing?"

Glancing toward the door, Adrian frowned as Lady Mowbray bustled into the room. "What is it, Mother?" he asked.

"I just came in to tell you I am leaving."

"Leaving?" he asked with confusion. "But you only just got here."

"Yes, but it seems that Clarissa and Lydia had a good talk this morning and are now trying to mend their relationship. I do not wish to intrude and possibly hamper their efforts. I am going to visit the Wyndhams for a bit, and will return once Lady and Lord Crambray leave."

"Oh." Adrian nodded, his gaze returning to the window and the past reflected in it. "Who told you about their talk? Kibble?"

"No. Clarissa did."

That got his attention, and Adrian turned a surprised gaze back to his mother. "Clarissa? But she just left for the village."

"They left for the village first thing this morning, and have been back for almost an hour now." She frowned. "You have been in here, silent as a mouse, for hours."

Adrian blinked, amazed that he'd spent so much time in reflection. Sighing, he glanced unhappily out the window again. The time had not been wasted. He *had* managed to come to a decision. Reginald was like a brother to him, and it was hard to accept that he would try to hurt anyone, let alone Clarissa, but it was time to know for sure, one way or the other. He needed to confront his cousin as soon as possible and learn the truth.

"Adrian," Lady Mowbray said quietly. "I hope you will not hamper their efforts either. I think a relationship would be good for both Lydia and Clarissa. It might even aid the relationship between Lydia and Lord Crambray. There is a lot of unhappiness there, but none of it irreparable."

"I will not interfere unless Lydia returns to her old ways and tries to hurt Clarissa," he said automatically. He would not allow anyone to hurt Clarissa. Not even his beloved cousin.

"That is as it should be," his mother said with satisfaction. She was silent for a moment, then suddenly moved between him and the window, blocking his view and forcing his attention to her. "It would be nice if you could see me off," she suggested firmly, hands on hips.

"Oh, of course. I am sorry." Rising abruptly, Adrian took her arm to lead her to the door. "I have to go out anyway. I shall see you out on the way."

Clarissa waited nervously by the front door as she heard her husband and mother-in-law's chattering approach. Fixing an anxious smile on her face, she tried not to wring her hands nervously as they appeared and joined her.

"Here she is!" Lady Mowbray smiled reassuringly as she pulled Clarissa into an embrace, then stepped back. "I shall miss you, my dear. You must make Adrian bring you to London as soon as he has finished with this business. He will resist — he does detest the season — but you must be firm. I shall take you shopping and instruct you on which parties to attend and which not, and you really must have a ball — your first as the Countess of Mowbray."

"Yes, my lady," Clarissa murmured doubtfully, not at all thrilled by the prospect of going back into society, even with spectacles. Lady Mowbray's expression seemed to say she was aware of as much, but the woman simply gave another reassuring smile, patted Clarissa's hand kindly, and turned back toward her son.

"Give Mother a kiss, dear," she murmured with amusement.

Bending, Adrian kissed his mother distractedly, not even seeming to notice a phrase that usually annoyed him. Eyebrows rising, the older woman glanced questioningly over his shoulder at Clarissa, but Clarissa had no idea why he had not reacted to the teasing, either. She shrugged helplessly.

Adrian straightened and took his mother's arm, walking her out to her carriage. Settling her inside, he closed the door, then banged on the side of it twice before stepping back. The coachman immediately cracked his whip over the heads of the horses, and the carriage jolted forward. Lady Mowbray's wide, concerned eyes peered worriedly out at Clarissa as the carriage moved off down the drive, her expression saying clearly that she believed something was wrong with her son.

Clarissa had to agree; there was definitely something wrong. Adrian had turned abruptly and moved off toward the stables. He had not even noticed the spectacles she wore.

Clarissa and Lady Mowbray had planned this scheme together as a way to reveal the spectacles to Adrian. The two women had talked after Clarissa and Lydia returned from the village, and it was then that Lady Mowbray had decided to do a little visiting, promising to return in a couple of days. But she had asked if Clarissa might see her way clear to telling Adrian about her spectacles before she went, so that she knew things were progressing in the right direction. Clarissa had reluctantly agreed, and they'd decided she should wait on the front step, wearing her spectacles as her husband saw his mother off.

Now the silly man had ruined all their plans. Adrian hadn't even noticed. In truth, he hadn't even seemed to really notice her presence, which was highly unusual. He'd acted terribly distracted. Something was obviously on his mind, and it wasn't pleasant, if she were to judge by his expression. There was a grim, determined cast to his face that made her anxious.

Frowning, Clarissa picked up her skirts and hurried after him. "Adrian?"

"Yes, my love?" he murmured, not slowing his steps.

She blinked at the term of endearment, startled, then shook off her surprise and asked, "Is aught amiss?"

"No, nothing."

"Then where are you going?" Clarissa asked with alarm. He had reached the stables and begun to saddle his stallion.

"I have to go to the Wyndhams'."

"The Wyndhams'," she echoed. "Your neighbors?"

"*Our* neighbors," Adrian corrected.

"Our neighbors," Clarissa repeated obediently. "Why?"

"Why, what?"

"Why are you going to the Wyndhams'?" she asked impatiently. When he hesitated over answering, Clarissa clutched at his arm and drew him around to face her. "What has happened?"

"Nothing," he said at once, but avoided her gaze by turning back to his horse.

Clarissa shook his arm. "Then why do you go see Reginald?"

Adrian stilled. He turned slowly to peer down at her. "You knew he was there?"

"Yes."

"How?" he asked harshly.

"We ran into him in the village today. He explained he was staying at the Wyndhams'."

"My God, he could have killed you," Adrian muttered in a horrified whisper. "Clarissa, you are not to go walking alone again."

"I was hardly alone, my lord. I had Lydia with me, and at least four servants trailed us to the village and back," she pointed out dryly. "And don't you start suspecting Reginald of this. I know Hadley does, but I thought you had better sense. Reginald would never harm anyone."

Adrian sighed impatiently. "Kibble has had men watching Lydia since she arrived. According to them, she could not have put the poisoned pie in your room. That really leaves only one person."

"Reginald?" She shook her head. "I do not believe it."

"Neither did I at first. But — according to Hadley — he needs money, and he *is* my heir if you are not . . . around. He is also the only other person who has been both here and in town with us. The Wyndhams live only half an hour away, easily close enough to slip in and leave the piece of pie by your bed."

Turning away, he cinched the strap on his saddle. "Stay close to the estate. In fact, stay indoors until I have returned." And without waiting for her agreement, Adrian led the horse out of the stables, mounted, and road off toward the Wyndham manor.

Clarissa watched him go with a frown. She did not believe for a moment that Reginald was behind all these accidents. It was obvious to her that Adrian wasn't thinking very clearly. Again, he hadn't even noticed the spectacles! Now the silly man was about to ruin a friendship he'd had since childhood. She sighed unhappily and turned back toward the house.

Adrian's words played through her head as she walked.

He is also the only other person who has been both here and in town with us. That was what the men were speaking about when she'd overheard them in the library. Whoever was behind the fountain incident, the fire, and the poisoning had to be someone who had been in London when she was, and who was out here in the country now.

There was Lydia, of course. In fact, Clarissa hadn't suffered any accidents here until Lydia's arrival. But according to Adrian, Kibble had ordered men to watch her stepmother, and the woman hadn't done it. Not that Clarissa would have believed it of her anyway. Still, it was good to have proof.

Reginald had also been in the city and was now in the country, but she found it impossible to believe that he was the culprit either. He had been very kind to her every time they met before the wedding, and even today in the village.

Nay, she thought unhappily. *There must be someone else. Someone . . .*

Clarissa's steps slowed to a halt as a sudden thought struck her. There *was* someone else who had been both in the city and here, she realized with surprise. But no, she thought at once, it could not be. Could it?

Frowning, Clarissa entered the house and headed for her room, then changed direction and headed for the library instead. She needed to think on this.

"Cousin!" Reginald entered the salon into which Adrian had been shown, a wide, welcoming smile on his face. "I thought you would be too busy with your new bride for visiting, else I would have ridden over to see you myself."

"I already have a houseful of guests," Adrian said. "One more would have been no bother."

"Actually, I knew that," Reginald admitted. "I did not think you needed another."

"How did you know?"

Reginald's eyes widened at his cousin's sharp tone. "For one thing, Aunt Isabel arrived here just moments before you and mentioned it. In fact, I was seeing her to her room when Lord Wyndham's butler came up to inform me that you were here."

"Oh." Adrian frowned. He'd thought he'd caught Reg out: If Reginald had been sneaking about Mowbray the last few days, that was one way he'd have known about the guests presently there.

"So, what can I do for you?" his cousin asked lightly, dropping into the chair next to Adrian. "Do you need help with your wife? Advice on wooing her or some such thing? I am at your service as always." He grinned.

Adrian's mouth tightened. It was so hard to believe that this man might be trying to kill Clarissa. In fact, all but one small corner of his mind did not believe it. But that uncertain little corner was causing him trouble. He had to know.

"The night of the Crambray ball," Adrian said abruptly, and Reginald's eyebrows rose in surprise.

"What of it?" Reginald asked.

"You did not give that letter to a lad to give to Clarissa, did you?"

"Of course not. I went to the ball to speak to her in person, and to send her out to you as planned. Why would I send a message?" He paused and frowned. "Though perhaps I should have thought of that. It would have saved my having to attend. That ball was really quite boring, even for the short while I was there."

Adrian frowned and glanced away, then asked, "What time did you leave?"

"Right after I talked to you. Well, not *right* after. I had a little difficulty finding Jeevers. But once I'd found him and told him I was leaving, I did so. I went to Staudt's and lost a small fortune."

Adrian's mouth tightened. Jeevers was Reg's friend who had actually been invited to the ball, and whom Reginald had accompanied to get in to speak to Clarissa. Staudt's was a gaming hell known for being shady.

"You went alone?" he asked.

430

"To Staudt's?" Reginald glanced up in surprise. "No, actually, I ran into Thoroughgood on the way and he came with me." He frowned. "Why all these questions, Adrian?" His mouth tightened when Adrian hesitated to answer, and he said slowly, "Aunt Isabel told me that Clarissa was poisoned the other day. I gather this means you were right about some of her accidents being attempts on her life."

Adrian shrugged and avoided his gaze.

"Aunt Isabel said that you, Hadley, and Lord Crambray are trying to sort out who might be causing Clarissa's 'accidents.' That you all are in accord that it must be someone who was both in the city at the time, and who is now in the country."

Adrian shifted uncomfortably in his chair.

"Like me," Reginald continued quietly. When Adrian flinched at the comment, he was suddenly on his feet. "You *do* suspect me!"

"I did not want to," Adrian assured him quickly, "but as you say, Hadley pointed out that it had to be someone who was both in the city and here, and . . . well, I preferred to think it was Lydia, but she has been proven innocent, and that left —"

"Me," Reginald interrupted dryly. "Well, thank you very much. After all I did to try to help you two get together — not to mention all the years you and I have known each other. You have now decided I am some mad killer?"

"Not mad," Adrian said quickly — but knew at once it was the wrong thing to say.

"Why on earth would I want to kill Clarissa?" Reginald asked. "Did this Hadley even consider that I do not have a motive?"

"Well, actually," Adrian admitted, "he supplied a motive."

Reginald blinked. In disbelief he asked, "What? What possible motive could I have to kill your wife?"

"It would appear he got hold of some rumors that you may be in dire financial straits."

Reginald snorted. "That is all it is, rumor. And one I started myself. Besides, that would be a motive to kill you, not your wife."

"You would not inherit if Clarissa were alive."

"No, but I could always marry Clarissa. In truth, if I were to enact such a wretched plan, I would be more likely to kill you and marry her. She is a lovely little bundle, which I noticed from the first, and absolutely charming. If only I had taken the time to get to know her better, and to realize that she was not refusing to wear her spectacles out of vanity, I might be the one married to her instead of you. Unfortunately, I could not get away from her quickly enough after she burned my piffle."

Adrian scowled at the suggestion of his cousin and Clarissa married, then asked, "You said the rumor of your financial difficulties is one you started yourself. Why?"

Reginald grimaced, and now he was the one finding it difficult to meet his cousin's gaze. He finally sighed and admitted, "I am interested in a certain lady who has come out this season. However, I have had it suggested to me that she is a fortune hunter. So I have dropped a word here and there suggesting that I am in dire straits in order to test her out."

"Really?" Adrian asked with surprise. He was amazed to see his cousin flushing in embarrassment. This seemed to suggest that Reginald was seriously interested in the woman in question. "Who is she?"

His cousin scowled. "Never mind that. Let us get back to the topic of Clarissa and her would-be killer."

Adrian sighed and nodded; he could ask about his cousin's love life later.

"If it is not Lydia, and it is not me — and I assure you, it is *not* me . . ." Reginald paused to glare at him coldly, then added, "You may ask Thoroughgood about that, by the way. He can tell you I was nowhere near the Crambrays' when the fire started. And you have my permission to ask my man of accounts about my true financial status as well."

"That will not be necessary," Adrian said, embarrassed even to have accused his cousin. He should have followed his instincts. Reginald was not a murderer.

"Hmmph," Reg muttered in disgust. "It would seem it *is* necessary, or you would not have come here looking to see if I was a killer."

"Look," Adrian said, "I am sorry about that. I did not really think you were, but I had to know for sure. *Someone* is trying to kill Clarissa, and I —"

Reginald waved him to silence. "Let us just stick to the topic of who it could be."

Adrian closed his mouth, exhaling a sigh through his nostrils. Reginald continued.

"Anyway, as I was saying, if you are sure it is not Lydia, and I know it is not me, whom does that leave?"

Adrian rubbed his forehead. "That just leaves the servants — or someone we are not even aware of."

Reginald pursed his lips. "The servants, you say?"

"Yes." Adrian frowned. "But none of them has a motive."

"Well, neither did I, but you thought I did it," Reginald snapped.

"Don't get angry at me about that. You are the idiot going around claiming to be broke, not I."

Reginald huffed again, then said, "Back to the servants."

Adrian shook his head. "As I said, there is no reason that I can think of for any of my staff to wish my wife dead. Besides, I have one staff here in the country and another in the city. None of them would have been able to attempt anything at both places, except for Keighley and Joan."

"Keighley and Joan? Joan is Clarissa's maid, is she not?" Reginald frowned.

Adrian peered at him closely. "What? I recognize that expression, Reg. Something has occurred to you. What are you thinking?"

His cousin shook his head, uncertainty filling his face. "It is probably nothing. I am probably mistaken."

"About what, Reginald?" he asked impatiently. "Anything you know, or think you know, may be of some help here. Just tell me, no matter how foolish it seems."

Reginald grimaced. "It is just . . . the night of the Crambray ball, when I went back inside . . . ?"

Adrian nodded.

"Well, as I told you, it took me several moments to find Jeevers."

Adrian nodded again. "Yes, yes. And?"

"By the time I found him and explained that I was leaving early, then finally made my way out to the hall, Clarissa and her maid were coming down the stairs, returning to the ball." He hesitated again, then sighed and said, "Her maid reminded me of someone, is all — but it could not be her."

"Could not be *whom?* Whom did she remind you of?" Adrian asked.

"An actress I saw several times onstage," Reginald said finally. "But it could not be her. I heard she died in a fire."

"In a fire?" Adrian felt a tingling along the back of his neck, some memory in his mind being activated. "What was this actress's name?"

"Molly Fielding," Reginald said.

Adrian's hand slammed down on the armrest of his chair, and in the next moment he was on his feet and hurrying for the door.

"Hey!" Reginald rushed after him. "Where

are you going?"

"Do you not recall the name of the man who kidnapped Clarissa and tricked her into marriage when she was a child?" Adrian asked as he strode quickly up the hall to the foyer. His voice was as hard as his heart had suddenly turned.

"Yes. That was Captain Fielding," Reg said. He followed Adrian out of the house and to the stables.

"And according to the tale, it was Captain Fielding and his *sister* who met her at the inn and traveled with her all over the place, and finally to Gretna Green."

"It could be a coincidence," Reginald warned. "I said the maid *looks* like Molly Fielding — besides, Molly died in a fire. That is why she was no longer onstage."

"Hadley said Captain Fielding's sister died in a fire. Molly Fielding has to be the sister," Adrian insisted. He began to walk the length of stalls in search of his horse.

"Okay," Reginald allowed. His cousin had stopped at the second stall and was opening it to let a horse out. Adrian recognized the roan as Reginald's mount. "But you just said she died in a fire. How can Clarissa's maid, Joan, be Molly?"

"I do not know, but it all fits." Adrian

finally found his own horse. He led the animal out beside Reginald's, and began to saddle him. "She was both in London and here. She had access to Clarissa's room, and easily could have left the piece of pie. And she is the one who called Clarissa away from the ball to receive the letter supposedly from me."

"But you said yourself at the time that she of all people would know that Clarissa could not read a letter. Why send her one?"

"I do not know," Adrian admitted. "Possibly for that very reason. She knows Clarissa cannot read without spectacles, and no one would think she would send a letter as a trap when Clarissa cannot read it. Which was a success. That was one of the reasons I did not suspect her," he pointed out. "Besides, if Joan is behind it all, and she arranged for that letter to be delivered, she could also have arranged for the time it was to be delivered — so that she could be nearby when the boy arrived. And, oh, how helpful she looked through it all," he added dryly.

"Why would Clarissa not recognize her?" Reginald asked with a frown.

"She cannot see without her spectacles," Adrian said. "And I do not think Joan has been with her long. Clarissa mentioned something about a maid, Violet, in the country. That woman served her mother before her, and was too old to be bouncing to the city and back. She retired when Clarissa left for London." He shook his head. "Clarissa has probably never seen Molly while wearing her spectacles. She . . ."

"What?" Reginald asked when he paused abruptly.

"Lydia sent for Clarissa's spectacles before the wedding. They apparently arrived the day before, and Joan rushed them upstairs, but Clarissa said she accidentally knocked them from the woman's hand with her blankets. I wonder now if Clarissa really did knock them, or if Joan just said she did and threw them to ensure that they broke and she could not see and recognize her."

"Hmm. That seems possible," Reg murmured. He frowned. "But why would Joan — er, Molly, if she is Molly — why would she even want Clarissa dead?"

"Fielding died in prison," Adrian reminded him, as they led their now saddled horses out of the stable. "Perhaps she blames Clarissa for his death. He was imprisoned for what he did to Clarissa, after all."

"Damn," Reginald muttered as they

mounted. "I say it over and over again; it is so hard to find good help nowadays. It's bad enough when they are robbing you blind, but now we have to worry about them trying to kill us?"

Adrian grunted in response, then put his heels to his horse, urging the beast into a run as he headed for home. He was glad his cousin had forgiven him enough to come; he was so angry at the moment that he could kill the maid with his bare hands. Of course if she'd harmed a single hair on Clarissa's head while he was gone, he would do just that. Even Reginald would not be able to stop him.

CHAPTER TWENTY

"Do not hover in the doorway, Joan. Come in," Clarissa murmured, glancing up from the book she'd been trying to read. The effort had been wasted; her mind was too preoccupied with thoughts, most of them about the woman presently crossing the library toward her.

Joan and Keighley were the only people besides Adrian, Lydia, and Reginald who had been in the city and were now here at Mowbray or in the vicinity. Clarissa did not believe either Lydia or Reginald could be the culprit behind her rash of accidents, and she certainly knew it was not Adrian. That left Joan and Keighley.

Joan was the more likely suspect. Keighley was an old man. Clarissa simply could not see him breaking into the London house in the dead of night to set a fire in the hall outside her door. Nor could she see him climbing the back gate, as Adrian had done, to creep about the footpaths and knock her unconscious.

Joan, on the other hand, wouldn't have had to break in. She'd always been present, and had been privy to information about Clarissa's location and whom she would be with. Joan was really the only viable suspect.

Clarissa's problem now was that she could not think of a motive for the woman to do these things. That, and the fact that she liked the girl, she acknowledged with a sigh.

Closing her book and setting it aside, Clarissa peered up at Joan as the maid paused in front of her desk. Her eyes immediately narrowed. She'd never seen the maid from this angle. Not while wearing spectacles. It allowed her to see the small raised beauty mark under the woman's chin. Clarissa had seen a beauty mark like it before, and in the exact same place. Ten years ago.

She stared briefly, then raised her eyes to Joan's face, looking her over more carefully before saying, "What is it, Molly?"

"I just wondered if you would like a cup of cocoa or tea while you are reading," the maid asked.

Clarissa's mouth tightened. Joan had not even noticed the name change. That and the beauty mark were proof enough for

Clarissa. "Not if it will be poisoned like the pie . . . *Molly,*" she said again.

The maid stiffened, her expression closing and her eyes suddenly wary as those of a cornered cat. "You know."

"I know who you are," Clarissa allowed. "But not why you have been trying to kill me."

Molly Fielding's hands clenched into fists at her sides. "My brother."

"Jeremy," Clarissa murmured, recalling the man. He'd cut a dashing figure in his uniform. At least, she'd thought so when she was young. He couldn't hold a candle to Adrian.

"And my mother," Molly added.

"I never even met your mother," Clarissa said with amazement.

"And me," Molly continued. She added bitterly, "When Jeremy was charged and sent to prison, we lost our support. I had to take to the stage to put food on the table. I'd led a sheltered life up until then. It was an eye-opening experience."

"I am sorry you had to do that to support yourself and your mother —," Clarissa began, but Molly wasn't finished.

"And it was all for nothing, really," the woman said. "I did it for Mother, but she died of a broken heart after the scandal hit and Jeremy was convicted. And then he died . . ." She lifted angry eyes to Clarissa, and rage made her words a growl. "You killed them both."

"I —"

"And I promised myself then that someday I would make you pay."

Clarissa sighed, gazing on Molly with pity. "And you have waited all this time to have your revenge."

"In truth, I did not expect ever to have the chance to get it," Molly admitted, picking up the letter opener off the desk and absently toying with it. "But then, at the beginning of the season, you and Lydia and her cronies showed up at a play I was in."

Clarissa blinked in surprise. She said, "A play? I have only ever been to one play in my life. It was one of Shakespeare's tales, when we first arrived here for the season." She frowned, unable to remember the title. She hadn't been able to see anything without her spectacles, and had fallen asleep listening. Giving up on the title, she asked, "You were in that play? As an actress?"

Molly nodded. "My character died in the first act. It was as I lay, supposedly dead, that I saw you up in one of the boxes. During intermission I slipped out to the lounge to get a closer look and to be sure it was you. I overheard Lydia saying that you needed a lady's maid, that your maid from home was too old to come to the city with you. I was standing right behind you, and you suddenly turned and glanced around. You looked right at me, and there was no recognition on your face at all. And then I realized you weren't wearing your spectacles."

"Lydia had already taken them away," Clarissa said quietly.

Molly nodded. "I am not sure I would have done anything even then if fate had not lent a hand. I went home that night exhausted and angry, and woke up in the middle of the night to the smell of smoke. Our row was on fire. I managed to slip out a window, but I hadn't had a chance to grab any clothes. I had to steal some. I lost everything in that fire. It wasn't until sunrise that I saw what I had stolen. I looked like a maid." She gave a short laugh. "It seemed almost providential. I did not contact anyone I knew from my life before. I let them all think I had died in the fire, and decided to apply for the position as your maid."

"Were you not afraid of being recognized?" Clarissa asked curiously. "If not by me, then by someone else? Surely, as an

445

actress, your face would be known."

"Not really. No one ever notices servants," Molly said with a shrug. She added, "I was more worried about whether I would be able to get the position. I knew nothing about being a lady's maid. But I guess my acting stood me in good stead. By that afternoon, I was your maid."

"And then the accidents began," Clarissa said. "I take it I have you to thank for falling down the stairs?"

"The item you tripped over was my shoe. I put it back on and rushed down to see if you were all right after you fell."

"And in front of that carriage?"

Molly shook her head. "That was just an accident. I had nothing to do with it."

"The poisoned pie?"

"I gather I did not use enough poison."

"Hitting my head and falling into the fountain?"

Molly's mouth tightened with remembered anger. "I hired the father of the boy who brought the message. He was only supposed to hit you over the head and knock you out. I was supposed to finish you off, but he got overexcited and tried to do it himself. He was trying to impress me," she said dryly.

Clarissa considered that, then asked, "The fire?"

Molly nodded. "I locked your door and started it in the hall, then slipped back to bed so that I could be startled awake when it was discovered."

Clarissa sighed and shook her head. "I am sorry about your mother, Molly. I lost my own, and know how hard that can be. But you have been blaming the wrong person. The scandal — all of it, really — was your brother's doing. And he died in prison. His death had nothing to do with me," she pointed out quietly.

"Nothing to do with you?" Molly echoed in disbelief, then pointed the letter opener at her and said, "He died in prison . . . where *you* put him. He never should have gone to prison. He was a good man; kind and sweet and —"

"I am sorry, Molly," Clarissa interrupted with amazement. "But you seem to forget your brother kidnapped me and tricked me into marrying him to get at my inheritance. I would hardly call that a good, kind, and sweet man."

"He loved you."

"He loved my inheritance, and devised a plan to get it," Clarissa corrected impatiently. "And — as all bad plans do — this one went awry. He was caught and forced to pay the price."

"There would have been no price to pay had he consummated the marriage."

Clarissa couldn't argue with that. Had Captain Fielding forced consummation on her, the marriage would have been irreversible. She would even now be stuck in a loveless match with someone interested only in her inheritance.

"Thanks to his kindness, he let you rest that night — and that kindness killed him," Molly said bitterly, tears glazing her eyes.

"Kindness, my arse!" Clarissa snapped irritably, recalling in stark detail that night and all its humiliation. She'd not told Adrian everything about her first wedding night; she'd not told anyone. Captain Fielding hadn't really asked if she was too tired when he broached the subject; he'd *stated* that she was and then left her alone. She was grateful now, but it had been a humiliating rejection for her at the time.

"Your brother did not consummate the marriage because he could not be bothered," Clarissa informed Molly grimly. "He did not find me attractive. My bosoms were not large enough, and the tavern maid at the inn was more to his taste."

"You lie!" Molly gasped. "It was his kindness that prevented his consummating the match with you. He told me so. His kindness got him killed. A little of that kindness in return from you would have saved him. But you gave none in return."

"I could do nothing once my father's men found us," Clarissa argued. And then honesty forced her to admit, "But even had I been able to do something on his behalf, I do not know that I would have. He was a stranger to me, and by the time the men found us, I knew it had all been a lie to get my inheritance."

"A stranger?" Molly cried with disbelief. "He *loved* you. He told me he fell in love with you the moment he saw you."

"Then he lied to you as well," Clarissa said firmly. "Probably to make his plan more acceptable to you, and to gain your help."

"Nay." Molly shook her head.

Clarissa *tsk*ed in irritation. "We never even met. How could he claim to love me?"

"He told me all about it when he was in prison. He said he ran into you at the theatre and —"

"Oh, bollocks!" Clarissa snorted. "I was never allowed anywhere alone at that age.

We had not met. Surely you remember, when I first arrived at the inn he introduced himself. Why would he introduce himself if we had already met?"

She saw the confusion on Molly's face as the woman was forced to recall their first meeting. Thinking it was working, Clarissa added, "And as for his loving me, that is not true either. I heard it from his own mouth. I had a nightmare the night we were married and went to find him. When I opened the door between our rooms, it was to hear him explaining to the maid — Beth, I believe her name was — that she was a lovely lass with luscious breasts, while his wife, alas, was as flat as a board and plain as a boot.

"When the girl asked why he had married me, he very kindly explained that, while my charms were on the light side, my purse was heavy. He then went on to flatter her further, telling her that she was the reason he had neglected to consummate the wedding, that he would attend that duty the next night on the ship if he had recovered sufficiently from his night with her, but that the whole time he was attending his duty, he would be imagining it was with her.

"Your brother then proceeded to service her as I closed the door. It seems his greed did not confine itself to money. Had he managed to control himself, he would have consummated our marriage, thereby saving himself." Clarissa shrugged wearily. "As it is, I have since been eternally grateful that I was still as flat as a plank at that age. And I was even more grateful when my father's men showed up."

"Lies. All lies," Molly growled, raising the letter opener.

"Are they? Come. You were there. I was as pliant and passive as a willow all the way from London to Gretna Green . . . until the last morning. Do you not recall how cross and contrary I was then? How I demanded to return home? Your brother said I was just overwrought, but when I continued to insist he slapped me. Do you not remember?"

Uncertainty crowded Molly's face, and the letter opener lowered slightly. The memories Clarissa spoke of had clearly come alive in her head.

"Yes," she murmured with a frown. "You were easily led most of the way, right up until . . ."

"Until that last morning, the morning *after* the wedding night that never happened."

The letter opener lowered even further, and confusion covered Molly's face. But when Clarissa stood up, Molly immediately jerked the letter opener back into a threatening position, anger filling her expression. "No. You are trying to trick me. He could not have lied to me."

Clarissa sighed. "Why? Have men never lied to get you to do what they wanted before?"

"Not Jeremy."

"He never lied to you? Ever?" she asked. "Not even to get out of trouble?" When doubt covered the maid's face once more, Clarissa tried another tactic. "When did he claim to have met and fallen in love with me?"

"He said he saw you at the theatre," Molly answered warily, as if expecting a trap.

Clarissa smiled. "See? Impossible. I had never been to the theater before this season — not before the night you saw me, in fact. I told you that not ten minutes ago, when you claimed that was when you first saw me again."

Molly's frown deepened, and her voice wasn't very convincing as she said, "You were probably lying even then."

"Why would I lie? I did not know then that he had claimed to see me there." Molly still looked unconvinced, and Clarissa shifted impatiently. "Why are you fighting the truth? Your brother was not the good, kind man you thought."

"He was. My Jeremy would never do what you are claiming. He must have loved you."

Clarissa felt pity claim her as she saw the betrayal and fear on Molly Fielding's face. She said gently, "Perhaps the Jeremy you knew would not have. But your brother had gone off to war, spent years there witnessing things we can only imagine. They say war changes a man. Perhaps the Jeremy that returned was not your Jeremy."

A sob slipping from her lips, Molly sank into the chair in front of the desk, the hand holding the letter opener dropping loosely to her side.

"What have I done?" she moaned hopelessly.

"Nothing irreparable," Clarissa assured her, taking a slow, cautious step around the desk. She paused abruptly when the girl released a bitter bark of laughter and raised the letter opener again, this time pressing it to her own wrist.

"Please do not come any closer, my lady. I . . ." Shaking her head, she glanced at the blade in her hand and back to Clarissa helplessly, hopelessly.

"Do not do anything rash, Joan — Molly," Clarissa corrected herself. "Everything will be all right."

"Easy for you to say. You are not the one facing prison."

"You will not go to prison," Clarissa assured her.

"How could I not? I have tried to kill you." Molly shook her head unhappily. "I saw enough of prison while visiting Jeremy. I would rather die."

"I shall not turn you in."

"But I tried to kill you," the woman repeated.

Clarissa sighed. "Well, you could not have been trying very hard. I am still here."

Molly sniffled, her head raising hopefully, as if Clarissa had proposed something that might redeem her.

"Well," Clarissa prompted, " 'tis true, is it not? I was blind as a bat and helpless most of the time. Had you really wanted the deed done, I am sure you would have accomplished it. Instead, you continually bungled the job. And as my maid, you were as efficient as can be. No, I do not think you truly had the heart to kill me."

"No," Molly admitted on a sigh. "I wanted to hurt you. I wanted you to suffer, but I could not seem to . . ." Pausing, she shook her head. "I fear it matters little whether you turn me in or not. If you were wise enough to figure things out, it is only a matter of time before your husband does. He will see me in prison."

Clarissa frowned as she realized Molly was right: Adrian would want her to be punished for sure. Her mind began to work, searching for a way out for the girl, and suddenly she brightened and blurted, "America."

Molly stared at her blankly. "America?"

"You could go there. I will pay your fare. You could make a new start. Fresh, without the fear of your past coming back to haunt you."

"I cannot afford —"

"I shall pay your way," Clarissa repeated firmly, leaning over the desk and pulling a piece of paper forward to scribble a note on it. "I will also give you enough money to start a small business of some sort — a boardinghouse, perhaps."

"Why?" Molly asked in bewilderment. "Why would you —"

"Because we both suffered at the hands of your brother, Molly. He tricked us both, and we have both suffered for it these last ten years. You more than me. Besides, Molly, I recall how kind you were to me on that trip, comforting me and assuring me that all would be well."

Clarissa signed her name to the bottom of the note and straightened to offer it. "Come.

Take it. I shall have the coachman drive you to London. You can collect your things, take this note to the bank to collect the money, then catch a boat to America."

When Molly hesitated, looking hopeful yet almost afraid to hope, Clarissa added, "You can start a boardinghouse there and a new life as a respectable woman. You can pay me back someday if you do well."

That seemed to decide her, and Molly reluctantly took the note.

Smiling, Clarissa took the letter opener away before the woman changed her mind, set it on the desk, then took her arm to lead her to the door, terribly aware that Adrian could return at any moment.

"Do you have anything here you need?" she asked.

"No, I did not bring much with me. Most of my things are back in London."

"Then you must collect them ere leaving," Clarissa murmured, opening the library door and leading Molly out into the hall. "All will be well. I hear that the Americas are becoming quite settled. Or you could go to France. You have many options. Do not even tell me which you choose. All will be well."

Espying Kibble moving up the hall, Clarissa called out for him to have the driver prepare the carriage and bring it around; then she led Molly to the front door and out onto the steps. "You need not leave England at all if you do not wish. I promise you shall not be pursued for what happened here."

Molly turned to face her, a wry grimace tugging at her mouth. "This is why I found I could not hurt you." When Clarissa raised a questioning eyebrow, she explained, "You are kind. I have seen how many women treat their servants. You are not like them. You were always kind to me, treating me as if my opinion mattered — as if we are equals." She smiled wryly. "I almost wish my brother had succeeded in completing the marriage. We would have been sisters then."

Clarissa smiled. "Yes, we would have. In fact, we *were* for a couple of days." She hugged the girl, then turned as the carriage appeared from the direction of the stables.

"If you need help, call on me," she murmured in the woman's ear, then straightened and urged her down the stairs. The carriage driver hopped down to open the door.

"Thank you," Molly whispered. Tears in her eyes, she squeezed Clarissa's hand and then stepped up into the carriage.

"Take her wherever she wants to go,"

Clarissa ordered. The driver closed the door. Turning, Clarissa moved back up the stairs as the coachman leaned into the window to hear a destination. By the time she reached the door, the man had gotten his instructions, taken up his seat at the reins again and was slapping them, urging the horses forward.

"You are too softhearted."

Clarissa turned sharply at those deep, low words, and found her husband standing behind her on the steps. Lord Greville filled the doorway behind him.

"How long have you been here?"

"Long enough," he answered. Then he repeated, "You are too softhearted, wife."

Ignoring his gentle criticism, she turned to watch the carriage roll off down the drive. She asked, "Are you two still friends?"

"Of course," Adrian said. He paused to glance sharply at Reginald, who answered at the same time, "I have not decided."

Clarissa smiled slightly at the two men; then she stepped past her husband to take Reginald's arm and walk him back into the house. "Come now, my lord; you must forgive my husband his false accusations. You must have realized by now that he can be quite dull-witted when it comes to those he loves. Why, just look at how he has not yet noticed that I wear spectacles."

Clarissa sensed her husband's step faltering behind her, and paused to turn back, holding out her hand to him in amusement. Adrian looked quite pale, his suddenly sickly gaze fixed on the wire rims of her spectacles.

"You can see me?"

"I have always been able to see you, my lord. I can simply see you better now," she informed him gently.

He stared, his face blank, and Reginald shifted impatiently beside her. "You really have been blind, have you not?" he asked derisively. "Did you not realize she was just nearsighted? Up close she can see quite well."

"I believe my husband thought that I could never see him," Clarissa murmured quietly. They were all silent for a moment; then Clarissa sighed and glanced at Reginald. "Perhaps, my lord, you could go inside and find yourself a drink in the parlor?"

Adrian's cousin grinned. "I have a better idea. I shall return to the Wyndhams', I think, and leave you to sort him out." And so saying, he paused to kiss her hand graciously, then moved back down the stairs they'd just ascended, hurrying toward the stables.

"You could really see me ere this?" Adrian asked once they were alone.

"Yes, my lord."

"When did you first see me?" he asked slowly.

"The night we met — as you leaned forward to speak. You got close enough that I could see your face and your beautiful, big brown eyes."

Adrian turned his head away, leaving his unmarred profile for her to look at, automatically hiding his scar. Closing the distance between them, Clarissa took his chin gently in hand and turned his face back toward her; then she kissed the mark he loathed so much.

Adrian flinched, fear on his face. "So you married me out of pity?"

"Pity?" Clarissa nearly laughed aloud. "Fie, sir! You insult yourself. You are a handsome man."

"I am a monster. Just a glimpse of my face has been known to make women swoon."

Clarissa shrugged. "Perhaps you were a sight after you were first injured, while the scar was still red and raw and new — but that was ten years ago. It has settled itself. Your scar is simply a part of you, a line down the side of your face. I think it is much larger in your mind than it truly is in reality."

"No. I have seen the women cringe."

"Did you see them cringe this season, my lord?" Adrian hesitated, and she nodded triumphantly. "I thought not. I imagine you even had a woman or two attempt to arrange liaisons with you while we were in London," she added archly, recalling Lady Johnson's indecent proposal.

Adrian gave a snort of disgust. "Only those wishing to experience a moment with a freak."

"Oh, I hardly think so." Clarissa smiled wryly, leading the way into the house and moving toward his office. "But pray, continue to think as you wish. I shall never need fear your being unfaithful if that is the case."

Adrian snorted again, following her into his office. "You need never fear that anyway. I am not interested in other women. I sowed my wild oats long ago."

"Hmm." Clarissa moved to the desk and seated herself carefully on the edge. "And do you think then that I want you because I wish to experience bedding a freak?"

Adrian frowned. "Do you still want me now that you can see me?"

"I have already told you, husband: I saw you on the first night we met, and many times since then. I have always wanted you."

"Seeing glimpses of me and seeing me fully and clearly and up close as I touch you are two different things."

Clarissa considered that, then nodded solemnly. "You are right, of course, my lord. They *are* two different things. I suppose that means that you do not want me now that I will again wear spectacles."

Adrian blinked. "That's not a fair comparison. You can take the spectacles off."

"Not if I wish to see," Clarissa pointed out. She slid off the desk and began undoing the fastenings of her gown. "Perhaps we should test it."

"What are you doing?" Adrian asked in dismay, whirling to push the door closed as she began to disrobe.

"Well, it seems to me, my lord, that we are in a bit of a quandary. I had no spectacles when we were married, so you might truly find me ugly with them. Not having spectacles, I also could not see you 'up close' as you touched me. Therefore we do not know — we might find each other thoroughly repulsive. It would seem to me that we must find out if that is the case, and if our marriage has any sort of a chance."

Adrian stared wide-eyed as his wife pushed

her gown off her shoulders, allowing it to pool at her feet. Her other garments quickly followed, leaving her standing before him as naked as the day she'd been born . . . except for her spectacles.

Swallowing thickly, he peered at her body, his eyes roving over her breasts, across her flat stomach and to the thatch of hair that nestled between her legs. A distressed sound drew his eyes quickly upward, and he saw that she cupped her full breasts and peered down at them in displeasure.

"It is as I feared," she said unhappily, and Adrian felt his heart stop at the words. Then she glanced at him and explained, "The very idea of enjoying the pleasure you give me with your body has made my breasts feel heavy and achy, my nipples puckered as if for a kiss."

Adrian swallowed again, his eyes fastening on the proof of her words, taking in those swollen breasts, their nipples hard and a dark cinnamon color. Then she moved one hand from her breast, sliding it down over her stomach to that nest of curls between her legs. His eyes widened incredulously as her fingers dipped down and disappeared.

"Oh, dear."

Adrian glanced up sharply again at that sigh, and she explained, "I appear to be already wet from the caress of your eyes. This is not working at all. How can I worry about your scar when your whole body, your very presence, affects me so?"

Releasing her breast, she held out her other hand to him. "Come," she whispered, and Adrian nearly tripped over his feet to obey.

He hurried forward, took her hand, then paused uncertainly as her gaze narrowed on him. "No, this does not appear to help, my lord. While I can see your scar very clearly, I cannot seem to ignore the rest of you to imagine the effect the scar alone might have on me." Her eyes shifted to meet his and she arched an eyebrow. "Did you not wish to join this experiment, husband, and see if you are repulsed by my spectacles?"

Adrian nodded dumbly, and she smiled. "Then why am I the only one naked?"

Adrian jerked his jacket off, tossing it across the room in his fervor, then began tugging impatiently at his cravat as Clarissa set to work on the buttons of his shirt. She had managed to undo only a couple by the time he'd loosened his cravat enough to rip it off over his head; then he settled the problem by ripping his shirt open. Buttons scattered everywhere. Adrian did not even bother to remove his jacket, but set to work on his breeches instead, undoing them and shoving them halfway down his hips.

His engorged member popped free, and Clarissa immediately caught it in one hand and squeezed it gently. She smiled up at him.

"It would seem my spectacles do not deter your ardor, my lord. I am vastly relieved."

Adrian groaned, affected as much by her words as her touch. He then caught her by the waist and lifted her onto the desk, covering her mouth with his own. Clarissa was still holding his penis, and he tried to brush her hand away to move closer, but her hand tightened instinctively on him. Adrian immediately stiffened and groaned, and he could feel her smile under his kiss. She loosened her hold enough to slide her hand down his length, caressing him. Adrian's kiss immediately became more passionate, more desperate, his hands clutching rather than caressing. He tried to urge her back onto the desk, but paused as she gasped in pain.

"I am sorry. What . . . ?" The question died on his lips as she slid off the desk and turned to peer at its cluttered surface. He'd forgotten to clear the desk first, Adrian realized, and he felt like an idiot for not thinking of it.

Clarissa leaned forward to begin shifting papers, and Adrian found his gaze dropping down over the curve of her back and lush behind. Unable to help himself, he reached out to follow the lines his eyes had traveled, this time with his fingers.

She stiffened, then slowly straightened. She started to turn to face him, but Adrian didn't let her. Catching her shoulder with his free hand, he held Clarissa in place and slid his other hand around to explore. He ran it over the soft skin of her hip, swept it around and up over the slight roundness of her belly, then up to cup one breast.

Clarissa sighed as his hand closed over her, her bottom pressing back and rubbing his erection as she arched into the caress, and Adrian moved his other hand to catch her other breast. He pulled her back tighter against him with his hold, then squeezed and pressed and fondled her nipples until she gasped and moaned by turn. Her bottom pressed against him more insistently. Adrian felt her head move against his chest and opened eyes he hadn't realized he'd closed, to find she'd tilted her head back, her lips seeking his. Adrian gave in to her demand, lowering his head to kiss her even as he let a hand drift down between her legs.

Clarissa cried out into his mouth, her hips

thrusting into the caress as he found her damp heat. She then began to suck eagerly at his tongue as Adrian rubbed his erection against her bottom. He wanted to be inside her, surrounded by her, taken home. And so, without further ado, he broke their kiss, bent her forward, and guided himself into the hot, wet heart of her.

Adrian saw Clarissa brace her hands on the desk surface, then he closed his eyes as she took him in and drove herself backward with a groan that spoke of both pleasure and need. He caught her hip with his free hand, his other hand returning to caress her as he drove in and out.

Clarissa allowed this for three or four thrusts; then she suddenly straightened and pulled away.

"What?" Adrian blinked his eyes open, and saw that she'd pushed the items on the desk out of the way and was now turning to face him.

"I want to see you while you make love to me," she whispered breathlessly. Reaching up and cupping the back of his head, she drew him down for a kiss.

Adrian kissed her back, but he still wasn't all that comfortable with the idea of her seeing his face. He knew she claimed it did not bother her, but . . .

Clarissa suddenly pulled back and raised herself up onto the edge of the desk, then reached out and caught him by his erection to draw him forward. "Make love to me, Adrian! Make love to me while I watch. I want to see the man I love make love to me."

Adrian froze, his mind spinning under the effect of her words. "You *love* me?"

Clarissa froze: then her expression softened as she saw the hope and wonder in him. "Of course I do. How could I not?"

"But —"

"There are no buts, husband," she interrupted. "I love you. I love your looks, your smile, your eyes, even your scar. I love all of you."

Adrian stepped between her legs, caught her hips, and slid into her.

"Oh." Clarissa's eyes briefly fluttered shut. A moment later she forced them open again and smiled at him. "I love you, Adrian. I shall surely say so until you are sick of hearing it."

Adrian stilled, his eyes locking on her face, and he saw there was no pity in the eyes behind the spectacles, no lie he could see, just pure, unadulterated pleasure, joy, and love. She peered up at him, then she leaned up to kiss his scar softly. "It is a part of you, Adrian. And I love all of you."

Adrian felt his mouth stretch into a wide, beaming smile, and he kissed her hard on the lips. But it was a quick kiss, and then he pulled back and said, "I shall never tire of hearing you say it. And I love you too, Clarissa. I love all of you — your body, your heart, your soul, your smile, your mind, and even your blind eyes. You are my heart. You've made me smile and laugh. You make life worth living. With spectacles or without, dressed or undressed, I love you all. And I always will."

He bent to lay a gentle kiss on her forehead, then added, "But, by God, at this moment I love you best naked."

Clarissa laughed. "I am so glad. Now, please make love to me, and make the aching stop."

Adrian tightened his hold on her hips, chuckling, and drove into her again, as deep as he could go. Her body welcomed him, squeezing warm and tight around his shaft as he withdrew and pressed forward. Each thrust was an affirmation. She had seen him with her spectacles on and still wanted him — loved him, even. She was his mate, his heart, his wife. Adrian didn't know what he'd done to deserve her, how the two of them had so blindly stumbled onto love, but he vowed to do everything in his power to keep her happy. Forever and ever.

ABOUT THE AUTHOR

Lynsay Sands has been writing since she was a child. She has a degree in psychology, enjoys reading both horror and romance, and believes a sense of humor can "see you through nearly anything."

The employees of Thorndike Press hope you have enjoyed this Large Print book. All our Thorndike and Wheeler Large Print titles are designed for easy reading, and all our books are made to last. Other Thorndike Press Large Print books are available at your library, through selected bookstores, or directly from us.

For information about titles, please call:
(800) 223-1244

or visit our Web site at:
www.gale.com/thorndike
www.gale.com/wheeler

To share your comments, please write:
Publisher
Thorndike Press
295 Kennedy Memorial Drive
Waterville, ME 04901